LIKE A DEE

He looked like a young Harrison Ford, with tousled brown hair, a square jaw, sparkling hazel eyes, and a long, lean body clad in jeans, a lab coat, and battered hiking boots. Okay, so maybe he didn't look all that much like Indy—there was no leather, fedora, or bullwhip in sight. But there was something about him that rooted her in place. And she wasn't one to grow roots.

Slightly uneven teeth flashed behind a charming smile, and a pair of killer dimples popped into view. "Doc Lopes retired and handed the practice over to me about six months ago. I'm Nick Masterson." Nodding to the blanket-wrapped bundle, he added, "Who do we have there?"

The question kicked Jenny's brain back into gear, bringing a flush and sidelining her surprise that Doc wasn't Dòc anymore—and the new guy was hot.

Also by Jesse Hayworth

Summer at Mustang Ridge
Sunset at Keyhole Canyon (A Penguin Special Novella)

WINTER *at* MUSTANG RIDGE

JESSE HAYWORTH

A SIGNET ECLIPSE BOOK

SIGNET ECLIPSE
Published by the Penguin Group
Penguin Group (USA) LLC, 375 Hudson Street,
New York, New York 10014

USA | Canada | UK | Ireland | Australia | New Zealand | India | South Africa | China
penguin.com
A Penguin Random House Company

First published by Signet Eclipse, an imprint of New American Library,
a division of Penguin Group (USA) LLC

First Printing, February 2014

ISBN 978-0-451-41915-6

Printed in the United States of America
10 9 8 7 6 5 4 3 2 1

To family

Dear Reader-Friends,

You know how sometimes things just work out the way they're supposed to? Luck, fate, destiny, vibrational energies aligning . . . whatever you call the moment. It's when, however briefly, things fall into place just the way they're meant to.

I had one of those moments not that long ago. Having decided that we needed a second cat (I love our Lucy dearly, but she's the anticuddler), I headed to the shelter two towns over. As I got on the highway, I worried over how to choose. How was I supposed to pick just one of the homeless kitties, and how could I guess which one would fit best into our little family?

Then, suddenly, the cars in front of me did the swerve-swerve-swerve thing that telegraphs "Eek! Something's in the road!" And, like the universe had answered my question then and there, a little black ball of fur went tumbling across two lanes, tossed out of a car window like so much trash.

Yep. Some cretin had thrown a kitten onto I-95, with wall-to-wall traffic going sixty and everyone honking—like that was going to help.

Near panic (That was my kitten!), I hit my hazards, pulled over, and got out . . . but there was no way I could get to the poor little critter, who was splayed flat three lanes away, trying to hang on to the road as the cars whipped by, blowing it around. So I crouched down and called, "Here, kitty-kitty!" while inwardly thinking, Yeah, like that's going to work.

But darned if that tiny black kitten didn't turn its head, lock eyes with me, and come racing over, dodging a whole lot of cars like a game of Frogger, to dive under my Subaru. Figuring I was about to get thoroughly clawed, I reached down, scruffed the kitten out from behind my back tire and held it to my chest . . . and little Pixel stuck her head under my chin and purred so loud, she drowned out the traffic noise.

Even a little banged up and a whole lot scared, she knew she had found her way home.

I felt the same when I wrote Winter at Mustang Ridge, *like I was in the right place at the right time to return to the Skye family's dude ranch and tell the story of a banged-up golden retriever, the prodigal daughter, and the hot new vet in town. I hope you'll love Rex, Jenny, and Nick together as much as I do!*

Love,
Jesse

1

Jenny woke to a quiet so profound it blasted her ear-drums, shocking her with the lack of parrot screeches and "get your butt out of bed" shouts from the other members of her film crew. But as she blinked around at the familiar yellow curtains and glossy white furniture of a room decorated in Early Teen, she realized it wasn't all the way silent. The old bones of the ranch house creaked a little in the cold, and muted noises from downstairs said she wasn't the first one up.

"Guess we're not in Belize anymore, Toto," she said, half expecting Jill to groan from the other side of the tent and tell her to shut up. But she didn't have a room-mate here, or a layer of mosquito netting draped around her bed. Which was just weird.

Ask any other member of her family, though, and they'd say it was the other way around. To them, this was normal. This was home.

A glance at the phone she'd dumped on the bedside table said it was just after eight, and the scents of coffee and cinnamon said it was time for breakfast. Her body wasn't sure what country it was in, never mind what time zone, but she levered herself out of bed anyway.

Because, hello, breakfast.

No stranger to catnaps, round-the-clock shifts and other o'dark thirty stuff, Jenny was clear-eyed by the time her feet hit the floor. She had slept in sweats and thick socks, but the cold cut through them, making her shiver as she dragged on another sweatshirt and stuffed her feet into a pair of sheepskin slippers.

"Brr." She headed for the dresser and snagged a fluffy red beret off the corner of the mirror, glancing at the photos her long-ago self had tucked in the frame.

She might want to deny that she'd ever curled and sprayed her hair so big or worn that shiny blue monstrosity to prom, but she was still darned proud of the six pictures she'd snapped during a summer storm when she was fifteen, one after the other, showing slashes of lightning spearing across Mustang Ridge. The photo series had won first prize at the local fair and made it all the way to state before getting beat out by a still life of fruit and old boots. Which had been seriously lame, but whatever.

Surprised by a kick of warmth that didn't have anything to do with fleece and cashmere, she grinned at herself in the mirror. "Welcome home, kiddo."

Granted, "home" for her was more of a base camp than a long-term residence, but it was where the big things stayed the same, year after year, and where she knew she'd find a hug and a hot meal no matter what.

She was lucky. Not everyone had something so rock solid to fall back on, thanks to a family dedicated to making sure it stayed that way, not just for her, but for all the people and animals that called Mustang Ridge their home.

The door to her room gave off the same three-note squeak it always had, and the wide floorboards in the upstairs hall creaked under her weight, making her feel like a rhino even though they'd been making those same noises since she was eight.

A moment later, there was a flash of movement at the bottom of the stairs and a familiar figure appeared, frowning up. "Did you hear—" Krista gasped, face lighting. "When did you . . . Why didn't you . . . Oh!" She flew up and grabbed Jenny in a huge hug. "You're here!"

As always, Jenny felt a shock of recognition at seeing herself in Krista, like she was looking into a not-quite-funhouse mirror that distorted things only slightly, giving her a long blond ponytail, coloring her high cheekbones with a flush of excitement rather than a sunblock-defying tan, and turning her into a country girl.

But then, as always, within those first few seconds everything clicked back into place, and something inside Jenny said, *Duh*. They were twins, after all.

Laughter bubbled up, and she hugged her sister, hard. "You sound surprised. Did you think I was going to bail on you?"

"No, never. But seeing you makes it feel like this is really happening!"

"I'm here, and it is." Jenny held Krista away. "But are you sure this is what you want to do with your time off? You're long overdue for a real vacation. You know, the kind with fruity drinks, pool boys, and sand?"

"Trust me, this *is* a real vacation."

"Six weeks of classes? Are you nuts?"

Krista grinned. "Four weeks of classes in a big city plus two more interning at one of the biggest dude ranches in California, which I'm guessing has fruity drinks and pool boys, and hopefully some tips on how to improve our services here. Maybe not to you, but it sure sounds like paradise to me."

"At least take an extra week for yourself on a beach somewhere. I've got the time before we start shooting the new season of *Jungle Love.*" Barely, but she would make it work.

"I couldn't ask you to do that when you've already rearranged your life to ride herd on this place while I'm gone." Krista hugged her again, tight enough to strangle. "I can't believe you're really here! When did you get in? I was heading out to pick you up in an hour!"

As a belated exclamation and some chair scrapes came from the dining room, Jenny said, "I caught an earlier flight and found a taxi driver who was willing to make the trip."

"That must've cost a fortune!" Krista socked her in the arm. "You should've called me."

Their father appeared in the archway leading to the dining room, saving Jenny from trying to explain a reluctance she wasn't even sure she understood. Heading toward him with Krista in tow, she stretched out her free hand. "Dad!"

His hug was big and burly, and carried a fresh-sawdust undertone that said he'd put in some early hours in his shop. But despite that familiar smell and the fact that Jenny had known her parents were back at the ranch, there was a moment of disconnect.

Easing back, she grinned. "Hey, big guy. I see you're back to rocking the lumberjack look." The last time she had visited her parents—a stopover at an RV campsite on Cape Cod—he'd been sporting loud prints, boat shoes, and a big hat, and looking as relaxed as she'd seen him in years. Now he was wearing a plaid flannel shirt, jeans, and a pair of thick wool socks that could've been holdovers from her childhood.

"When in Wyoming," he intoned, but then shot her a wink that said, *It's all good*.

"Where's Mom?"

"She left last night, headed for an estate auction on the other side of Laramie, with some stopovers at a few antiques places along the way. She'll be gone a few days, but said to tell you hi and that she's sorry she missed your first day back."

Just not sorry enough to change her plans. "An estate sale? Antiques stores? When did Mom go *American Pickers*?" Last she knew, her mother had been into French cuisine and the Food Channel.

"The write-up on the auction said they're selling some nice Depression-era glass," her father said in a good-natured nonanswer.

"Speaking of rocking the lumberjack look . . ." Krista gave Jenny's sweats-on-sweats outfit a pointed up-and-down. "What are you wearing? Everything?"

"Shut up, it's freezing in here!"

"Pansy. I was just getting ready to open a window and let out some of the cooking heat." Krista looked perfectly comfortable in yoga pants, a tank top, and flip-flops.

Beneath her fuzzy hat, Jenny scowled. "Try it and I'll toss you in a snowbank."

"No you won't. That'd mean going outside, and there's no way you're setting foot beyond the front door without more clothes." Krista's grin took on an edge. "Like, you know, one of those survival suits they use in the Bering Sea."

"Ha. You willing to bet on that?"

"Time out." Their father made a T sign with his hands. "Breakfast first, then snow fights."

"Aw," Jenny and Krista said together, harmonizing, and then laughed and hugged again as the three of them trooped into the main room, with its exposed beams and tasteful—if you were into that sort of thing—taxidermy.

It didn't look exactly the same as it had when they were kids, but it wasn't all that different, either. The couches and chairs were new and overstuffed, the carved wood mantel over the fireplace held landscapes rather than family photos, and just inside the door was a polished wooden counter-slash-computer stand that served as the registration desk and hub of guest services. The comfortable jumble was gone, the afghans folded, the pillows plumped, and the corners neatly swept, but the homeyness was there, and not just in the welcome smell of coffee and muffins.

There was still a dog bed near the fire—it had been a while since their last house pup passed on, but a few of the wranglers had working dogs that occasionally snuck in for a nap—and the twelve-person dining table still took up the back half of the room, sheltered by big bookcases that gave the dining area some privacy without cutting off the straight-through view of the snow-shrouded fields, distant mountains, and leaden sky.

During the summer, most everyone ate in the hall that had been added on to the other side of the expanded kitchen, leaving the dining area for the occasional special event. In the winter, though, the hall was closed off and meals were held at the long, wide-board dining table. Krista, Jenny, and their father sat together at the end nearest the fireplace, where the open hearth held a gray soapstone stove that gave off mellow waves of heat.

Jenny snagged a mug off the sideboard and poured herself a cup of thick, black coffee that practically stuck to her teeth when she took her first sip. She sighed in appreciation. "Mmm. Hello, caffeine. I've missed you."

"They don't have good java down south?" Krista asked.

"It's not cowboy coffee." After a second deep swallow that burned its way along Jenny's throat and heated her stomach, she set down her cup and motioned to the hallway that led to the big commercial kitchen. "I'm going to go say hi to—"

"Jenny?" A figure bustled through the arched doorway, nearly lost in a ruffled blue apron. Bird-small and delicate, with silver hair and quick eyes, she brought with her a gush of sugar-laden air and a bright smile. "I thought I heard you out here! Oh, sweetie!"

"Gran!" Jenny met her halfway and leaned into the embrace. Inhaling the scents of baking and lavender bathwater, she sighed and breathed out a tension she hadn't even been aware of. *This*, she thought. This was what she had missed the most. Emails and Skype just weren't the same as a hug that smelled like a bakery and stayed tight, like it wasn't ever going to let go.

Then again, that was Gran. She was the glue behind the scenes of Mustang Ridge, sticking them together with love, stubbornness, and baked goods. She had been the first one to see that the old ways weren't cutting it anymore, the first one to throw her support behind Krista's crazy-sounding plan to herd dudes instead of cattle. And, bless her, she had been the only one who hadn't seemed surprised when Jenny announced she was leaving. Instead, when the time came, Gran had hidden a Ziploc bag full of cookies and five hundred dollars in her luggage, and hugged her good-bye.

Now they hugged hello for the first time in more than a year.

"Let me see you!" Gran drew back and frowned. "You look tired, baby."

"I am, but it's nothing a good night's sleep won't fix.

My body isn't sure what day it's supposed to be, never mind what time." She looked past her grandmother. "Where's Big Skye?" Her gramps wasn't a fan of crowds—or the transition from cattle station to dude ranch—but given that it was the off season, she would've expected him to be either bellied up to the table or mooching bacon out of the pan, giving Gran a wink and a kiss when she scolded him.

"He's got a cold, which has him stuck in bed and cranky as a mustang with a burr under his saddle. But he'll want to see you, if you can stand it."

"I'll walk down to the cabin after breakfast." Cranky or not, Big Skye was always a hoot to be around, with a caustic wit and a story for every occasion, most of them starting with, "There was this one roundup . . ." or "I was in this honky-tonk one time . . ." Some of them were even true, though she didn't have any problem calling him on the tall tales.

Funny, wasn't it, how families worked? She could spar with her grandfather all day long, but five minutes with her mother in hobby mode put her seriously on edge. Krista, on the other hand, would bend over sideways to keep the peace with their mom, but did the duck-and-shuffle with Big Skye.

Gran patted her cheek. "You're a good girl. Sit and relax. I'll be right out with the food."

Knowing it was no use offering to help—the kitchen was Gran's domain—Jenny sat. Warmer now, thawed out by family and the heat of the wood stove, she pulled off her hat.

Krista froze with her mug suspended midair. "Ohmigod, did you dye your *hair*?" She might as well have said "You got a *face tattoo*?" or "You ate a *puppy*?" There was that much horror in her voice.

Resisting the urge to put the hat back on, Jenny gave a *no biggie* shrug. "Why? Don't you like it?"

"It's not that. It's just . . . Wow, it's so dark! And short!" Krista reached over and rubbed a couple of strands between her fingers. "It makes you look so different. Like, I don't know. A movie star or something."

Jenny batted her hand away. "Knock it off. It's no big deal." Or maybe it was; she hadn't decided yet. She'd only had the new hairdo for a couple of days, and the brunette color was a far cry from their natural blond. Maybe it had been a last act of defiance before coming home . . . or maybe self-defense. Either way, she hoped it would make the locals stop and think before confusing her with her sister.

"Hello. It's a big deal to me." Krista's eyes lit. "Did you do it for the show?"

"No way." Jenny almost laughed at the idea. "As long as I'm more or less presentable, they don't care what I look like. I'm behind the camera, remember?"

"You don't need to be. I bet they'd take you as a contestant in a heartbeat. Especially looking like this! It's got total wow factor." Krista made another grab for her hair.

Jenny waved a fork to fend her off. "I'd let parrots peck my eyes out before I signed on for *Jungle Love*." It was one thing being a cameraman for the exotic reality dating show. It was quite another being a contestant—she didn't know which would be worse, dealing with the people or being on the wrong side of the camera.

"Then why'd you change your hair?"

"Because I felt like it. And stop touching me."

"Am I going to have to separate you two?" their father asked mildly over his coffee.

"Nope, because here's the food." Jenny sniffed appreciatively as Gran appeared pushing a server loaded with berry pancakes, scrambled eggs, and crispy bacon. "Mmm. I'm starving."

"Come on," Krista said. "What have you got against going on the show? I mean, Mike and Niki from season two are engaged. It can happen."

As far as Jenny was concerned, Mike Neils was a jerk, Niki French had more mileage on her than the average commercial Boeing, and their engagement was as fake as Niki's boobs. But her contract was very clear on what would happen if she leaked, so she went with a noncommittal: "I'm not interested in dating on national TV." And it wasn't like her occasional hookups would be good fodder, anyway.

"But it could be fun. You'd get to go cave diving, treasure hunting, riding in the rain forest . . ." Krista ticked off the made-for-ratings group dates on her fingers, sounding dreamy.

"Live with eleven other women who want me dead," Jenny added. "That's assuming, of course, that I didn't get kicked off in the first episode."

"With that haircut? You'd totally score."

"We could take a swing by Harry's later, get you one to match."

"I—" Krista lifted a hand to her ponytail. "Um."

"Didn't think so." Jenny grinned as Gran took the seat opposite her, and added, "Besides, I'm not here to talk about the show. Rumor has it that I'm in charge of the guest stuff for the next six weeks. So . . . what do you guys say? You ready to bring me up to speed?"

2

"Morning, Ruth," Nick said as he hip-checked the door open and let himself into the clinic's waiting area, carrying coffee for two. "How was your weekend? Did you and BillyBobScott hit it off?"

From her seat behind the reception desk, his assistant—aka Queen of All Things Important at the Three Rivers Veterinary Clinic—made a face. "Not really. The pictures he posted had to be a good ten years old, and if he's six feet tall, then I'm a Labrador. All of which might've been okay if he hadn't also been boring and a bad tipper. Oh, and his real name was Doug."

Ruth had purple hair, thick tortoise shell reading glasses, a sweater set for every day of the week, and a clause in her contract that said she got to leave at four thirty on Wednesdays for Bingo. Nick had thought he had her pegged when he took over the office a few months earlier . . . but, boy, had he been wrong. It hadn't taken him long to discover that Wednesday night Bingo was the local seniors' equivalent of a pickup joint, and

Ruth approached dating with the verve and dedication of an Olympic athlete.

He handed over her coffee and took a healthy swig of his own. "Then why did he have BillyBobScott as his user name on the dating site?"

"Redneck schizophrenia?"

Chuckling, he picked up the list she had printed out of his morning rounds. "And that's a turnoff?" Ruth might be pushing AARP eligibility, but her views on men were pretty liberal.

"Not necessarily. Could make for some interesting role-playing. No, it was the boring thing. And his breath. Day-old egg salad just isn't something a girl can get past, not even with wasabi on the table."

Trying not to think about Ruth and role-playing in the same sentence, Nick focused on the call sheet. It looked like he'd be doing a follow-up on that gelding surgery over at Mustang Ridge Ranch, shooting another set of digital rads on Missy Simms's laminitic pony to see if the corrective shoeing had helped, and checking out a half-dozen sheep at the Plunkett place. And, of course, whatever emergency calls the day might bring, along with small-animal office hours this afternoon. "Maybe he was just nervous," he suggested. "Trying to impress you."

"That might account for the fifteen-minute monologue on his new shoelaces, but not the egg breath."

"Which could just be a onetime thing, too." Nick folded the call sheet and stuck it in his pocket. Ruth would've sent the info to his phone, but the local cell service was spotty and there were places where even his GPS got confused, so he had learned the value of keeping a hard copy on hand. "Maybe you should give him another chance."

"Hello, pot? This is the kettle. If anyone in this room is too picky, it's you."

Translation: He had ducked all of her efforts to set him up. "Well, anyway. I'm sorry BillyBobScottDoug was a dud."

She shrugged. "I'll keep looking. Mr. Right is out there somewhere."

"Not Mr. Right Now?"

That got a sly grin. "I've found plenty of them, thanks." But then her smile got crooked. "My Charlie is going to be a hard act to follow, but I know that one of these times it's going to click."

"I'll keep my fingers crossed for you. Meanwhile, do me a favor and manage things while I'm out."

"Don't I always?"

Yes, she did. Ruth ran his office, triaged the calls, made sure he got where he was going more or less on time, soothed ruffled feathers when he couldn't, and gave him the lowdown on his clients, which was crucial in an area like Three Ridges, Wyoming. But more than that, she had a huge heart and a wicked sense of humor, and when she was in the mood she made blissfully sweet poppy-seed muffins the size of his head. And she had loved her Charlie dearly.

Knowing it would make her laugh, he leaned over her desk and wiggled his eyebrows. "Forget about trying to hook me up with other women. You know I'm just waiting for you to give me a chance."

She put her hand to her heart and sighed with the drama of a soap opera diva. "Alas, our love is doomed before it even gets started. I don't have many rules when it comes to men, but not dating the boss is one of them."

"I could fire you."

"You won't. But I keep telling you, Doc"—Ruth wagged a finger at him—"you should give the ladies around here a chance."

After breakfast, Krista and Jenny adjourned to the office at the back of the house.

"I consider myself lucky that Dude Ranch 101 is only offered in the dead of winter," Jenny said, snuggling into her coat. She had put her hat back on, but with her system busy digesting a short stack of pancakes and too many cheesy scrambled eggs, she was feeling the cold.

Krista shot her an amused look. "Was that sarcasm?"

"Nope, I'm serious. I'd rather freeze my butt off than get dropped into the deep end come summer, with forty dudes who don't know which way the saddle horn goes."

"We max out at around twenty-five guests. Thirty if we push it and have multiples bunking together in the bigger cabins."

"Still." Jenny faked a shudder. "I know you love meeting new people and thinking up ways to entertain a new rotation every week, but it's not for me."

"How is riding herd on two dozen guests any worse than chasing desperate, fame-hungry singles through the rain forest with a camera? Seems to me like our jobs are pretty similar."

"Not even close," Jenny said firmly. "I'm trying to get my people into trouble and film what happens, with bonus points for tears and drama. You're trying to keep yours *out* of trouble and minimize the drama. That's way harder."

"Lucky for me, the location does most of the keep-'em-happy work, and the horses do the rest." Krista spun away from the big, messy desk. Tipping back in the battered chair, she put her feet on the windowsill with a contented sigh. "Isn't it incredible?"

Beyond the double-hung glass stretched a panorama that looked like it couldn't possibly be real, a huge expanse of unbroken snow rising up to the ridgeline, with jagged, iced-over mountains in the distance and a colorless sky that made it hard to tell where the snow ended and the atmosphere began. But although it made Jenny's fingers itch for a camera, it was also very big, very monochrome, and very cold looking.

She'd take bugs, butterflies, and greenery any day, thankyouverymuch . . . but she wasn't going to whine about that, or how it'd been eighty-five and sunny a day and a half and several thousand miles ago. Not when she owed her sister big-time for keeping the family business alive and kicking. And not now, when Krista needed her to pitch in, if only temporarily. Sure, she had tried to duck the chore—*Can't Foster do it, or*

Shelby?—but now that she was stuck here for the next six weeks, she was determined to handle everything and let Krista have some fun.

Plopping down in a chair on the other side of the desk, Jenny whipped out her app-laden phone. If it kept her organized in the midst of a brutal shoot, with a half dozen voices yapping in her headset while the singles scattered like deranged sheep, it would be more than sufficient for the day-to-day at Mustang Ridge. "Okay, let's hear it. What do you need me to do?"

Krista spun back from the window and let her flip-flops hit the floor. "Let's start with the reservation database. If we're not booking cabins for the summer—or, better yet, next summer—then we're not paying the bills."

They spent the next couple of hours going over the nuts and bolts of Krista's usual winter workday, which was a mix of advertising, customer relations, and supplier negotiations, plus a sprinkling of ranch chores.

"Foster is going to handle all the outdoor stuff," she assured Jenny. "I just need you to keep up with the office work."

"And come up with photos and videos for Shelby to use in her new grand plan." Jenny hadn't met Foster's fiancée yet, but she'd heard all about the former Boston advertising exec, who had started her own advertising firm out here in the middle of nowhere and had big plans for taking things up a notch at Mustang Ridge.

"Well, yeah." That got her a rueful grin. "Noticed

how I slipped that in, did you? It's just that she's got all these great ideas for branding and advertising, and you're here, and—"

"Stop right there. You think I don't want to play with my cameras? Hello, this is me we're talking about."

"I don't want you to feel obligated. You get paid a ton for your work, and—"

"And you can shut up anytime now. I'd love to do it." In fact, Jenny already had a flock of ideas zinging through her head. "I'll go through the pictures I took during my last couple of visits for spring and summer shots, and right now is perfect for winter landscapes. What are you guys looking for, specifically?"

They spent the next ten minutes going over the ranch's new advertising strategy, which would include a Web site overhaul, updated brochures, and a series of short videos.

"At first I was thinking of doing a longer overview piece," Krista said, "but given how fast the world moves these days, Shelby suggested that we break up the video clips and sprinkle them through the Web site, post them on public sites, and promote them via social media."

"She's right. It's all about making content bite-size these days." Jenny finished keying the topic list into her phone and hit the Save key with a flourish. "I shot a little video of the Fourth of July Roundup the summer before last, and I can take care of the local interviews and historical stuff now, keeping the winter backdrops to a minimum. That should give you a

bunch of clips to start posting now, and then next summer I'll come back for a week or two and get the rest of
the pretty-pretty."

"Or if that would be too much for you, we could fill
in the gaps with phone videos."

"You didn't just say that." Jenny stuck her fingers in
her ears. "I can't hear you. La-la-la-la."

Krista laughed. "Okay, okay. No camera phones. But
I don't want you to feel like you have to go nuts with
this, either."

"What, me go overboard on a film? Never." Okay, so
maybe she had gone a little crazy with a few of her film
school projects, but that had been part of the fun. Besides, it had been years since she'd had full creative
freedom. "Anyway, we don't have to nail down all the
details right now. I'll pull some stuff together and then
hook up with Shelby and see what she'd like tweaked."
In her experience, that was generally easier than starting with a totally blank slate. Besides, she wanted to
meet the woman who had snagged Mustang Ridge's
famously solitary head wrangler.

"That sounds like a plan, if you're sure this isn't going to be too much."

"Are you kidding me? This is going to make the next
six weeks bearable." The moment she said it, she
wished she hadn't. She hated seeing Krista's face fall.
"I didn't mean that the way it came out."

"I know this is an imposition—"

Jenny held up a hand. "Don't. Seriously. Thanks to

you, I've got someplace to come home to when I'm not working. Maybe the idea of being a full-timer gives me hives, but I love knowing that the ranch is still in the family. And, better yet, it's flourishing. If keeping it that way means that I need to put in some time now and then, so be it. Seems to me that this is long overdue."

"But—"

"No buts. I'm staying, you're leaving, and you're going to have an awesome time. And when you get back, I'll have lots of pics and video for you to wade through."

Krista drew breath to argue, but then hesitated and let it out again. "Okay, but I owe you one."

"Nope. Not even close."

"Still, thanks."

Jenny waved that off. "What else do I need to know?"

"Businesswise? I think that's about it, though I'm sure I'll think of a dozen other things between now and when I leave. And, of course, you can always call me with questions, or ask one of the others. Gran knows all about the special services we're starting to offer, Foster is the man when it comes to the horses and other animals, and Dad is our handyman for the winter, since they're not traveling."

"Speaking of the *Rambling Rose* . . ." That was what Ed and Rose Skye had dubbed their RV, but it fit their mother all too well these days, both in geography and interests. "What's with the *Antiques Roadshow* routine?"

Krista hesitated. Then, apparently deciding not to

tell Jenny to lighten up on their mom—a familiar refrain—she said, "The battle over kitchen space died down once the guests left."

"Once the audience was gone, you mean."

"Be nice—she's a good cook."

"They both are, but Gran cooks ranch food, which is what this place is all about. People don't come to a dude ranch to eat fondue and frogs' legs."

"That's what I thought at first, but lately I've been reconsidering. It might be fun to add Foodie Week to the roster, or have Mom do a few meals per week as a change of pace. Or . . ." Krista trailed off, shrugging. "Regardless, you shouldn't have to deal with any kitchen issues. She's redoing her and Dad's suite. Last I heard, she was rabid to find some forties perfume bottles and a spindle-leg dressing table."

Jenny rolled her eyes. "Thus, the buying trip."

"Would you rather be mediating a kitchen turf war?"

"No, it's just . . ." She sighed. "I miss the old Mom. You know, the pre-midlife crisis version that didn't make you feel like you'd gotten in the way of a fluffy bulldozer."

"She's not that bad," Krista protested, not quite hiding her grin. "Look at it this way—at least she's out of Gran's hair."

"There is that." A *beep-beep* from the front of the house brought Jenny's attention around. "Are we expecting someone?"

"I . . ." Krista checked the time. "Wow, is it that late already? That'll be Doc, here to look at Lucky's man parts . . . or what used to be man parts, anyway. He got gelded last week. Lucky, I mean, not Doc. You want to come on out and say hi?"

Doc Lopes was pushing seventy and moving slower by the year, but he still had a cowboy's reflexes when it came to dodging a flying hoof. With a dry wit and little patience for foolishness, he was a fixture around Mustang Ridge.

Jenny shook her head. "No, thanks. I think I'm going to bond with the woodstove for a while, maybe poke around the databases and see if I have any questions before you're wheels up."

"Of course." Krista pulled her in for a one-armed hug. "Thanks for coming, Jen. I need this break."

"You more than earned it." Jenny nudged her toward the door. "Go on, deal with not-gonna-get-Lucky's vet visit, and then get yourself packed. I'll take care of everything here, I promise." She crossed her heart like she would've when they were twelve, promising never to like the same boy.

And she meant it, too. She had hung suspended over a gorge to film a ziplining date, swum into an ancient cave with her camera on her head to catch the contestants stripping down, and white-knuckled her way through a flash flood that had nearly decimated the crew's main camp. She could handle six weeks at home.

3

The following afternoon, Krista slung her last bag over her shoulder, hugged everyone for the umpteenth time, and headed out the door. She was borderline late to leave, having taken too much time fussing over last-minute details.

Despite the freezing cold and a darkening sky that threatened more snow, Jenny trailed her across the parking lot, shivering inside an old down parka. "Wow. Is this what it feels like to be the one staying home?"

"Ha. Welcome to my world." But despite Krista's teasing tone, her eyes held question marks. "Jen, are you sure—"

"Positive." She poked her twin toward the idling truck, where Junior, one of the ranch's assistant wranglers, was waiting to take her to the airport. "Get your butt in that truck before you miss your plane or I turn into a Popsicle."

Krista laughed and hugged her tight. "We need to put some Wyoming back in your blood."

No, thanks. "I'll work on it. Safe trip. Call when you get to the hotel, okay?"

"Will do." Krista headed to the truck and tossed her bag in the front, then shot Jenny a final wave before she bounced up into the vehicle. The door slammed, the engine revved, and Junior headed out with a cheerful horn blast.

Jenny watched the truck churn up the long driveway, its taillights glowing cherry red as it crested the hill.

A moment later, it was gone.

"Okay. Here goes nothing." Resolved not to let Krista down, she turned and headed for the main house. She should probably check for messages and make sure she really, truly knew how to update the reservation database without deleting the whole shebang. Granted, Krista would be only a phone call away, but she wanted to let her sister have her so-called vacation in peace.

She had one boot on the porch stairs when her phone gave a muffled bleat from the bottom of her downpoufed pocket. She checked the ID, saw it was Krista, and laughed as she answered. "You couldn't even make it out the driveway? Everything's fine. I haven't had time to mess up yet."

"Get in the Jeep and come up to the main road, quick!"

Krista's tone put an *uh-oh* in the pit of Jenny's stomach. "Did you crash?"

"No, there's a dog up at the end of the driveway,

probably a drop-off. I need you to grab him before he gets hit!"

"A . . . Seriously?" Jenny didn't know why she was surprised—dumped pets had always been a fact of life at Mustang Ridge, and it had only gotten worse with the shaky economy. The ranch was home to untold barn cats, ancient saddle horses, and past-their-prime cows, but softhearted Krista always found room—and vet money—for one more.

"Would I kid about this?" Her sister's voice climbed. "He looked like he was in pretty rough shape, and with the snowbanks from the plows, he's going to get hit for sure. But if Junior and I turn back for him, I'll miss my plane, and—"

"I'm on my way."

A few minutes later, armed with a flashlight, a lead rope from the barn, and a package of mini bratwursts she'd found stashed in the back of one of the refrigerators, Jenny parked Krista's Jeep at the end of the wide driveway and climbed out.

Big solar-powered lanterns topped the stone columns on either side of the entrance, lighting a generous semicircle of the main road. There was no sign of the dog, but Krista was right about the danger. The plowed snowbanks narrowed the shoulders of the two-laner, leaving little room for evasive maneuvers.

"And some creep dumps a dog up here, not even bothering to get it down the driveway," Jenny said, disgusted. *Probably told the kids it went to live at a nice farm, too.* Crossing her fingers, she gave a sharp whistle and called, "Here, puppy, puppy, puppy. Who's a good puppy?"

The only answer was a low, eerie moan of wind through the welded horseshoe sign that arched over the drive, welcoming people to Mustang Ridge.

Should've asked what it looked like, she thought as she clicked on the flashlight and started up the road, scanning both sides. Jack Russell? Great Dane? Something in between? Was it big enough to jump up on one of the banks, or was it stuck in the roadway canyon? Sure, she could call Krista back and get more deets, but she didn't want to waste the time . . . or get her sister's "Jenny can't handle it" radar going in the first ten minutes. Especially when she could handle it.

A deer trail cut through the snow and across the road, but that was the only sign of life. Mostly, things were too iced over to hold tracks. Was she even going the right way? She had turned in the direction Junior would've driven, but there was no telling if her quarry had doubled back.

She opened the package of finger-size sausage links, crinkling the wrapper extra loud. "Are you hungry, buddy? Want some dinner?" She wasn't sure if the odor would carry on the leaden air, but she didn't want to start tossing pieces at random. It wasn't like she was chumming for great whites. Instead, she stood in one spot and swung the flashlight in a wide arc, calling, "Come on, puppy. Help me out here. Don't you want a nice spot by the fire?" It sure sounded good to her.

Suddenly, not twenty feet from the mouth of the

driveway, a canine head popped up from behind the snowbank on the opposite side of the road. Caught in her flashlight beam, the large, floppy-eared dog blinked and shifted, looking poised to bolt. But its eyes were locked on her hands, like it wanted those brats, bad.

Jenny's pulse kicked up a notch. *There you are!*

She didn't let herself react, though—she might've been out of the ranch loop for a while, but she knew enough not to rush a spooky critter or make too much eye contact. Instead, aiming the flashlight off to the side, she broke off a piece of sausage and tossed it to land a few feet away from the dog, up on the snowbank.

The animal flinched when the brat landed, but it didn't run off. Instead, it hesitated and then crept onto the plowed-up berm to gulp the food, watching her with worried eyes.

"You're okay," she said softly. "Everything's okay." But the dog's matted fur hung in ropes and it was favoring one front leg. Drop-off or stray, it'd been a while since this guy had been loved on.

Heart twisting, she tossed the rest of the brat so it landed at the base of the embankment.

The dog hesitated, but hunger overrode caution and he scrambled down and snapped up the tidbit. Then he crouched, shaking all over and whining low at the back of his throat. And, with the flashlight full on the dog and the gleam of snow behind it, Jenny could see why Krista had sounded so emotional on the phone.

He looked like their old golden retriever, Rusty.

Not just a little. A lot.

Dark, honey-colored hair shone through the dirty, ice-crusted mats, and if the dog wasn't pure golden, it was darn close, with the heavy bone structure and wide-browed head of the breed. And more than just the basics of color and shape, there was something about the dog's expression that tugged at Jenny's childhood memories, taking her back to thousands of games of fetch, hundreds of rides with Rusty tagging at her horse's heels, and countless hours spent sitting down by the lake, with him curled up next to her as she looked out over the water and tried to work out a future that didn't look anything like Mustang Ridge.

It was his eyes, she thought, and the shape of his muzzle. The way he tilted his head like he was really listening.

"Handsome boy," she said automatically, like she used to do with Rusty. "Good man."

The end of his tail twitched, but when she took a step forward, the dog emitted a low growl.

This isn't Rusty, she reminded herself. *Don't assume anything*. The last thing she wanted was to start her stint at the ranch with a course of rabies shots.

Crouching, she broke off another piece of sausage—keeping it small so the dog wouldn't fill up if this took a while—and tossed it very near his nose. It disappeared with a *slurp-gulp* and the growl diminished.

"That's a fine fellow. Want another?" This one fell shorter than she intended, landing well onto the road. Grateful that there was almost zero through traffic, especially this time of year, she crooned, "Come on, buddy. You know you want it. Brave boy."

It took her a solid ten minutes to get the dog over the center line, and another five to get him to the point that he would dart within a few feet of her to snatch up the thrown food before retreating out of reach. By that time, however, she was running low on bribes and he was backing off farther each time, no doubt because he had nearly a pound of sausage in his belly. And she was freezing, her hands and face most of the way to numb.

She had options. She could leave now and come back in the morning with more food, or have Foster set a live trap. But there was no guarantee the dog would still be around by then. He could wander off, get run over, be attacked . . . She didn't like any of the alternatives, and she didn't want to have to answer Krista's inevitable "Well, did you get him?" call with "Not yet."

Mostly, though, she didn't want to leave him behind when his growl said *I can take care of myself*, but his eyes telegraphed *Please help me*.

So, with the lead rope clipped onto itself in a crude lasso and held casually at her side, she tossed the last bratwurst a couple of feet away.

The dog's eyes locked on it and his body vibrated with the force of his anxious whine. Jenny didn't say anything, just stood there, looking off into the darkness like she had all the time in the world. She was aware of everything, though—the cold that had seeped into her bones, the tug of hunger in her own belly, her sick anger at the poor creature's condition, and most of all, the dog's slow progress as he edged closer with one eye locked on the brat, the other on her.

Come on, she urged silently as she closed her fingers on the soft cotton rope. *You can do it. Just a few more feet . . .*

And then she heard a low vibration in the distance. *No!* She kept the word to herself, but a pit opened up in her stomach as the noise became an engine rumble, that of a heavy truck downshifting to start up the incline on the other side of the ridge.

Another minute, and it would be right on top of them.

Her pulse thudded in her ears, fast and urgent. *Rock meet hard place.* If she chased the dog out of the street, she'd shatter his fragile trust. But they couldn't stay where they were, and—

The dog lunged forward and grabbed the sausage. Jenny's body moved before she was aware of making the decision, tossing the lead over his head with a quick, practiced flick, and then yanking back to set the loop, like she was roping a steer. *Gotcha!*

Yelping, he exploded, lurching up and away from her, pulling the rope even tighter.

"I'm not going to hurt you." She said it automatically, not that he would believe her as she hauled him back and got him by the scruff, dodging teeth as a pair of headlights crested the hill and started toward them. "Come on, we've got to get off the road!"

Grateful for her heavy clothing, she lifted the panicked animal partway off the ground and started for the driveway at a shambling run. She could feel his bones beneath her gloved hands, but even emaciated, the dog weighed enough that his struggles nearly knocked her off her feet.

"Hang on!" she shouted over the climbing engine noise. "We're almost there." Just a few more steps and—

The truck's horn blasted, like she didn't already know she needed to get the heck out of the way, and the air brakes kicked on with a thunderous racket that hammered at her eardrums. The dog let out a howl, lunged forward and then yanked back, throwing her further off balance. She stumbled and went partway down, banging one knee on the pavement, and the dog tore free.

"No!" she cried as the lead whipped from her gloved fingers, her cry barely audible. She flung herself up against the snowbank as the dog bolted across the road. He slipped, skidded, and—

VAROOM! The truck and tandem trailers blasted through. Running lights flashed past in amber blurs that didn't light the trailer logos, and all she saw was a HOW AM I DRIVING? sign with the phone number scratched off. Then, engine howling, the truck flew off into the night.

When it was gone, Jenny shoved away from the snowbank, moaning, "Oh, no."

The dog lay on the other side of the road, unmoving.

*   *   *

With Ruby gone for the day and no overnight guests of the small or large animal variety, the clinic was dead quiet by six. After a quick phone call to his father—their usual "Yep it's cold; nope the fish aren't biting; how's the clinic?" routine—Nick focused on banging out the last of the day's paperwork.

"Want some?" He broke a corner off his pizza slice and held it out to Cheesepuff.

The fat orange tabby gave the offering a suspicious sniff, then turned away with a sidelong look that said *Hypocrite.*

Okay, so maybe he'd given Ted Dwyer a lecture on not feeding his lard-ass hunting dogs so many table scraps not an hour ago. And, yeah, the Puffmeister wasn't exactly svelte.

"No? Your loss." Nick ate the last of the day-old Di-Giorno's, washed it down with some root beer, and let out a satisfied sigh. "I think that does it for today. Don't you? Want to roll upstairs?"

The cat flicked one ear back, then yawned.

"Your call. I'm heading up." Another guy might be worried about getting caught talking to his cat, but a vet could get away with stuff like that without losing his man card.

After draining the last of the root beer and three-pointing the can in the recycling bin, Nick shucked off his lab coat and headed across the office to hang it up. He was halfway across the room when the buzzer rang, letting him know someone was coming down the long driveway. A moment later, headlights crested the hill and lit the picture window out front.

"Guess I spoke too soon, huh?" But, hey, at least he was still downstairs, and not in the shower, wearing nothing but shampoo. Been there, done that. And, besides, this was part of the deal when you ran a one-vet clinic and lived on-site. "Let's see what's up."

He pulled the coat back on and got it buttoned, and headed out into the reception area just as snow boots thudded on the front porch and the door swung open. A blast of frigid air swept in, haloing a bundled figure that stumbled past him into the waiting area. The furry pink boots and five-foot-something height said female, possibly young, but the rest of the details got swallowed up in a huge pink parka, blue wool hat, and a striped scarf. And the sight of a big, blanket-wrapped dog in her arms and smears of blood on her coat.

Never a good sign.

Adrenaline kicking in, Nick did a quick mental rundown of which pieces of equipment would need time to warm up. "Come in, come in. You can go straight back to Exam One."

Instead she swung back and gaped at him, her bright blue eyes widening in the gap between hat and scarf. "You're not Doc!"

4

Maybe it was the adrenaline coming from the near-miss with the truck plus the rushed drive to the clinic on a road that got slippery when the snow started to fall, or the relief of getting there in one piece, but Jenny's mind blanked at the sight of the stranger standing in Doc's office.

Brain freeze. Nada.

He looked like a young Harrison Ford, with tousled brown hair, a square jaw, sparkling hazel eyes, and a long, lean body clad in jeans, a lab coat, and battered hiking boots. Okay, so maybe he didn't look all that much like Indy—there was no leather, fedora, or bullwhip in sight. But there was something about him that rooted her in place. And she wasn't one to grow roots.

Slightly uneven teeth flashed behind a charming smile, and a pair of killer dimples popped into view. "Doc Lopes retired and handed the practice over to me about six months ago. I'm Nick Masterson." Nodding to the blanket-wrapped bundle, he added, "Who do we have there?"

The question kicked Jenny's brain back into gear, bringing a flush and sidelining her surprise that Doc wasn't Doc anymore—and the new guy was hot.

"I don't know. He was up by our driveway. I was trying to get him, almost had him, but . . ." Her voice cracked. "He got away from me and wound up under an eighteen-wheeler. I don't know how bad he was hit."

His eyes sharpened on her. "Are you okay?"

She shook her head no, then changed it to a nod. "I'm fine. But the dog—"

"I'll take him back and see what we've got." He held out broad, competent-looking hands to take the blanket-wrapped bundle. "Or do you want to stay with him?"

Over and over during the drive to the clinic, she had reminded herself: *This isn't Rusty, and it wasn't your fault.* And if she kept telling herself that second part, eventually it might start feeling like the truth. "No. I'll . . . ah, I'll wait out here. Unless you need help?"

"Not for the initial look-see." He took the dog gently in his arms, showing none of the strain she had felt at lugging the fifty-some pounds of deadweight. "I'll be a few minutes." As he headed down the short hallway that led to the exam rooms, he said over his shoulder, "In my office, there's soda in the fridge and a friendly orange cat sacked out next to the computer, if you could use either. Through the door behind the reception desk."

Then he disappeared into one of the exam rooms,

leaving her alone in the waiting area, surrounded by empty chairs, well-thumbed animal magazines, and posters that alternated between ADOPT A PET NOW and info on the life cycles of fleas.

Gravitating to the fleas, she stuck her hands in her pockets and read up on third-stage larvae. Except when she was done with the short paragraph, she couldn't have repeated any of it—her mind was stuck on the *varoom* of the truck and the way things had gone to hell in a split second.

If she had just held on to the dog, they'd be sitting next to the woodstove right now. Or maybe tucking into Gran's chicken and biscuits.

"Hang in there, buddy," she said softly. "There's a dog bed back home with your name on it."

Part of her wished she had followed the vet into the back room, but even if the dog regained consciousness, it wasn't like her being there would help. Besides, she needed a minute to regroup. She'd driven up here expecting old Doc Lopes, and instead gotten a guy who looked like he'd be right at home in a mosquito-netted tent, with a very different world outside.

The disconnect was the same as seeing her dad back at Mustang Ridge, like the scenery and the people didn't go together.

Flea eggs take two to fourteen days to hatch. Hatching occurs only when the environmental conditions are exactly right for their survival.

"No problem there." Jenny sighed. "These conditions aren't right for anything. Except maybe making daiquiris." Not that she would want a frozen drink right now. She was only just beginning to thaw out in the clinic's warmth, enough that her feet ached and her fingers were going pins and needles.

When conditions are warm and humid, the flea egg will hatch and the larva emerges.

"They'd like Belize," she mused.

"Never been there."

"Oh!" She spun, flushing inside her layers when she found the vet standing behind her, looking amused.

"I talk to the cat all the time. Never tried the artwork before." Taking pity on her, he continued. "I've had a look at the dog, and wanted to talk to you before we go any further."

The flush cooled. "Is it bad?"

"He's in pretty decent shape, all things considered. It doesn't look like the truck wheel rolled over him, which is good, but I won't know how good until I take some X rays and run a few tests. Beyond that, he's got a healing wire cut on a front paw and he's skinny as heck. I'd say it's been a while since he saw any love, though he's friendly enough that he must've at some point."

Jenny's chest tightened. "Poor old guy."

"He's actually not that old. I'd say three or four years, which is going to be in his favor for recovery."

"Good." Relief came out of her in a whooshing breath. "That's good. Do what you can for him. I'll cover the bill and give him a home." Granted, she was making a promise that Krista and the others would be keeping when she left, but any of them would've said the same thing.

The vet hesitated. "It could get expensive if the damage is worse than it looks."

"I'm good for it. X rays, tests, surgery, whatever he needs."

"Is there someone you should check with first?"

"Are you trying to talk me out of it?" *Or fishing for whether I'm taken?* He wasn't wearing a ring, but she didn't think that was where it was coming from. Either way, the conversation felt out of sync, like she was missing something.

"I'm just making sure you know what you're getting into."

That was when she realized what was so strange. He wasn't treating her like she was an extension of Mustang Ridge, wasn't assuming that she knew the drill.

Wow. Weird. And kind of nice, actually.

"I can handle the dog and the bill. Run a tab, Doc, and let's get this party started."

A crooked smile crossed his face, making her think of Indy again. And the fact that there hadn't been any really good adventurer movies out recently.

"Yes, ma'am." He turned away and headed for the reception desk. "I'm going to need you to fill out some paperwork. You can leave it on the desk, along with a number where I can reach you with an update."

"Can I wait here until the X rays are done?" She didn't know where the impulse came from, but it felt right.

"It'll take some time. An hour, maybe longer."

A glance out the window warned that the snow was still falling, but the Jeep had four-wheel drive and there was no rush getting back. "Like you said, it's been a while since anybody cared about him. I'd like to wait."

He handed over a clipboard with a pen stuck at the top. "Make yourself comfortable. There are magazines in the basket over there, and a restroom on the left." With a half wave that wasn't quite a salute, he disappeared into the exam room.

Not letting herself glance back over at the fleas—had he really caught her talking to a *poster*?—Jenny dropped into a chair and fumbled for the pen. It wasn't until her gloves got in the way that she realized she was boiling, and not just from embarrassment.

How had she not noticed that she was overheating inside her Stay-Puft Marshmallow of a coat and six-mile scarf? *Because for the past couple of days you've spent way more time shivering than sweating*, she thought, and shucked off her vest, hat, and hoodie, piling them off to the side. Which left her sitting there in jeans and a clingy turquoise thermal that had come out of the high school section of her closet.

She dragged her fingers through her hair, like that was going to fix anything. She had asked the film crew's hair stylist for an Audrey Hepburn do, and with a little work she could come close to that mark. Add in some hat head, though, and she was more hedgehog than Hepburn.

And she was primping. Which was ridiculous.

Okay, so Nick Masterson was seriously yummy and

he seemed like a nice guy, but she was here to work, not play. And he was a local.

Focusing on the clipboard, she skipped all the fill in the blanks and wrote *Bill to Mustang Ridge* across the bottom, along with her name. For phone numbers, she left both her cell and the landline in Krista's office, knowing there were no guarantees when it came to cell service up on the ridge.

She returned the paperwork to the reception desk, grabbed a magazine at random, and sat back down. After using her phone to shoot off a text to Krista—*Dog got hit, at vet's now*—she flipped open the magazine. She was halfway through an article on knitting sweaters out of pet hair when something warm and soft bumped against her shins.

Looking down, she discovered a sturdy orange tabby winding between her legs. "Hey, cat. What's up? You volunteering for sweater duty?"

He hopped up on the bench beside her, gave her wadded-up parka a sniff, and then climbed up on her lap to sit square on the magazine, purring a cheerful chainsaw buzz.

She scratched behind an ear, and he tipped his head and leaned into her fingers. Settling back and pushing the mag aside, she made a more comfortable lap for the big cat, who lurched up in an affectionate head butt.

Leaning back to avoid a mouthful of fur, she said, "Well, it's nice to meet you, too."

"See? I told you the cat was a good conversationalist."

Jolting, she looked up, surprised to find the vet not just in the room, but practically standing over her. "Oh!" she said as their eyes met. "I didn't know you were there. How do the X rays look?" *Please say they're okay*.

He didn't answer at first, just stood there, staring at her like he'd caught an invisible hoof upside the head. Then, slowly, he said, "You must be Krista's sister."

It took a second for her to reorient, another to quash the stupid tug of resentment at being pigeonholed. Then, scooting the cat off her lap, she stood and faced Doc Hottie. "That's right. How is the dog?"

"Not bad, considering. He has a couple of cracked ribs, but no displaced fractures." Nick's answer was automatic. Which was lucky, because the rest of his brain was jammed up with a whole lot of *wow*.

She was a few inches shorter now that she wasn't wearing the hat. Wasn't wearing much, in fact, and it was an effort not to stare at the way her blue-green shirt clung to her. She was slender and delicately curved, yet her stance made her appear to take up more space than she actually did. Short, chocolate brown hair framed a delicate face with high cheekbones, vivid blue eyes, and a wide, luscious mouth.

Twins, he thought, though the woman in front of him was far from a double of her sister. Where Krista rarely bothered with makeup, her twin's lips were full and dark and her thick eyelashes made her eyes more intensely blue. And while he liked Krista plenty, and respected her as a client, an animal lover, and all-around nice person, she had never put a sizzle in the center of his body or made him stumble over his words.

He cleared his throat. "You're Jenny, right? The photographer?"

"How'd you know that?" she countered with a bit of an edge to her voice. Worried or defensive? He wasn't sure.

"I was at the ranch the other day checking on one of the horses, and Krista told me you were filling in for her while she's on the coast. Nice of you."

Seeming to relax a little, she lifted a shoulder. "I had some time off coming."

Krista had made it sound like it had been a bigger deal than that, and like she'd had to do some convincing to get her sister to come home and ranch-sit. He didn't figure that bore repeating, though, so he said, "Sorry I didn't recognize you under all those layers. I wouldn't have given you the 'this could get expensive' lecture."

"Is it going to? Get expensive, I mean."

Okay, so she didn't want to talk about the ranch. Or maybe she was wishing he would get to the point already. Reorienting, he forced his brain back on track. "I don't think it's going to be too bad, all things considered. I'd like to keep him for the next twenty-four hours. I'll run some blood panels to make sure there's nothing shutting down internally, and also make sure he's heartworm negative. He'll need his vaccinations, but I'd suggest letting him heal up a bit first. He's already neutered, so we don't need to have that conversation. And, well, he stinks."

Her lips twitched. "You volunteering for bath duty?"

"Ruth likes a good grooming challenge, though be warned, she's got a thing for polka-dot bows and perfumed shampoos."

"I bet Old Man Plunkett loves that."

He snorted at the thought of Ruth getting her hands on the crotchety old farmer's livestock guardian dogs—a pair of Great Pyrs that tipped the scales near one seventy each and patrolled their flocks like militant yetis. "Okay, that cinches it. You're definitely a local."

She made a face. "Recovering local, please."

"That's right. Krista said you travel all over filming documentaries and TV shows."

"Mostly TV these days. It's steady work and the location rocks."

"Belize?"

"How did you . . ." Her frown cleared and she actually cracked a smile, which he considered progress. "Right. The fleas. Yes, I've been rain foresting it for the past few years. The next go-round starts taping in seven weeks, and I plan to be there."

"What's the quarantine like?"

"Why . . . Oh, I get it. No, when I head back our newest family member will stay at Mustang Ridge, aka Doggy Paradise." Her expression softened. "Krista and I had a goldie when we were kids. I'm pretty sure I'm speaking for everyone back home when I say it'll be nice having another one around."

And the universe had put the dog in the right place at the right time, Nick thought, grateful that he wouldn't have to scramble to find a home for yet another stray. "Well, then, I guess there's only one thing left for me to say."

"Which is?"

"Congratulations on your new dog."

5

By midmorning the next day, Jenny had gained a new level of respect for her sister's ability to keep her cool.

"Okay, then," she said into the phone. "I'll check on that and get back to you."

"Can't you just fix it now and send me a new confirmation email?"

"As I already explained, I need to run this change past our head of guest services."

"Don't get snippy with me, young lady."

Don't tempt me. Trying to find some amusement in being "young lady'd" by someone she suspected wasn't much older than she was—or at least she sure didn't act it—Jenny said, "That's absolutely not my intention, ma'am." *Ha, I'll see you a "young lady" and raise you a "ma'am" or two.* "However, the week you wish to switch your reservation to is already at capacity." She managed not to tack on, "as I already explained." Stifling a sigh, she tried again. "If you could come the following week instead—"

"No, no, that won't do at all. This is for our anniversary."

Then maybe you should've gotten the date right three months ago when you made the reservation. If Krista had been sitting in the chair opposite her, they could've traded eye rolls. As it was, all Jenny could do was stare out the window while Missy Mackey explained for the third time about plane tickets and childcare, like that was Jenny's problem.

Then again, it kind of was, because she had Krista's voice in her head, reminding her that the customer was always right and it was up to her to make nice. So when Missy finally ran down, she said, "I understand your situation, really I do. But I don't have the authority to make the change. I'll work on it and get back to you."

There was a chilly pause. "I'd like to speak with your superior."

It was tempting to transfer the woman to Big Skye, but that definitely didn't count as making nice with the guests. "This is a family organization, ma'am, and I'm the ranking family member currently available. I'm afraid you'll have to wait for a call back."

"This simply won't do. Your brochure promises satisfaction guaranteed."

"What can I do to satisfy you, ma'am? Would you like to cancel your reservation?" Okay, so that wasn't exactly making nice, either, but what else could she do? She wasn't about to overbook the cabins or try to move people around without talking to Krista first.

"I . . . No. No, don't do that." Missy gave a put-upon sigh. "You'll have an answer for me this afternoon?"

"If not today, then tomorrow at the latest." *As I already said*.

It took Jenny another five minutes to get the woman off the phone, and the moment she had the handset back in its cradle, the darn thing started ringing again, like it had been doing pretty much all morning.

She didn't know how Krista did it. She really didn't.

Summoning a cheery tone that made her molars ache, she answered with, "Mustang Ridge. This is Jenny Skye. How can I help you?"

"You're not answering your cell phone."

Her stomach lurched as she placed the resonant male voice. A glance at her cell had her scowling. "Darn it, no bars. Sorry, Doc."

"Nick."

"Nick, then. Anyway . . ." She took a deep breath to beat back the sudden flutters. "How's our patient doing?"

"He's good. Actually, I'd say he's better than good, maybe all the way up to rock star status. He's alert, hungry, heartworm negative, and friendly as all get out, especially once he figured out that Ruth and I come bearing biscuits." He paused. "Now we just need to cross our fingers that he's housebroken and doesn't like to eat drywall."

Warmed by the good news and the sound of his voice, she tucked the phone tighter to her cheek and made a teasing *pffft* sound. "Drywall? Please. This is Mustang Ridge. We're all about lumber and cowhide."

He chuckled. "What was I thinking? Anyway, I'd like to check him back over later this afternoon, and if everything looks good, you can pick him up this evening. Sound like a plan?"

"Absolutely. Gran and my dad are eager to meet him." Her grandfather, too, though Big Skye had grumbled about retrievers having no business on a working ranch, and why couldn't she have found a cattle dog or a collie? "When can I spring our new family member?"

"Let's aim for six. That'll give Ruth time to work her grooming magic, and me time to finish up his lab work and discharge instructions. I'll call you if anything changes."

It wasn't a date, shouldn't have felt like one. But it gave her a buzz to say, "I'll see you then, Doc. Oh, and you'd better use this number if you need to call. Apparently, Krista's office is a cellular void."

"Ah, well, dead zones happen . . . usually at the most inconvenient time possible. You know, like when you break down twenty miles from civilization."

"With your provisions limited to half a granola bar and a can of Coke."

"In the middle of the desert at high noon."

"Wearing a cocktail dress and four-inch heels," she finished, grinning.

"Hey, have you been stalking my blog?"

"Are there pictures?"

"If there were, Ruth would probably have them front and center on the clinic's Web site. And speaking of Ruth, I need to hit the road before she comes looking for me."

Jenny suffered a bump of disappointment, like she was a teenager and her mom had just come in and booted her off the phone in the middle of some juicy gossip. "Good luck with, well, whatever you've got on your to-do list."

"Four spay and neuters, three ailing heifers, two lameness rechecks—"

"And a partridge in a pear tree," she singsonged.

"A healthy one, please. Birds hate me."

She laughed. "Bye, Doc."

"I'll see you at six."

Fortunately, there was nobody there to see her goofy grin as she disconnected.

Nick was whistling as he came out of his office. "I'm off to play large-animal vet. Be back in a few hours."

Ruby raised her eyebrows. "Somebody took a happy pill. Do I want to know what you were doing in your office just now?"

"Can't a guy be in a good mood?"

"Sure, but there are good moods and then there are *good moods*, if you know what I mean."

He was pretty sure he didn't want her to explain the difference. And, besides, it had just been a quick conversation. Nothing earth-shattering. Just . . . fun. So he said, "Guess that second cup of coffee is catching up with me."

"Or maybe you got a sext you don't want me to know about?"

"A what?"

"A sext. You know, a sexy text message."

He didn't know which was worse—that she knew sext was a word, or that he didn't. Clearly, he needed to watch more TV. Or hang out at Wednesday Bingo. "Nope, no, er, messages to speak of."

"If you say so." Grinning, she waved him off. "Drive safe and watch the ice. Call me if you get lost."

"Count on it." He pulled on his parka and gloves, and shot her a wink as he headed out the door, suddenly in a hurry to get through his day.

By midafternoon, Jenny had dealt with most of her to-do list and needed a break, so she bundled up and followed the path down to the neat little split-log cabin at the bottom of the valley. She let herself in through the kitchen door, calling, "Knock, knock."

A gruff voice called from the next room, "Who's there?"

"Bear," she said as she crossed the kitchen and tiptoed into the living room, where Big Skye was kicked back in his recliner, facing the sliders that looked out on the snow-covered ridgeline and the mountains beyond.

"Bear who?" he demanded.

She put her hands over his eyes and leaned in to say, "Bear with me while I come up with a better punch line." Then she gave him a smacking kiss on the cheek before she let go and danced away.

"Ah, go on with you." He made a face and swiped at the spot she had kissed. "And if you catch this lung crud of mine, don't say I didn't warn you to keep your distance." But his voice was stronger than it had been a few days earlier, suggesting that the antibiotics were doing their job against the sinus infection that had knocked him off his boots.

Grinning at him, she tossed her coat, hat, and gloves onto the floral sofa, and perched on the arm closest to him. "Was that the official diagnosis? Lung crud?"

"Close enough." His eyes went to the window. "Nice day. Looks like it'll stay that way for a bit."

With anyone else, that would've been small talk. With her gramps, it was sixty-some years of reading the sky and the way the sunlight fell on the mountains. "Think we'll get a melt?" she asked.

"In January?" He looked at her like she had just suggested he trade his rigging for a sissy English pancake saddle.

"Right. What was I thinking?" Wishing, more like it. She had shivered awake that morning, despite a space heater and pile of blankets. Maybe Krista was right about her needing to get some Wyoming back in her blood. Temporarily, anyway.

"Jenny?" Gran poked her head in from the back hallway. "Hello, sweetheart. Are you visiting, or did you need me?"

"Both, actually. I've got a guest question for you."

Big Skye harrumphed. "Dang foolishness, all of it."

"Foolishness that's keeping this family together," Gran said with a definite edge to her voice, suggesting that he wasn't the only one feeling cooped up with him riding a recliner rather than a fence line. To Jenny, she said, "Come into the kitchen, sweetie, and tell me all about it."

The invitation was as familiar as the spindle-leg piano beside the kitchen door and the decorative cast iron trivets that hung near the ceiling. The cabin was only five or six years old, built to give Gran and Big Skye a one-level refuge from the guests, but to Jenny it seemed that they had never lived anywhere else, like they had transplanted everything that mattered—and not just the furniture and stuff—from their former rooms in the main house.

Jenny paused just inside the kitchen, where her grandmother already had the kettle on, the oven preheating, and her head in the fridge. "Can I help?"

"Poosh, no. You just sit and relax a minute while I get these guys going." Gran pulled out a mixing bowl and slicked off the wax-paper covering to reveal chilled cookie dough, golden brown and loaded with chocolate chips.

"Mmm," Jenny said, picturing them warm, right out of the oven. But then she cocked her head. "Don't you get enough of cooking up at the main house?"

"Not during the wintertime. Besides, where do you think I test my recipes before they go on the menu?" Blue eyes dancing, she tipped her head toward the living room. "Don't tell him that, though."

Jenny grinned. "It'll be our secret."

"Here." Gran set a mug of tea in front of her, blue earthenware in a matching saucer. The tea ball was another old friend, as were the scents of the herbs she dried herself.

"Chamomile and lemon," Jenny said, inhaling the fragrant steam. "Guess I must look pretty stressed out."

"Maybe not on the surface, but it's in there." Gran retrieved two cookie sheets from the cabinet to the left of the stove, just where they had been in the old kitchen up the hill. She lined up the sheets on the counter and, using two spoons so gracefully they could've been extensions of her fingers, began dropping perfect teardrop-shaped clumps of dough in ruler-straight lines. "Tell me about this guest. What's the issue?"

"Her name is Missy Mackey, and she's . . . Well, let's just say that if we met at a party, we'd probably annoy each other. Anyway, she booked a romantic getaway for her and hubby's third anniversary, and just realized she put in for the wrong week. Now she wants us to fix it. And by 'wants' I mean 'will likely trash us on every review site known to mankind if she doesn't get her way.' Problem is, her anniversary falls on the one week next summer that Krista is already fully booked. First week in June."

Gran made an "ouch" face. "Ricci-Norris week. Doesn't that just figure?"

"What's a Ricci-Norris?" Jenny had thought she knew all of the theme weeks Krista put on to help entice guests to the ranch, everything from Singles Week to Rodeo Week, but she'd never heard of that one.

"Not what, who. Antonia Ricci and Dale Norris. It's a wedding."

"A . . . oh." She took a sip of tea, remembering her sister's enthusiasm over the idea of adding wedding planning to the ranch's repertoire last year. *Shudder*. "Good for Krista."

"But too bad for Missy."

"Who is *not* going to be happy about this. Ten bucks says she cancels, demands her nonrefundable deposit back, and then complains to anyone who'll listen." Which could mean a hit to the ranch's rep, given that most people would rather read a scathing rant or watch idiots scheming against one another for a million-dollar prize than read a complimentary review or watch a solid documentary.

"So give her a reason to stick with her original reservation and be happy about it."

That brought Jenny's head up. "Like what? A discount?"

"I was more thinking along the lines of up-charges." Gran slid the cookie sheets into the oven and set the timer. Then, cupping her mug in both hands, she leaned back against the counter, eyes narrowing in concentration. "Is her current reservation a week early or a week late?"

"Late."

"Perfect."

"Says who?"

"Me." Smiling now, Gran sipped her tea. "Tell her to make it a surprise for her husband. She'll need to have him take that week off from work, but she can turn the rest of it into a big mystery. And then, for the day of their anniversary, we'll ship a special picnic basket—cheese, cookies, champagne, that sort of thing—and she can make a big announcement about their upcoming Wild West adventure."

Jenny nodded, wheels starting to turn. "Good. That's good. And exactly the sort of thing I think she would go for." Over the top, with no extra effort on Missy's part. "We can include information on the ranch and a big card inviting them for their special anniversary celebration the following week. So they're actually celebrating twice, and Missy looks like a star for planning everything out. She can even have a party back home on the day of their actual anniversary, so there's a public unveiling of her big gift, with lots of *ooh*s and *aah*s."

"And some free advertising for us," Gran put in, eyes twinkling. "We can also do a private catered dinner on the last night they're here. Table for two under the gazebo, candles, even a fiddler or guitarist if they'd like."

"Let's not go overboard."

"Poosh. It's not the first or last time we'll do a little extra for a guest. And charge them for it, of course. Just because the customer is always right, doesn't mean they get it for free. Especially when they start off by giving us grief."

Jenny laughed. "Amen to that." She lifted her mug and was surprised to find it empty. Setting it back in the saucer with a click, she stood, crossed to Gran, and kissed her cheek. "It's perfect. You're the best." Enthused by the solution, she twirled away. "I'm going to deal with this right now."

"Do you want to wait and bring some cookies up with you?"

"Tempting, but I need to call Missy while things are still fresh and I don't feel like strangling her. Rain check?"

"I'll bring a few up when I start dinner."

"You're the best. Seriously." Riding high, Jenny blew her grandfather a kiss he pretended to ignore, snagged her layers, and dragged them on as she headed back through the kitchen with a "Love you, Gran. See you at dinner, and thanks again!"

Not even the subzero temps outside flattened out the bounce in her step as she headed for the main house. See? She could totally handle this. She just had to ask the right people the right questions, and remember that no matter how cranky a guest she was dealing with, or how weird the request, it probably wasn't a first at Mustang Ridge.

Now she just had to make sure she didn't blow it with Missy.

"I'm sorry," she said, trying out the tone as she boot-thumped her way up the porch steps and pushed through the door into the warm entryway. "We're unable to move your reservation to the week you've requested. However, I think you'll find that's a good thing. Just listen to what we've cooked up especially for you and your husband—"

"Jenny, darling!" The lilting call came from upstairs,

in a familiar voice that stopped her dead in her tracks with her coat half off.

Pivoting toward the staircase, she looked up. "Mom?"

Rose Skye stood on the second step with her hand on the rubbed-smooth banister. Wearing tailored navy pants and a soft ivory sweater, with her steel gray hair swept up in a twist that had relaxed to let a few wisps fall free, she looked professionally elegant, and nothing like the jeans-and-flannel mom of Jenny's childhood.

Eyes alight with pleasure, she stretched out a hand and drifted down the last two steps. "Come here! Oh, it's so good to see you!"

Crossing to her, Jenny leaned into a cloud of unfamiliar perfume and returned her mother's hug. "You, too, Mom. You're back early."

"I couldn't wait to see my baby." Rose let go and stepped back, face lighting. "Besides, I found some amazing pieces for the bedroom, and I wanted to get back here with them."

Sigh. "Dad said you were on the hunt for a dressing table. Did you find what you were looking for?"

"It's beautiful. Come and see!"

"I need to make a phone call first. Guest issue, you know. Can you give me ten minutes, maybe fifteen?"

"This won't take long." Rose pulled a bright plum-colored parka off the rack near the door.

"We're going outside?"

"Of course, silly. Do you think the pieces are going to carry themselves in?"

"Carry . . . Right." Jenny shot a look out the back

window, but there was no sign of life in the workshop. "Where's Dad?"

"He had to run to the hardware store."

"How about Foster? Junior?"

Her mother's eyebrows climbed. "Jennifer Lynn Skye. Since when do you need a man to carry your bags for you? I taught you girls better than that."

Jenny wanted to point out that it wasn't about testosterone and she had work to do. But it wasn't like Missy was sitting by the phone, waiting for her to call back—or if she was, that was Missy's problem, not hers. And the guests weren't the only ones she was supposed to be making nice with. "Okay, okay, you got me. Let's go unload your booty."

She stifled another sigh, though, as she dragged her parka back on. Darn it. She really should've waited for those cookies to come out of the oven.

6

Nick's morning flew and he was back at the clinic by lunchtime. With an hour free before his first small-animal appointment, he headed for the back room, where he found the golden retriever on the grooming stand with a dog-size pile of hacked-off fur off to one side and Ruth going to town with a pair of scissors.

"Whoa there Three River Scissorhands," he said. "He's a dog, not a topiary!"

She spared him an eye roll. "You want to get in here with the detangler and a brush, be my guest. You want me to do it, then keep the comments to yourself."

"In that case, he looks great."

"Good call."

Nick patted the dog's shoulder. "Hey, buddy. You behaving yourself?"

"He wasn't too sure about getting up on the stand at first, but he's a sucker for a biscuit or two. He started by sitting and offering me a paw to shake, so I'd say he got decent training at some point, maybe with a prior owner."

"The scanner didn't pick up any microchip, and the local animal controls don't have an APB on a missing goldie."

"Can't say I'm sorry to hear that."

Given the condition he'd been in, neither of them was in a hurry to return the dog to wherever he'd come from. Besides, the most likely scenario was an all too common story these days—pet owner one loses a job or house and has to move on, and gives Fido to owner two, thinking they're doing the right thing. In some cases—most cases, Nick liked to think—it worked out just fine.

Not always, though. Sometimes it was the start of a downward slide. Which was why it felt so darn good when things worked out for the better, like they were in this guy's case.

"I'm going to check his labs."

"Don't forget Binky the Pug at two." Taking a few steps back, Ruth surveyed her handiwork. "There. That's better, don't you think?"

Not so much. "He certainly looks more comfortable." She had cut off the ropy mess that had hung under the dog's belly and snipped out the worst of the tangles on his chest and jowls, leaving the dog looking ragged, but relieved.

She grinned over at Nick like he had said the first part out loud. "Just wait until after I've got him bathed and brushed. Besides, the Skyes know how to look past the rough bits and see diamonds underneath." As Ruth started running warm water through the spray nozzle in the big stainless steel tub, she said conversationally to the dog, "I bet Jenny's gran is going to sneak you treats from the kitchen, and Ed is going to make noises about building you a top-notch dog house, but then skip it because you wind up spending most of your time indoors, next to the fireplace. And even if you're not fully trained—which my gut says you are—Krista and Foster will have you civilized by the time the first load of guests rolls in next summer."

"Jenny found him," Nick commented, "and she seemed mighty attached. Said he reminded her of the dog they had when she was a kid. Maybe she'll work with him." He wasn't fishing; just making conversation.

Ruth made a *that's neither here nor there* face. "Jenny's different. She might've been born at Mustang Ridge, but there's not much rancher in her. Sure, she knows how to go through the motions—she rode like a dream and could cut a cow with the best of them—but after she lit out for school she didn't do much looking back."

"She came home when her family needed her. That's got to count for something."

"It counts for plenty, but this guy," Ruth gave the goldie a pat and set his wispy tail to wagging, "is going to need to bond with the others, because she won't be here for long. Where Krista's got roots, Jenny's got wings."

Yeah, he knew how that went.

"Want me to get him in there for you?" he offered, with a nod toward the tub.

"I wouldn't say no."

Brightening his voice to a tone of *who's a good boy?* he said to the dog, "What do you say, buddy? Are you ready for a B-A-T-H?" Not waiting for an answer—or to see if the goldie could spell—he got the big dog in an easy chest-and-rump cradle that wouldn't twinge his injured ribs and lifted him the short distance to the stainless-steel tub, with its grippy rubber bottom and steamy spray.

The dog didn't struggle or try to jump out, just sighed and took it like a man. A dog. Whatever.

As Nick stepped back, Ruth shot him a look under her lashes. "Why the interest in Jenny?"

"Just curious."

"A hot and heavy kind of curious?"

"Ah, Ruth. Always the romantic. Nope, I'm not going there. Not even thinking in that direction." Okay, maybe he was, a little. But not in any serious kind of way.

"Because if you were, I'd have to suggest you think more in Krista's direction. They're twins, after all, and she's still going to be in town come spring."

"Like I said, not going there." Especially when Krista wasn't the one who'd left him grinning after only a few minutes on the phone.

Jenny parked the Jeep in front of the vet clinic at six on the dot, snagged the picnic basket from the passenger's side footwell, and climbed out into a night that had gotten darker and colder during the twenty-minute drive from Mustang Ridge. Or maybe—probably—she was feeling the cold because she had swapped out her down parka for a trim ski jacket, wanting to look less like a teenager and more like . . . well, herself.

Maybe Gran's eyes had been laughing as she handed over the basket, and maybe Jenny had taken an extra five minutes on her hair, but what was the harm? She could think of far worse ways to pass the next five weeks and five days than flirting with the local vet.

She stepped onto the porch, the door opened and there he was, just like last night. Only this time she was carrying treats rather than an injured dog, and she didn't look like the Michelin Man and smell like bratwurst.

Hopefully.

Nick was wearing the same lab coat, thermal shirt, and jeans routine as yesterday, but unlike her, he hadn't had any ground to make up in that department. The light loved him from every angle, putting sexy shadow-smudges along his cheekbones and jaw, and highlighting the waves of his finger-rumpled hair.

"Right on time," he said with an easy grin, ushering her in and closing the door behind her. "You ready to bust your newest family member out of this joint?"

Her flush didn't come from the warm air inside; it was all about the full-on eye contact he was giving her. Still, she managed to come up with a breezy, "Definitely. The others are dying to meet him."

"If that's your dog crate," he said with a nod at the picnic basket, "I've got bad news for you."

"Nope. It's for you." She held it out. "A thank-you from my gran."

Eyes lighting, he took the basket. "Tell me she sent cookies."

"Double chocolate chunk, along with peanut butter brownies and apple cinnamon muffins."

"Score." He flipped up the lid and took a deep breath, which was a pretty universal response where Gran's cooking was concerned. Then he set the basket on the reception desk. "I'll have to scarf the muffins before Ruth gets in. I wouldn't want her to think I was two-timing her."

"Good plan. They're sworn enemies on the local bake-off circuit."

"And Bingo?"

"No, Ruth's got the edge there."

They shared a grin that went on a beat longer than required and put a flutter in Jenny's chest, one that said, *Oh, yeah*, like an oldie-but-goodie Kool-Aid commercial. He wasn't anything like her usual type, but maybe that was part of the attraction.

He held out a hand. "Can I take your coat?"

"Sure. Thanks." Coming from a world where she opened her own doors and schlepped her own equipment, it felt strange to hand over her ski jacket and gloves. Strange and kind of girly, which wasn't necessarily a bad thing, she decided as he hung her stuff on a rack beside the door.

"Your guy is waiting in my office. He looked so sad in his cage, I took pity once Ruth left for the night."

"Ah, you're a sucker."

"Guilty as charged." He opened the office door with a flourish. "Ta-daa!"

Jenny did a double take at the sight of a big golden retriever rising slowly from a nest of blankets in the corner. Because while the dog might be moving like an old cowboy who'd hit the dirt a few too many times, he looked like a million bucks, at least in comparison. The tangles were gone, his honey-colored fur was soft and flowing, and he smelled like lemons rather than funky wet dog and neglect.

And best of all, his eyes were warm and soft, and as he took a couple of old-man steps toward them, his tail wiggled like he wanted her to know he'd be wagging furiously if he wasn't so sore.

Her grin felt wider than her face. "Wow. You guys did a great job!"

"The clip is rough, but he was pretty tangled up."

"Considering what he looked like before, I think it's better than a show trim." She crouched down. "Hey, buddy. Remember me? I kind of hope you don't, but if you do, I'm sorry for what happened with the truck."

He didn't bother sniffing her fingers, just shoved his head into her hand for some scritches.

"I'd say you're the only one beating yourself up on that one," Nick said, leaning a hip against the desk. "How about you cut yourself some slack and lose that guilt?"

"I will. I am. It's just . . ." Stroking the soft, smooth fur, she nodded. "Okay, you're right. Consider it gone.

And consider yourself a hero, because this guy looks great. It's hard to believe this is the same dog I brought in here yesterday."

"It looked worse than it turned out to be. Which is something I wish I could say about all my patients."

"Nice of you to let him hang out in your office."

"Like you said, I'm a sucker. Though Cheesepuff is in the back room, sulking."

She kept patting the dog, but her attention was on the man—not just the way the light curled around his face and long, lean body, but the way the rise and fall of his deep, mellow voice sent an answering hum through her system. "That would be the chubby orange tiger cat I met the other day?"

"Big boned, please. And, yes, that's Cheese. Normally he'd be in here with me after hours, making sure I minded my Ps and Qs."

"Oh? Does he often need to worry about that?"

A gleam entered his eyes, but he shook his head. "Not so much these days. And what does that even mean, anyway? Pints and quarts? Pens and quills?"

"I think it was from old-timey printing presses, where the letters were backward and easy to confuse. Though, why it's not 'mind your lowercase Bs and Ds,' I couldn't tell you."

"Glad we don't have to deal with that anymore. I'm bad enough at reading my own chicken scratches, which is why you should be grateful I've got a computer and a printer. Speaking of which . . ." He tapped a couple of pages on the desk. "These are yours."

"The grand total?"

"Nah, we'll get you for that later. They're discharge instructions, otherwise known as 'the quieter he stays, the faster he'll heal.' Keep him on limited activity for a couple of weeks—indoors, leash walks, that sort of thing—while his ribs knit. After that, you can start letting him have more freedom." He shifted a small white paper bag to join the instructions. "These are his meds. Painkillers for the next few days and a course of antibiotics to get that infection on his leg cleared up. Directions are on the bottles."

"Is the infection a big deal?"

"I'd say we've got it on the run. He might always have a limp, though. Time will tell."

"Considering some of Krista's rescues, that's pretty minor." She ruffled the dog's fur and took a look around the room, part curiosity, part stalling. "I like what you've done with the place."

Where Doc Lopes had packed the built-in shelves with yellowed journals and lined the walls with file cabinets, Nick had streamlined things way down, with just a desk and a couple of chairs. A sleek laptop was hooked to a flat-screen TV and keyboard, and the shelves held personal mementos ranging from a neon green Slinky and a battered Rubik's Cube to a couple of diplomas and a framed photo.

"Thanks," he said. "It's starting to feel like home base."

She stood and crossed to the picture. "Do you mind? Occupational hazard."

"Be my guest. Doubt it's up to your standards, though."

Maybe not as photos went, but the candid snapshot brought an instant grin and an inner *bingo* at the sight of him wearing sand-colored pants and a sun-bleached khaki T-shirt, with his boots planted on baked dirt and a couple of kids flanking him, one with a stranglehold on a happy-looking brown mutt, the other hanging on to a spotted goat. They grinned into the camera like someone had just said the local equivalent of "cheese," and the background sported lots of baked earth and blue sky, and a single baobab tree.

She touched it. "Africa?"

"Far away from the land of ice and snow."

"Amen."

He chuckled and moved up beside her, close enough that she felt an echo of his body heat as her skin prickled to sudden awareness. "I was part of the Africa Twenty-Thirty Project. It's an international group that's working toward a set of pretty ambitious goals to be met by the year 2030, everything from building new roads and hospitals to educating farmers on how to improve yields from their crops and livestock. That was where I came in."

She glanced back at him, eyebrows raised. "Impressive."

"It will be. They're in the middle of a massive survey right now, analyzing which interventions have had the biggest positive impacts. Based on those results, they'll tweak the next set of projects for maximum effect. Even if they don't hit all the big goals, they're changing lives."

"I can't believe you gave up Africa for Three Ridges."

"Life happens. Things change. Speaking of which . . ." He backed off and ruffled the fur on the dog's upturned head. "You should probably get this guy home, so he can start getting used to his new life. I snagged a collar for him out of our Lost and Found." He turned away to buckle the blue nylon strap in place.

In other words, end of discussion. Jenny stuck her hands in her pockets and rocked on her heels. "Sorry for being nosy. Like I said, occupational hazard. You can quiz me back if you want."

The lines around his mouth eased up, like he'd been expecting an interrogation. "That sounds fair . . . But how about over dinner? Friday night? Pick you up at eight?"

A sizzle of surprised pleasure was followed by an inner happy dance. "I thought you'd never ask."

He moved closer, turning the happy-happy into a serious case of butterflies at the thought that he was going to kiss her. He lifted a hand, touched her cheek, lingered there . . . and then tucked a strand of hair behind her ear. "Guess I should walk you out."

Torn between frustration at the *kissus interruptus* and amusement at his unexpected flair, she clipped her lead on to the dog's collar. "Guess you should. This guy has a family to meet." And, come Friday, she had a date.

7

When Jenny got home, she found her parents and grandparents gathered in the front room, lined up behind the couch like they were just waiting to throw confetti and yell "Surprise!"

Given the way the dog was pressed up against her leg, suddenly tense and worried, she really hoped that wasn't the plan. He had handled the car ride just fine, but when they hit the parking lot and she opened the door, he had flattened out on the backseat and started shaking. She had coaxed him up the stairs and through the door, but had a feeling she was pushing it.

She had him on a short leash, so she wasn't afraid of him bolting and hurting himself. But she really wanted this to go well.

"Easy, guys," she warned. "He's a little wigged out."

Gran, bless her, stepped forward and crouched down, becoming very small and nonthreatening. "Who could blame him after what he's been through? Poor boy. But, oh, aren't you a handsome fellow?"

The goldie gave a low whine, but stayed put, leaning against Jenny. The pressure was kind of nice, making her feel like she was his protector, his safe place. Granted, she was the only thing around that was even slightly familiar, but still.

Going down beside the dog, she edged around so the others could see him, saying softly, "Nothing to worry about here, buddy. They just want to get to know you." Even her mom was smiling, standing there next to her dad, and Big Skye might've been giving one of his *goldens aren't ranch dogs* scowls, but there was a suspicious twinkle in his eyes.

"Turn me around," an unexpected voice said suddenly. "I can't see him!"

Jenny's jaw dropped. "Krista? What are you doing back— Oh!" She grinned when her dad reached over to an end table and reversed an open laptop, and she saw her sister on the screen. "Hey!"

"Hey yourself. Who have you got there?"

"Don't you recognize him? Imagine him wearing five pounds of matted fur and wishing he could jump in the truck with you and Junior."

"Wow, he looks great! What did Nick say about his ribs?"

Hoping the sudden heat in her face was of the invisible variety, Jenny played it cool. "We're supposed to keep him leashed or confined for the next week or so, then gradually increase his exercise, etcetera. Otherwise he looks good. His blood work is fine and he's heartworm negative."

"That's a relief."

"I'd say he dodged a few bullets. You here to chime in on names?"

"You betcha!"

All eyes went to the dog, who had come out to stand in front of Jenny with the leash slack and his tail doing a hesitant back-and-forth as the sisters chatted. Now, he cocked his head, eyes a little worried, as if to say *Do you like me? Am I being a good boy?*

Jenny heard the words in a goofy, hopeful voice. "I was thinking maybe we could call him Rusty Too," she said. "R2 for short."

Krista gave a *meh* shrug. "I think he deserves his very own name. Weasley?"

"Because a *Harry Potter* reference is more original than naming him after Rusty?"

"Hello, R2-D2?"

Their dad put in, "If we're going for *Star Wars* references, how about Chewie?"

"Gimpy?" Big Skye suggested. "Stumpy?"

"If he was a she, we could've called her Biscuit," Gran said wistfully. "Or Cinnamon."

"What about Emeril?" said their mom.

"Or Drop-off?" Big Skye added unhelpfully.

"Mack, for the truck that almost got him?" Krista offered with a grin.

"No, and not 'Roadkill,' either, thankyouverymuch." Jenny ruffled his fur. "Come on, people, let's help the poor guy out! No clichés, either. Not Fido, Yeller, Lassie, Rex—"

The dog's head whipped up and he gave a low

"whuff." It was the first noise he'd made since coming into the house.

Jenny looked down at him. "You're kidding. Your name is Rex?"

His eyes were bright, his body quivering. "Whuff!" *Yes, yes, that's me!*

"Seriously?"

Their dad chuckled. "If that wasn't his name before, I'd say it is now. What do you say, Rex?"

When that got another indoor-voice bark, Jenny threw up her hands. "Okay, cliché it is. Welcome to the family, Rex m'boy." She patted the dog bed by the fireplace, with its laundry-smelling cover and newly donated fleece blanket. "I think you should park it here. You're supposed to be taking it easy."

The dog obediently curled on the bed, forming a loose ball of reddish guard fur and rabbit-soft undercoat, and looked up at her as if to say *Now what?*

And suddenly Jenny knew exactly what came next.

"Come on, everyone." She waved toward the hearth. "Get yourselves organized. It's family photo time."

As she headed up the stairs for a camera, she heard her mother say, "I should go change. And my hair—"

"Looks great," her father interrupted firmly, wrapping an arm around her waist.

From her bedroom, Jenny snagged the big padded bag that contained her second-best yet absolute favorite camera, a Nikon she called Old Faithful. Back downstairs, she found her whole family—including Skype Krista—gathered around the dog bed. Her gramps stood in the back wearing his *this is ridiculous* face, but the others were bumping shoulders to sneak a pat of the golden fur.

And the dog, thank goodness, was soaking it up. *Smart guy.*

"Everybody ready?" Jenny asked, lifting Old Faithful and tweaking things for an inside shot.

Gran beckoned. "You should be in here, too."

"My tripod is packed and the timer died on Machu Picchu." She lifted the camera and framed her family. "Squish in closer around the dog."

"His name is Rex," Krista reminded her

"Right. Cuddle up, everyone, and say 'Sexy Rexy'!"

By quitting time on Friday, Jenny felt like she was starting to get the hang of the make-nice-to-the-guests thing. She had turned Missy around by hitting the "he'll love the surprise and you can throw a party to announce the trip" angle exactly right, and had dealt with a minicrisis with one of the suppliers. She had even upsold a few cabins and two more of Gran's special-occasion packages to new guests, and was surprised by the sense of accomplishment.

Then again, it had helped to have the advertising project to fall back on when the ranch stuff made her want to poke her eyes out with a Bic.

She had gone through the photos she'd taken around Mustang Ridge over the past few years and pulled together some possibilities, and sketched out ideas for the short interview clips. She was meeting with Shelby next Thursday, and wanted to have at least two videos to show her. Which meant it was time to get down and dirty with Old Faithful and Doris, her trusty digital vidcam.

But not tonight. Tonight, she had plans.

"Happy date night to me," she said, pushing away from the desk and opening her arms wide in a back-cracking stretch.

Rex gave a hopeful chuff from the corner, where he was sacked out in a nest of old blankets. The dog had settled into the family like he'd been raised beside the woodstove, even staying off the doily-studded frou-frou pillows that Jenny's mom insisted looked just dar-ling in the rustic living area. The dog had proven to be a cheerful, easily distracted fellow with good manners, at least so far. He was still moving slow, favoring his injured ribs and gimping on his infected paw, so Jenny had been keeping him close by her side most of the time, either in the office or her bedroom.

She gave him a sympathetic ear rub. "Sorry, buddy. You're not invited. Come on, let's see if you can hang with Gran in the kitchen."

That got her an enthusiastic tail wag. *Cookies?*

But the kitchen was deserted, with even the ovens powered down, suggesting she wasn't the only one with Friday night plans.

"Gran?" Jenny called, walking back into the main room with Rex padding unevenly behind her. "Dad?" When there was no answer, she tagged on, "Mom?"

There was no answer from that quadrant, either, and

guilt stung a little that she didn't have a clue what her mother was up to, or if she was even around. Jenny hadn't been avoiding her, exactly, but they had both been busy with their own stuff.

"Well, then, I guess we'll have to put you in my room. I'll leave the TV on for you, okay? What do you say, *Animal Planet* or *Jerry Springer* reruns?"

She went for *Animal Planet*, and patted the yellow patchwork bedspread she had picked out of a catalog for her sixteenth birthday. "Here. You can have the bed."

After a brief hesitation, he hopped up, did his customary two and a half circles, and lay down with a sigh that was clearly designed to make her feel guilty for leaving him behind.

"Suck it up," she advised, but gave his ruff a scratch and added, "I won't be too late."

At least she didn't think she would be. Nick had called earlier to confirm and suggest dinner at the Steak Lodge, earning points for avoiding Three Ridge's more traditional first-date, linen-tablecloth restaurant in favor of talking animatronic taxidermy and killer onion rings. And after that . . . well, they would see how it went.

She didn't intend to rush into anything—if nothing else, Krista would kill her if she made things awkward with Mustang Ridge's main vet. But she and Nick were both grownups, and it wasn't like he was a born-and-bred local. Besides, if the Twenty-Thirty Project was anything like the relief group she had embedded with for a three-month stint before joining *Jungle Love*, he wouldn't be any stranger to people coming and going, and the potential for a no-strings fling as a stress reliever.

Maybe. Possibly. But first they would start with dinner.

She hopped in the shower, then gave her hair a quick blow-dry and fluff—*thank you, short haircut*. Coming back into her bedroom, she gave a silly twirl. "What do you think, Rex? Jeans and the dark purple sweater that shows off the goods, or black pants I practically have to paint on plus something loose up top?"

That got her a "whuff," but no clear vote either way.

"Black it is," she said, deciding to take it up a notch. There was that zing to think about, and the way her stomach had fluttered at odd moments through the week, in anticipation of tonight.

She paired the pants with a tight black shirt and a soft sea foam sweater with a dramatic cowl neck, tapped her feet into silver-toed black boots, added an extra two minutes to her five-minute makeup routine, and was ready to roll.

Doing her best not to collect too many dog hairs, she gave Rex a good rub that set his tail thumping on the mattress. "See you later, buddy. Be a good boy."

He wiggled and slurped her hand.

Out in the hallway, the floorboards did their *creak-creak-creak*, but she did a little dance with her boots, drowning them out.

The doorway at the far end of the hall swung partway open and her mother popped her head through. "Jenny! Sweetie, I was hoping I'd catch you."

"I'm on my way out. Nick is picking me up in a few minutes." More like fifteen, but the last thing she wanted to do right now was unload dusty old stuff from the van and schlep it upstairs.

"This won't take long. I need your opinion." Rose beckoned. "Come on."

Admittedly curious about all the noises that had been coming from her parents' suite over the past few days, Jenny headed up the hallway. "You promise no heavy lifting?"

"Oh, you." Rose looked both ways, as if making sure nobody was hiding in the bathroom or linen closet, just waiting for an opportunity to rush the master bedroom, and then stepped back and cracked the door a few inches wider.

Stifling the urge to hum the theme from *Mission: Impossible*, Jenny slipped through. Then, as her mother closed and locked the door behind her, she blinked around.

Wow. Things had really changed in the four days since she'd last been in here.

The main room had been cleared of furniture, the carpet tarped over, and the windows taped. In the dressing area beside the bathroom, the spindle-legged dressing table and boxes of art glass sat under clear plastic, nestled up against the dispossessed bedroom furniture. Next to that, incongruously, sat a huge red-and-white structure that looked like a one-tenth scale model of a New England barn, but might've been a cabinet. Or a chicken coop. Maybe both.

What the heck?

Rose bounced a little on her paint-speckled sneakers. "What do you think?"

Um . . . "I thought you were doing Depression era?"

"Not for the whole thing, silly. That would be like reproducing your Nonnie's house on purpose."

"What's that?" She pointed to the coop.

"It's an armoire for all your father's things! Isn't it darling?"

"Has Dad seen it yet?"

"Of course, silly. He loves it." She beamed at the monstrosity. "I'd show you the inside, but I'm waiting on the hardware. Besides, I know you're in a hurry. We wouldn't want to keep Dick waiting, would we?"

"It's Nick."

"Over here." Rose caught Jenny's arm and urged her to a wall, where six irregular squares of paint had been slapped up in two rows of three. At first they all looked like the same color of pale apple green, but as Jenny got closer, she saw the small differences in shade and tone.

"Guess you're going with green."

"Just for this wall." Rose stepped back with a wide sweep of her arm, like she was Vanna revealing the grand prize. "Which one do you like better?"

"Ah . . . the green one?"

"Very funny. Which one says 'mossy riverbank seen through a thick morning fog' to you?"

Suppressing questions like "Is that what you're aiming for?" and "Why, exactly?"—which would only hurt her mom's feelings or, worse, spark a lecture on interior design—Jenny indicated the one that looked the least like melted lime sherbet. "Middle bottom."

"No, no. That one won't do at all. It's got too much blue in it." Rose stepped up and trailed her fingertips over an upper square. "This one is much better. It's got more balance to it, and a fresher look."

Then why did you ask? Reminding herself that she didn't need to get it as long as her mom was happy—and out of Gran's hair—Jenny said, "I think it's lovely."

Rose's face brightened. "Do you really think so?"

"Absolutely. It's going to look great." She gave her mom an awkward one-armed hug. "I've really got to go."

"Then what are you waiting for? Have a nice time with Dick."

"It's Nick."

"Have fun!"

Jenny escaped into the hallway and beelined downstairs, determined to make it out before her mother decided she needed her opinion on something else. But as she shrugged into her ski jacket, the cell phone in her pocket did its vibrate-buzz-ring routine.

Nick's name popped up on the caller ID, putting a lilt in her voice as she answered. "Hey, there! Are you on your way?"

"I'm pulled over just shy of your driveway, actually."

"You didn't see another stray, did you?"

"No. Unfortunately, I just got an emergency call for a sick horse on the other side of town."

Her stomach dropped. *Drat, drat, drat!* "How bad is it?"

"I'm not sure. The owner isn't super experienced. From the answers to my twenty questions, it could go either way, so I don't dare tell her to give him a couple of bute and call me in the morning. I'm really sorry, but I'm going to have to bail on dinner."

"Of course. Rain check." She tried to keep the disappointment out of her voice.

"Definitely. Thanks for being cool about it."

"You're a vet. Comes with the territory. I . . . um, I don't suppose you're looking for a ride-along?"

"Seriously?"

Noting that he hadn't hesitated, had even sounded pleased, she said, "Sure, why not? I know my way around a barn."

"No kidding. That's why I didn't figure you would want to spend your night hanging around someone else's."

"Emergency farm calls might be old hat for you, but not for me. And I'm always up for an adventure. So what do you say?"

His voice deepened. "I say keep an eye out your front window, because you're going to be seeing my headlights in a couple of minutes."

She laughed, relieved that her night out hadn't entirely disappeared, just changed direction. "Give me five to pull on my thermals and barn clothes, and I'll meet you out there!"

8

He was waiting for her when she came out, leaning back against his truck, which was a dark green late-model Ford with an extended cab and the white compartmentalized hard shell that—to a ranch-raised girl, at least—said "traveling Vetmobile."

As she came down the path, he pushed away from the truck and opened the passenger door. "For the record, I was going to come up to the house and knock, but you were pretty specific that you'd meet me out here, so I figured there was a reason."

Her grin felt sheepish. "Just trying to escape some family weirdness. It's . . . Well, it's not important. I'm just glad to be shifting gears for a few hours." No point in airing family stuff, especially when the family member in question wasn't really doing anything wrong. And even though it wasn't turning out to be the night she had expected, she was looking forward to her ride-along date with Doc Hottie.

He was taller than she remembered, or maybe the heavy fleece made him look bigger. There was a layer of warmth around him, an energy that made her want to move closer and soak him in, take a taste. But she didn't want their first kiss to be a *Hey, how are you?* in her front yard, so she took the hand he offered and let him help her up into the cab of the truck.

She had been scrambling up into Ford F-250s un-aided pretty much since she could walk, but it was a nice gesture.

As he climbed into the driver's side and closed them into the warm interior, he glanced over, one corner of his mouth kicking upward. "By the way, I looked nicer when I left the house. I keep a change of clothes in the truck for when stuff like this happens."

"Lucky you were driving your Vetmobile."

"More experience than luck. Emergency calls come at the darnedest times."

"I'm pretty sure that's a corollary of Murphy's Law. And since we're doing *for the records*, I, too, looked less like the Michelin Man in my original ensemble." She unzipped her heavy parka in the truck's warm interior, but left it on, figuring she would be cold soon enough.

"You're a good sport."

"Like I said, I'm always up for an adventure." It was pretty much her motto. Granted, she could have found a solo adventure, but she had wanted to spend the evening with him.

They got under way, turning out of the driveway toward town. The radio was turned on low, playing Johnny Cash, and the hum of the truck's knobby snow tires on the road combined with the heat blasting from the vents soothed her, taking away the last of the edgy frustration her mother invariably kicked up.

"How are things going at the ranch?" he asked as they rolled along. "You doing okay with the guest stuff?"

"So far, so good."

"But it's not your dream job?"

She rolled her eyes. "Hardly. I don't know how Krista does all the politicking. If I'm not busting my butt to satisfy the one nit-picky potential guest we get out of every fifteen good ones, I'm having to alternate between butt-kissing and hard-assing to make sure the suppliers are staying on track."

"How many supplies do you need in the dead of winter?"

"You'd be surprised how much of the summer stuff gets done ahead of time. I know I am. Not to mention that Krista is continually upping the bar on the ranch's services. This winter she set out to create a line of Mustang Ridge merchandise that guests can buy when they're here, or order online. Which is cool and all, but it means I'm fielding logo proofs, samples, and a whole lot of questions I'm not qualified to answer, especially when I'm trying to bother her as little as possible." She paused. "Some days, I wonder if I'm being hazed."

"You'd know if you were," he said with a grin. "Trust me on that one."

"Oh?" She glanced over, lips curving. "Let me guess. Fraternity? Vet school tradition?"

"Worse. The Bingo ladies."

A laugh bubbled up. "Oh, this I've got to hear."

His chiseled face was a study of light and dark cast by the dashboard illumination. It eased into amused lines as he said, "My first week in Three Ridges, this little old lady comes in with a big, mean-looking buff-colored Persian that had to be seventeen pounds. His name was Cutie Pie."

"Naturally."

"Naturally. I, having checked through my day's appointments and seen that said beast needs his five-year rabies booster, start readying the injection. Except his owner, Miss Patty, gives me the full-on fisheye and says, 'That best not be for my Cutie Pie. He's got a heart murmur and can't be sedated.' When I explain it's his rabies booster, she shakes her head. 'Oh, no,' she says, 'he's not here for a shot. It's time for his lion trim.'"

"She wanted you to *shave* him?"

"Down to the skin, except for his head and the tip of his tail. She said old Doc Lopes used to wrap him in a towel and clip whatever part was sticking out. She even brought his favorite towel with her. White, with pink flowers."

A giggle escaped. "Did you do it?"

"I got him wrapped up nice and tight, with part of his big old belly hanging out. I was headed for him with the clippers, ready to go at it, when Miss Patty suddenly remembered she had someplace to be, popped him back in the carrier, towel and all, and hustled out the door. Leaving me standing there, shaking my head and wondering what I had gotten myself into with this place." He chuckled. "The next day, though, I got a six-pack of pink frosted cupcakes from Miss Patty, along with an invitation to sit next to her at Bingo any-time I want. So I'd say I did okay."

"I'd say you did better than okay. I wouldn't even get through the door on Bingo night."

"You want me to arrange an invite? Though you might have to shave a cat first."

"I'm good, really." And she was, she realized as they cruised through town. Better than good. She was out with a handsome man on a Friday night. The details didn't matter. "Have you seen Cutie Pie since?"

"Only for his five-year rabies shot, which I did by taking the top off his crate and sticking my arm in, rather than trying to haul him out and pin him down. Got a dozen cookies on top of my fee for my trouble. They weren't as good as your gran's, of course."

"That goes without saying. There might be some de-bate over the annual muffin title, but Gran won the bis-cuit and chocolate chip cookie divisions so many times they finally gave her a perpetual title and asked her to be the judge."

"Speaking of Mustang Ridge, how's the dog doing? Does he have an official name yet?"

"Rex. And he's great. We really won the stray lottery with him."

"Did you name him or was it a family effort?"

"He named himself." She told him the story while

the truck rolled through Three Ridges, which was so much bigger than it had been before. Not box-store big, but more than the feed store, grocery and two restaurants of her earliest childhood. "After that, we didn't have the heart to call him anything else."

"Some people think it's bad luck to change a pet's name."

"I don't know about that, but I figure he had a good life at some point. He's too nice to have been a neglect case all along."

"Ruth and I thought the same thing. Here we are." He turned up a wide paved driveway, drove past a McMansion-style house, and pulled up in front of a new-looking barn that was burning so many lights that it cast an orange halo in the night sky. "The owner's name is Michelle, the horse is Nero. She's got three of them, all quarter horses. Decent pleasure types, pretty healthy overall."

Jenny cocked her head. "I hear a 'but' in there."

"But she's a horse newbie surrounded by people who were riding before they could walk. She's trying to catch up as fast as she can via the Internet, and doesn't have a great filter."

"Ah. Like an amateur photographer who has all the latest gadgets and no idea how to use them."

"Or a hypochondriac who spends way too much time on WebMD."

A tall woman with curly dark hair stepped into the lit doorway and waved at Nick, looking both worried and relieved.

Aware that she was about to dive into the Three

Ridges rumor pool, Jenny said, "I don't mind hanging here."

He raised an eyebrow. "Too cold out there for you?"

"More that I'm not sure you want the Bingo crowd to have us engaged by noon tomorrow."

Dimples deepening, he winked. "Michelle is new to town, so I'd say we're safe. Besides, it's not much of an adventure if you sit in the car."

"Fair enough. But don't say I didn't warn you." Zipping up, she piled out of the truck and came around the hood.

"Dr. Masterson, thank you so much for coming out on a Friday night." Michelle shook his hand, then turned to Jenny. "And your assistant."

Deciding not to correct her, Jenny shook the offered hand. "I'm Jenny Skye."

The name apparently didn't register, which was nice. Michelle beckoned. "Come in, come in. It's freezing out here. I've got Nero on the crossties for you."

The interior of the glossy, tricked-out barn was varnished wood, the stalls assembled from top-end kits, and the center aisle was a smooth river of concrete covered in rubber pavers that gave gently under Jenny's boots. Halfway down the aisle, a large dark bay gelding stood on the crossties with a back foot cocked and his head hanging in a way that suggested he was either asleep or felt like crap, possibly both. His weight was good, but his coat had that fluffed-out, dry look that spoke of a fever, and all four lower legs were swollen so badly it was hard to tell where the joints ended and the long bones began.

Two stalls farther down were occupied, the horses blowing softly and moving around with crunches of hay and the sprinkling sound of shavings.

"He's been tested for HYPP," said Michelle. "Of course you know that, since you did the retest last month. He's negative for PSSM, too, and he wasn't worked hard or anything. Could it be PHF? EHV-1? I heard there was an outbreak a few months ago."

Jenny translated the abbreviations, which ranged from a debilitating genetic condition to tick- and mosquito-borne diseases that most horses were vaccinated against. Internetitis, indeed.

Nick just let it roll off him as he examined his patient, starting a thermometer going, and then checking the gelding's eyes and gums, palpating the nodes under his jaw, and taking the horse's pulse. When the owner ran down and moved to Nero's head, he said, "The first thing you noticed was that he didn't clean up his breakfast?"

"Yes, but he's not always the best eater. I took his temperature, and when it was normal, I put them out like I do every day. He looked okay at lunchtime, but when I brought him in I saw that his legs were getting puffy." One of her hands fluttered up to her throat. "Then I took his temperature, and it was one-oh-five!"

Jenny winced. Normal was around a hundred, and horses tolerated being too cold much better than they did being too hot.

"Well it's down some now," Nick said after checking his thermometer. "He's at a shade over one-oh-two."

"I gave him Banamine like you said."

"It helped."

She rubbed the gelding's forehead in a compulsive circular motion. "I was so worried when I saw his legs, and then his fever. What if it's lymphangitis? Or even strangles?" Glancing over her shoulder at Jenny, who had been staying out of the way farther up the aisle, she said, "You probably think I need to back slowly away from the Internet."

Jenny held up her hands. "Hey, it's easy to work yourself up over stuff like this. I once convinced myself I had Ebola when it was really just a bad batch of chili. Good news is, you've got a great vet on call."

Michelle's smile warmed. "That's nice of you to say."

"You shouldn't ever feel like you have to apologize for caring. Within reason, anyway."

Jenny glanced at Nick, hoping she wasn't overstepping, and got a covert thumbs-up. A moment later, he went out to his truck and returned carrying a plastic tote containing a variety of syringes and tubes.

Melissa visibly braced herself. "What's the diagnosis, Doc?"

"The best I can do is ADR-FUO."

She heaved a sigh. "That's what I was afraid of. What's the plan?"

"Well, he's a bit dehydrated, so I'm going to tube him with some fluids. That'll get him feeling a whole lot better, on top of the meds you already gave him. We'll keep after him with the Banamine for the fever and watch him for a couple of days. If he gets worse or the blood tests come back positive for something, we'll adjust from there."

It took twenty minutes for Nick to administer the fluids, take several tubes of blood, and set Michelle up with the meds she would need for the next few days.

The worried owner dogged Nick's heels as he cleaned up his equipment and reloaded the truck, peppering him with questions that he fielded with lots of "We'll see how the next few days go" and "Call me if he gets worse." He took quick looks at the two other horses and checked their temperatures. Straightening, he announced, "They're both WNL." He grinned in Jenny's direction. "Within normal limits."

Michelle chuckled. "Okay, if you're teasing me, I know he's going to be okay."

"Which isn't to say that you shouldn't have called. That high of a fever isn't something to mess with." He gave her a few more instructions, then gripped her shoulder. "Now go inside and get something to eat, okay?"

"I . . . Okay." She smiled ruefully. "Peter's probably missing me. He's good about the horses, but still." She sketched a suddenly shy-seeming wave in Jenny's direction. "It was nice to meet you. I'm sorry I interrupted your evening."

"What, you're not buying me as an assistant?"

"Not when Nick is prepping and schlepping his own syringes."

"Shoot. I'll have to remember that next time." Jenny dug in her pocket, and came up with one of Krista's cards. She held it out. "Nick said you're new to town and haven't been into horses for too long. I'm at this number for another five weeks, and then it's my sister's number. She's my twin. Anyway, give me a call if you'd like to get together sometime. Or if we don't connect, give Krista a shout-out. She's always up for talking horses, and she loves making new friends."

They left amid Michelle's effusive thanks, piling back into the truck and cranking the heat as Nick punched a few notes into his phone. When he tucked it away, he shot Jenny a sidelong look and an approving smile. "You're quite a lady."

The simple statement went straight through her, warming her more thoroughly than the hot air being pumped out of the vents. "I didn't do much."

"You did plenty." He drove away from the barn, *toot-toot*ing the horn as they went by the house. "Michelle could use some horsey contacts."

"I liked her. And we've all got to start somewhere." She paused, glancing over at him. "What does ADR-FUO stand for?"

"You haven't heard that one? It's a vet-school special that means the horse ain't doin' right, due to a fever of unknown origin. ADR-FUO."

She giggle-snorted, clapping a hand over her mouth. "In other words, you don't have a clue why he's sick."

"Yeah, but I gave it a name, which made her feel better even though it doesn't really mean anything specific. And the meds will make Nero feel better, so it's a win-win."

"You're not worried that it's serious?"

"Any fever that high is serious in its own right, but it's responding to the Banamine, which means we can keep his temp in a safe range. Most likely it's a stray virus that might or might not hit the other two horses—the stocked-up legs have me leaning in that direction. I'll run tests, of course, and maybe something will pop up. Or else he might develop another symptom or two. My money says this'll be the end of it, though. And in a few days Michelle will probably find some other reason to stress about him or one of the others."

"Hypochondria by proxy?"

"Maybe a little. I'm not going to fault her for wanting to do right by her horses, but I'm also trying to guide her a little on learning to do the basics for herself."

"Not keen on spending every other Friday with Nero and his buddies?"

He lifted a shoulder. "No reason she should spend for an emergency farm call if it's not really an emergency."

She studied him, liking what she saw. "You're a good guy, Doc."

"You sound surprised."

"That you're a good guy? No. That I'm here with you? Maybe a little."

"You don't usually date locals?"

I don't usually date mature, self-sufficient adults. The thought showed up out of nowhere, popping into her head like someone had whispered it into her ear. "Something like that."

He paused at the top of Michelle's driveway. "It's not too late. You hungry?"

"Gosh, yes. Bring on the golden arches."

"I think we can do better than that."

"Would you mind if we didn't?"

He laughed over at her. "Jonesing for grease?"

"Gran doesn't believe in fast food. Which, of course, means I crave it the moment I set foot on the ridge."

"I know just the place, then. It doesn't look like much, but the food rocks."

"Sounds like my kind of dive."

Sure enough, when they walked into a small, brightly lit diner a half hour later, she closed her eyes and inhaled the scents of grease and powdered sugar, and reached out to squeeze his hand. "This is exactly what I had in mind."

Better yet, it was an unknown quantity, a small place tucked into a strip mall outside of Three Ridges. She was pretty sure it had been a Blockbuster or something the last time she had paid attention. Now it was the sort of place that didn't look like much from the outside, mostly plate glass and a menu stuck above the OPEN sign, with vinyl booths and mushroomlike stools at a Formica counter. But it was nearly two-thirds full at ten p.m., which was always a good sign.

"Dining in or takeout?" asked the hostess, a bottle blonde with wide-set eyes and a pointy chin, who Jenny thought might have been a year or two ahead of her in school.

"Takeout okay?" she asked Nick.

"Works for me."

"Cool." She gave the menu a quick glance and went with the burger that had the longest list of stuff added on top. "I'll have a rustler's special with fries and a large Diet Coke, please, and . . ." She flipped the menu and drew a finger down the desserts. "A slice of chocolate-pecan pie. To go."

When the waitress transferred her attention, Nick held up two fingers. "Make that two of the same." As she moved off, scribbling, he said, "Nice to know you're not one of those 'I'll have a salad with the dressing on the side, and water with a lemon' girls."

"I have my salad days. This ain't one of 'em."

"Word."

They sat companionably close at the counter for the ten minutes it took their food to appear, making small talk about the giggling teens, hustling waitresses, and decor.

"It's homey," Jenny decided, "though my mom would probably come up with some highbrow name for it. Vintage-inspired Western Kitch, or Mid-Century Rodeo."

"Retro Yard Sale Cowboy?" Nick suggested.

"Ooh, that's a good one."

The waitress plonked a couple of bags down in front of them, along with a ticket. "Pay up front. Have a nice night."

They wrangled briefly over the bill, he paid, and they headed back out into the chilly night. "Where to?" he asked as they reached the truck.

She shot him a sidelong look. "Have you been to Makeout Point yet?"

He did a double take, and then gave a long, slow grin that came with lots of dimple action. He eased in until she was leaning against the passenger door, blocking her with his body in a move that sent a skitter of warmth through her as he said, "Jenny Skye. Are you asking me to go parking?"

9

Nick had expected to be attracted to Jenny—heck, he had been looking forward to their date all week. But he hadn't expected to be charmed. He was, though. Not just by her enthusiasm for riding along with him or the way she and Michelle had connected, but also by the way she grinned up at him in challenge now.

"Maybe I *am* asking you to go parking," she teased. "Are you shocked?"

"It'll take a whole lot more than that to shock me, darlin'." He leaned in, saw her expression change as she readied for the kiss he knew they were both anticipating . . . and then he reached past her and opened the truck door. "Shall we go?"

Her face blanked for a second, and then she laughed, balled up a fist, and socked him in the arm. "Beast!"

"And here I thought I was being a gentleman." He offered his hand to help her up into the cab, and squeezed her fingers before letting go and shutting the door. When he climbed in on the other side, he added, "But if you want me to be a beast instead . . ."

"Oh, just shut up and drive."

"Yes, ma'am!"

Hunger got the best of them, and they ate their burgers and fries on the short drive out of town, chasing ketchup and special sauce with napkins and good humor. Jenny directed him along secondary roads that got progressively narrower as they went, with snow under their tires and packed in berms on either side. The only illumination came from the truck's headlights and the sliver of moon overhead, intermittently visible through thick stands of pine.

"The turnoff is up there." She pointed to a gap in the trees. It proved to be a plowed one-lane road that wound through the trees for about a mile before ending in a wide turnaround. There, wind had scoured the ground nearly bare, revealing a rocky outcropping that speared out past the tree line. Beyond it, the world fell away.

He rolled the truck to a stop. "Should I drive out there?"

"We used to when we were kids, but let's not risk it. I'd hate to see the Vetmobile go poof."

"The Vetmobile, eh? Do I get a cool theme song?"

"We'll see." She lifted the last two takeout containers. "Want to take our desserts mobile?"

"Absolutely. Let me grab a couple of flashlights." He expected to freeze, even in his heavy coat and ski pants, but when they got out of the truck, he was pleasantly surprised. "Hey, it's not so cold here."

She took a deep breath of the pine-laden air. "It has

something to do with the trees and the air currents, though there's supposed to be a hidden hot spring involved, too. Every few years, a group of kids—or adults who should really know better—gets in trouble trying to find the hidden springs, and Search and Rescue has to come in and pull them out of wherever they've gotten stuck, lost, or otherwise incapacitated."

"Think we could find it? I'm up for some spelunking, if you know where to start."

"I'd suggest waiting until summer for that one."

"We could use melt patterns and steam to find the hot spots."

She looked momentarily intrigued, but then shook her head. "Nah. Krista would kill me if either of us wound up out of commission."

Enjoying her mix of irreverence and family loyalty, he took the containers and offered her the crook of his arm. "Shall we?"

They walked together along the point, not needing the lights because the moonlight amped as they broke out of the trees.

For a make-out spot, it had a hell of a view.

Nick gave a low whistle as he balanced himself and looked out over a sheer forty-foot drop. The cliff face was featureless save for a few ledges that offered far more sharp rocks than soft landing spots, and dark, jagged stones speared through the snow at the base. But beyond that ruggedness, the snowscape smoothed out, flowing away from them almost as far as he could see in the moonlight, until it butted up against the distant foothills.

"The land down there isn't part of Mustang Ridge, is it?" He thought they were still too far south, though he didn't have the area fully mapped out in his head yet.

"No, it's state land. We used to see mustangs down there all the time—little family groups, sometimes bigger herds on the move. I'd come out here by myself, bring my camera, and just sit here until dusk, waiting for the perfect shot." She scanned out to the horizon. "I don't see any tracks. They must be ranging someplace else for the winter."

He looked around. "I should've brought a blanket or something for us to sit on."

"Ah, let me show you the trick. Come on, this way. Watch your step." She flicked on her flashlight.

To his surprise, she led him back to the tree line near the parking area, and then down to what looked like a fault line in the stone, but turned out to be a narrow path that ran below the promontory to a small sheltered area he hadn't seen from above. There, old, worn logs were set in a semicircle around a fire pit that was lined with stones and blackened with soot.

The logs were carved with a myriad of names and dates, some in hearts, others with threats or boasts, and a few RIPs, spelling out the history of a generation or two of teens. The nearby stones were bare of graffiti, though, and there wasn't any trash, suggesting that either the local rangers patrolled the area, or the kids had a code of conduct when it came to using the point.

Jenny sat at one end of the center log, leaving room

for him to sit beside her as long as he didn't mind squeezing in with their bodies pressed together from knee to shoulder.

He didn't mind that. At all.

"Here." She handed him a fork and took one of the dessert containers. "Keep track of your trash. We carry out at least as much as we bring in around here."

Which answered that question. "Thanks." He took a bite and looked around, appreciating the shelter, the view, and the company. "This is definitely better than the diner. As long as we don't go over the edge, that is."

She bumped him with her shoulder. "I like living a little dangerously."

He could relate, but it also brought a twinge of *been there, done that, learned my lesson*. He wasn't the same guy he had been before, though, and they were just having fun. "Is that what got you into photography?" he asked. "The call to adventure?"

"Either that or vice versa. Chicken, egg, who knows? According to my parents, when Krista and I got chicken pox—we were maybe ten or so—I recovered first and was driving everybody nuts because I wasn't sick enough to stay in bed, wasn't well enough to be out doing much, and was bored with everything in between. So Gran gave me her instant Polaroid and two boxes of film, figuring that would kill an hour or so."

"And an artist was discovered?" He liked the image.

"Something like that. Two days later, I had my first showing." She grinned. "I matted the photos on construction paper, hung them along the hallway leading to the kitchen, got Gran to make cookies, and—if you believe my father's version of the story, anyway—tried to charge admission."

He chuckled. "Way to be an entrepreneur."

"I didn't get away with selling tickets, but my parents got me a few more packs of instant film, which I burned through in a weekend. A few days later, Dad handed me his thirty-five-millimeter camera—a decent Canon with a zoom and everything—and told me that he would buy the film, but I had to pay for the developing out of my allowance."

"Which, I'm guessing, taught you not to waste your shots."

"Yep. It also motivated me to do extra chores, which I suspect was part of his plan. Anyway over the next few years, I took some classes, won some prizes, and did most of the yearbook candids and a bunch of the senior pictures. It was a natural progression to head for film school, even if it meant moving out of state."

"And from there, to Belize."

"Actually, it was an internship in Kenya first, followed by a couple of bottom-barrel jobs in L.A. and New York, where I clawed my way up to the camera crew. Then I worked on documentaries in the UK, Ireland, and central Texas before signing on with *Jungle Love* because I was ready for some rain forests and parrots. So far, I've done two seasons in Belize and one each in Honduras, Guatemala, and central Mexico."

"Impressive. I bet your passport is even prettier than mine."

"We can have a stamp-off if you like."

"You'd win. And I think mine's expired."

"Not mine," she declared, and dug into her pie. "I can't wait to get back on a plane headed wherever."

Again he felt that twinge.

"What does your family think about you living abroad?" he asked. When she hesitated—maybe?—he added, "You mentioned wanting to escape some weirdness earlier. I thought they might be leaning on you to stay on at the ranch."

She shuddered. "Yeesh. Don't even say it. No, they're used to me being gone. As for the weirdness, that would be courtesy of my mother. These days, she and I make oil and water look like best buddies."

"Really? I'm surprised." He had only met Rose Skye a couple of times, and had the impression of a cheerful—if somewhat formidable—woman who didn't have much to do with the ranch operations. "She seemed pretty mellow to me."

"You must've caught her on a down day." She closed her take-out box and set it aside.

"Sorry. I didn't mean to pry."

"I owe you a couple of personal questions, remember? Besides, it's something I've been thinking about lots since I've been home. It's the first time the two of us have been under the same roof in . . . I don't know. Five years? Six? I don't know if it's gotten worse recently, or if I'm just noticing it more."

On any of the other first dates he'd been on in the last couple of years—not that there had been many—he would've steered things in some other direction, keeping things light and fun. And, yeah, he and Jenny were just having fun . . . but they were also friends of a sort, and he wanted to help. "What is she doing that has you worried?"

"When I was growing up, she was totally normal, you know? She wasn't perfect—who is? But she worked in the ranch office, drove me and Krista around, nagged us to do our homework and chores, rode out with the roundups, and she was, well, Mom. And when it became obvious that Mustang Ridge was going to have to make a change if it wanted to stay afloat, she got right behind Krista's idea of a dude ranch. She helped design the cabins, the theme weeks, even the dining hall and the original Web site."

"I take it something changed?"

"When it was all up and running, and Krista was finding her balance being in charge of things, our mom and dad announced that they were retiring, buying an RV, and taking off. Which I totally get—my dad should've been an engineer or an inventor or something, but there was no way he was going to let the ranch leave the family, so he became a cattleman instead. He never loved it, though. Not like he's loved traveling." An utterly fond smile softened her face in the moonlight. "You should see some of the things he's engineered in the RV—little machines that let him brew coffee in the galley while he's sitting in the driver's seat, spring-loaded gizmos in the sleeping compartment that make it easier for my mom to lift the mattress and get to the storage area underneath, that sort of thing. And he's made friends all over, not just because he's the kind of guy people want to be around, but because he can fix almost anything. Your taillight is wired wrong? Let Ed Skye take a look at it. Got a problem with your plumbing? Eddie can help. He'll take a beer in payment, but never anything more." Her eyes went soft in the moonlight. "He still gets emails from all over the country asking him how to fix this or that."

"He sounds like a neat guy," Nick said. "I should've made more of an effort to get to know him when I was out to Mustang Ridge for farm calls."

"Not your fault. These days he spends most of his time in the workshop, hiding from Mom." She sighed. "I shouldn't say that. It's just . . . she's gone crazy with this retirement thing. Where he gets a kick out of helping other people, she's gone the other way. She latches on to hobbies, becomes obsessed by them and loses track of the people around her." She pried a frozen pebble off the ground and tossed it in the fire pit, where it clinked and slid to the bottom. "Like when she's on a cooking kick and invades Gran's kitchen. Or when she goes on a decorating binge and moves her and Dad into a tiny guest room with just a double bed in it. And when you try to talk to her about it, she just steamrolls right over the top of you, acting like nothing's wrong. Because to her, nothing *is* wrong. It's everyone else who's got the problem. Not to mention . . ." She stopped suddenly, expression rueful. "Not to mention, I'm babbling."

"Seems like you had some pressure built up there."

He took her hand, linked their fingers. "I don't mind listening, if you want to talk."

"That's nice of you to say, but I think we should even things up, here. Can I ask about your family?"

"How about next time?" He stood and held out a hand to help her up. "I think my core temperature is about bottomed out."

She hesitated, then smiled. "What do you know? Looks like I'm getting some Wyoming back in my blood, after all."

They walked back to the truck hand in hand. When he fired up the engine and the clock came to life, she squeaked. "It's not really that late, is it?"

He looked at the three-digit number. "Technically, it's early."

"Yeah, if you're talking about tomorrow."

"It's all a matter of perspective." And from his perspective the hours had flown. More, he was strongly tempted to head back to the diner, grab a couple of coffees, and keep on talking until it was time to order breakfast. But they weren't nineteen anymore and he had clinic appointments starting in just over seven hours, so he navigated back out to the main road and headed for Mustang Ridge.

The drive passed in warm, comfortable silence, with them holding hands on the center console. As they turned into the driveway and rolled under the WELCOME TO MUSTANG RIDGE sign, she stirred and said, "I'm going to hold you to that 'next time' on telling me about your family. Count on it."

"I'll take that as fair warning," he said. "How about Sunday?"

Her lips curved. "You're not a slouch-in-front-of-the-TV-and-watch-football guy?"

"I can adjust my slouching schedule. Besides, I owe you a real meal."

"You don't owe me anything. I had fun tonight." She slid him a sidelong glance. "If you want to try again for the Steak Lodge, though, Sunday sounds good."

"I'll pick you up at seven thirty."

"Trying to avoid the six o'clock–special crowd?"

"Something like that," he said as they rolled into the parking lot and he killed the engine. The image of Ruth and her cronies watching from a nearby booth was enough to make a man shudder.

"It's a date." She reached for her door.

"Wait. Let me get that for you." He ushered her out, then trailed her up the shoveled path to the main house. The porch stairs amplified their bootfalls, making him grin. "Hard to be subtle around here."

She leaned back against the door, eyes alight. "There's that gentlemanly streak again, walking me home like we're seventeen and coming home from prom."

"Sometimes tradition can be its own sort of adventure," he said. And, going with tradition, he leaned in and kissed her good night.

10

Jenny had been kissed many times before. She had even been kissed before in this very spot, and on chilly nights like this one. Except where those long-ago kisses had come from boys, this one came from a man.

And what a man.

If she had thought he was big before, now he seemed huge as he enfolded her in his arms, pressing through the layers of their jackets to mold their bodies together. There was no hesitation, no pause to see if she was on board with a good night kiss. Or if there was, it was lost beneath the rush of desire that flared through her at the touch of his tongue against hers.

Her hands found their way up to his shoulders, where she dug in and clung, because without him to anchor her and the door at her back, she was sure she would've melted into the wide-board floor of the porch. Even at that, she was barely conscious of anything beyond his lips and tongue, and his body against hers. Desire pulled her in and whirled her around like whitewater, except if she had been in a river she would've tried to fight free and reach the shore. Here, she dove in for more, not caring that she couldn't breathe.

He broke the kiss with a groan, then eased back and looked down at her with eyes that had gone dark and intense.

Suddenly, she could breathe again, ribs heaving like she had come through the other side of the whirlpool. Reeling, she fought to keep the porch floorboards steady under her feet. "Wow," she said, too shaken to go for subtle. "That was . . . Wow."

He shook his head, though she didn't know if he was trying to deny what had just happened between them, or attempting to stop his ears from ringing. "I should . . . I'm going to go now."

She shouldn't even entertain the thought of sneaking him inside or, worse, upstairs, where if the floorboards didn't give them away, Rex certainly would. Besides, too much, too soon, and hey, what about that whole *I'm not rushing into anything* vow? Still, it was a long moment before she said, "Yeah. You probably should."

He leaned in and brushed his lips across her cheek. "I'll see you Sunday."

"See you then."

Reaching past her, he pushed open the door. "I can't leave until you're inside. It's part of the Guy Code."

"Not the guys I've known."

"The Gentleman's Code, then." And, like a complete gentleman, he shoved her over the threshold and pulled the door shut between them.

Laughing, she yanked it open. "Hey, Nick?"

He turned back on the shoveled pathway, and cocked his head. "Yeah?"

"Thanks for tonight. You give excellent first date."

His dimples popped. "Would it be gentlemanly to say the same about you?"

"It would be ungentlemanly not to say it."

"Then consider it said. Now get inside before you let out all the heat, or your father comes down to see what's taking me so long to drive off."

The next morning, Jenny slept in deliciously late, spared some sympathy for a certain vet who had to work today, and—after a brief internal debate—sent him a text of the "thanks for last night, looking forward to Sunday" variety. She hadn't ever seen the point of playing hard to get. She liked him, he liked her, the chemistry was whizz-bang off the charts, and he knew full well she'd be gone in five more weeks.

Four weeks and six days, actually. Not that she was counting.

The sunshine streaming in through the window showed a gorgeous day outside, all blue skies and puffy little clouds. There was still way too much white and not enough green, never mind the distinct lack of parrots and butterflies, but she was getting used to it. Besides, with the office line going to voicemail and a Saturday free to do what she wanted, her fingers were itching for a camera.

"Come on, Rex," she said, swinging her legs to the side of the bed. "Breakfast calls."

He lurched up with a happy "whuff." *Oh, boy! Breakfast!*

In the kitchen, Gran was shaking toasted coconut shavings over the tops of a dozen perfectly plump muffins. When Jenny came in with Rex at her heels, she turned, face lighting. "There you are! We were starting to wonder if you made it home last night, or if you'd be doing the walk of shame come lunchtime."

"You did not just say *walk of shame*." Jenny reached for one of the muffins, then hesitated on the theory that it would be bad karma if they were destined for a church bake sale or a get-well basket. "Are these for us?"

"They're for the Paw Pals silent auction, but I made extra." Gran set a steaming mug of coffee on the counter at Jenny's elbow, then bustled off to let Rex out the back door, where they had shoveled a spot for him to do his business. When she returned, she said briskly, "Well? Are you going to make me drag it out of you?"

"Drag what?"

That got her a narrow-eyed look. "Don't mess with me, missy, or I'll cut you off."

Laughing, Jenny grabbed a second muffin just in case. "It was fun. Better than fun." She waved the muffin in emphasis. "Dates like the one I had last night are the reason why us females don't give up after the sixth bad first date, or the twentieth. We keep hoping that lightning will strike."

Gran's eyes widened. "Lightning? Really?"

"Not like that," Jenny warned, knowing her gran

wouldn't object to being a great-gran sooner than later. "It was one of those nights that just worked, you know?" And then there was that kiss . . . ."How were things here?" she asked before the date recap turned into twenty questions.

"Quiet. Not like today." Gran's lips pursed. "Your mother has been thumping and banging around upstairs all morning. I'm surprised the noise didn't wake you."

"I'm used to commotion." In fact, the noises were probably why she had slept so soundly. Her subconscious hadn't been straining to find some background noise in the winter quiet. "How is Big Skye feeling?"

"Like he's traded the flu for cabin fever. I had to threaten to withhold cookies to keep him from riding out with Foster today, but the doctor said he needs to take it easy until his recheck on Tuesday."

"Think he'd be up to telling some old-timey stories on camera? Like an interview?"

"Oh, goodness, yes." Gran's expression smoothed to one of entreaty. "Please. I'm begging you. It'll make his day."

Jenny laughed. "Okay, I'll call down and give him a ten-minute warning so he can get camera-ready."

It was more like fifteen before she finished her coffee, suited up for the cold, and headed out of the house with a pair of padded bags—one for Old Faithful, the other for Doris—looped across her body like bandoliers. Rex elected to stay behind and doze next to the fire, smart dog.

Whistling, she headed down the shoveled path toward her grandparents' cottage. She wasn't in a rush, though, and let her eyes roam.

Caught by the way the snow draped down off the pitched roof of the barn and furred the Dutch doors like impatient eyebrows, she pulled Old Faithful out of the worn bag, tweaked the settings, and then framed and focused, the actions as natural as breathing. As she took the first shot, a male cardinal zoomed past her and lit on the edge of the gutter, putting a splash of crimson center stage.

"Right on cue," she murmured, and snapped several frames at increasing zoom. Then she shifted over a few paces, until she thought she was at the same angle and distance as she had been during her visit last summer, and took a few more photos as the cardinal obliged by cocking his head and watching her with bright eyes.

Nice. The matching winter and summer shots would have an impact. Maybe not for the planned advertising, but she was starting to see a calendar taking shape, or maybe a coffee table book they could personalize by slotting in a few shots of the guests during their stay at the ranch.

Look at her, brainstorming merchandise.

She was tucking Old Faithful back in his battered bag when a sharp whistle cut through the air. A joyous bark answered, and as Jenny followed the path around the side of the barn, she saw a black-and-white border collie dolphining through the snow toward a mounted man who could've been Wikipedia's poster boy for the entry labeled *cowboy*.

Utterly in his element astride a compact dark bay gelding, wearing batwing chaps, a battered shearling coat, and a black felt Stetson that would soak up the sun and keep his head warm, Foster could've been one of his own great-great-great ancestors, riding out to check on the stock after a storm.

"Gotcha!" Jenny said as she raised the camera and hit the trigger, taking frame after frame as the dog whisked from side to side, the horse churned through the knee-deep snow and snorted plumes of white vapor, and Foster's body shifted to absorb the movement.

A year ago she might've thought twice about paparazzi-ing the ranch's taciturn, ultra-private head wrangler, but he had lightened up considerably since meeting his lady love. He smiled more, laughed occasionally, and had even started a couple of conversations with Jenny that hadn't been strictly about ranch biz. Which had her looking forward to meeting Shelby in person later in the week.

The woman was clearly a miracle worker.

Man, horse, and dog forged up the incline, leaving a chopped-up trail in the snow. When they reached the top, Foster turned his mount and raised a hand in a wave that was part "Hey, there" and part "Yeah, I totally know you're there" like he had eyes in the back of his Stetson.

Jenny got the last laugh on that one, though, because it made a hell of a shot—the horse and rider in perfect profile with the snow at their feet and the blue sky at their backs, and his hand raised in a wave that, no matter its real intent, would read like he was welcoming the viewer to his world.

"Congratulations. You just made the calendar's cover." Which would no doubt horrify him.

Cheered by the thought and the knowledge that she had already nailed a couple of pictures, she stowed Old Faithful and continued on to the cottage. After a quick *rat-tat-tat* knock, she swung open the kitchen door. "Yoo-hoo. Anyone home?"

"Come on back," came Big Skye's reply, sounding hale and hearty, like he had finally kicked the lung crud.

She stowed her outer clothes and boots near the door and headed for the living room, swiping a couple of peanut butter cookies off the cooling rack and devouring the first before she was through the door and past the piano. Around half of the second cookie— excessive, granted, after the muffins, but she had zero willpower after being baking-deprived for so long— she said, "You ready to be a YouTube star, big guy? We work this right, and you could go viral."

"I'm on antibiotics."

She grinned, adoring him. "Which kill bacteria, not viruses. And, besides, in this case *viral* is a good thing. It means getting the sort of attention that snowballs, with two people each sending the link to a couple of their friends, who each send it to a couple of their friends, and so on, until a quadzillion people are talking about your video."

"Those are probably news reports. Not an old man talking about his family farm."

"Actually, it's more like piano-playing cats and drunken bridesmaids falling into pools," she said cheerfully as she unfolded Doris's tripod. "Want to get started?"

"Harumph." He shot her a glare over a pair of reading glasses, and set his cattleman's mag aside. "If more people turned off their computers and got their butts outside, we'd all be a durned sight better off."

Yet he was wearing creased jeans, a snap-studded shirt, and the fawn brown Stetson he saved for date night, and his thin white hair was slicked down on the sides, with wet comb marks showing where he had worked to get it tamed.

"You're absolutely right." Jenny looked through the viewfinder, then made a face at the way the snow glare from outside was muddying things. "Do a one-eighty." She twirled her finger. "I want the wall behind you as my background, not the window."

He scowled. "The window's the best part. Have you ever seen anything prettier than those mountains?"

"Sure, they're pretty. They're also really white. Someone sees that in the middle of summer, and they're going to think it snows year-round up here."

"Anyone who thinks that is an idiot."

She did a finger twirl.

Grumbling, he about-faced it, so he was looking out at his beloved mountains.

She got the camera reoriented, took another look, and nodded. "Now we're talking." The pale wall color

helped the eye focus on his face; the exposed beams that
flanked him on either side made her think of log cabins;
and the age-faded photos behind him—pictures of the
ranch's old chuck wagon in action during a roundup—
spoke for themselves. "Okay. How about you introduce
yourself to your fans-to-be?"

His eyes took on a gleam. "Are you taping?"

"It's not really tape anymore, but, yeah, we're rolling. So let's start with who you are and how you came
to be part of Mustang Ridge."

"I was born here," he said simply, squaring his
shoulders beneath his stiff-looking shirt. "Under a full
moon in the hot of summer, when my daddy and the
others were out in the fields, dodging storms to get the
hay put up for winter. The way my mama told it, I was
out there with them, not three days old, sleeping in a
sling hung around her shoulders while she drove the
big tractor, freeing up another pair of hands for the harvest."

Rather than telling him to keep it short, sweet, and
quotable, Jenny let him roll with it, nudging him from
one familiar story to another. Like how Jonah Skye had
struck it rich, not on his gold claim, but filling an inside
straight in a high-stakes poker game, and how his wife,
Mary, had urged him to buy land instead of another
claim.

The minutes disappeared beneath the creaky ca-
dence of his words, but by the time he got around to
describing some of the roundups he had been on, first

as a kid and then as the boss, his voice was starting to get scratchy so she called it quits.

"You rock." She plucked off his date-night Stetson and gave him a smacking kiss on the top of his head. "Seriously. That was awesome."

He craned to watch her disassemble Doris and the tripod. "When can I see it? When is it going to go typhoid?"

"Viral. That'll be up to Shelby and Krista, and probably won't be for a few months. But how about I do some rough edits over the next few days, and we can all watch it together? Light a fire, pop some popcorn, pass some beers, that sort of thing?"

"I'll ask your gran to bake something special."

"Then it's totally a date." Jazzed by the interview, she snagged another peanut butter cookie and headed back to the main house with her camera bags slung over her shoulder and a bounce in her step as the video clips started to take shape in her head. It was easy to see where some of the breaks would go, and where a few nips and tucks could get them to the payoff faster. And although she had been planning on sticking with a straight interview format, now she was seeing where she could splice in some of the grainy old family photos that were up in the attic.

The huge collection had some gems in it, from nineteenth-century tintypes to her and Krista's baby pictures, and she had only been through maybe a quarter of the file boxes. Who knew what else might be hiding in there? Besides, she had been talking about cataloging the collection for years now. With the office stuff more or less under control, maybe now was the time.

She swung through the door and started shucking off layers, excited to get to work.

A door slammed upstairs followed by hurried footsteps, and her mom appeared on the landing, beaming. She was wearing pale wool slacks and a plum-colored cowl-neck sweater that was nearly the same color as her dangling earrings and a shade darker than her lipstick. With her hair upswept and her eyes outlined in heavy swipes of mascara, she looked great, but seriously overdressed for painting trim.

"You're back!" she said, like Jenny had been missing. "Where have you been?" She came down the stairs in a rush and reached for the camera bags. "Let me get those. Which one do you need?"

Jenny hooked them out of her reach. "For what?"

"The reveal, of course. Didn't you get my text? We've been waiting for you!"

"You . . . oh." A check of her phone showed that she had missed two texts.

One was from her mom, letting her know that the bedroom was finished and she wanted to film the big unveiling. Which explained the stage makeup. The other, earlier message was from Nick: *I'm dragging, but it was so worth it. Call you tonight?*

Grinning like a fool, she tucked the phone away. "Sorry. I had it on quiet mode while I was interviewing Big Skye."

"Do you have enough film left?"

"It's digital."

"Then let's go!" Rose headed back up the stairs, calling, "Eddie? It's time!"

Jenny hesitated at the base of the stairs, but then shrugged and went with it. Who knew? Maybe she could get her mom on one of those "next great designer" shows. If nothing else, it'd keep her out of the kitchen for a while longer.

11

By the time Jenny got Doris set up once more, her father was there, looking tolerant in the blue pants, button-down shirt, and dark tie he wore on the rare occasion he needed to wear something other than work clothes. She started rolling but didn't announce it, having learned that a minute or two of candid video could be a gold mine for honest images. Or blackmail.

Her mom beamed up at her dad, hands fluttering in a small show of nerves. "Are you excited to see our new room, Eddie?"

He brushed his lips across hers. "Absolutely."

Jenny glanced away from the viewfinder, throat tightening. Of all of them, her dad had the most reason to be irritated, yet he ate the crazy food and slept in temporary quarters without complaint, and when she had flat out asked him about her mother's behavior the other day, he had gone into woodworker Zen mode, patted her hand, and said, "She'll figure it out."

If he wasn't frustrated with the way her mom had gone hobby junkie, why should she be? Who knew? He might even care about the difference between two nearly identical shades of green.

"We're rolling," she announced. "What do you say I slip inside and set up facing the doors, so I can get some reaction shots when Dad sees it for the first time?"

The next half hour was more fun than she would've expected. To her surprise, the pale green paint pulled the space together; accents of darker green and plum in the interiors of the built-ins and closets added some drama; and even the chicken coop–themed armoire made sense somehow, tucked into an alcove with its barn doors open to showcase her father's clothes.

He got a real kick out of it, in fact, playing with the doors and drawers and exclaiming over the craftsmanship while her mother stood off to the side and beamed. Jenny shot them from every angle and prompted her mom to talk about the spindle-legged desk with its artfully arranged perfume bottles, and her foggy-day color scheme. She actually made a pretty good subject, telling little stories about her shopping trips and gazillion visits to the hardware store in town.

"Okay," Jenny decided finally, "that's a wrap." She powered down Doris and started putting things away while her father made a few more approving noises and then left, shucking off his tie before he was even clear of the door. Smiling to herself, Rose drifted around the room, brushing at invisible smudges and shifting knickknacks by millimeters. Enjoying the low-grade buzz that came from a solid shoot, Jenny said,

"I'm going to get to work editing the clips of you and Big Skye. I should have something to show you by tomorrow afternoon."

"Can you make it all nice, with music and everything?"

Tempted by thoughts of the *Austin Powers* theme, or possibly Darth Vader's march, Jenny grinned. "I can probably come up with something. Do you have a title in mind? *Ranch Reno*, or *Barnyard Bedroom*, perhaps?"

"Very funny." But there was actual amusement in Rose's voice. "Let me think about it."

"No prob." Jenny shouldered her bags and headed out of the bedroom. "You know where to find me. Come on, Rex. We've got work to do!"

As he bounded down the hall beside her, there was something very satisfying about his goofy, galumphing stride and the way he was so darn excited for everything. *We're going upstairs? Yippee! We're going downstairs? Yahoo! We're going to the bathroom? Awesome!* She wasn't sure whether it would be fun to have that much enthusiasm, or just exhausting.

Her mom followed them into the hallway. "I was thinking . . ."

"Yes?" Jenny said as she ducked into her bedroom to snag her laptop. When she turned back, her mom was standing in the doorway, looking around the room. Rex sat in the hallway with a doggy grin on his face. "You were thinking . . ." she prompted.

"That we should do this room next. You and me together. Wouldn't that be fun?"

Jenny's heart probably didn't shudder for real, but it sure felt that way. She managed not to say *Dear God, no*, but all she could come up with in its place was "Um."

"It's a small space, so we wouldn't want to do too much." Rose crossed the room, wiggled the footboard, and then headed for the closet.

"Mom," Jenny said, but it was like her mother had suddenly gone into a decorative fugue, tuning out the rest of the universe while she paced off dimensions and muttered to herself about pink being a creative color. "*Mom!*" she said again, loud enough to make Rex twitch.

"You don't have to shout. What do you think of raspberry?"

"Good on chocolate cake, not on walls. And thanks but no, thanks. I like this place just the way it is."

"You and I decorated it together for your fourteenth birthday. Don't you think it's time to let it grow up?"

She didn't know where the sudden pressure in her chest had come from, wished it would go away. "It's a room. It doesn't care what color it is."

"I do."

"Me, too, and I like yellow walls, white furniture, and dorky photos of myself." Okay, so maybe she was digging in for the sake of digging in, but still.

Her mother looked at her—really at her, rather than through her to something else—and gave a sad little half smile. "Nothing stays the same forever, sweetie."

Of course not, Jenny thought, working hard to stifle a pang. When she was fourteen, the ranch was over-flowing with cattle, Krista was determined to marry

Joey Fatone, and their mom worked a full week and volunteered with 4-H. "Talk to Krista," she suggested, doing her best to keep the edge out of her voice. "Maybe she'd like to change up her room." She managed a grin. "Midcentury tack room is so last year, you know."

"But—"

"Sorry, Mom. I appreciate the offer, I really do. But I like things just the way they are."

With his overnight patients tucked away, his paperwork done, a sandwich on one side of him and a beer on the other, Nick kicked back on his leather couch and did what he had been looking forward to doing all day. He dialed Jenny's number.

She picked up on the second ring. "Mustang Ridge Insane Asylum. Do you know your party's extension?"

He chuckled. "Crazy day?"

"Nobody is dead, hospitalized, or incarcerated, so I suppose it could've been worse."

"Did an enormous Great Dane barf two pounds of ground beef and a package of craft-store googly eyes on you?"

"Um, no. Did that happen to you?"

"All those eyes." He made a shuddering noise. "Hundreds of them, staring off in all different directions."

Her laugh vibrated on the airwaves. "That sounds . . ."

"Creepy?"

"I was thinking existential," she said, "but creepy

works, too. And no, my day didn't include vomit or googly eyes, though there was an armoire that looked like a chicken coop."

"Falling under the category of 'crimes against interior decorating' I take it?"

"Smart guy. I think I diverted Mom from tackling my bedroom next, though. I told her she should send in an audition tape for one of those design star shows. Said I'd help her."

"Devious. I like it."

"Hey, as long as she stays out of my stuff."

"And the rest of the craziness?"

"In addition to some computer wonkiness, I had a conversation that was so circular it was a danged spiral, with a guest who didn't want to hear that the ranch has a no-pets policy."

"That's just common sense. The last thing you need is someone turning loose a city dog with a high prey drive in the middle of a herd of range cattle."

"Or to spend the whole week looking for Muffy Frou-Frou when she escapes from her cabin on day one. I get that, and you get that, but Mr. I Can't Possibly Leave Killer at Home thinks I'm just being a pill."

"Give him the clinic's number. We board."

"Already did. Gran said you're the go-to in this situation. Why it took forty minutes to talk the guy off the ledge is still a mystery to me."

"We'll put a silver star on his chart."

"Meaning that he's a pain in the butt?"

"Yep, silver if it's the client, gold if it's the patient.

Safer than writing stuff like *Beware: Cujo* or *Owns a new Mercedes, but constantly whines about the bill* in the file where the client might see it."

"If I were you, I'd charge this guy an up-front annoyance tariff, because he's guaranteed to be a pain. Not to mention that he probably hasn't had Killer fixed or trained. He seemed like that sort." Her sigh echoed down the line, but it was tainted with amusement. "How was your day overall? Get any bloodthirsty parrots in need of a pedicure?"

"Fortunately, no. And no emergencies to speak of, either." He settled deeper into the couch, nudged Cheesepuff away from his sandwich, and took a swig of his beer. "Let's see. Skimming over the part where I hit Snooze way too many times and then doubled up on the coffee because *somebody* kept me up way past my bedtime, my day started with Ruth quizzing me on who I brought to the diner last night. I guess her spies must've reported in."

"Uh-oh. Busted." Jenny didn't sound upset, which he took as a good sign. "What did you tell her?"

"That you and I had discussed hopping a plane to Vegas for a quickie wedding, but settled for burgers and Makeout Point instead."

"Sounds reasonable."

"Just kidding. I told her you came out on a call with me and we grabbed dinner, and managed to avoid telling her when and where we were getting together next."

"Trying to avoid a stakeout?"

"Wouldn't put it past her. After that, I saw a Siamese cat with a flea allergy and an impressively large vocabulary, did a couple of routine vaccinations, and dealt with an elderly basset with ear problems. And then came Bobo, the Great Dane."

"Who puked googly eyes on you."

"And then, feeling better, attempted to lick my face."

She snickered. "Was that the high point of your day?"

"Nope," he said, shifting so Cheese could get comfortable sprawled halfway across his lap, halfway across the arm of the sofa. "This is."

"Awww. Smooth talker."

"Just calling it how I see it." And there were far worse things than talking to a beautiful, interesting woman while his clinic-slash-house settled around him for the night. "I'm looking forward to dinner tomorrow."

"Me, too, even if 'dinner' turns into visiting a sick cow in the middle of a very cold field."

"Don't even joke about it," he said mock-sternly. "We're going to dinner, darn it, and we're going to make it all the way from drinks to dessert."

"Have some experience with interrupted dates, do we?"

"Fewer than you'd think."

"I guess there's not a lot of formal dating when you're doing relief work, huh?"

She would get that, wouldn't she? "Not a lot of

restaurant choices, and 'your place or mine' doesn't have the same ring when you're already living on top of each other."

"And, if it's anything like being on a film crew in an out-of-the-way location, there's a whole lot of hooking up without much in the way of pairing off, at least not long-term."

He winced. "Okay, then, it sounds a lot like being on a film crew."

Something must have come through in his voice, because she said, "Uh-oh. Did I hit a nerve? Sorry."

"Don't be. Just that something I thought was long-term didn't turn out that way." And, hey, look at that. He had a new candidate for understatement of the year.

"Want to talk about googly eyes instead? Or maybe what disguises we should wear tomorrow to foil the Bingo Brigade?" Her tone conveyed sympathy as she offered him the easy way out.

He surprised himself by not taking it. "Does this mean there's no angsty filmmaker waiting for you back in Belize?"

"The angsty ones don't usually end up in reality TV. Or if they do, they don't last long—you need a certain sense of humor to survive a group hot tub shoot—or for that matter, a one-on-one hot tub shoot. Which, depending on the one-plus-one, can be far worse than the group deals." She paused. "Let's just say it's been a while since my last . . . well, whatever it was, and I'm not the sort of girl that a guy waits around for." Her voice had gone more serious, as if she realized they were shifting gears a little.

Keep it light, he reminded himself, and went with, "In other words, the guys you hang around with are idiots."

That got a laugh out of her. "Thanks for the compliment, but no, it's not that. Some of them—most of them, really—are really cool. It's more that everybody goes into things knowing it's just for fun, gonna end, that sort of thing. Like a vacation fling. It's better that way. Nobody gets hurt, nobody waits around, and nobody gets left behind." She paused, voice going wicked. "Now, about those disguises we're going to wear to dinner . . ."

He chuckled. "I think we're out of luck on the stealth-dating front—where Ruth is concerned, the cat's already out of the bag, the horse is out of the barn, and the cows have come home."

"Sounds like roundup day here at the ranch."

"Except that we'll be at the Steak Lounge. You still up for it?"

"Drinks to dessert, Doc," she vowed. "Drinks to dessert."

They talked for a few minutes more and then said their good-byes, lingering long enough that when Nick finally did hang up, he sat there for another couple of minutes, staring out the window and grinning like a fool. He hadn't thought he was in the market, but it looked like he had found someone. And she was a heck of a someone. "Like she said, short-term, no harm, no foul," he said to Cheesepuff. "I can do that."

The cat stood, stretched, and gave him a look of *Really, dude?* And then he did a one-eighty and sat on Nick's sandwich.

12

Jenny spent Sunday morning finishing up the rough cuts on her mom's video and getting started on the first of the Big Skye clips, and then rewarded herself with a trek up into the attic.

The huge, wood-beamed space followed the peaked roof, angling down to crawl spaces on either side. Aside from a cleaning fit every decade or so, little had been done to keep the stuff under control for the past . . . well, Jenny didn't have a clue beyond a really long time. Near the stairs, stacks of Tupperware tubs marked *Kitchen* had a couple of familiar pieces of bedroom furniture pushed up against them, where her mom had no doubt shoved them in her hurry to move on to bigger and better. Beyond that, Jenny worked her way past dusty layers of once-favorite toys, Archie Bunker furniture, and boxes labeled with things that had no doubt made sense at the time, like *Spare pigs* and *Glow stuff*. The old photos were about halfway back, stacked in boxes almost directly over Jenny's bedroom. The two neat rows of three made it look like they were far more organized than they actually were, though—she had transferred the family archive from moldering shoeboxes to archival cases a few years ago, but hadn't gotten any further in the filing department.

She hefted the first two. "Well, gotta start somewhere!"

Rex whuffed from off to one side, where he was sniffing around an old steamer trunk with a whole-body wiggle that suggested she shouldn't look in there unless she was prepared to deal with whatever he was smelling.

"Come on, buddy. Back downstairs."

His wheeled around. *We're going downstairs. Oh, boy!*

As he thundered ahead of her, tail going like a metronome, she could hardly believe he was the same dog she had lured with bratwurst up on the main road, or carried into the vet clinic. Had it only been a week? It seemed impossible, like too much had happened for so little time to have passed.

He had already gained weight and a bloom in his coat, and his limp had smoothed out some. He knew when to be in the kitchen to mooch the best treats from Gran and when to sneak up onto the couch in the family room to score scritches from multiple people during TV time. And darned if it didn't seem like he had been there forever.

"All the way downstairs," she said when Rex paused at her bedroom door. "We've got more work to do before we call it a day." And in a few hours, it would be time to get ready for her date. Even thinking it put happy flutters in her stomach as she hit the first floor.

Rex whuffed from the office. *Hurry up!*

"I'm coming, I'm coming. It's not like you offered to help carry this stuff, you know. In fact—" She missed a step at the sight of her mom sitting behind the big desk, ruffling Rex's fur while the dog danced around like it had been days since he'd last seen her, rather than breakfast. "Hey, Mom. I thought you headed into town."

Rose looked up, face bright. "I hurried home."

"To see your video?"

"That can wait. I've got something incredible to show you!"

Biting back a snippy comment about having her hard work tossed on the back burner, Jenny set the boxes on the floor and took the visitor's chair. "Okay, what's up?"

Rose pushed her laptop aside, clearing space in the middle of the desk, and then, with a flourish, produced a foam-core board. It was maybe two feet square, plastered with paint chips in shades of berry and flamingo, cutouts of ornate gold mirrors and fussy tufted pillows, and small squares of pink, gold, and white fabric, all spiraling around the central image of a glossy red, rabid-looking ceramic horse. The whole effect was one of a multimedia scrapbook gone very wrong, yet her eyes gleamed. "Don't you just love it?"

Gawd, no. "What is it?" Jenny asked carefully.

"It's an inspiration board," her mother answered, and she might as well have added "duh." The tone was definitely there. "Decorators use it as a springboard for discussions with their clients, so I thought it would be fun for us to have one for our project."

When had the office floor turned to quicksand? "Project?" *Please don't be talking about what I think you're talking about.*

"Your bedroom, silly. We discussed this."

It was an effort to stay planted in the visitor's chair. "Yes, we did. What part of 'no, thanks' did you not understand?"

"Oh, you." Rose tinkled a laugh and waved it off. "It'll be fun!"

Frustration kicked, though she tried to hold it in check. "What if I upgraded it to a 'hell, no'?"

"You'll love it." Her mom stroked the paint chips and fussy little fabrics, looking utterly besotted. "We'll do the darker colors on the bed and keep the walls light since it's such a small room. But if we put the striped cloth on the biggest wall and add the mirrors, we'll get the illusion of more space."

"*We* aren't doing anything of the sort." It came out sharp, but that didn't seem to matter. Jenny could've been talking to herself, for all the impression it made.

Rex came around the desk and pressed against her leg, looking up with worried eyes. *Everything okay?*

Not really, but scaring the dog wasn't going to help. At this point, she didn't know what would. Forcing her voice level, she said, "Look, Mom, I know you mean all this in the best possible way, but I need you to understand something: I like my room just the way it is. I like that it hasn't changed since I was fourteen, and that no matter what tent I've been living in, I always know what I'm coming home to."

"I . . . Hmm." To Jenny's relief, her mom actually seemed to hear her that time. She frowned down at the board, fingering the striped fabric. "I thought that you of all people would understand needing a project."

Ouch. Not much she could do to counter that when there were half-finished clips on her computer and dusty boxes at her feet. But at least it was something that made sense, maybe even a tiny, shifting piece of common ground. "Okay, I get that. But there's got to be a better option, a bigger space you can work with." She snapped her fingers. "How about you redecorate one of the cabins?"

"They're not heated."

"The bonus house, then." The former bunkhouse had been relocated to the other side of the property, with its own driveway, eco-friendly solar panels, and a cistern. With Foster now living at the Double-Bar H, it was empty.

"Krista hasn't decided whether to offer it to an employee or use it as a private guest retreat. Until she makes that call, there's no point in redecorating. And, besides, that's too big a project for the middle of winter. I need something small, where I can make an impact."

"How about . . ." *Come on, come on.* There had to be something else.

Rose reached out and touched Jenny's balled fist. "Please, sweetie. I really want to do this for you. What's more, I want to do it *with* you."

Right then, Jenny would've given almost anything to be back down south in the jungle, where she could occasionally tell the producers where to shove their ideas. She couldn't do that to her mother, though. Especially not when she was pulling the *I want some mom-daughter time* card.

The sigh felt like it came all the way up from her toes. "No pink," she said firmly.

Her mom's eyebrows rose. "What's wrong with it?"

"If we're going to do this, it's going to be yellow and white, just like it is now."

"I . . ." Rose paused for a moment, trying to look disappointed. But the corners of her mouth curved in victory. "Yellow and white, with a few pops of color."

"We'll discuss the pops later." Jenny stood, looking at the clock on the wall. "I've got to go change for dinner." She practically sprinted up the stairs with Rex galumphing after her, knowing full well that she was running away.

There was no doubt that she had lost that round. But as she jumped in the shower, she announced, "Take a note, Rex. I hereby swear there's no way I'm going to let that creepy-ass china horse watch me sleep!"

"You totally caved." For some reason, Nick seemed charmed by her wimpitude. He leaned in across their table at the Steak Lodge, a romantic two-top directly beneath a wall-mounted bison she was pretty sure was animatronic. "Does this mean you've got a chicken coop armoire in your future, or maybe a bed shaped like a giant camera?"

"No way. And I'm also not going to live with walls the color of a strawberry shake at Mickey D's, or any ceramic animal that looks like it's plotting my imminent demise." She leaned in to meet him, though, liking the way his green button-down was open at the throat, giving her glimpses of his collarbones and smooth masculine skin. Lowering her voice, she said, almost in a whisper, "I'll tell you a secret, though, if you promise it'll stay between the two of us."

He made a show of crossing his heart. "Scout's honor. And, yes, I was actually a Scout. Made it all the way to Eagle."

"You did? What was your final project?"

"Organizing a low-cost spay and neuter program."

"Awww. Should've guessed. You really are one of the good ones, aren't you?"

"Flattery will get you most anywhere, except out of telling me your deep, dark secret."

"Ah." She looked to the left and right, and then whispered, "You're right. I totally caved. But I promised Krista I would do whatever it took to keep Mom out of Gran's hair for the duration."

"That's it? Lame. I totally could've guessed that. And what's more, it sounds like your mom figured it out, too."

Jenny leaned back, sighing. "Yeah, you're probably right." She wasn't even that put out about it, either—at least not right now. It was awfully hard to be upset about much of anything when she was sitting opposite a handsome, interesting guy whose eyes gleamed like that when he looked at her.

There was a whirr and a click from overhead, and the buffalo came to mechanical life, batting its feathery eyelashes and cocking its huge furry head to look down at them. Mouth moving a little out of sync with the recording, it said, "Hey, there, pretty lady. You look like you could use a kiss." The creature turned its head to fix Nick with a plastic-and-fur *come on* look. "What do you say, buddy?"

He grinned across at her. "You heard the bison."

"Yes, I did."

They met halfway across the table in a kiss that was as thorough as it was gentle, yet more or less PG rated, earning scattered applause from the tables nearby. Jenny's heart gave a giddy flip-flop, and she worked not to look like a total dewy-eyed sap when they parted.

She cleared her throat. "That ought to give the Bingo Brigade something to talk about."

"Do you mind?"

"Actually, no."

"You sound surprised."

"It used to bug me how everybody was up in each other's business here, and how a girl couldn't do anything naughty without her mom finding out within the hour."

"Define naughty."

"You've got an imagination. Use it." She chuckled,

leaning back a little, though their hands remained linked on the tabletop. "I guess having spent a bunch of years living with even smaller groups made up of way nosier people has put things into perspective."

"Not to mention the whole *Jungle Love* thing. Talk about dating in a fishbowl."

She winced. "If you're a fan of the show, we are so over."

"No worries. I caught a couple of episodes online, but it was strictly for research purposes." At her raised eyebrow, he grinned. "It was kind of fun, thinking that the girl who took me parking down by the point might've filmed this scene or that one. As for the show itself? Not really my cup of tea."

"Mine neither, but Belize rocks."

The waitress appeared with their drinks, set out bar napkins for each of them, and deposited their beers. "Your meals will be out in a minute."

"Thanks," Nick said. Then he studied the woman, eyes narrowing. "You didn't happen to tip off the bison, did you? I'm guessing that particular program doesn't run when there's, say, a serious business meeting going on at this table."

Her lips curved. "Sometimes it does, just for our amusement. But, yeah, maybe I put in a good word for you."

He toasted her with his beer. "Appreciate it."

Jenny laughed as she moved off. "And here I thought the fix was already in."

"It would've been if I'd thought of it." He raised his

glass again, this time in her direction. "To a beautiful lady, talking taxidermy, and a night with no emergency calls."

"I'll so toast to that." They clinked and sipped.

"So, tell me. What's it really like, being behind the camera on a show like that?"

Usually, she fobbed off questions of that sort with a breezy nonanswer and changed the subject. Now, though, she took a sip and thought about it. "Some days I look around and think 'I can't believe they're paying me to do this.' The country is flipping gorgeous, and when we get time off, we'll group up and head off on side trips. One time, we followed an underground river through these cave systems you wouldn't believe, filled with all these crazy stone formations and old Mayan carvings and stuff. Another time, we went to a friend-of-a-friend-of-a-friend's village for a harvest festival. I don't know the names of everything I ate, but it was incredible." She smiled at the memories, a little surprised by how far away they felt, like she was remembering a vacation rather than this being her hiatus and the other stuff belonging to her real life. "As for the work . . . it's a mixed bag, really. Because of all the competitions, group dates and one-on-ones, there's a whole lot less sitting and waiting than when you're shooting a straight documentary, or even a less scripted reality show. But at the same time you've always got to be on the lookout for a catfight or other drama that's going on outside the organized stuff."

Studying her over the rim of his glass, he said, "You enjoy it."

"I do. It started out as a fill-in gig while a friend waited on funding for a documentary. But the project fell through, so I stayed on another season while I looked for something more serious. By season three, I stopped looking." She shrugged. "It suits me. I like the people and the locations, and even though the show follows roughly the same pattern each cycle, we bust our butts to come up with new settings and crazy things for the contestants to do. So it never gets too boring, you know?"

She paused while the waitress set their meals in front of them. As they started on their steaks, he said, "What was your favorite shoot so far on the show?"

"That depends. Are we talking about favorite setting, favorite activity, favorite blooper, or favorite 'awww, that's so sweet' moment?" She wouldn't have bet a nickel on most of the so-called couples that had developed during filming, but one or two of them had made her think there was a glimmer of hope.

"I want to hear all of them," he said promptly. "But bloopers first, of course."

"Of course." Around bites of a perfect medium sirloin and loaded baked potato, she hit the highlights of the wardrobe malfunctions, awkward blunders and outright pranks she had filmed over the last few years, along with some of her favorite scenes and people.

Most everything had found its way into the show or

online, so it was fair game. She added her own take on things, though, and delighted in hearing his laugh roll across the busy restaurant. It was nicer than she would've thought to talk about the show with someone who wasn't in the business, wasn't angling for an audition or an introduction to one of the show's singles. He just wanted to hear about it because it was important to her.

Before she knew it, the waitress was clearing the last of their plates and asking if they wanted to see the dessert menu.

"No, thanks," Nick said. "It was excellent, but we'll take the check now." As the waitress walked away and Jenny tried to decide whether she was annoyed that he hadn't asked her—*hello, chocolate cake?*—he shot her a slow smile that said he knew exactly what she was thinking, and said, "I've got other plans for dessert."

13

When Nick steered the truck onto the snowy track leading to Makeout Point, Jenny shot him a side-long look. "Dessert, huh? What are we having?"

"You'll see." He parked at the end of the lane, where the world seemed to fall away, and popped open the rear door to retrieve his duffel and a roped bundle of firewood.

Her eyes gleamed in the pale illumination from his flashlight. "I see you came prepared."

"Like I said, I was a Scout."

"Can I carry something?"

"I've got it. You lead." They picked their way down the narrow track to the little alcove with its old-timey fire pit. It was colder than the other day, but he decided that the Arctic air made it extra satisfying to stack the wood in a careful teepee and tuck smaller sticks and curled slivers of pine underneath.

Jenny watched the proceedings from one of the log benches, huddling inside her ski jacket. "Here." He stripped off his parka and draped it over her shoulders, leaving him relatively warm in the wind-blocking sweater he had pulled on in the truck.

"Thanks." She tugged it closed around her neck. "A small part of me says I should go back to the truck for my own parka, but I'm going to have a little cuddle with yours first."

The sight of her wrapped in his jacket made him want to peel it back off again, maybe sling her over his shoulder and carry her back to the truck for some— *Focus*, he told himself. If he was going to channel his inner caveman, he should at least prove he could make fire first. Clearing his throat, he said, "Hopefully we'll have some heat going in just a minute here."

Eyeing his duffel—high-end trekkers' gear that wore its years hard—she said, "You're not going to start the fire with a couple of sticks, are you?"

"I could if you want me to, but I was going to cheat." He pulled out a barbecue lighter shaped like a dachshund. When she laughed, he held it up and pulled the trigger-tail, and a small flame came out of the dog's mouth. "In my defense, it was a gift from a client."

"If it lights the fire, I'm a fan."

It did, indeed, and a few minutes later he had a respectable little blaze going, enough so he could add a couple of the larger logs. As he settled beside her, he could feel the first real tendrils of warmth starting to radiate into the little hollow. "I think we're getting somewhere."

She sent him a sidelong smile. "Yes, I'd definitely say we are."

And darned if his heart didn't take on a thick, heavy beat—the kind that said there was more going on here than he had meant for there to be. Or if there wasn't already, they were on the edge of it.

Clearing his throat, he dug into his duffel and came up with the Tupperware and thermos he'd stashed right before leaving the clinic. "Double fudge brownie and white chocolate cocoa?"

She moaned at the back of her throat, making his body come to life. But her eyes were on the chocolate booty. "You baked?"

"I did the cocoa, which I don't think counts as baking."

"And the brownies?"

"Courtesy of Ruth." Who had given him a *I bet I know what you're going to do with these* look when she handed over the requested baked goods, but he didn't figure Jenny needed to know that part.

"Gimme. Just don't tell Gran I cheated on her with another woman's brownie."

"My lips are sealed." He uncovered the sweets and held them out.

"Hang on." She unzipped his parka and started worming her arms out of the sleeves. "I'm warming up."

He shifted closer and wrapped an arm around her, tucking her close to his side. "Keep it. I'm fine, really. Like you said, the fire is doing its thing. And, besides, we've got chocolate."

"That we do. You mind sharing the thermos cup?"

"That's a rhetorical question, right?"

She took an experimental sip of the cocoa, then smiled. "It's good."

"I didn't burn the water? That's a relief."

Her chuckle vibrated against him, making him very aware of her body tucked against his, and how well they fit together. "You're not much of a cook, I take it?" she asked.

"My mom did her best with me, even had me cooking dinner once a week when I was in my teens. Only let me serve frozen pizza and salad once a month, too. The rest of the time I actually had to make stuff." He grinned down at her. "I can rock spaghetti, burgers and Shake 'n Bake, thanks to good old Mom."

"She sounds like a neat lady."

"She was." It was out there before he could call it back. Not that he wanted to, really. It was part of who he was, just not one he tended to talk about.

Jenny looked up at him. "Oh."

He tightened his arm around her, giving an *it's okay* squeeze, and for a moment they concentrated on their brownies and hot chocolate, and the *hiss-pop* of the fire as it ate away at the two bigger logs. The silence was friendly, but it said she would listen if he wanted to talk.

Caution said he should pull back, keep it light. They were just making time together, spending a few fun weeks while it was convenient. But that was the beauty, wasn't it? They could say what they wanted to and be themselves, without adding expectations to the mix.

And it felt strange sometimes, being back in his home state, yet surrounded by people who hadn't known his family for decades and didn't know the whole story. "We lost her just over two years ago," he said. "Lung cancer, even though she quit smoking when I was just a kid. She . . . um." He took a slug of the cocoa. "She went downhill fast. It wasn't much more than a month after the diagnosis." Which still seemed impossible, even though he had lived through it.

Jenny leaned into him, not saying a word. Somehow, though, the press of her face against his upper arm loosened the tightness inside him.

That made it easier to say, "I got the message in plenty of time, but it was the rainy season and travel was tough. Between breakdowns and flooding, it took me almost two weeks to get home. I made it, but . . ." He stared into the fire, seeing the sudden peace that had overtaken his mom's face when he'd walked into her room, and feeling the guilt that still hung in there, even though he'd made it home in time. "Everyone who loved her got to say good-bye."

The fire crackled in the silence that followed. After a moment, Jenny threaded her fingers through his, and squeezed. "I haven't really lost anyone, so I don't have the right words. But I think . . . I can imagine that on one hand the closure helps, but on the other hand it doesn't help a damn bit, because you don't want her to be gone."

"Something like that." Exactly like that, in fact, though he'd more or less dealt with the anger that used to grab him out of nowhere, making him want to put his fist through a wall. "After that . . . I guess I lost my taste for being overseas. It was just too far to fly if things went wrong back home."

She eased back to look up at him. "And, I'm guessing, because your father needed you."

"He and I kept his clinic going for almost a year before he called it quits. He didn't want to walk in and see someone else at her desk, didn't want to be around people who saw him and thought of her. Most of all, he didn't want to be a vet anymore." It was tough to say, tougher to remember those months, and not just because of his dad's retirement.

"Lots of changes," she said softly.

He cleared his throat, not wanting his voice to go gruff, though he was feeling it suddenly. More than he would've expected. "There was another clinic in town. Doc Sharma was happy to take his patients, as it gave her an excuse to add a second vet to her practice and upgrade some equipment. Dad sold the house and bought a hunting lodge in the foothills north of Three Ridges, so he'd be within shouting distance of me." He nodded to the dark bulk of the mountains on the horizon beyond the fire. "He lives there year-round now, and he's doing okay. Better than okay. He's happy."

"And you?"

He tipped his head back and watched a couple of sparks head for the stars. "I like it here. More than I thought I would. And if Dad needs me, I'm just a couple of hours away."

She shifted away from him, and when he looked over, he found her shaking her head at him.

"You don't think I'm happy?" he asked.

"You're the only one who can make that call. I was more thinking that you're one of the good ones, Doc. And you're way out of my league."

He snorted. "On what planet?"

"On the one where you traded Africa for Three Ridges because your father needed you."

"You would've done the same thing." And he didn't want her to think he was any kind of hero. He was just doing what needed to be done, making the choices that needed to be made, and doing his best to find things to like about his new life rather than missing the pieces he'd left behind.

"I practically have to be bribed to spend some time with my mother," she pointed out.

"You rearranged your life to come home when Krista needed you."

"Only temporarily."

"It counts."

Expression softening, she tugged off a glove and reached up to lay her palm on his cheek. "And here you are, trying to make me feel better."

Still not a hero. Not wanting to look too closely at why the idea bothered him, yet stirred by the light in her eyes, he captured her hand and held it against his face. "I have an idea about making you feel even better."

Her lips curved and her fingers flexed beneath his

touch. "Oh, really? I'm sure I have no idea what you're talking about."

"Then let me show you." He leaned down and covered her mouth with his in a kiss that surrounded him with warmth, the taste of chocolate, and the sense of being exactly where he was supposed to be. Which shouldn't have made any sense with them sitting outside in the bitter cold, huddled together over a fire, but somehow made all the sense in the world.

14

The next morning, instead of being exhausted from her and Nick having put Makeout Point to good use until the wee hours of the morning, Jenny was up early, bubbling with an energy that sent her dancing into the kitchen with Rex bouncing along beside her. "Treats! We need treats!"

Gran looked up from her recipe box, face lighting with amusement. "I take it we're celebrating a successful second date?"

"What date? I'm excited about getting back to my video clips. You should see Big Skye on the screen. He's such a handsome devil."

That got an eye roll. "Devil is right, at any rate. He was on the phone first thing this morning to see if the doctor could fit him in any earlier. Though I won't be sorry to get him out of the house and back out riding the fences. Do us both some good, that will." She wagged a finger at Jenny. "But you're trying to change the subject."

Maybe a little, Jenny realized, which in itself was a

surprise. Where usually she would be happy to pour herself a cup of coffee and postmortem a date, now she hesitated, rummaging in the dog-shaped cookie jar to buy herself a minute.

Rex happily scarfed the biscuits, then galumphed over to Gran, tail wagging in happy swipes that were getting faster by the day as he healed, projecting the doggy version of *Got anything good? I like muffins, you know.*

"They're yesterday's," Gran warned, breaking off a piece of apple cinnamon for him.

"Like that'll slow him down?" Jenny headed for the fridge and pulled out some nonfat yogurt and blueberries, figuring she should take a stab at a healthy meal. Then, knowing Gran would read too much into it if she kept quiet, she said, "It was a really nice night. We went to the Steak Lodge, got heckled by a mechanical buffalo, and talked pretty much nonstop through dinner."

"And?"

"And what? We had a nice time. He's a nice guy." And she needed to stop saying "nice." It didn't even come close to describing the reality. And, like silence, probably said way too much about how it had felt to be wrapped in layers of him—his parka, his arms, his kiss . . . Her lips curved and her body heated a couple of notches at the memory.

"Late night for just dinner," Gran remarked.

"You want details about our trip to Makeout Point?" Jenny quipped. "Maybe some video?"

That got a girlish giggle and a flip of a kitchen towel.

"Oh, you. Fine. Don't tell me where you really were. See if I save you any macaroons."

"Macaroons?" Jenny straightened, looking around. "Where?"

"Not yet, but check back this afternoon. If all goes well at Dr. Moore's, I'm going to be celebrating the liberation of my living room."

By the time Jenny had finished uploading the final version of *Rose's Boudoir*—yeesh on the title her mom had picked, but whatever—it was midafternoon, with the wan sun on its downslide toward the quick winter dusk. Pushing away from the desk, she gave a shoulder-popping stretch and exhaled. "Okay. Next crisis."

Actually, it had been a pretty tame day, with only a few eye-roll-worthy calls and an email exchange that had left her wondering if the sender was actually a psych student testing to see how many times she could ask the same four questions before the answers started getting snippy. So far, they were up to three rounds, and Jenny hadn't even let fly with an "As I already mentioned." She was giving herself points on that one.

Rex, sacked out on his blanket nest in midafternoon nap mode, acknowledged her with a single tail thump.

"I'm sorry. Am I disturbing you?" She scooted around in her chair to reach down and ruffle his belly fur, just as the landline started ringing. "Hold that thought," she said, and grabbed the phone. "Mustang Ridge, this is Jenny. How may I help you today?"

"By telling me you're nice and toasty warm in that

office," Nick said wistfully, his voice muffled by a bad connection and engine noise.

Heart giving a giddy thump, she tucked the receiver close to her face. "Is that code for 'what are you wearing'?"

That got a chuckle. "It wasn't, but now I'm curious."

"Sorry. Wish I could say something about a bath and a layer of bubbles, but at the moment you'll have to settle for jeans, fleece, and bunny slippers. You headed out on an emergency call?"

"Just finished with one," he said. "Turned into a long day."

"After a short night," she agreed. "I recommend hot chocolate, or a beer. Possibly both, though I don't recommend mixing them."

"What, you've never had chocolate beer?"

"Ew, no, and as far as I'm concerned, chocolate goes with almost anything. In fact—" She broke off at the sound of her name coming from the front of the house. "Hang on." Putting her hand over the phone, she raised her voice to call, "Gran? Is that you? I'm in the office."

"Jenny!" Gran hurried into the office still wearing her boots and coat, and trailing snow. "I'm sorry to interrupt, sweetie, but have you seen your grandfather?"

"No, not since this morning. Do you need help with something?"

"Yes. Finding him." Gran clutched her hands together in front of her body, suddenly looking very small and pale. "I'm probably overreacting, but he's been so sick. After the doctor's appointment, he said he was just going out for a short ride. An hour, maybe two."

Jenny rose to her feet, but it felt like her stomach stayed put in the chair. "When was that?"

"Right before lunch."

Oh, that wasn't good. Not good at all. Unbidden, her eyes went to the cold white world beyond the window. "Did you check the barn?"

A shallow nod. "Bueno isn't in his stall."

"Jenny?" a tinny voice said from the phone. "Can you hear me?"

"Oh!" She raised the handset as her stomach gave a nervous churn. "Sorry. I'm sorry. There's . . . a situation."

"I heard. Hang up and start looking for him. I'll be there soon to help."

"You . . ." She wanted to tell Nick not to bother, that it was some sort of mistake. But the words wouldn't come. Not when Gran was standing there, looking on the verge of panic while beyond her, through the window, a gust of wind kicked up a whirl of white along the ridgeline. "Okay."

He hung up, or maybe she did—her priority was Gran, who was too pale, her eyes too big. "Nick is on his way. Who else is here?"

"Nobody. Foster went home, Rose and Eddie are out, and everyone else is done for the day." Gran's voice trembled slightly. "If he fell off Bueno and hurt himself—"

"He didn't," Jenny said. "I bet he just lost track of time." She hoped. "Does he have his phone with him?" It was a house rule that everyone had to carry a cell, especially when riding out alone—even with sketchy reception, the phones were better than nothing—but she wouldn't put it past Big Skye to "forget" his.

Sure enough, Gran shook her head. "No. It's still in the cottage. He probably figured he was just going for a short ride . . ." She swallowed, eyes filming. "I need to get a grip."

But her worry was fueling Jenny's. "Maybe he already came back, stripped Bueno down, and turned him out to have a roll in the snow. Let's take a look. Come on, Rex. You're on bloodhound duty."

"Whuff!" The dog wagged his tail as hard as she had seen him manage so far, his eyes glued to her and Gran like he was trying to promise that whatever suddenly had them so worried, he was there to help.

Jenny wasn't sure he would be much use, but his enthusiasm was contagious. "We'll find him." She gave Gran a quick, hard hug. "And he'll be fine. This is Big Skye we're talking about. There's no way he's putting himself back on bed rest."

"If he does, I'm moving his bed in here and telling your mother it's her turn."

"That's the spirit. Let's go find him."

But a thorough search didn't turn up any sign of Big Skye, his tack, or his favorite horse, and it didn't look like he had taken a radio, either—all the walkie-talkies were lined up in their chargers, most of them dusty from winter disuse.

"Guess we'll have to do it the old-fashioned way," Jenny decided. "Will you go grab the Remington and some shells for me?"

Gran's face cleared. "Signal shots! Absolutely."

"And while you're in there, call Mom and Dad back. Foster, too. We may need to ride out." She glanced at the sky. "The sooner, the better. I know it'll annoy Gramps if we make a fuss—"

"Good," Gran said primly. "Then next time maybe he'll bring his phone with him." She headed for the main house with Rex on her heels.

Jenny watched her go, envying her gran's ability to mix her huge capacity for love with the spine and practicality of a lifelong rancher. Still, she was all too aware of the fading light, the bone-chilling cold, and the wall-to-wall snow that was broken only by the packed-down trail leading up the ridgeline. Big Skye had no doubt followed it, but for how long? Had he turned off on the other side of the ridge, or had he ridden all the way up to the high pasture, making his usual self-appointed rounds of the fence line? The big predators should be in their dens, but that wasn't a guarantee. And with the weather being what it was, everything from a thrown shoe to a bad fall took on a whole new level of danger.

She worked to suppress a shiver.

Gran's hurried footsteps sounded as she came down

the path carrying the shotgun and wearing a grim expression. "Your parents and Foster are on their way, but it'll be at least an hour, maybe more."

Jenny took the Remington. "Let's see if he's within earshot. You want to hang on to Rex for me?" The last thing they needed was to send him running for the hills.

It felt strange to hold the weapon. The shotgun was good for fending off bears and big cats because it could hold multiple shells, but that made it solid, almost too heavy. The strangeness wore off quickly, though, as her muscles remembered the routine: check the safety, check the chamber, load the shells, rack a shell into the chamber and take the safety off. She scanned her surroundings, saw that Gran had moved closer to the house and had a good hold of Rex's collar. Then, aiming at the big, empty white of the ridgeline, she fired off three shots at two-second intervals—*blam, blam, blam*. The recoil jerked against her shoulder and punched the air from her lungs, making her feel like she'd just jumped into a gully and landed too hard. The echoes ricocheted off the buildings and surrounding hills, tickling her ears long after the last shot had peppered a spray-can splotch in the snow.

And then, nothing. The fading day was silent, save for the sound of Rex panting some distance away.

Slowly, she turned to Gran. "Guess he's out of range." There was no question that Big Skye would be armed—he might leave the house without his phone, but never without a gun.

"Or else he's hurt." Gran's voice was almost inaudible.

"He's . . ." Jenny shook her head, knowing they were running out of options, out of time. "I'll ride out now. The others can catch up with me when they get here, or fan out and search other trails."

"Wait," Gran said, starting toward her. "You don't have to . . ." She stopped and stomped a booted foot, eyes welling. "Darn it. When he gets back, I'm going to glue that phone where he can't reach it. See if he ever leaves it behind again."

Trying to imagine where, exactly, her gran planned on sticking the phone, Jenny found a weak grin. "Maybe this is just his way of getting me back on a horse."

"You could take one of the snowmobiles."

"There are too many places out there that a snowmobile can't go. Besides, a good horse will help me look for his buddy, and keep me out of trouble when the going gets rough." She didn't know the trails as well as she once had, and horses had far better instincts than machines. "Don't worry about me. I haven't forgotten how to ride."

Krista had pointed out a couple of reliable saddle horses, in case Jenny wanted to throw a leg over. At the time, she had scoffed. Now, she ran through the mental checklist, knowing she couldn't afford to waste time, but she wouldn't be any use if she disappeared out there, too.

"But . . ." Gran trailed off, hands fluttering helplessly as Rex pawed at her leg, whining. "I should go with you."

"No." No way in hell. "I need you here to call me back when he rides in, complaining because we raised a fuss."

That took some of the strain out of Gran's face. Not much, but some. "Are you sure?"

"Positive. Can you grab me some extra clothes for him? Whatever you think makes sense."

"Of course. I'll bring them to the barn. And some extras for you, too, along with snacks and coffee."

No point in arguing that, if she had even wanted to. Which she didn't, because the doubts were creeping in. It was cold, night was coming, and it had been years since she had tracked anything but reality TV stars, longer since she had done it from horseback in the snow. But if she waited and they reached him too late, she would never forgive herself. "Maybe leave Rex in the house when you come back," she said to Gran. "I don't want him following me."

In the barn, Jenny grabbed Krista's tack and one of the knapsacks that went along on every guest ride, pre-filled with a first-aid kit, heat packs, foil blankets, rations, and a fire-starting kit. Stacking the equipment in the aisle, she headed for the lower paddock and brought in all of the riding horses, sticking them in stalls for when the others arrived. Just as she ran the stall door shut behind Doobie, the sturdy mustang she planned to ride, she heard the deep rumble of a truck's engine and the crunch of tires on snowy gravel out in front of the barn.

Heart thudding, she hurried toward the sound, reaching the main slider just as Nick swung down from his truck. Wearing heavy layers and a fur-lined hat she hadn't seen on him before, he looked capable and cowboyish, and like he fit right in with the rugged landscape.

Relief poured through her. "You came." She walked straight into his arms, needing the contact. "Thank you."

He gripped her tightly, burrowing in for a moment, then easing away as Gran hurried up, her arms piled with clothes and food. "I take it he's not back?"

"No," Jenny said, "and the others won't be here before dusk." She looked at him, measuring his worn jeans and sturdy boots, surprised to realize how little she really knew about him. "Can you ride?"

"Try and stop me."

The rush of gratitude was stronger than she wanted to let on. Inhaling a deep breath, she nodded. "Thanks." To Gran, she said, "We'll bring him back in one piece."

She didn't promise, though. Didn't dare.

It had been a few years since Nick had done any serious riding, but the motions came back quickly enough as he slapped borrowed tack on Roman, a solid bay gelding with an aquiline nose and a reportedly unflappable temperament. He was aware of Jenny keeping an eye on him as he buckled on the last of the gear, then double-checked his cinch. "I think I'm good to go," he said.

"I'd say you are." Despite the underlying strain, her eyes warmed as she crossed to him, reached up on her tiptoes, and kissed his cheek. "Thank you. Gran is relieved you're going with me. So am I."

Dropping a kiss on her forehead, he said, "Two sets of eyes are better than one. Or four versus two, if we're counting the horses. And we need to get moving if we're going to beat the dark." He didn't think she would want to hear there was no way he would've let her go alone, even if it had meant chasing her on foot.

As it was, they would likely be riding past dark, hoping to hell that the sky stayed clear, the moonlight strong enough to light the trail. And hoping they had loaded themselves and the horses with the right supplies. "Give me a minute to grab a few things out of my truck?"

She nodded, face setting in resolute lines. "I'll meet you around the side with both horses."

It didn't take him long to load a battered knapsack with the supplies he thought he might need—the moves were ingrained after so many years of doing his job on the fly, in situations that would've made his "sterile field is everything" vet school professors cringe. He had already changed into his heaviest clothes, so he just had to add an extra pair of gloves, and he was good to go.

In the plowed-clear section beside the barn, Jenny sat astride a chestnut gelding who mouthed the bit and stomped a forefoot, wanting to be moving. Beside her, Gran held Roman's reins and craned to see the horizon.

As Nick took the reins from the older woman, who looked so much smaller out here than she did in her big, homey kitchen, he said, "Go get yourself thawed out and make sure Rex isn't too worried. We'll be in touch."

After giving the cinch a final tug, he swung up into the wide saddle while Jenny bent down to give her grandmother a hug. With Gran raising a hand in farewell, they reined the horses away and headed along the wide hoof-packed trail leading out of the homestead valley, their progress accompanied by the crunch of ice beneath the horses' sharp-shod hooves, the creak of cold leather, and the jingle of the long-shanked bits.

As they crested the ridge, where the wind had scoured the snow from the three-rock pyramid that landmarked the ranch valley, Jenny reined her horse to a restless halt. Nick rode up beside her and scanned the next valley, where the snow stretched to the horizon, unbroken save for the main trail and the shadowy veins where other riders—or perhaps animals—had broken off and forged their own paths.

"There's no sign of him," she said tightly. "I was hoping . . ."

He bumped his knee against hers. "Chin up. He knows this land and its winters better than any of us. If he got into trouble, he's probably made camp by now."

Her smile was wan, but real. "And he'll be ticked that we came out after him. In fact, he'll probably act like he had planned an overnight all along, wanting some time away after being so sick." Her voice trailed off on the last, though.

"He's tough as nails, Jenny. He's going to be okay."

"Thanks. I know I'm saying that way too much, but seriously, thanks. For being here. For trying to cheer me up. For looking seriously hot in the saddle. For all of it."

His grin got real. "I was going to tell you to stop thanking me, but I think I just changed my mind."

"Too bad, because I'm done." Centering herself in the saddle, she let out a steadying breath. "Okay. We're going to follow the main trail until it intersects with the upper pasture, then follow the fence line uphill. That's Gran's and my best guess on where he would've gone."

"You got it."

A nudge sent her horse onward and down the sloping trail, the muscles of its haunches bunching and shifting beneath the supplies lashed behind the saddle. Nick followed, staying back and off to one side, so if one horse slipped and fell, it would be less likely to take out the other in a tangle of legs and equipment. He strained to detect anything out of the ordinary, but heard only the wind. More tellingly, the horses kept their attention on the trail, with none of the pricked ears or whinnies that would indicate they had sensed another horse in the distance.

Over the next hour as they rode along a series of lower, snow-shrouded hills, they kept conversation to a minimum. Jenny's face was set, resolute, but each time they passed a smaller, offshoot trail and saw the prints of a shod horse in the snow, she patted her horse's neck and whispered praise to the little chestnut. It reminded Nick of the way his father had sat at his

mother's bedside those last few days, his thumb stroking the back of her hand over and over again, as if
afraid that if he stopped, she would, too.

"Come on, old man," he muttered under his breath.
"Where did you get off to?" He was still hoping for that
stopped-and-made-camp scenario, but as the yellow
sunlight bled from the sky and there was no evidence
of woodsmoke up ahead, it got far too easy to imagine
that Big Skye had been thrown and stranded on foot, or
worse.

"Let's try the shotgun again," Jenny said, though he
wasn't sure if that was because she had heard him or
not. He hadn't meant for her to, wanted to keep his
input wholly positive. But then again, they both knew
the odds.

"The horses going to be okay with it?" he asked as
she loosened the scabbard.

"Should be, but I wouldn't throw my reins away."

"Noted."

He took a feel of Roman's mouth as she aimed and
fired three shots over ten or so seconds. The blasts
cracked through the cold air, echoed off the surrounding hills, and brought the horse's heads jerking up, but
that was it.

They sat for a moment, straining to hear a far-off
reply.

She let out a frustrated sigh. "Damn. Okay, let's— "
A gunshot sounded suddenly from up ahead, cutting
her off. As her face lit, it was followed by two more in
rapid succession. "There he is!" Jenny whooped and

sent her horse bounding forward, shouting, "Hey! Hey, Gramps! It's Jenny!"

"Wait! Be careful— " Nick bit off the pointless warning and gave Roman his head instead. "Go on. Get them!"

15

Jenny's heart sang as she and Doobie pounded up a slight rise to the ridge beyond. They had found Big Skye, and he was in good enough shape to fire off a few rounds, and that was the hugest relief she could imagine. Then she crested the hill and started down, and she let loose with a disbelieving laugh at the sight of a strange parade: a bundled human figure trudging along the trail, leading a horse with a leggy black calf tied across the saddle, with a rawboned black cow bringing up the rear, bumping anxiously from side to side.

Not only was Big Skye okay, he was on a flipping rescue mission.

"Hey!" she called, reining in some distance away, not wanting to spook the little herd. "Who do you have there?"

Her grandfather raised a hand in greeting, but didn't say anything right away, looking torn between embarrassment and relief. After a moment, he grumbled, "Good to see you haven't forgotten how to ride. Is that the vet with you? Come on down here, Doc. These two could use some help."

A laugh got stuck in Jenny's throat. "Nice to see you, too, big guy." Not that she needed hugs and gratitude, really. All that mattered was that he was in one piece.

She and Nick quickly secured the horses and got a rope on the agitated cow, who wanted to be in the thick of things.

Two, maybe three weeks old, the wolfhound-size calf was limp and exhausted-looking, and had blood seeping from fresh bite wounds on its ribs and neck. "Heard some coyotes getting after something, and went to have a look-see," Big Skye explained as Nick moved in. "Found them worrying at this guy while his mama tried to drive them off." He patted the pistol on his hip. "Gave the varmints something else to think about."

"Late baby," Nick said, checking the calf's gums, which were dangerously pale. "Or early, depending."

"They're not ours. Must've wandered in, or been dropped off."

"Some folk are looking to be done with their livestock these days, just like their dogs." Nick unshouldered his knapsack and started rummaging for supplies. "Is this the worst of the bites?"

"Looked it to me. You want to untie him, give him a good going-over?"

To Jenny's immense gratitude, Nick shook his head. "He's shocky, but I don't see fresh blood. I think we should get him stabilized, then head for home." He glanced over at her. "Want to break out some snacks, and we can do a quick refuel while I get some fluids into this guy and take a quick look at his mama?"

Big Skye visibly perked up at that. "Got any cookies?"

Her heart turned over—not just at how pale her grandfather was, or the little stumble when he turned toward her, but at how Nick had made it the most natural thing in the world for her to break out the thermos of thick, hot cowboy coffee and hand it to her gramps. "Drink up. And, yes, Gran sent cookies."

He took a deep draught, then exhaled a relieved sigh. "What a woman."

Jenny handed over a cookie. "She made us bring extra clothes for you, too. You'd better put some of them on, or we'll all hear about it."

She doled out extra socks, air-activated hot packs for his hands and feet, a second parka and a fur-lined hat, interspersing the articles with cookie bribes. And, as he struggled with the clothing in a way that was more than the cold and fatigue, she looked away, chest tightening. His hair was so thin, the last of the steel gray turned white seemingly overnight, and his shoulders were stooped beneath the layers of goose down and nylon.

He's getting old. No matter how hard she tried to quash the thought, it stayed put, rooting itself in her brain alongside things like *they're not going to be around forever*, and *what will happen when they're gone?* Maybe the fears had been there ever since Nick had told her about his mother's death, bringing the niggling thought that it could've been her getting the "come home now" call, only to return and discover that the things she had depended on to stay the same, suddenly weren't anymore. Or maybe it was all about today—seeing the fear in Gran's face, feeling it herself as they had ridden over hill after hill without any sign of him. And even now, the nerves wouldn't let up.

What if he got sick again? What if the next time things didn't go so well? What if, what if, what if?

Turning away so Big Skye wouldn't see the sudden film of tears in her eyes, she cleared her throat. "I'll call Gran, let her know we're on our way back."

"Guess we don't have to put the vet on standby," Big Skye said, stomping back into his boots, "seeing as he's already here."

Yes, he was, wasn't he? The knowledge eased some of the tightness in her chest as she turned to look at the small mixed herd, where Nick was moving around the skittish black cow, talking soothing nonsense and keeping close, so if the animal did kick him, the blow would lack its full punch. He was big and solid beneath his layers, someone she could depend on. And where at first she had thought him an outsider like her, someone who didn't fit in with the cow-and-ranch thing, now she realized he was utterly in his element.

Giving the cow a final pat, he looked over at her. "You ready to move out?"

The warmth deepened to an inner glow of gratitude— that he had taken care of the calf without pointing out that the harsh economics of ranching argued for a bullet instead; that he had maneuvered things so Big Skye had accepted food and clothes without a fuss; that he was so darn good at everything he did. Going on impulse, she crossed to him, went up on her tiptoes, and gave him a big, smacking kiss. "Thanks, Doc. You're the best."

He grinned down at her. "I thought you were done thanking me for today?"

She patted his cheek. "I am now, hotshot. Let's get this show on the road. And by the way? I'm riding with you."

Even with Roman carrying a double load, with Jenny's arms around Nick's waist in what he decided was a nice perk, the ride back seemed much shorter than the trip out had been. Still, it was full dark before they crested Mustang Ridge, passed the marker stones, and looked down on the homestead, which spread out in the bowl of the valley in a wash of yellow light.

"Hello, electricity," Jenny said, leaning to look around him. "Looks like they've got every bulb in the place lit."

"Guess they wanted to give us a big target." He clucked to Roman and they started down the path. "Looks like there's a welcoming party, too," he added as figures emerged from the barn and main house, half a dozen humans with a pair of dogs racing around them in giddy circles. A chorus of barks carried across the snow.

"Stuff and nonsense," Big Skye muttered behind them. "When this was a real ranch, it was rare for a man to get in before dark. Don't know why all the fuss now."

Fighting a grin at Jenny's low growl, Nick said, "Blame it on the winter. These days, we'll take any excuse for a little excitement."

"Humph."

Nick chuckled at that, and Jenny poked him in the ribs. There wasn't much of a tickle through his heavy clothes, but he caught her gloved hand in his and held it tight, so her arm was snug against him as they passed through the outer gate, into the fenced-in confines of the ranch proper.

If he had been on foot, he might have hesitated briefly before entering the loose semicircle made of Gran, Rose and Ed Skye, and the wranglers, Foster, Stace, and Junior—which, along with Big Skye and the absent Krista, basically amounted to Jenny's family and friends, and the heart of Mustang Ridge. But Roman had no such qualms, eagerly marching into the brightly lit parking area and stopping in front of the barn, one ear flicking back in a clear indication of "Okay, that was fun. Now get off and feed me."

Jenny squeezed Nick's hand, then swung off the gelding's haunches. "Look what we found!"

It wasn't clear whether she was talking about the stray cattle or her grandfather, but the others flocked around her, then surrounded Big Skye as he climbed stiffly down from Doobie, grumbling about having to ride in her too-small saddle. Most everyone was talking at once, asking for details and making lots of "we were so worried!" noises. Foster was the exception, breaking off to give the horses and cows a quick once-over.

Nick hung back from it all, not really sure of his footing. He had crossed paths with each of them in the course of his work on the ranch, granted, but that had been before he got involved with Jenny, making this an odd sort of meet-the-parents-but-not-really moment.

"Hey, Doc," Foster said casually, "you want to help me get these two into the barn?"

"Sure." Heck, yeah. Nick took hold of the calf's back end and between the two of them, they got the limp little creature off Big Skye's horse and carried it into the barn, followed closely by the black cow, who stepped on their heels, and didn't at all appreciate being shut in a separate stall. Bumping the wall hard enough to make the two-by-twelves creak, she mooed protest.

Foster straightened away from the calf, which lay quietly on an old blanket, eyes at half-mast. "I'll get you some warm water. Need anything else? Coffee?"

"I wouldn't turn down a cup."

"Coming right up."

Nick made a trip out to his truck and came back with more fluids, along with his suture kit and a selection of meds. Big Skye had been right about the bite marks—Nick had already seen the worst of them, and if there was other damage, it wasn't obvious from the outside. The bleeding had stopped on the ride, though a sluggish ooze started up from some of them as the calf warmed up.

Digging into his equipment, Nick came up with a light tranq and a pair of cordless surgical clippers. "Okay, there, little buddy. Let's see what we're really dealing with, shall we?"

Over the next hour, he carefully clipped the baby-fine coat down to the dark skin, scrubbed and flushed the wounds, and stitched where stitching made sense. Foster came and went several times, seeing to the horses and tossing hay to the black cow, who settled in quickly enough to suggest she wasn't anyone's wild range beef. Then, toward the end, as Nick was snipping off the last of the sutures and feeling the ache in his neck and shoulders, Jenny's father came in.

Suddenly very aware that he hadn't gone one-on-one with the father of a girl he was seeing since high school or thereabouts, Nick said, "Evening," and squelched the urge to tack on a "sir."

Hands in his pockets, Ed Skye leaned against the open stall door and took a look at the patched-up calf. "Neatly done, Doc."

"Hope it holds." Nick smeared on a thick coat of ointment. "Teeth can be nasty things—ragged edges, punctures, and lots of bruising—and coyotes are worse than most. I left plenty of drainage space, though, and I'll hit him with some antibiotics now and leave you more for later."

"Think he'll make it?"

"I'd say he's got a decent chance." The warmth and

fluids had perked up the little guy's systems, pinking his gums and filling out some of the hollows, though it would be a little while yet before the calf woke from the tranq. "That's assuming he doesn't get sick from exposure, and there isn't anything going on internally." He glanced over. "Lot of work for someone else's calf. Even for one of your own, really."

Ed shrugged. "A rancher has to pick his battles. Sometimes he picks one that doesn't seem worth fighting, but that's okay. It's part of being human."

"Ah, a rancher-philosopher."

"I prefer to think of myself as a tinkerer."

"That's right. Jenny said you fix things."

"Things, maybe, but not people or animals. A living being is a far more complex system, so my hat's off to you."

"Thanks, though most of what I do is pretty straightforward—plug this, unplug that, convince owners that it's in the animal's best interest to be confined, even if it seems cruel. Hardest part is that my patients can't tell me exactly where it hurts, at least not in words. So there's more than a bit of guesswork involved."

"In my experience, there's a fair bit of guesswork involved with people, too." One corner of Ed's mouth kicked up. "That's why I like my tools. No opinions to deal with except a stubborn bolt or two."

Nick chuckled and stood, feeling his knees pop from having been down on the stall floor for too long. "You don't miss living on the road?"

"I do, but Rosie wanted to come home." His smile

was utterly fond, and didn't seem to echo any of Jenny's worries about her mom. "I've had my turn," Ed added, "and now it's hers. Speaking of which, I should get back in there, make sure Big Skye is playing nice." Pushing away from the doorframe, he stuck out a hand. "Thank you for riding out tonight, Doc. Mustang Ridge owes you one."

Nick shook on it, and got a firm, no-nonsense grip in return. "I was glad I could help, and glad it all turned out okay."

"That it did." Ed's eyes went to the black mama cow. "We'll call around, see if anyone is missing these two. Probably haul the old man back to the doctor tomorrow, to be on the safe side. Couple of days and things will be back to normal . . . but I mean it. We owe you one."

"Send some cookies my way the next time your mom makes a batch, and we'll call it even," Nick said, having learned that, especially as the only vet in such a small, close-knit community, it was better to suggest a small token than refuse gratitude.

"Count on it. And you're welcome at our table anytime." With that, Ed sketched a wave and headed for the main door.

Nick stared after him for a long moment, wondering just how much he should read into that parting shot. Had it been standard country courtesy, a sort of neighbors-helping-neighbors thing, or had it been a paternal stamp of approval?

He was still trying to figure that one out fifteen or so

minutes later, when the door rolled open a crack and Jenny slipped through. Her eyes warmed when she saw him standing in the aisle, packing his gear. "All done?"

"For tonight, at any rate."

She crossed to peer in the open stall. "How's he doing?"

Leaning on the divider next to her, their elbows bumping, he looked in at the calf, who had wobbled to his feet. "He would've been a goner without your gramps—that's for sure."

"Don't tell Big Skye that. He's already riding the 'nobody needed to come get me, I was perfectly fine' high horse. He doesn't want us to fuss over him, doesn't want to hear that we worry about him. And . . ." She blew out a breath. "And I shouldn't complain. Things could have turned out so much worse than they did, thanks in no small part to you. Which is the long way of saying I'm sorry this is the first I've gotten out to see you since we got back. I got caught up."

"No need to apologize. You've got family to deal with. I understand." And maybe he missed that sort of big, boisterous drama more than he had realized. Away from the old hometown, it was down to just him and his dad. Slipping an arm around Jenny's waist, he brushed his cheek against her hair. "So . . . Friday night?"

She tipped her head to look up at him, blinking in pretend confusion. "What about Friday night?"

"You. Me. A date. What do you say?"

Her eyelash-batting dissolved to a smile. "I say absolutely yes. It'll give me something to look forward to as I slog through purchase orders and run interference between my grandparents over the next few days."

"You want something to look forward to? How about this?" He covered her smiling mouth with his own in a kiss that was as stirring as it was sweet, and that reminded him once more that it didn't matter what anyone else thought about him and Jenny, because the two of them were on exactly the same page.

16

It was Thursday before Jenny knew what hit her. The excitement of Big Skye's adventure had worn off in a couple of days, pretty much as soon as the black cow and her healing calf had been picked up by their grateful, chastened owner two spreads over. Beyond that, the week had disappeared in a blur of phone calls, film clips, and digging through the family photos. And then, once she had exactly the right images, picking her grandfather's brain on names, dates, and locations before she slotted the pictures into place in the first two official Mustang Ridge video clips. But she was getting close to having things nailed down. As she bent over her computer, the center of her chest had the tingly feeling that meant a film had started gelling, elevating itself to a sum greater than its parts.

"Just a few more hours," she said, tipping back in the desk chair and spreading her arms to stretch out the kinks.

Rex lifted his head to give her an inquiring "Whuff?" *Are we doing something?*

"Two more hours, maybe three, and this is going to knock Shelby's socks off."

They had rescheduled their meeting to Friday when Shelby's daughter, Lizzie, had come down with a short-lived bug, and the delay had given Jenny the time to hone her first two clips from rough cuts to Sundance quality.

Okay, that was pushing it. But still. There was that happy tingle in her chest.

And, yes, some of those inner sparkles were because of Nick. They had talked every night and texted at odd hours of the day, and were firm on their Friday night rendezvous. And she. Couldn't. Wait. She didn't care where they went or what they did, as long as they were face-to-face.

"Tomorrow's going to be a good day," she told Rex.

His tail thumped.

"You're looking forward to the snow?" her mother's voice asked from behind her.

Spinning around in the desk chair, Jenny let her boots fall to the floor. "Snow?"

Her mom was wearing gray slacks and a soft-looking sweater in her beloved raspberry. Propping her shoulder against the doorframe, she lowered her voice to a conspiratorial hush. "Haven't you heard? There's a big storm coming in."

"Nope, not buying it. I've got plans for tomorrow."

"Ah. Snow denial. Let me know how it works for you."

"It can snow on Saturday." When she and her mom were supposed to go shopping for bedroom stuff.

"Whether or not the storm has moved on by then, the roads will be a mess."

"Bummer. I was looking forward to shopping." Sort of. Not really.

Rose beamed. "Me, too. That's why I think we should go now."

"I'm really—" Jenny stopped herself, thought for a second, and then reached out to close the lid of her laptop. "You know what? You're right. Let's do it." The videos were close to finished, and shopping would kill the rest of the day. If nothing else, she could protect herself from Pepto pink walls and rabid ceramic animals. She'd finish up the videos later tonight.

Two hours later, after parking in the heart of the Three Ridges shopping district, Jenny warily followed her mom into Kitty's Kountry Kitsch, worried by the shop's name, the thick aroma of cinnamon, and the sight of a whole lot of calico.

"Oh!" Her mother made a beeline for a display of granny dolls with dried-apple heads and detergent-bottle bodies, wearing stiff gingham dresses and expressions that made them look like they were thinking: *Braaaains!* "Look at these beauties," she cooed. "Aren't they fabulous?"

"Assuming I never want to sleep again." Jenny imagined a half dozen of them lined up on her dresser with their freaky little eyes glowing red in the dark.

"Oh, you." Rose flapped a hand at her. "Always

teasing. Come on, let's see what other new things she's gotten in!"

Fortunately, the store's creep factor decreased once they got past the apple dolls. Folding three-quarter walls divided the good-size store into smaller areas that reminded Jenny of movie sets—living rooms, dining rooms, bedrooms, and playrooms, all done in versions of Country Bear Jamboree. She eyed an explosion of gingham ruffles that looked more like a bed tutu than a dust ruffle. "I don't know, Mom. This isn't really my style."

That got an eye roll. "Your idea of decor is mosquito netting and a photo collage thumbtacked to the wall."

Sounded pretty good to her. "Then why am I here again?"

"To tell me what you like, sweetie."

"I like yellow, white, and simplicity." Lowering her voice so as not to offend the orange-haired, stick-thin woman who was bearing down on them, she added, "Ikea delivers, you know."

"That's not funny. Come on, we're going to pick a few rustic pieces here and then go vintage-retro on the soft goods. You'll love how it turns out, I promise."

"Hiya, Rose!" The stranger turned, did a double-take, and then beamed. "Jenny! Well, I never. When did you get home?"

It took a second, but the woman's features came into focus and Jenny's brain did a remember-when back to junior high science class. "Mrs. Cosgrove?"

Her laugh was the same hee-haw bray that had

earned the biology teacher a slew of lunchroom nick-names. "It's Kitty now, even to my former students." She indicated the room with a wave. "As you can see, I branched out from worms and weather patterns. What do you think?"

Remembering field trips to the local forestry service and getting extra credit for a photo essay documenting a band of wild mustangs, Jenny went with, "It looks like the junior high's loss was the shopping area's gain."

Kitty beamed. "Why, aren't you sweet?" She brushed a hand over one of the apple creepies. "I try to show-case local artisans, and of course I buy Wyoming-made products as much as possible. Business was slow at first, but lately a few people—like your mom here—have been redecorating, which has helped. Speaking of which, if you're here to pick up more of those lace pillows, Rose, you're a few days early."

"We're redecorating Jenny's room, and of course this had to be our first stop."

That brought Kitty's bright, interested eyes back to Jenny. "You're staying?"

"Oh, no." Hell, no. "We're just updating my room a little, bringing it out of high school and into the adult zone."

"And why not? You've got your own in-house dec-orator." To Rose, she said, "I just got in the most divine bureau from Billy Fox's woodshop. You know, down toward Laramie? The front is carved with these amaz-ing horses, a whole herd of them coming down around the sides and galloping across the front." She sighed happily. "Gorgeous."

"I'd like to see it." Rose shot Jenny a look that was almost a smile. "Don't worry. It'd be for Krista, not you. Or maybe the bunkhouse, depending on how high-end she wants to go." To Kitty, she said, "My Jenny likes things clean and simple, and set up for a quick getaway."

As Kitty's brow furrowed a little on that one, Jenny added, "Bonus points for yellow and white."

Her mother opened her mouth to protest, but Kitty brightened. "If you're after yellow and white, I've got just the thing. Follow me!" She led them through a maze of little scenes, a whole lot of them featuring bedrooms that were made from bark-on pine trees and birch, and looked like something out of a hunter's catalogue. Hanging a left at a rabbit-themed nursery, she breezed past a whole bunch of antlers and stopped in front of a bedroom set that looked nothing like the others. "What about something like this?"

The cubicle-size display held a glossy white queen-size bed done up in a diamond-pattern quilt in three different shades of lemony yellow against a creamy white background. A gorgeous afghan lay folded at the foot of the bed, knitted in stripes of the same yellow, and the throw pillows that drifted up against the headboard wore yellow and white flowers with pops of a lovely sky blue.

"I don't think—" Rose began.

"It's perfect," Jenny interrupted. She reached out to

her mother, intending to grip her arm but catching her sleeve instead, like she was tugging and going "Mama, Mama, I want this one!" Which in a way she was. "I'll make you a deal—if you go with me on the bedding and the color scheme, I'll let you pick the rug and the curtains. No fuss, no arguments. Free rein."

Her mother's eyes narrowed. "Free rein?"

What was the worst that could happen? "Cross my heart. Is it a deal?"

"I want to pick the mirror, too."

"You . . . Okay, but no antlers. No offense, Kitty, but they're not my style."

"Mine, either," the shop owner said cheerfully, "but sometimes a girl has to go where the money's at."

"Words to live by," Jenny agreed. Because, hey, she had wanted to do documentaries, not a dating show. "What do you say, Mom? Deal?"

"Deal." They shook on it.

"Sheesh. You drive a hard bargain."

"Big Skye used to say the same thing," Kitty remarked, "back when you were just a baby."

Jenny looked over at her. "Oh?"

"My dad was a wrangler at Mustang Ridge, and I part-timed at the ranch during the summers when I was a kid, doing chores, helping put up hay and such."

"You . . ." Okay, it made sense, small town and all that. But Jenny was having a hard time picturing the woman opposite her slinging square bales. "What was it like? As a girl, I mean, working with the cowboys back in the day?"

"Oh, it was great fun! Lots of work, mind you, but loads of fun. My daddy kept an eye on me, of course, so there wasn't much fuss about me being a girl. And, besides, everyone knew Mustang Ridge wasn't the place for anyone who thought cowboying was a man's job. She was a tough one, your mom, but fair. And like I said, there wasn't anyone on that ranch—maybe even the town—who could beat her in a negotiation. Supplies coming in, cows going out, payroll, you name it, if it had to do with the business end of things, you went to Rose."

Jenny glanced over at her mother, who at that moment was fluttering over a blue ceramic vase filled with dried twigs, cooing things like "darling" and "evocative." *How times have changed.*

"And the roundups!" Kitty threw up her hands. "I know I don't need to tell you how exciting it is the first time you ride out with the herd. I pretended I was Mercy Skye, running the ranch after her Jedediah was gunned down by those rustlers, or Pansy Skye and the other women riding out when the men got sick at the poisoned watering hole."

"Wow. You really know your Mustang Ridge history."

Kitty pressed her lips together, then confided, "Well, your daddy was a handsome man who didn't mind telling campfire stories. You can say I paid better attention than I would have otherwise."

Jenny liked where this was going. Okay, not so much that her science teacher used to have a crush on her dad—*squick*—but the roundup stuff rocked. "Would you be willing to tell some of those stories on camera?"

Kitty's brows drew together. "Excuse me?"

She explained the video project, adding, "We could do a short piece on the store, too. You could put it on your Web site, share it around, get some more buzz going."

"You'd do that for me?" Kitty's voice nearly squeaked in her excitement.

"Sure. Why not?" It would only take a few hours, and if she could survive postproduction on *Rose's Boudoir*, she could handle calico ruffles and dried-apple zombies. "We could do it one day next week."

"Oh, my, yes! Wow, thank you! That sounds like so much fun." They chatted for a few more minutes, going through the do's and don'ts of an on-camera interview. While they talked, Jenny's mom puttered around the store, adding things to a rapidly growing pile on the counter. By the time the three of them convened at the register, with Jenny carrying the quilt and afghan, and Kitty following with an armload of pillows, the pile had become a mountain, with an avalanche threatening.

Jenny eyed the jumble, but didn't bother trying to dissect it.

"Should I put this on your tab?" Kitty asked.

"No," Jenny said, at the same time that her mother said, "Yes."

Kitty blinked. "Which is it?"

"I'm paying," Jenny said firmly, pulling out her

credit card. Her mom grumbled but gave in, and wandered deeper into the store as Kitty rang her up. And kept ringing. Jenny frowned at the mounting total. "Did I okay all that?" She only remembered about half of it.

"Trust me." Her mother appeared behind her with an armload of apple grannies, making her twitch. "We'll take these, too."

Kitty beamed. "Aren't they just darling? They're each one-of-a-kind. A woman over in Calverton makes them from windfall apples she picks out of her nephew's pasture. She swears the apples that land in the cow patties make the best grannies."

Jenny stifled a laugh. Only in Three Ridges would the presence of manure be considered a selling point when it came to home decor. *I think we'll leave that out of the advertising.* Then again, far weirder things had gone viral.

Once they were back outside, loading their smaller purchases into the car, Jenny said, "Those dolls are so not going in my room."

"I was thinking they would make a real statement in the dining area."

"What, abandon hope, all ye who enter here?" Gran would have a fit.

"Hush," Rose said primly, but with a thread of amusement. Slamming the rear door, she pointed across the street to the hardware store. "Next stop, paint."

"I want white."

"Which shade of white?"

Jenny would've argued that white was white, but her inner photographer rebelled on that one. "How about pizza? We could hit Harry's for a Hawaiian." She and her mom were the only two people in the family who dug ham and pineapple on their pies.

"Paint before pizza, young lady."

Jenny hung her head. "Yes, Mom." But she bumped Rose with her hip as they started across the street, and ducked a return hip check, dancing aside as laughter bubbled up.

Turned out this mom-daughter stuff wasn't so bad, after all.

Jenny stayed up late and got up early to put the last few polishing touches on the clips of her gramps talking about Mustang Ridge. As she worked, new scene snippets kept sneaking into her brain, forcing her to jot them down so she could clear some space for the work at hand. Just past ten thirty, when she really needed to be heading out to meet Shelby at her in-home office, Jenny pushed away from the desk and blinked at the screen, where Big Skye's weathered face was frozen in a John Wayne grin.

"Gotcha." This time she said it out loud, putting the word to the certainty that had lodged itself in her belly. "Done and done." And, damn, she was glad this hadn't turned into an epitaph.

Rex's tail thumped twice, giving her words a synco-pated backbeat. The big dog was sacked out on his bed near the space heater, replete from all the bacon and toast that had snuck its way under the table during breakfast.

"Thanks, buddy." She didn't remember the last time she had actually built a film from the ground up, even a five-minute short like this one. Sure, she knocked off *Look what I've been up to!* clips every month or so and sent them to the family email loop, but that wasn't the same as a fully produced piece.

It felt good. Really, really good.

As she was getting ready to leave, with her computer packed and ready to roll, the office phone rang.

"Leave a message," she sang out, but then checked the caller ID, in case it was Shelby needing to rearrange things. The sight of Nick's cell number in the display put a light, happy pressure in her lungs. She picked up the handset. "Hey, there! This is a nice surprise. I figured you'd be jammed up, trying to get all of today's and tomorrow's patients seen." With the storm predicted to hit overnight, he had already cancelled his Saturday appointments.

"I am." His voice, warm and mellow, came through the phone and seemed to surround her like a down parka that carried his warmth and scent. "I snuck out between an abscess and a tartar scrape so I could wish you luck on your presentation."

Sweet warmth stole through her. "Thanks."

"How do the clips look?"

"At the risk of total immodesty, they rock."

"When can I see them?"

"How does tonight sound?"

"Sounds good to me. Let's keep an eye on the storm, though. The weather hens are starting to do their the-sky-is-falling routine on this one, making blizzard noises and saying it might start more like late this afternoon. I guess one front stalled right on top of us, but the other one is moving faster than expected."

"Nope," Jenny said, "not going to happen."

"What's not going to happen?"

"I'm not going to let snow mess with date night."

His chuckle carried down the line. "Alas, I don't think the Wyoming weather cares about our plans."

"You'll see," she predicted.

"How about I call you after I'm done with my patients, and we can go from there?"

"Sounds good. Right now, I should hit the road."

"Me, too. My halitosis hound awaits." He paused. "Drive safe, okay?"

"Will do." She wanted to linger over the good-byes, but wasn't sure how long it would take her to get out to Foster's family ranch. "Thanks for the call."

"Knock 'em dead."

She hung up, grinning, and then slung her computer bag over her shoulder and patted her thigh in invitation. "Come on, Sexy Rexy. Last one out to the Double-Bar H is a rotten egg."

The goldie lurched to his feet with a "whuff" and a wiggle, all but dancing with glee. *We're going somewhere! Yippee!*

17

"You should see the databases they're running here!" Krista gushed along the storm-static'd cell connection. "They're seriously drool-worthy."

With twenty minutes until her meeting and only a couple of miles left to drive, Jenny had pulled the Jeep over to take her sister's call, killing time while Rex hung his head out the window, seeming delighted to scan the winter landscape from inside the warm vehicle. "Is that all that's drool-worthy?" she asked. "Lame."

"I'm here to learn how to ramp things up a notch at the ranch, not add a notch to my bedpost."

"Which would bring you up to a grand total of, what, two notches?" Krista's one serious relationship had been in college, and there hadn't really been anyone since then. Which was another way the two of them differed—Krista did Deep and Meaningful in the guy department, while Jenny, well, didn't.

"Speaking of notches," Krista said, paralleling her thoughts, "how are things going with Nick? Have you seen him since the two of you played Search and Rescue?"

"Are you asking me to kiss and tell?"

"That depends."

"On?"

"Whether the kisses are worth telling about."

Most definitely. But where she and Krista usually told each other anything and everything, now Jenny hesitated. "How about this—you find someone to kiss out there in Cali, and report back. Then I'll tell you all about things with Doc Hottie."

Krista hooted with laughter. "Doc Hottie? Oh, I am so calling him that the next time he's out to the ranch."

"Don't you dare."

"Why not? You'll be long gone."

Ouch. Unable to argue the point, Jenny said, "Uh-oh, I'm down to eight minutes. I don't want to be late meeting Shelby."

"Don't stress over it. She's figured out that time is relative out in the backcountry."

"Still. I'm going to get going."

"Are you dodging the question?"

"Don't make me do the *sssssss . . . You're breaking up . . . sssssss* thing. Besides, this meeting is for your advertising project. I'd think you'd want me to be on time."

"So go already. But don't think I missed your not so subtle subject change. I want details, sister. Preferably juicy ones I can use for blackmail when I get home."

"*Sssssss . . .* What was that? I think the clouds are messing with the signal."

"Fine, be that way. I'll talk to you later." Laughing, Krista killed the connection.

Refusing to replay too much of that particular conversation—or her own responses—Jenny said, "Hey, Rex, you want to get your head back in here?" When the dog complied, she buzzed up the window and got them back on the road.

The Double-Bar H took up a shallow bowl of a valley that was undoubtedly "ooh, stop and look" gorgeous when everything was green and lush. Foster had bought the family acreage back from an absentee owner just this past summer, and he and Shelby were renovating the place from the ground up while living there. According to Shelby, they had floors, a table and a couple of chairs, plus heat and WiFi—and what more did they need?

Jenny liked her already, and not just because Foster was head over heels.

Shouldering her computer bag, she headed along the shoveled path to the main house, with Rex right behind her.

The door opened as she came up the steps, and a vivid brunette stepped out, seeming not to notice the cold, even though she was only wearing jeans, thick socks, and a fuzzy sweater. Spreading her arms wide, she said, "Jenny! I've been dying to meet you! And Sexy Rexy!"

"Shelby, hi!" Coming up the last steps, Jenny did the hug-and-air-kiss thing. "I feel like I already know you."

"I know what you mean, but I didn't want to say it

because I thought it would come out like 'Krista and I are friends, therefore you and I are friends.' I didn't know if you were touchy about the twin thing."

Feeling that whole-body relaxation that came from meeting a kindred spirit, Jenny shook her head. "Not so much anymore, and I wouldn't have taken it like that anyway, coming from you. It's because we're working on a project together. If you're lucky enough to get along, working together breaks down the barriers fast. If you're not lucky . . . well, then the project is pretty much guaranteed to be a headache, or worse."

"Been there, done that. But why are we standing out here like half-frozen fools? Come inside. It's a disaster area, but it's home."

Shelby waved them through, giving Rex—in full wriggle mode—a thorough head rub on the way by.

While the house wasn't quite a disaster area by Jenny's definition, it definitely smacked of a renovation, complete with the smell of sawdust and latex paint. The open-concept living, dining, and kitchen areas were a patchwork of old surfaces and new drywall, suggesting they had recently been the smaller, interconnected rooms of the usual family ranch home, circa eighteen-something. The furniture was equally mismatched, with a folding table and aluminum chairs taking the place of what would be a breakfast bar when the granite went in, opposite a pretty oak buffet that would probably make Jenny's mom drool.

It was a mishmash, admittedly, but Jenny could see what they were going for, and that it would be amazing

when it was done. Better yet, a blanket of warmth
wrapped around them as they entered, making her
sigh with pleasure. "Oh. That's nice. I'll take a project-
in-progress as long as I'm not freezing my butt off."

"Me, too, which is why we splurged. Put radiant
heating in the floors as soon as humanly possible, and
hooked them to the big solar panels on the roof."
Shelby glanced out a window. "Not that there's much
in the way of sun today. Here. I'll take your coat."

"Boots off?"

"Your call. With a kid, a dog, and a cowboy who's
known to forget his spurs, I've given up on keeping the
floors pristine." Her tone was fond, her face soft.

"Lizzie's at school?"

"For a few more hours yet. She didn't want to miss
another day, which is a very nice change from how she
was back in Boston."

"I'd like to meet her." Shelby's nine-year-old daughter was the reason Shelby had come to Wyoming in the
first place. Foster, though, was why they had stayed.

"Check your barn on the weekends. She's usually
out there with Foster—or, rather, with the horses."
Shelby's lips curved. "Krista's yearling, Lucky, is a particular favorite of hers. She was there when he was
born. Anyway, let's go into my office." She gestured to
the dining area, where a gorgeous mahogany table with
ball-in-claw feet was covered in a drop cloth and a
layer of books, papers, and a sleek laptop hooked to a
flat-screen monitor. "Rex can have the dog bed. Vader
won't mind sharing."

The goldie did his two and a half circles, flopped down, and started gnawing on a well-used bone.

Jenny looked over Shelby's setup with interest. "I would've thought a workspace would've happened before even the floors. Home business and all that."

"That was the original plan, but I decided I wanted warm feet more than a real desk. It's funny how quickly I went from Type A ad exec to 'work at home, uh-oh, the UPS guy is here, better put on a bra.'"

Given the way the other woman was rocking a pair of Wranglers that looked like they'd been made for her, along with a sweater that screamed "cashmere" and "European," Jenny had a feeling that was an overstatement. "You don't miss it?"

"Miss what, the city? The pressure? The rush-rush-rush, and the feeling that my career hangs on every meeting, every concept?" Her teeth flashed. "Heck, yes, I miss it. Sometimes I miss it so much that I drive into Laramie just to breathe the exhaust and buy over-priced coffee from a cranky barista."

Jenny laughed. "Done that." Though in her case it usually required a two-day trip on dirt roads and puddle jumpers, not just a few hours on the highway.

"The trade-off is so worth it, though, to live in a place like this, raise my daughter here. And, honestly, could you see Foster in Boston?"

Jenny thought about it, surprised that the answer wasn't immediate and easy. "You know what? I have a feeling he'd do okay. He's a smart guy. Adaptable, though he hides it behind that *why are you in my space?* scowl. At least he used to. Less so since he met you."

That got her a considering look. "It took me a while to see that part of him—he even offered to come back east with me, so we'd have a chance to see if we could make it work. In the end, though, there was more for me here than there was back home, so we stayed." Shelby looked utterly at home in her skin and her space as she pulled a rolling desk chair up to the dining table and sat, tucking her feet underneath herself.

"Boston's loss, Three Ridge's gain."

"You're sweet to say so."

"Nope, and not just because I like you." Pulling up another chair, Jenny plonked down beside her and dug into her computer bag. "Like I said on the phone, I love the idea of forming symbiotic relationships with local businesses, not just on the Web site, but in terms of merchandise and services. Got a suggestion there, by the way: Kitty Cosgrove over at Kitty's Kountry Kitch. It's actually way cooler than it sounds, and she buys local as much as possible. Not to mention that she used to work at the ranch and is going to give me an interview."

"Sweet. I'll put her on the list." Shelby rat-a-tatted the info into her laptop, typing blind while she watched Jenny hook up the secondary monitor, so they could both look at the on-screen images without bumping heads. "That's quite a setup."

"Betsy? She's only really portable in the loosest sense of the word, but she's got a memory like a thousand elephants and refuses to crash, no matter what I do to her." Jenny patted the computer, which was darn near indestructible in its military-grade ballistic housing. "I've got her baby sister for when I need to move fast, but for stuff like this, she's my go-to girl."

"Any other thoughts on local vendors?"

"Not off the top of my head, but I can ask my mom for suggestions. She's the champion shopper in the family." Fingers skimming the touchpad, she pulled up the first of the files she had collated for Shelby. "I figure you and Krista have the vendor stuff pretty much nailed down, anyway. Your concepts really rock, assuming your photog—me—can pull it off."

"I'm not worried. Krista showed me your work."

"Please, not *Jungle Love*."

Shelby chuckled. "I haven't missed an episode since season two."

"You should be ashamed."

"It's research. Pop culture, trends, that sort of thing."

"Suuure."

"Anyway. Krista showed me one of your documentaries, too. The one about U.S. doctors who went overseas to help out after that earthquake, and wound up triaging radiation workers at a failing nuke plant. . . . That was powerful stuff."

"I should probably say something like 'it's old, just a film-school project,' but I won't, because I'm still darn proud of it."

"You should be. Those images of the workers sleeping in stairwells between their shifts until the doctors

and nurses pulled strings to get cots, along with supplies for the wounded . . . Well, it all stuck with me—
that's for sure."

Nostalgia tugged and Jenny found herself smiling.
"Thanks." She hesitated for a second before she opened
up the first file, the one with the pictures from her last
couple of visits. *She wants pretty, not editorial*, she told
herself, and went ahead and spun the second monitor
toward Shelby.

"You're wel—" Shelby's jaw dropped. "Ohmigosh.
You took all these?"

The screen showed thirty-five miniature versions of
the high-res pictures she had selected. They ranged
from long-range field-and-mountain landscapes that
were *ooh-ahh* pretty but—at least to Jenny—ultimately
boring, all the way to more interesting—and less
advertising-relevant—close-ups of leaves and birds,
and a few action shots of the herds that gave Mustang
Ridge its name.

Arrayed together like that, she had to admit they
were pretty darn impressive.

"Yep, over the last few years. It's a habit, something
I don't always realize I'm doing. You know how some
people have tics and twitches? Well, I take pictures."

Shelby practically glowed. "They're yours, free and
clear? We can use them?"

"Yes, and duh. That's why I'm showing them to
you." But her reaction was more than flattering. "I took
this batch for my own entertainment, so they may not
be geared in the direction you're going. I'll come back

this summer to get some guest interviews, and can get some additional stills then. Unless that's going to be too late?"

"We'll be changing things up every few months, keeping it fresh, so I'm sure we'll take you up on that. For a first pass, though, these are perfect. Better than I had even dared hope, and my hopes were pretty high after hearing Krista sing your praises."

"Don't get too excited until you've seen the rest of it." Jenny paused. "Strike that. Feel free to get excited, but at the same time don't be afraid to tell me where I'm hitting the mark and where I'm missing it."

They went through the winter photos together, with lots of "what if we . . ." and "do you think it would work to . . ." and both of them taking notes on their computers.

Then it was time for the videos.

Jenny's pulse bumped with a combination of nerves and excitement as she cued up the first of Big Skye's videos. "Now, I know Krista said just interviews, but I spiced it up with some stuff from our archives—aka, the attic. Feel free to tell me it's too much." *Please don't tell me it's too much.*

"If your photos are anything to go by, I'm going to love it."

In a perfect world, they would've been in a screening room where Jenny could've killed the lights, not just to improve the picture, but also so she wouldn't have the option of darting nervous looks over at Shelby, trying to judge her reaction as the video began with a black screen and the soft strum of a lone guitar. Then the black warmed to a sepia-toned image of a man and a woman posed stiffly together, a dollar photograph from back when a dollar might be a cowboy's wages for the whole week.

After a moment, Big Skye's voice said, "In 1869, two years after the Union Pacific Railroad came through Wyoming, a railroader-turned-gold prospector named Jonah Skye won five hundred head of cattle and some money in a poker game. His wife, Mary—tired of moving around and living on the fringes—pressured him to cash in his gold and build her a proper home in a valley they knew of, near a little town that didn't even have a name yet. A year later, they drove a hundred head down to the railhead, where they were fattened up and shipped for slaughter. Two years later, it was five hundred head. By year five, when this picture was taken, the cowboys of Mustang Ridge Ranch were running several thousand head and making good money. More, Jonah and Mary had added a son to the family, little James Skye."

The picture dissolved to Big Skye's image, and darned if you couldn't see Jonah Skye in the shape of his face. "My name is Arthur Skye, and I'm James's four-times great-grandson. Mustang Ridge Ranch is, and always will be, my family's legacy."

The narration paused and the background guitar strum came up over a montage of the oldest pictures Jenny had managed to find. Most of them were posed shots of family members, but there were a few candid photos of caballeros wearing batwing chaps and knotted neck rags, and cowboys on horseback amid huge herds, looking like their upper bodies were floating above the backs of the cows.

Then the screen went dark again, the music paused, and the simple title came up: *Mustang Ridge: The Early Years*.

Into the brief silence, Shelby said softly, "You're flipping brilliant."

"We can change the title, or whatever you want. This is just a first pass at—"

"Shut up. You're messing with my moment."

Jenny leaned back, let out a long, slow breath, and let the video play out.

For the next eight and a half minutes—she just hadn't been able to keep it to five—her gramps told them about the cattle rustlers of the Keyhole Canyon gang, and how the interconnected *MRR* of the ranch's brand was designed to be almost impossible to alter. He recounted fortunes won and lost with the draw of a card or a gun, and how the cattle business had boomed as the population exploded. Always, though, the stories came back to family, and how when you lived in the middle of nowhere, it was family that counted.

Even though she had seen it a zillion times already, Jenny's throat still lumped up when the clip finished with Big Skye looking into the camera like it was an old friend, and saying, "Throughout our history, the men and women of Mustang Ridge have always been a family, whether by blood or by heart. We stand by each other, and we stand for the land and the creatures entrusted to us. I think—I hope—that Jonah and Mary would be proud of the family we've made here."

His face stayed on the screen for a beat, and then dissolved to a picture of his younger self astride a bay gelding, wearing batwing chaps and a wide-brimmed hat as he rode off along the fence line and into the setting sun.

Slowly, the guitar faded out. Then, the image did, too.

When the screen went to credits, Jenny hit a button and froze things.

There was a three-count of silence. And then Shelby, still staring at her monitor, said, "Oh. My. God. Where were you when I had huge budgets to work with?"

"Belize, probably. I guess that means you like it."

Shelby turned to her, eyes shining with more than just appreciation. "Perfect. That was absolutely perfect. And . . . I can't believe you got your grandfather to do this. He hates the dude ranch thing!"

"He loves being on camera more."

"Krista never said."

"She might not have known how deep his camera whoreness goes."

Shelby belly laughed. "You did not just call your grandfather a whore."

"If you tell anybody, I'll deny it. Or, better yet, I'll say you said it."

"You wouldn't."

"Watch me."

They grinned at each other like a couple of fools, and then Jenny said, "You want to see the other one?"

"You did two of them? Already?"

"And a vanity piece for my mom."

"Is she still—" Shelby's phone rang, interrupting. She checked the ID and frowned. "It's Lizzie's school."

While she took the call, Jenny rose and went to the dining room windows.

Rex leaped up and followed, excited. *Are we doing something cool?*

"I'm just having a look-see, buddy."

The windows were marked out with a huge rectangle of painter's tape that went all the way to the floor, suggesting that they were slated to become French doors in the near future. The view was a doozy: a tractor shed on one side and a falling-down barn on the other, with snow draping the buildings like it had been put there on purpose to turn them from dilapidated to picturesque. But that wasn't what caught Jenny's attention so much as the leaden gray of the horizon, and how she couldn't see the mountains anymore.

"They're letting the kids out early," Shelby said, coming to join her at the window. "The bus is on its way. I guess the storm is moving faster than the forecasters thought."

Well, darn. Jenny scowled at the sky. "No fair. I've got a date tonight."

"I'm thinking that's going to need a rain check. Or would that be a snow check?"

"It's annoying, that's what it is." Jenny sighed. "Either way, I should probably hit the road. I'll leave you with a flash drive that has most of what I just showed you on it. If you change your mind on any of it—"

"I won't."

"Good to hear. Okay, so if you have any more ideas on how I can contribute, or suggestions for the interviews, you've got my numbers and my email. Meanwhile, I'll do the additional interviews we talked about. We can meet again in a week or two, if you like."

"Absolutely. And I was thinking we should get together outside of work stuff and have a couple of drinks or a meal and a movie, or something. Do a girls' night."

The invite brought a flush of pleasure. "I'd like that. I haven't been out since I've been back."

"Not big on hooking up with old friends for a round of remember whens?"

"Not many old friends, at least not that I've kept in touch with." None, really. "The kids who left after high school are long gone, and the ones who stayed or came back after college have their own friends and families to hang with. When I try to add myself on without Krista there to run interference, everybody gets weird and awkward, like they don't know what to say."

"You're a celebrity."

"More like an escapee."

"Okay, I get it. You're out of the local scene. Their loss, my gain." She held out Jenny's coat. "Next week?"

"Would it be okay if I invite another newbie along?" she asked, thinking of Michelle.

"The more, the merrier. How does Wednesday sound?"

"Great, assuming we're dug out by then."

"Don't even joke about it." Shelby made a face. "It's

my first winter out here, and I'm told we've been lucky so far."

Jenny shouldered her bag. "Did the school say when the snow is supposed to start?"

"Sorry, no. It's an automated system. Want me to call Foster and see how things look up on Mustang Ridge?"

"That's okay. Even if it's started dusting a little by the time I hit the high country, the Jeep can handle it." She leaned in and gave Shelby a half-hug with her free arm. "Great to meet you, totally yes to girls' night, and I'm out of here. Come on, Rex!"

"Go!" Shelby waved them through the door, then called, "Do you want me to call the ranch and let them know you're on your way?"

"Yes, please! 'Bye!"

Foster was just pulling in as Jenny pulled out, and he gave her a thumbs-up that she took to mean that the roads were okay. Still, she kept the pedal down and the speedometer up as she headed for home, hoping to beat the snow.

13

"Here's the last of today's charts," Ruth announced, as she bustled into Nick's office. "I'll put them away, and then I'm going to boogie. The snow is piling up fast."

He looked up from his notes. "Leave 'em. I'll do the filing."

"Are you sure?"

"You're the one who has to drive home, so scram already. Drive safe and text me when you get there."

She gave him a fond smile. "Yes, dear." She headed for the door, but turned back to say. "Sorry about your date."

"Me, too." He was itching to see Jenny again, and she wasn't going to be in Wyoming forever. "Hopefully this storm won't sock us in for too long."

She shot a dubious look over her shoulder. "I wouldn't count on it." Then she brightened. "Lucky for you, we live in a brave new world of technology. You can have a Skype date."

"My nose looks huge on Skype."

"So put your computer on a couple of books to get the camera looking down at you," she said like that should've been obvious. "A glass of wine, a couple of candles, some music in the background and voila! Instant romance. Or you could stream the same movie, sync it up, and watch it together."

"True." But after four days of phone calls that could have—and a few times had—lasted for hours, he wanted some one-on-one time, up close and personal.

"I know it's not the same," she said with a wink. "But you can still have fun if you get creative. Ask me how I know."

I'd really rather not. "I thought you were boogy-ing?"

She laughed and left.

Twenty minutes later, as he was finishing up in the office, tucking away the last of the files, her text came through: *Home safe. Stay warm. C u Mnday.*

"Ah, Ruth." He shook his head. "I suppose I should be grateful you don't use text-speak in the office." Cheesepuff jumped off his desk, landed with an audible *thud*, and walked over to the door, tail flicking. "What, you want to go outside, too?" Nick dumped his lab coat and followed the cat to the waiting area, giving a low whistle at the wall of white outside. "That would be a no on going outside, then." Having grown up a few hours south of Three Ridges, he'd thought he had known what to expect around here. Half a winter at this elevation, though, had taught him different. Up on the ridgelines, the storms came in fast, hit hard, and stayed put. "Okay, upstairs it is. How does popcorn and some Bond sound to you?"

As he followed the cat up the stairs, he composed a message to Jenny. *Done for the day, but socked in. You home safe?* He debated turning it into text speak for a laugh, but couldn't bring himself to mangle the English language like that.

He didn't get an answer right away, but they were in the Land of Dead Zones, after all. He figured he'd give it a half hour, then make a couple of calls. Not to stalk her, so much as to make sure she'd made it home okay from Shelby's. Grinning at the prospect of her giving him the "I've been handling myself for a long time, Buster, so don't think you're going to do it for me" attitude that he had glimpsed a few times before, he snagged his popcorn out of the microwave, grabbed a soda, and headed for the couch. "Come on, cat, let's have some guy time."

The opening chase scene unfolded with the usual collection of gunshots, screeching tires, and improbable stunts, and with Nick checking his phone every couple of minutes, just in case.

Bond was zooming along an eyebrow road in a fast car that'd taken a serious beating when something went *thudda-thud* downstairs.

"Did you hear that?" Nick muted the movie, figuring Daniel Craig could kick ass with or without volume, but there was no way he could hear anything over the chop-socky on the screen.

In the sudden quiet he was very aware of the whited-out window and the wind that lashed at the building, sounding annoyed that it couldn't get past all the weather stripping and spray foam he'd slopped around when the first cold snap hit. The noise—if there had even been a noise—didn't repeat itself, but silence didn't mean there wasn't a problem.

"Think someone's out in this garbage?" he asked Cheese, figuring those radar-dish ears could outperform his own any day. He had learned to kill the driveway buzzer during a bad storm—better that than listen to the darn thing false-alarming every few minutes, so that couldn't have been it. But he'd thought . . . "Or am I imagining things?"

He was halfway down the stairs when footsteps thudded on the front porch, followed by a weather-muffled knock and a faint call of, "Hello? Nick?"

"It's open!" He hollered, coming down the rest of the stairs in a rush, adrenaline starting to pump. That had sounded like . . . "Jenny?"

The door flew open and banged on its stop as a whole lot of icy-cold rushed in, along with a snow-crusted figure, petite and female, wearing a familiar ski jacket and fuzzy hat, and carrying a computer bag strapped across her body like a bandolier. Behind her was a four-legged snowman of a dog.

They stumbled in as he wrestled the door shut, muting the roar of the storm.

"S-surprise." The word came from between her chattering teeth as Rex shook, spraying snow in all directions.

"What the devil do you think you're doing?" The bellow surprised him, as did the emotions that punched him in the chest. Bringing his tone down a notch, he demanded, "Are you okay?"

"We're f-fine. Just got caught, that's all." She fumbled to lower the computer bag, which landed amid melting shards of ice. "Thought I had enough time to make it back from the Double-Bar H, but it turned out I didn't, so I decided to come here, instead." She fumbled to pull off her gloves, unzip her ski jacket, and drag it off. "Almost made it, too."

"Almost?" He looked out the window, his gut doing a somersault. "Where's the Jeep?"

"In the ditch around the corner from your driveway." When he emitted a low growl, she narrowed her eyes. "It's no big deal."

And there it was, the 'tude he'd been wishing for earlier. Only now it was more irritating than adorable. "You should've stayed at Shelby's."

Crossing to him, she reached up and cupped his jaw in her cool palms. "I'm okay," she said firmly. "And, yeah, I probably should've turned around when things got messy. But I decided that if I was going to be snowed in with anyone, I wanted it to be you."

Danged if that didn't make him melt faster than the snow. Not just because of what she'd said, but because she was right—she was safe. And, better yet, she was here. He brought his hands up to her hips, caging her against him. "You did mention that you weren't going to let any wussy old storm mess with date night."

"I'm a woman of my word."

He leaned in, skimmed his lips across hers. "My nose really looks huge on Skype."

"What?"

"Never mind," he said, and kissed her.

Before their kisses had said *I like you* and *This feels good*. Now this one said *Thank God you're safe* and *I'm glad you came here*. More, there was a deeper, darker edge, an urgency that acknowledged what was going to happen next—they were going to go upstairs together and wait out the storm.

Her lips warmed beneath his, but he was all too aware that her fingers were cool on the back of his neck and her clothes were damp and chilly. And Rex wasn't doing much better.

"Let's get you two upstairs," he said in a voice that didn't quite sound like his own. "Warm you up, dry you off. That sort of thing." He wasn't quite tongue-tied, but he didn't feel like his usual more or less charming self, either, like that part of him had been temporarily stripped away.

She eased back and toed off her boots, then retrieved her computer bag, which looked reassuringly waterproof. "I wouldn't say no to a cup of coffee. And Rex could probably use a couple of towels, maybe a blow-dryer."

"That I can do." He snagged the dryer from Ruth's grooming supplies and led his guests through the Employees Only door, and up the stairs to the second floor. "Er, do me a favor and excuse the mess."

"Please," she scoffed as she opened the door and stepped into his apartment. "I'm sure I've seen—" She stepped into his living room-slash-man cave, and laughed. "It's not that messy, but, hello, bachelor pad."

He came in behind her and took a look around, confirming that the mess factor was pretty low, thanks to his most recent herding of dirty dishes and laundry. Looking at it through her eyes, though, he imagined that a room empty of everything but a double recliner couch, huge flat-screen, and gazillion gaming components probably screamed "arrested development" rather than "I'm used to living out of a duffel."

Then again, this was Jenny. She probably got the second part.

Seeing her glance at the screen, where Daniel Craig was kicking butt on mute, he said, "Cheese and I were burrowing in for a snow day and waiting for you to text us back and let us know you made it home safe."

Her lips curved. "I did. Just not all the way to Mustang Ridge."

"Hallelujah," he said fervently, getting a laugh out of her. "You want to let them know where you are? Landline's in the kitchen if your cell doesn't want to play."

"Thanks. I'll give them a call."

"I'll dry Rex off here in the kitchen. You take the bathroom. Hop in the shower, get your body temp back up." He pointed. "Down that hallway, first on the left. I'll leave a set of sweats outside the door."

"I'd accuse you of trying to get me naked, but I'll admit it—I'm freezing."

"And I'm a doctor," he said piously.

Laughing, she disappeared in the direction of the bathroom. A few minutes later, as he was rifling through the shelves in his closet, he heard the shower go on. As a gentleman, he didn't picture her naked.

Not much, anyway.

Tapping on the bathroom door, he called, "Clothes are out here."

"You're a prince." Her voice was muffled by the door and the noise of running water, and all those sounds together combined to put a hitch in his breathing. He liked having a woman in his shower, for the first time in his new place.

More, he really liked that it was Jenny.

Figuring it was best not to look at it any closer than that, he focused on getting Rex dry. Three soggy towels and a few minutes later, he had a damp, wiggly dog that was warm enough that he'd rather explore than sit for any more grooming.

"Jenny's right. You've got some focus issues." He released the dog. "Go on. But don't say I didn't try!"

The goldie bounded out of the kitchen, did a loop of the living room, and bounced up on the couch to sniff Cheesepuff. The tabby hissed and swatted at the dog, and when Rex retreated, the cat puffed up to twice his already considerable girth and gave chase.

Nick stepped between them with a stern, "Quit that.

You guys met downstairs and did just fine." He put his hands on his hips and gave Cheese a mock glare. "And since when do you bother with dogs?"

That got him a rear-end view and a tail flick he interpreted as *Since he's upstairs, in* my *space*.

"Well, deal with it."

When the animals seemed ready to ignore each other, Nick made a quick circuit of the apartment, ensuring there wasn't anything too embarrassing out in the open. He was only using four of the eight rooms— there were six on this level and two more downstairs, behind the clinic—so it didn't take long. He stashed a few dishes in the dishwasher, kicked a few socks in the closet, and pulled his bedspread more or less smooth, kind of wishing he'd assembled the steel bed frame that had come with the mattress and box spring rather than just setting them up on the floor. Not that he was assuming anything. But it was a nice change to even have the thought.

The guest room—which he'd furnished in case his father wanted to crash with him—didn't need any work because he was almost never in there. The pullout couch was folded up, the framed prints were straight, and there weren't any hairballs on the rug. He was good to go.

Back out in the living room, he draped the fuzzy brown blanket more artfully over the leather behemoth, fished a couple of pillows off the floor, killed the TV, and tuned the radio to a local station that played a decent mix of music and gave good weather.

Cheesepuff watched him with a look of *Dude, really?*

"Stuff it," he said mildly. "We've got company."

Standing in front of the flat-screen, he took a look around, and decided it might come across as a bachelor pad, but at least it didn't look like a scuzzy one. Most of the stuff was new, after all. It hadn't had time to earn its rips and duct tape.

The cat's ears flicked when the water went off, and again when the door opened and a bare arm snaked out to snag the sweats and socks Nick had left in the hallway. Rex's head came up and he gave a low "whuff," but he seemed content to stay flopped out on the rug in front of the sofa.

Still not imagining Jenny naked—not much, anyway—Nick headed for the kitchen and considered his options on the warm-the-body-up front. When he heard footsteps behind him, he said, "I can offer you coffee, hot chocolate, chicken noodle or cream of mushroom. Which, for the record, I thought was another can of chicken noodle when I bought it."

"Can I get my hot chocolate with those little petrified marshmallows in it?"

He turned to look at her, and swallowed a grin at the sight of her in his drawstring sweatpants, with the legs cuffed to show a pair of thick wool socks that flopped at the toes. The sweatshirt fit a little better—it was one of the ones he'd shrunk before figuring out the dryer—but it still sagged off one shoulder, giving him a glimpse of skin.

What were they talking about again? Oh, right. Marshmallows.

"What does this look like, base camp? Here at Chez Masterson, you've got your choice between full-size marshmallows that aren't even stale yet, or a slightly used tub of marshmallow fluff. And the hot chocolate is Keurig-ized and close to sinful."

"What, no hand towels, but he has a Keurig?"

"The gadget gene is on the Y chromosome. Is that a yes on the hot cocoa?"

"If you'll join me."

"Count on it. In fact, how about you pull out the milk and chocolate syrup? I like to layer."

"On it." She pulled open the fridge, and laughed. "Bread, eggs, and milk, huh? Did you have to fight for them at the grocery store?"

"Just about." He shrugged. "It's a blizzard, which means we're constitutionally obligated to eat French toast. Or maybe egg-in-toast with a glass of milk."

"Or scrambled eggs with toast on the side."

"Where's the milk in that scenario?"

"You put it in the eggs to make the texture smoother."

"Your gran teach you that?"

"I got banned from the kitchen the second time I used baking soda instead of cornstarch in a recipe that also involved white wine." She pulled out the milk and Hershey's syrup, bumped the door shut with her hip, and slid him a look. "You know the vinegar-and-baking-soda volcanoes you make in science class? Yeah. It was like that."

He held up his palms in surrender. "Just hand over

the milk and chocolate syrup, nice and slow, and nobody will get hurt."

"Ha-ha." She faked a toss with the half gallon, then crowed, "Made you flinch."

They teased their way through prepping the hot chocolate, and the back-and-forth leveled things out between them. But although he stopped feeling like he had to watch what he was saying, that didn't mean the sizzle had died down. If anything it was stronger, connecting them when their bodies brushed in the small galley-style kitchen, making him want to move in and hold her tight.

He didn't, though. Instead, he made himself enjoy the anticipation.

The storm winds pounded the building intermittently, but the sturdy timbers held without protest and the weather stripping dulled even the rattle of windows, making his quarters feel snug and the rest of the world seem very far away.

"How's your dad?" she asked. "Are you worried about him being up in the foothills, all alone?"

"Yes and no. I wish I could get him to spend more time down here, especially in weather like this. But at the same time, I know he's in good shape up there. He's got backups for his backups, and enough know-how to be on one of those survivor shows. He said he'd check in tonight. How about you? Did you phone home?"

She nodded. "My gran said to say hi and my mom said, 'I can't believe you're not here to help me paint.'

Which, for the record, is the first I've heard about us having a painting date this afternoon."

He chuckled. "How is the redecorating going?"

"Honestly? Better than I expected. I think having negotiated the terms of my surrender helped. She's been good about getting my approval on most everything, and the stuff that she's picked out isn't nearly as crazy looking as I was afraid it might be. So far, anyway."

"Good to hear." He held out her mug. "Cocoa's done. You ready to have your world rocked?"

"Fluff *and* marshmallows? You're really pulling out all the stops."

"Let's call it a blizzard special for my special lady."

"Your special lady," she said softly. "I like that." And there was something new in her eyes. He couldn't identify the deep, drugging emotion, but it reached inside him and cranked up the heat and the tenderness. More, it made him want to haul her into his arms and carry her to the bedroom.

When she reached for the cocoa mug he didn't let go, so their fingers overlapped, the pressure as tangible as the way their eyes synced up. "Jenny," he began, and then stalled, caught in her gaze and the push-pull of wanting this, yet wanting it to be right for her.

"Yes?"

"This," he said. And instead of giving her the cocoa, he reached past her to set the mug on the counter, then slid his hand up her arm to the back of her neck, and kissed her. The heat that had been on a slow simmer all week boiled over in an instant, but he held himself in check, loving the smooth suppleness of her skin against his, and the way she murmured softly at the back of her throat, wrapped her arms around his neck, and returned the kiss with a sweet, wondrous enthusiasm that said this was all exactly right.

19

Ever since Jenny had decided to turn toward Nick's clinic rather than home, the question had been there, running beneath the surface like a delicious itch. *How far are we going to take this?* She would be spending the night; that much was clear. But would she be in the guest room or his bed? She hadn't been sure. Now, as he kissed her with all the pent-up heat that had been building since the first moment she walked through his door two weeks ago, she still didn't have any of the answers, but she wasn't sure she cared. Because if she knew one thing, it was that she trusted him. Whatever happened—or didn't happen—next, they could talk about it, figure it out together. And that was a wondrous thing.

Parting her lips beneath his, she sighed into his mouth and let him in. Their tongues touched, stroked, and he pulled her against his body, banding his arms around her and holding tight. He tasted sharp and intoxicating, making her head spin like she'd been sitting around a campfire, passing around a bottle of something strong and spicy.

He changed the angle of the kiss, diving in, devouring, enfolding her. Warmth went to heat, and from there to an inferno.

On one level, she was aware of the howling wind and lashing snow, and the way it made his place into a warm, safe shelter. On another level, though, the storm was inside her, making her want to rake her fingers through his hair and down his back. Making her want to accept all that he was giving her, and then take more.

Instead, he eased back and let out a long breath that was almost a growl. Then, taking a moment to pull himself together, he reached past her once more, handed her the mug, and took a big step back. "Drink."

Shaky enough to follow his order without protest, she took a sip. Then, as the spicy chocolate and almost too-sweet sugar of the marshmallows hit her tongue, she moaned and took another, longer drink.

"Don't do that," he warned.

"Do what?"

"We need to have a serious conversation, and it's not going to happen if you make chocolate orgasm noises."

"Then you shouldn't have added the fluff."

The laugh lines deepened at the corners of his eyes. "Noted."

She took another sip, then studied him over the rim of her mug. "Would it help if I said I've got a hard-and-fast rule about not doing what I think we're talking about doing until at least the fifth date?"

It was a good rule, one that had kept her from making several hormone- and cocktail-driven blunders over the last few years. If a guy didn't want to put in at least a little effort to get to know her—and vice versa—then sex was a bad idea. But this was different, wasn't it? She already knew him better than she had known her last few just-for-fun guys. She liked him, trusted him, wanted him. . . . The thought of being with him sent her senses into overdrive, heating her center with a low throb and making her very aware of his cracked-open bedroom door. Something inside her held back, though. Maybe it was the suspicion that the storm was moving up their timeline, or the way he was so different from the guys she usually went out with. He was settled, centered, landlocked.

And the next time she came home, he would still be here.

Whatever the source of the impulse, she found herself wanting to cling to the five-date rule.

"Yeah, that helps." He took a slug of his own cocoa and shifted in place, as if he, too, was itching for the sensation of skin on skin, but holding back. "How many actual dates have we had, do you think?"

Relief bubbled up in a laugh. "I think we can call this number four."

"You're counting the farm call to Michelle's as a date?"

"Well, you did buy me dinner."

"Clearly, excellent planning on my part. And going after your grandfather?"

"A romantic moonlit ride. And there were snacks involved. Work with me here."

"Trust me, I am. Okay, so we're on date four. Good

to know." He looped his free hand into the pocket of his worn jeans and cocked a hip, looking more relaxed suddenly, now that they knew where things stood. Or maybe that was an illusion, because if he was feeling anything like she was at that moment, his blood was still running hot, his lips tingling from a mix of kisses and cocoa. "You hungry?"

"For French toast?"

"Actually, I was thinking of cheese and crackers, maybe some grapes and apple slices. I've even got some wine to go with it."

"Somebody send you a gift basket?"

He grinned. "Grateful client."

"Lucky us. And, yes, that sounds perfect." Wine and cheese with a handsome vet, tucked in together during a storm along with his cat and her dog. It certainly wasn't what she had been expecting when she got off the plane in Laramie two weeks ago.

It was infinitely better.

For the next hour or so, they cuddled together on the couch and demolished the gift basket while 007 did his thing on the TV, and Rex and Cheesepuff mooched slivers of cheddar and pepperoni. The whiteout beyond the windows had turned gray-blue by the time the credits rolled. As Jenny cleaned up the leftovers, Nick went into the kitchen and poured wine into a pair of coffee mugs.

He made a mental *remember to buy wineglasses* note, then handed over her mug and held out his own. "To blizzards."

"To blizzards." She clinked and sipped. "Mmm. Nice. Another gift?"

"How'd you guess?"

"You seem like more of a beer guy."

"Is that a good thing?"

"Definitely." She said it with such conviction that he laughed. "What about—" His phone buzzed from the living room, then pounded out the *Indiana Jones* theme, which had Jenny clapping a hand over her mouth to stifle a whoop. "Hold that thought," he said. "That'll be my old man checking in."

He snagged the phone and answered it. "Hey, Dad. How are you holding up?"

"Like a maiden cow, son," Bill Masterson said in a humor-filled voice that cracked around the edges. "Tight as a tick."

Nick stifled a chuckle. "Glad to hear it. Power's still good? Got enough food to make it through?"

"You worry too much."

"I'll take that as a yes and yes. How's Molly handling the weather?" His father's constant companion was a big, rangy dog with a lot of shepherd and maybe a little wolf in her. Well trained and confident in her old home, she had come partially unglued when they moved up to the cabin, going overboard on protecting her human and her territory. An experienced trainer, Bill had worked hard to get her comfortable in her new surroundings, but any animal could get a little wonky during a big storm.

"She's okay. We heard some wolves just before the

weather hit, and that got her blood up, but after wearing a track by the front windows for a while, she's finally settled down."

"Glad to hear it."

In the kitchen, Jenny was chatting with Cheesepuff while Rex did a wiggle-dance at her feet. Fed up with being ignored—at least in his doggy brain—he hopped up, put his paws on the edge of the counter, and gave a big "whuff!" right in the cat's face.

The tabby hissed, swiped at his nose, and bounded down the other side of the breakfast bar while Jenny ordered Rex to go lie down in the corner and behave himself.

"You finally get yourself a dog?" Bill asked, interest lighting his voice. It had been a bone of mild contention ever since Nick had moved to Three Ridges, with his father insisting that a man needed a dog of his own.

Up to this point, Nick had stuck to answering "I'll get around to it," part of him hoping his old man would drop it while another part warned that his father would just move on to the next step in the house-plus-dog-equals-settled-down equation. Not that he was against starting a family—it was in the five-year plan he was going to initiate one of these days. It just wasn't in the cards anytime soon.

Now, he said, "Rex belongs to a friend. They're hanging out here for the duration."

"A lady friend?"

He glanced at Jenny, who was fussing over an indignant Cheesepuff. "You could say that."

"Is it serious?"

"It's . . ." He couldn't say yes and didn't want to say no, and he'd be darned if he copped out with "complicated." Especially when it wasn't complicated at all—there weren't any games here. Just two people who enjoyed each other's company.

"Never mind, forget I asked. That's your business, not mine."

"I'm not keeping secrets. I just don't have a good answer."

"I should go anyway. Molly is scratching at the back door like she needs to go out."

Nick was grateful for the subject change, but not so much for the image of his father following the wolf-dog out into the storm. "Keep her close to the house. Did you set up a tether rope to the woodshed and back?"

"Stop fussing. I'm fine. Go back to . . . whatever you were doing."

"Watching a movie. Call me tomorrow?"

"Will do. And maybe you could come out to the cabin with your lady friend. I'd like to meet the woman who's got you second-guessing yourself."

The line went *click*, leaving Nick to groan and give a good-natured curse.

"Something wrong?" Jenny asked from the kitchen.

"My dad has this thing about getting in the last word. But no, nothing's wrong. Sounds like he's doing just fine up there." And Nick wasn't second-guessing himself about anything. He liked where he and Jenny were right now, liked where they were going. And he didn't need a dog. He had Cheesepuff.

"Good to hear. Want to cue up another movie?"

"Got anything good on that computer of yours?"

"What, like Netflix?"

"I was thinking more along the lines of a Jenny Skye original."

She blinked, lips curving. "You want to see the videos?"

"I thought you'd never ask."

A few minutes and an HDMI cable later, she had her computer hooked to his TV and a prompt showing on the screen.

"Want more?" he asked from the kitchen, lifting the wine.

She held out her mug. "Definitely. In fact, maybe just bring the bottle in here." She pressed a hand to her stomach. "I'm nervous. Why am I nervous?"

"Rex and I are on your side, but Cheese can be a tough audience." He topped off her wine and settled them on the couch, with him and Jenny twined together on a reclining section, Rex on a blanket beside them, and the cat perched Sphinx-like on the high leather back, glaring down at the dog as if still offended. Or plotting revenge.

"Ready?" Her finger hovered over the touchpad.

"Still nervous?"

"Nope," she said, but didn't quite meet his eyes, like she wanted to impress him but didn't want to admit it.

Thing was, she had already impressed the heck out

of him in a hundred different ways, from saving Rex to working at finding a middle ground with her mother. The cool factor of her career was just an added bonus. Grabbing a remote, he killed the lights, plunging the room into a darkness broken only by the glow from the flat-screen. Then, taking her hand, he folded their fingers together and squeezed. "Okay. Now I'm ready."

She hit the button, the screen faded to black, and a few notes sounded from a single guitar, low and weepy. Slowly, an image coalesced in gray scale—a grainy black-and-white photograph of a dark-haired boy, maybe eight or nine, wearing a kid-size cowboy hat and chaps, and riding a full-size horse along the edge of a huge herd of cattle. He had a stiffly looped rope in one gloved hand, the reins in the other, and a look of fierce concentration on his face, like the fate of the world—or at least this part of it—depended on him not letting the animals stray out of formation. At the horse's heels loped a lean black-and-white border collie, ears up and alert.

After a moment, a man's voice said, "Back then, we didn't use satellite phones or walkie-talkies, and helicopters were for the military or a rich-man's toy, not herding cattle. We rode out on mustangs that we caught and gentled ourselves, with the help of dogs that ate from our tins and slept on our bedrolls. It was the same way our grandfathers had gathered the herds, and their grandfathers before them. It was the cowboy way."

The screen faded back to black, and then a title came up: *Mustang Ridge: The Cowboy Way.*

The back of Nick's neck prickled as it hit him hard and fast that this wasn't just a YouTube clip or an advertisement. He had expected it to be good, of course. This was Jenny after all, and he was rapidly learning that she didn't do anything halfway. But he hadn't expected to be unable to pull his eyes off the screen, hadn't expected the words and music to surround him, making him feel the sunlight on his skin and taste the trail dust at the back of his throat.

Then the title faded, a new image came to life, and he was looking at Jenny's grandfather, face etched with character, faded blue eyes looking faraway. "The cowboy way wasn't something a boy learned back then, wasn't something you printed on fancy signs or slapped on a T-shirt. It just *was*, deep down in your bones. I knew to walk my horse the first mile out and the last mile back, not just because my pappy would tan my hide if I ran my horse in wet and bothered, but because my horse depended on me, just like I depended on him."

The screen went to a slide show of old photographs, a flip book of years as the dark-haired boy aged. Black-and-white went to grainy color. His clothes changed, his horses changed, even the dog disappeared and was replaced with another, fluffier version. But always there was that look of do-or-die concentration, the rope in his hand, the border collie at his heels.

As the images played out, Big Skye shared stories from the trail, interspersing them with pieces of advice, like "Don't kick dirt in the fire or another man's meal" and "Always triple-check your cinch."

The montage ended with a photograph of the boy-turned-man, riding at the front of the herd now rather than its flanks, leading the way through the wrought-iron arch that welcomed visitors—and tired, trail-worn cowboys—to Mustang Ridge Ranch.

In a beat of silence, the image shifted, centering on the figure and then zooming to his face, looking grainy in the close up for a moment. Then the pixels dissolved to Big Skye looking solemnly into the camera. "The most important part, at least to me, is that a cowboy, especially a trail boss, sees to his horse, his men, and his family before he sees to himself. That's how it's always been at Mustang Ridge. And, God willing, that's the way it always will be."

His eyes held the camera for a two count, and then the screen went black and the guitar picked out a few more chords, then fell silent.

Jenny froze the image and looked at him sidelong. "Well? What do you think?"

I think that you amaze me. That you're selling yourself short doing what you do . . . and that there's no way you belong in a place like this. The last part came out of nowhere and felt like it came from somebody else, a guy who was actually thinking along those lines. A guy who wished she would stay, wished that what they had was more than temporary. "I think it's amazing," he said, able to put that one out there, at least. "Seriously incredible, and not just as an advertising piece. It's a little movie, all wrapped up in what, five minutes? Eight? But the advertising works, too, because after seeing that, I'm so going to jump in on Roundup Week next summer. You just juiced every cowboy fantasy I ever had, and even added a few new ones."

"That was all thanks to Big Skye. And Gran, too. She's the one who started pulling the photos together a few years back. I just picked up where she left off." But Jenny's cheeks were pink, her lips curved.

"The stories and pictures are pure gold, but it's the filmmaking that wraps it all up and ties a big fat bow on it." He leaned in and planted a quick kiss on her. And then, compelled by the taste of her lips and the buzz from watching her movie, he went back for another that lingered.

She murmured and shifted against him, making his body suddenly very aware that they were curled together, practically horizontal. He rose over her, letting his lips trail across her jaw to her neck, the dip of her collarbone. Rather than pushing him away, she slid her hands under his shirt and along his ribs, leaving little licks of fire behind.

Groaning, he pulled back. "Jenny, I—"

"Whuff!" Rex's bark was close to a howl as he shot to his feet and shook off twenty pounds of aerial tabby attack. When Cheese just clung, Rex bolted off the sofa.

"Ow!" Nick rolled, shielding Jenny from the canine stampede, which was followed by a blur of stripey orange. "Darn it, you two!"

Cheesepuff disappeared around the corner into the spare room, flicking his tail.

Nick felt a tremor beneath him, and looked down to

find Jenny laughing silently, with both hands clapped over her mouth and her eyes filled with mirth.

When their gazes met, she lowered her hands and wheezed. "What a pair of brats!"

"Not to mention a buzzkill." He levered away from her. "Yes?"

"More like a reality check." She straightened and ran her fingers through her hair, smoothing the sleek, dark strands. "I don't want to seem like a tease—"

"You're not. We just got carried away."

She slid him a sidelong look. "Started to, anyway."

"Yeah . . . so." He stood and held out a hand. "Want to play a game?"

"What, Halo?"

"I was thinking more along the lines of backgammon or a puzzle or something. It's a family snow-day tradition."

"Aw, that's nice. Not to mention that it'll keep our hands busy."

He hauled her to her feet and patted her on the behind. "Smart lady. No wonder I like you. Games are over here. They came with the house, along with an extensive collection of VHS tapes that I Freecycled."

She peered at the stacked boxes in the built-in. "You have any preference?"

"Scrabble?"

"You have a second choice?"

"How can you not like Scrabble? It's a classic."

"Not to sound like the blonde that I am underneath

the dye, but I'm Scrabble impaired. I even suck at Words with Friends." Eyes lighting, she reached for a different box. "Aha! Trivial Pursuit."

"How is that less mental effort than Scrabble?"

"It's the Silver Screen Edition."

"In other words, I'm doomed." But he took the box and headed for the couch. "What color do you want?"

They were more evenly matched than Nick had predicted—Jenny kicked butt in the on-screen stuff, but it turned out that he had an edge when it came to titles and settings. He won the first game by a few moves, but she trounced him in game two. By the time they neared the end of game three, pretty much neck and neck, Rex was fast asleep on the floor and Cheesepuff was sacked out on the couch, stretched out to cover more square inches than seemed possible.

The humans had switched from wine to water by unspoken consent, so she was stone sober, but there was nothing cold about it. She was warm and flushed all over, and entirely aware of Nick as he sprawled out opposite her, loose and limber, like a high school jock all grown up into a man's body.

He picked a card and read. "What movie won best picture in 1981?"

She didn't care anymore, didn't want to play anymore. "*Gandhi?*"

"Nope. *Chariots of Fire.*"

"Drat," she said, but without much heat. She was six

spots short of the center of the wheel, and he was only three. But it didn't matter who won—all that mattered was what happened after the game.

What was she trying to avoid here? Why? She wanted him, he wanted her; it ought to be an easy choice.

He rolled. "Three! I'm so making it to the middle." He moved his game piece.

"What category do you want?"

"Titles, baby."

Snagging a card, she scanned the question, lips curving. "This is a tough one. A silent romantic comedy from 1925 starring Marie Provost, with no known copies in existence."

Dimples deepening, he sat up and leaned across the board. "Kiss me again."

Stomach flip-flopping, she obliged, moving in to brush her lips across his and then find his mouth in a deep kiss that was familiar yet not, as if her body was just beginning to recognize his. Against his mouth, she murmured, "You're stalling."

He drew away, grin going cocky. "No, I'm not. That's the title of the movie: *Kiss Me Again*."

"That's—" She looked back down at the card. "You're joking." But he wasn't. Laughing, she swept the board aside and closed the small gap between them. "Well, never let it be said that I can't obey orders when it suits me."

She leaned in to him, kissed him, and let the rising heat wash away the lingering nervousness. And when the kiss ended, she rose to her feet and held out her hand. He took it but didn't put any pressure on her, even though she could feel the tension in his big body, see it in his eyes. "Time to call it a night?" he asked with a rough catch of desire in his voice.

"That depends. Is it past midnight?"

"Yes, why? Are you going to turn into a pumpkin? Or wait. Are we having a *Gremlins* moment here? Should I not feed you?"

"Actually, you should. Then, between us having a meal together and it being tomorrow, it'll count as our fifth date."

20

Nick's lips curved in that slow, cocky smile she was rapidly becoming addicted to, and then he took a quick scan of the room. Spotting the remnants of the microwave popcorn they had decimated during game two, he scooped up the bowl, snagged one of the last few ragged bits at the bottom, and held it to her lips. "Here."

She accepted the morsel. "What? No chocolate-covered strawberries and champagne?"

"I'll do better next time. Right now, I need to do this." He moved in and kissed her, and there was no mistaking the message he was sending her. *I want this, want you. Here. Now. Hard and fast.* His mouth covered hers, plundering as he took the kiss deeper, banding his arms around her and pressing their bodies together.

Heat flared deep inside her, and this time she didn't need to keep some part of herself in control. Grateful, relieved, excited, she sank into the kiss. Her hands streaked under his shirt and found the wonderful contrasts of silken skin and wiry hair, of soft spots and hard muscle. Groaning, he pressed his lips to the corner of her mouth, the side of her jaw, the hollow of her throat. Desire coiled from the points of contact, spiraling in to tighten her inner muscles, making her yearn. "Nick," she whispered, letting her head fall back in surrender. "Yes."

"Not here. Not like this." He swung her into his arms in a single smooth, powerful move, and turned for the bedroom.

Jenny curled her arms around his neck and kissed his throat, his jaw, tasting the faint saltiness of his skin and reveling in the feel of being held so carefully. So much for the whole *I can take care of myself* thing. Apparently part of her really dug being swept off her feet.

The bedroom was dimly illuminated by a nightlight that gave off soft sepia tones, like they were inside an old tintype. The mattress and box spring wore a dark comforter, the chair in the corner held a pile of folded clothes, and the nightstand was two milk crates fastened together with a couple of zip ties. The combination made her smile—maybe he wasn't so landlocked, after all.

"I can give you the name of a fabulous decorator," she offered.

"Maybe later," he said, and tossed her.

She shrieked and windmilled, but made a soft landing on what proved to be a decadent foam mattress that yielded perfectly beneath her. "Wow," she said, stroking the coverlet. "This is . . . Wow."

There was a low "whuff" from the door, but Rex

seemed to understand that she wasn't in any danger. More, he got that he wasn't invited. Doing a one-eighty, he disappeared, claws clicking on the tiles as he headed back toward the living room.

After a glance at the doorway, Nick followed her down and rose above her, supporting his weight on his arms while their legs tangled and their bodies aligned so naturally that it felt like they had been lovers for years. Yet at the same time, everything was sharp, new, and bright, like the sensations had turned to colors in the monochrome room.

Leaning down, he brushed his lips across her cheek. There was a chuckle in his voice when he admitted, "I splurged on the mattress."

"I guess you did." She wrapped her arms around his neck and gave a couple of test bounces, only to find almost no rebound. "It's squishy. How is it for what we're about to do?"

"We're about to find out." He kissed the side of her neck, then moved downward to lift the hem of her shirt and kiss the flesh he had revealed. Fleetingly, she thought that if she had known all this was going to happen, she would've worn a prettier bra. She hadn't planned on seeing him right after her meeting, after all.

And, thinking that, she remembered what else she hadn't planned for.

She shuddered under his touch, skin going hot-cold-hot, and moved her legs restlessly against his. "Reality check. Condoms?"

He looked up at her, eyes dark and intense. "Top egg crate."

"Right. Boy Scout."

He slid both hands under her shirt and peeled it off, and then took a moment to just look at her, eyes heated and approving. Then he said, "I bought them the other day, not because I was assuming anything, but because I wanted to believe we'd end up here."

"We did. We are. Now, take off that shirt before I have to hurt you." She caught her breath as he complied. He looked like a bronze statue in the burnished light, all golden skin and bulging muscles, but with the lean ropiness that spoke of hard work outdoors rather than reps at the gym. "And again—wow. Only this time I'm not talking about the mattress."

He wiggled his eyebrows. "You will be in a minute."

She laughed as he lowered himself to her, and then gasped softly at the first real press of skin on skin, and the good, solid weight of his body against hers. He kissed her long and hard, and the world threatened to spin away. How long had it been since she had felt like this? Had she ever? The faint whisper of nerves that sparked at the thought was quickly lost to the desire that twined through her, following the path of his fingers, his lips.

They undressed each other piece by piece, chasing the clothing away with kisses and soft noises of pleasure. By the time they lay together, naked, her sighs had turned to moans, his hissed-out breaths to groans.

Part of her couldn't believe that she was doing this, but at the same time she couldn't imagine holding out any longer.

She welcomed him when he rose over her, surged into her, the two of them together forging a tight fit. They found their rhythm together, slow at first as their bodies asked and answered—*yes, there, like that*—and then gaining tempo as the storm inside them swelled and intensified, turning primal. She clung to him, surged beneath him, matching him stroke for stroke and then racing ahead toward the peak. She found her release first, tightening beneath and around him, mouth open in a wordless cry that was echoed moments later in his deeper baritone.

His body bowed as his hips jerked against her, wringing additional pleasure. Then he eased, relaxing into her and letting his brow rest on hers, though he kept his full weight on his arms. Their breathing aligned, their bodies moving together as they had just moments before, only softly now, gently. Then, with a final, almost reverent kiss on her lips, he rolled aside, onto his back, and nestled her against him. And even though she had never been much of a postcoital cuddler, she found that her head fit in the hollow beneath his shoulder, her hand between his pecs.

"So." The word was a rumble in his chest, followed by a pause, like he was weighing something. After a moment, he said, deeply serious, "How was the mattress?"

A laugh bubbled up alongside relief. They could

keep this simple, she thought. They really could. "Superlative, really. I'm going to have to see about getting my own."

"You can borrow this one a few more times if you'd like."

She kissed his cheek. "Generous guy."

"It comes natural when I'm with you."

"I think it comes natural for you, period."

His arm tightened around her. "Seriously, Jenny. You make things easy on a man. You don't play games, don't make me guess. Instead, you make me think. You make me laugh. And you make me happy."

Her throat tightened with emotion, but in a good way. There was no sense of "uh-oh, what have I done?" because he got it. He got *her*. And, best of all, he liked her just the way she was.

She tipped her head up and found his lips for a soft, sweet kiss. "There isn't anybody I'd rather be stranded with, Doc. You're something special, and I consider myself very lucky that our paths crossed."

"We'll have to thank Rex for that."

"The next cheese plate is all his."

"As his vet, I'd advise against that," he said solemnly, then wiggled his eyebrows. "As the guy who just got lucky, I'll spring for the deluxe tray with the cocktail wieners."

She gave him a smacking kiss on the lips, still a little dazed by the sex, dazzled by the fact that it didn't seem to have changed things between them. "Such a prince."

Alerted by the conversation or the sound of his

name, Rex reappeared in the doorway, tail making happy thumps on the frame. *Are you guys coming back out here for more snacks?*

Jenny glanced at the window, which was pitch-black except where snow crystals had stuck in the lower corners, turning them round and furry. "I should let him out," she said, totally not looking forward to getting cold and wet.

"I'll do it." Nick rose, found his jeans, and pulled them on.

The desire to stay put warred briefly with guilt. "I should—"

"You should stay right there and build up lots of nice body heat so you can thaw me out when I get back." He shrugged into a fleece. "Five minutes, maybe less."

He was back in four, with a big glass of water and a soggy dog who went straight to a fallen blanket on the floor, did his two and a half circles, and plopped down with a happy sigh.

Nick eyed him, amused. "I'll get us another blanket."

As he draped it over her, Cheesepuff jumped up and proceeded to pace the length and width of the huge mattress, looking for the perfect spot. Which, it turned out, was directly behind Jenny's knees, leaving her unable to move much when Nick shucked off his clothes and got back into bed.

Not that she wanted to move, really. He was snowman cold and his hair was damp, but where a couple of week ago she would've protected her warmth at all costs, now she curled an arm around his cool torso and rubbed her cheek on his chest, trying to bring him back up to temp. "How bad is it out there?"

"It's snowing like crazy, and it doesn't feel like the wind has let up any. There's probably a foot on the ground, maybe more. You might be stuck here for a while."

"Better here than anywhere else," she said drowsily, then tensed, wondering if that was taking it too far.

But he just kissed the top of her head. "Yeah. That was what I was thinking. Get some sleep, darling. We'll make a snowman in the morning."

"Is that another Masterson snow-day tradition?"

"If not, it should be."

They fell silent, listening to the storm. The wind lashed snow pellets against the glass with a rushing hiss, occasionally rattling something outside. It made her feel very snug and safe, being wedged between a cat and her lover, with the dog at their feet. She snuggled in, her brain gone astonishingly quiet. There was none of the usual background chatter, no flashes of things she had seen during the day, images she had filmed or—worse—missed filming. No mental list of the things she needed to do tomorrow, the places she wanted to go. There was just . . . contentment.

Lulled by his and Rex's breathing and the warm weight of the cat, she was too comfortable to move, too relaxed to do anything but—

Sleep.

*   *   *

The next morning when twenty pounds of tabby thudded onto Nick's stomach and padded up his torso with pointy paws, he fought consciousness like the devil, trying to hold on to his dreams, which had been a delicious mix of sexy skin, soft touches, and—

Jenny.

A whole-body shock went through him, and he opened his eyes and turned to find her there, snuggled into a pillow with her eyelashes fanned out across her lightly freckled cheeks.

A big orange head loomed over him, blocking out the light.

He nudged the cat aside. "You'll wake her up."

Or maybe not. She looked deeply under, breathing softly. They had turned to each other twice more during the night, once in the wee hours and again not long ago. He should let her rest. Granted, he hadn't gotten any sleep, either, and he had that tired-legs, whole-body ache that came from what they'd been doing—and doing well—since just after midnight. But at the same time, he felt like he could take on the world, like a movie superhero. He was energized, loose, relaxed, and totally ready to roll. And hey, what do you know? It was still snowing—big, fat flakes that drifted down rather than pelting sideways, but wouldn't be any easier on the roads. Which didn't just mean another snow day. It meant another snow day with Jenny.

He couldn't think of anything better.

Claws sank into his shoulder, and he got a loud "Mrwow!" right in his ear, followed by a "whuff" from down below and the *thump-thump-thump* of Rex's tail.

"Okay, okay, I'm up." He peeled himself out of the bed, pulled on sweats and socks, and then turned back and tucked the blankets around Jenny. Leaning in, he kissed her brow. "Don't get up. We've got all day."

She smiled and gave a sweet murmur. With the diffuse white snow-light illuminating her, she looked like a portrait done by a master, with a glow to her skin offset by her dark hair and rose-tinted lips. The image caught him, engraving itself on his retinas.

If he had been the photographer, he would have gone for his camera. But all he had was his phone, and he didn't want to come off as creepy.

"Go on, you two." He waved the critters toward the kitchen. "Let's see what we can do about breakfast." He wasn't sure if this was a continuation of his and Jenny's fifth date or the beginning of their sixth—or whether they had stopped counting—but he definitely wanted to do better than leftover popcorn.

Jenny woke slowly, like she was surfacing after holding her breath underwater. The sinful mattress cushioned her, tempting her to slip back under and rest some more, but when she stretched beneath the soft sheets, unfamiliar twinges reminded her of the new reality.

Opening her eyes, she looked around the room, lingering on the window, where the snow was still drifting down. She stared at the patterns made by the flakes and tested out the thought: Nick was her lover now. It tightened her throat and put a shimmy in her stomach, even though she had thought she was past the nerves. There wasn't anything to worry about, was there? He understood her, and she thought she understood him.

Like his bedroom. Another woman might see the bed on the floor, the cobbled-together nightstand, and the shelves he was using in place of a dresser, and think that he needed a keeper. She, on the other hand, felt right at home, because it was a pick-up-and-go place. This might be his place, but it wasn't his home yet. He was just camping out, waiting to see what happened next.

She totally got that.

The door bumped open and Cheesepuff sauntered in, testing the air and pretending he wasn't checking to see if she was awake.

"Hey, buddy." She patted the bed. "Come on up."

Instead, he about-faced and headed back for the door with his upright tail curled at the end like a candy cane. He bumped the door farther open on his way through, letting in the tantalizing smell of coffee and the sounds of good stuff happening in the kitchen, just like home.

Only this wasn't the ranch, and that definitely wasn't Gran in the kitchen.

Pulse kicking at the thought of seeing Nick—which was silly, really—Jenny got up, pulled on the borrowed sweats, visited the bathroom to finger brush her teeth and tame her hair to not so angry hedgehog status.

Then, taking a deep breath, she headed out into the kitchen.

"There she is," Nick said cheerfully from the stove. Wearing baggy sweatpants and a hoodie, he looked comfortable, casual, and just as tasty—if not tastier— than the thick slabs of bacon he was cooking on the front burner. The light angled down on his cheekbones and emphasized his dimples when he smiled, and if she could've framed the moment and clicked the shutter, she would've called it *Hottie at Home*, or maybe *Beefcake and Bacon*.

"Good morning," she said, crossing to where Cheese was winding around his legs, begging. Dodging the cat, she got in close enough to smell the soap and shampoo that said Nick had already showered. She started to reach for him—

And stalled.

What now? Should she hug him? Kiss him on the cheek? The lips? She was so used to the friends-with-benefits thing that she didn't know how to handle something more. Panicking, she stuck out her hand. "Nice to see you again."

Really? She could just die.

Face lighting, he shook her hand. "Nice to see you, too."

"Um. Okay, then." She retrieved her hand. "Glad this isn't at all awkward."

He chuckled. "Guess I'm out of practice."

"It's not you. I just . . ." She shrugged, not liking how it was going to sound. "I don't usually stay for breakfast." And she hadn't really realized it until just now. "I mean, I've had breakfast, you know, the morning after. But with a group, or out." Not at home, with her dog under the table, licking his chops.

"Chill. I know what you mean. Guess I've got another reason to be grateful for the storm." He turned away from the stove, caught her hips in his hands, and backed her up a couple of steps until she bumped into the opposite counter. Voice going low, to a sexy rasp that woke up her nerve endings and made her think of the things they had done to each other in the darkness, he said, "How about we try this instead?"

The kiss was firm and no nonsense, with a whole lot of full-body press and hands-on action that reminded her what they had been up to for the past eight or nine hours, and suggested they should try some more of it, real soon. But more than that, it centered her, settled her, brought things into perspective.

He lingered at her lips, then leaned in to press his brow to hers. "Better?"

She cupped his jaw, which was roughened with stubble. "Much." Then she stood on her tiptoes to peer past him. "There's my French toast! Now it feels like a snow day."

"Sit." He nudged her toward the breakfast bar, then placed a coffee mug in front of her. "It'll be ready in a few minutes. You can supervise."

"That's no hardship." In fact, she couldn't take her eyes off him as he moved around the small space, poking at the sizzling bacon, adding a dusting of sugar to the French toast, and loading a pair of plates.

"Madame's breakfast," he said, setting one in front of her, along with utensils and a woven basket holding a stack of paper napkins. "Hope you like your French toast stiff and your bacon limp."

"There's a joke in there somewhere."

He opened his hands away from his body in a come-at-me gesture. "Bring it on."

"Nah. You're feeding me. That gets you a pass for most anything."

"I'll keep that in mind." He grabbed his own plate, checked both their coffee levels, and then sat beside her at the breakfast bar, angling his stool so their knees bumped. "Dig in."

"Thanks." She waited a beat, until he looked over at her and their eyes met once more. "I mean it. Thanks." For making last night special. For not letting her make this morning weird.

He leaned in and kissed her cheek, as easy as breathing. "You're welcome."

She was surrounded momentarily by him—his scent, his warmth, the buzz of energy that came with the brush of his lips across her skin. Enjoying the moment and the man, she forked up a fluffy bite of egg-laden bread, dipped it in a pool of syrup, and sampled. "Mmm. Not bad, Doc. In fact, it's pretty awesome."

"I can handle breakfast, especially when I've got a beautiful woman in my bed."

"Oh? Does this happen often?" It wasn't until he eased back that she realized she was venturing toward sticky territory. The kind that was posted with WARNING, GIRLFRIEND STATUS AHEAD signs. And that so wasn't where she had meant to go. "I was teasing, not fishing," she said quickly, then turned her attention to the window. "It's still coming down out there, huh?"

And, yes, she was talking about the weather.

His shoulders loosened a notch, though, and he followed her lead. "It's stickier now. Better for snowballs."

She lifted a slice of bacon and bit in. "Or a snowman?" Rex, who had been watching the bacon like it was in danger of going extinct, gave a low whine. She grinned down at him. "What was that? You want us to make a snow retriever?"

Nick dimpled. "I think we can handle that."

"What do you think, Rexy?" When he gave his low, indoor-voice bark, she flipped him her last slice of bacon.

"You're spoiling him," Nick said mildly.

"News flash. Your cat's on the counter."

"Or for the love of— Cheesepuff, get down!"

They kept it light for the remainder of breakfast, wrangled good-naturedly when she insisted on doing the dishes, and then geared up to venture out into the storm. The phone rang while she was putting on her boots. Nick answered, and almost instantly slipped on an invisible white coat and went into vet mode, saying things like, "Well, some dogs aren't sensitive to chocolate, but it's better to be safe than sorry, especially in a blizzard."

He stood staring out into the storm as he talked the woman through giving the pooch a slug of Ipecac to clear out his stomach, letting Jenny do some staring of her own. The storm light put faint hollows beneath his strong cheekbones, reminding her of what he had looked like naked in the golden glow of the nightlight. Desire thrummed through her, along with the pleasure of knowing that she had said the right thing just now, done the right thing. Because if he was going to take her the way she was, then she needed to do the same for him.

Turning away, she rummaged through her computer bag, came up with her cell phone, and put in a call to Mustang Ridge. To her surprise, it went through, and her mom picked up with a trilling, "Hel-lo, sweetie. Are you coming home to paint?"

"Um . . ."

"I'm teasing. You stay right where you are until the storm lets up. I'm assuming you're having fun?"

Ignoring whatever undercurrents might or might not be in the question, Jenny said, "Sure am. How are things there?"

"You know how your father is. He'd rather make a couple of extra passes with the plow than overstress the engine by trying to move the snow all at once."

In other words, he had escaped the house to play on the tractor. "I was wondering if you could do something for me."

"Oh?"

"I didn't get a chance to clear the decks in the office

yesterday. Could you check the voicemail and emails, and see if anything looks mission critical? I could do it remotely, but it's a pain."

"Of course, sweetie. Do I need passwords?"

Jenny talked her through the procedure, made her promise twice to call her or Krista if she had any questions, and rang off. To Rex, she said, "Mom said to give you a biscuit for her, but I think we'll wait on that for now. Nick is right about the treats, even if it is a snow day."

"Geez, make me out to be the bad guy, why don't you?" Nick protested. But he was grinning, leaned hip-shot against the breakfast bar. "And did I just hear you giving your mother marching orders?"

"Just a little office work."

He crossed to her, kissed the top of her head. "Nice job."

"It wasn't a big deal."

"You know what *is* a big deal?"

"What's that?"

He tossed her parka at her. "Snowball fight. Last one out the door is making lunch!"

21

Jenny didn't remember the last time she'd had a full-on snow day, the kind that had nothing to do with real life and everything to do with having fun. She and Nick shoveled the snow a little, wrestled in it a lot, and built a snow family complete with a snow retriever. Given the number of calls he fielded while they played—none of them true emergencies, fortunately—it was shaping up to be a busy couple of days when the roads cleared.

Until then, though, it was just the two of them.

After a late lunch of grilled cheese and soup, they cuddled up on the couch and watched a gloriously silly movie while the dog snored at their feet and the cat mooched belly rubs. Then, as the credits rolled, they turned toward each other and kissed. Naturally, easily. Like they were alone in the world with no cares, no complications. Nothing but the two of them.

They kissed on the couch while the snow sifted down and heat spiraled inside her, intensifying with every beat of her heart. They kissed as they walked up the short hallway together, stumbling in their haste to reach the bedroom and skim out of their clothes. And they kissed as she sank into the soft cloud of his mattress.

His skin was hot, his muscles taut, and when she wrapped her legs around him, it felt like the rest of the day had been leading up to this moment.

She moaned and flexed her fingers on his hips as he moved against her, and then again as he entered her. As before, there was a moment of surprise at the tight, perfect fit; another at the sense of rightness. And then he began to thrust, setting an even, controlled pace that said "I can do this for hours."

Which he more or less had done the night before. But now, in the muted light of day, a new, different urgency raced through her. Levering herself up, she wrapped her arms around his neck, took their next kiss deep, and kept on going up and over, reversing their positions.

He made a low sound of masculine pleasure, eyes gleaming as he looked up at her. "Oh?"

"Yes," she purred, bowing over him for another kiss. And then she began to ride, slow at first, but quickly gaining tempo and intensity as the heat rose up inside her.

Oh, she thought, and, *Yes*. She had wanted him like this, the two of them together, the give and take of pleasure. And then he dug his fingertips into her hips, bucked up beneath her to meet the rhythm she had set, and she couldn't think at all. The sensations overwhelmed her, consumed her, left her unable to do anything but meet him stroke for stroke as passion built. Peaked. Crested.

Jenny shuddered against him, tightened around him, and came. Fingers pressing into her hips, he groaned and followed her over, bucking his hips beneath her and eking out the pleasure all the way to a last long, slow roll that left her boneless, breathless.

Utterly satisfied.

Letting out a moaning breath, she sank down along his body and off to the side, so they cuddled together like a lock and key.

"Oh, baby." He hugged her close and kissed her brow. "You rock my snowstorm."

Outside, the day had gone blue-black, but the atmosphere seemed lighter, the flakes finer. She brushed her cheek across his pec. "I'd be okay if it snowed all day tomorrow, too."

"Or we could pretend we lost power and play hooky."

"Could we?"

He hesitated, but then shook his head. "Probably not."

Given what she had overheard of his phone calls, she wasn't surprised. She was a little startled, though, by the sting of disappointment. "Too bad." Summoning a grin, she gave him a come-hither eyebrow wiggle. "Guess we'll have to make good use of tonight."

"How about we start with what's left of the grilled cheese? Or we could go old school, with Saltines and fluff."

"I've got plans for that fluff."

"Oh, really? Hold that thought." He kissed the tip of her nose. "I'll be right back."

He sauntered out buck naked, with the animals competing for who would make it through the door first. Rex won by a nose, claws skittering a little on the polished floor.

Jenny snuggled down in the warm bedclothes and dozed. Her mind was like a warm, fuzzy version of the world outside: gentle swirls, soft and undefined, with no details beyond the window.

"Room service." He swept back in with the food and drink, but without the pets. "Sorry it took so long. My dad called to check in."

"He okay?"

"Snug as the proverbial bug."

She looked past him to the empty doorway. "What did you do with our furry friends?"

"I let Rex out and gave them both dinner. I kept it light, figuring they've been snacking all day, but they would just bug the bejeebers out of us if they didn't get something that looked like a meal."

"Spoken like someone who understands them very well."

He set out the food and climbed back into bed, bringing cool air with him. "I've always understood animals better than people."

"I wouldn't say that." She piled a couple of slices of slightly stale cheddar on a cracker, added a sliver of pepperoni, and handed it over. "From where I'm sitting, I'd say you do awfully well with people, too. Not to mention that you've got a seriously cute domestic streak." She held up a small sprig of grapes. "Dinner in bed? That's hot."

"You want hot? How about . . ." He produced the tub of marshmallow spread. "I believe madame requested this?"

"Madame most definitely did." She crooked her finger. "Come over here, and I'll show you what I have in mind."

The snow stopped overnight, and—despite Nick's fervent wish that things would be slow to get back under way—the main roads were clear by late morning. Soon after that, Robbie Peet plowed out the clinic and delivered Jenny's Jeep. Which unfortunately meant they didn't have any more excuses.

Still, as Nick waved Jenny off and got a tap of the brake lights and a cheery *beep-beep* in return, he darn well knew he didn't have anything to complain about. They had gotten two wonderful days together, and while they had just said a lingering good-bye-for-now, they had plans to talk later and hopefully hit a movie. And, well, other things.

He chuckled to himself, heard the rusty sound, and laughed aloud. "Boy, you've got it bad." And he was talking to himself now. But he didn't care because, well, he had it bad. Or maybe it would be more accurate to say he had it good?

Jenny was . . . Wow. The sex was amazing and the

other parts were equally incredible. They thought enough alike to be simpatico, different enough to make things interesting, and he didn't remember the last time he'd so enjoyed just hanging out with a woman. Or the last time he had wished he worked the kind of job he could blow off to do it some more.

That wasn't an option, though. She had things to do at Mustang Ridge and he had at least ten appointments to get through, priority clients that had hung on through the storm, but needed some hands-on attention.

"So let's get this started," he said, clapping his hands and turning back toward the clinic, where Cheesepuff sat in the window, looking at him like he was nuts for being out there a second longer than absolutely necessary.

Just then, Ruth's boxy red SUV crested the hill and came toward him with a cheerful *beep-beep* very like the one Jenny had given him just a few minutes earlier. He waited while Ruth parked next to his truck, idly wondering if she would notice the fresh tire marks in the blown-over snow.

She popped out of her car. "Was that Jenny pulling out as I came in?"

Busted, he thought, but couldn't do anything but grin. "You know darn well it was."

"And . . . ?"

"And a gentleman doesn't talk behind his lady's back."

She pouted. "I tell you about my dates."

"Fine. We ate soup and cocoa, busted out the cheese and crackers Mrs. Donohoe sent, and played board games."

Misting up a little, she smiled and sighed. "That sounds lovely. Just like the kind of things Charlie and I used to do when we were snowed in. Well, that and boink like bunnies, of course."

"And we have a Too Much Information buzzer on the play," Nick announced, holding up his arms like a ref. "Five yard penalty, loss of down. Which means it's time for us to buckle down and get back to work. Especially since our first appointment is Elvie Peet and Crisco."

Which, he knew, would change the subject pronto.

Sure enough, Ruth made a face. "She's going to want to tell me all about her brother, Silas, and how he'd be perfect for me. He's been happily married for going on forty years and has three grown kids and a bunch of grands, but Elvie's sure he'll figure out soon what a witch he married." She snorted. "She's the witch, more like. I'd hate to have her as a sister-in-law."

"You could handle her, one way or the other. And I could always help you hide the body."

"Awww." She bumped him with her shoulder as they headed for the clinic. "You'd do that for me?"

"What are friends for?" He bumped her back, glad to have gotten off the other subject.

But as he held open the door for her, she said, "When are you going to see her again?"

"Who, Elvie? She's probably already on her way.

You know she likes to get here early and rip coupons out of the magazines."

Ruth smacked his arm with the end of her multicolored scarf. "No, doofus. Jenny. When are you going to see Jenny again?"

"Tonight, if things don't get too hectic here or at Mustang Ridge." And he was going to do his darnedest to make sure the coast was clear on his end, maybe even lay in some munchies—and some more marshmallow fluff—upstairs in the hopes that they would end up back at his place to play a few more hours of hooky.

"You want some pointers?"

"You want another TMI penalty?"

She made a *pfft* noise in his direction. "If I know one thing, it's how to have a great date in these parts. I could give you some suggestions. You're going to have to work to give Jenny a new experience around here, you know."

Okay, she had a point there. The Steak Lodge had been fun, but he didn't know if the talking bison would be as cool the second time around. At the same time, he didn't think he wanted dating advice from someone who had once texted him pictures from a cage fight, declaring it her favorite third date of the year. "Maybe later."

Giving him a look like he had said the rest of it aloud, she tapped a finger on his chest, right over his heart. "If you want her to stay, you're going to have to show her that there's more variety around here than she thinks, and that even the little things can turn into adventures if you've got the right attitude."

"If I . . . Whoa." He put up both hands like she had just pointed a Taser at him. "Nobody said anything about her staying."

"She might, though, if you played it right."

"I don't want . . . That's not what's going on here. We're just having a good time."

"Well, isn't that the point? Why be with someone if you're not having a good time?"

"There's a heck of a leap between having a good time with Jenny and asking her to— Look, I appreciate that you want what's best for me, really I do. But a long-term relationship doesn't make the cut for me right now, and it's not on Jenny's top ten list, either. So do me a favor and be happy for us while it lasts, okay?"

"It's just . . ." She sighed, shaking her head like he was missing the whole concept of one plus one equals two. "Okay, I'll butt out."

"That wasn't exactly what I said, but thanks. Besides," he said, watching out the window as a wiry seventysomething climbed slowly out of an all-wheel-drive Subaru that had seen better days, "I'd say you've got your own love life to worry about for the next half hour or so. Elvie and Crisco are here."

Elvie was wearing a pink pom-pom of a wool hat and an insulated canvas trench that fell in folds around her slight body as she opened the rear car door. A pure white West Highland terrier wearing a tartan doggie coat jumped down and did a couple of excited one-eighties at the end of his leash, but then settled down as his mistress began making her arthritic way up the clinic steps, ignoring the wheelchair ramp that ran around the side.

"Repeat after me," Ruth muttered. "I don't date married men!"

Taking pity on her, Nick pushed open the door. "Mrs. Peet, welcome! And hello to you, Crisco. How about we go straight back and get started?" He ushered a slightly startled Elvie through the lobby and into Exam One while Ruth beat it in the other direction. To Elvie he said, "Now, last night you said Crisco had vomited a couple of times, and then began refusing food. Has anything changed since then?"

One down, nine to go, he thought, determined to make the rest of his day fly by. Because quitting time was Jenny time, and that was rapidly becoming his favorite part of the day.

It was ridiculous to feel like she had missed curfew, Jenny decided as she sat in the Jeep, staring at the main house. Not to mention, it was ridiculous for her to sit there replaying the past forty-eight hours in her mind, feeling like some of it was going to disappear the moment she walked through the front door.

Those were her snow days, her memories, and she wasn't going to let anyone mess with them.

"Whuff?" Rex pressed his head against her arm and looked up at her with a charming mix of *Are you okay?*

and *Are we going to sit here all day? I bet there are cookies in the kitchen.*

It was the thought of cookies that got her moving. Not because she was hungry, but because the kitchen meant Gran, and she could use a dose of Gran right now. "Okay, we're going," Jenny said. "You ready to brave the cold?"

"Rworf!" *Oh, boy, oh, boy, we're going inside!*

With Rex bounding ahead of her, barking and wriggling with a pointless enthusiasm that would no doubt make Big Skye roll his eyes, she pushed through the main door, knocking snow off her boots as she called, "Hey, gang. I'm home!"

"In the kitchen!" Gran called, and Rex charged down the hallway. But as Jenny turned to follow, a head popped through the office door.

"Hello, sweetie." Her mom beckoned. "Come here. See what I've done!"

Oh, heck. Whatever had happened to the office, it would be Jenny's fault, because she was the one who had invited Hurricane Rose over the threshold. Like a decorative vampire or something.

Braced for raspberry with flamingo accents—or vice versa—Jenny took a deep breath, held it, stepped into the office . . . and let it out again, because everything looked the same. White walls, wooden shelves stuffed with books and folders that Krista had claimed were organized by subject and date, big desk dominated by the computer, phone, printer, and an in-box that wasn't as overflowing as it had been when Jenny arrived—it was all there, exactly the way she had left it.

Thank heaven.

Relief brightened her smile. "Hey, there. What did you want me to see?"

"This!" Rose lifted a three-ring binder, then sank into Krista's chair and motioned for Jenny to take the guest chair. Again. "Sit. Have a look!"

Figuring that whatever it was, it had to be easier to explain to Krista than an unwanted office redo, Jenny sat, took the binder, and flipped it open.

"What— Oh! You organized all the guest add-ons." They were all there in the table of contents, with chapters alphabetically ordered from Anniversary to Wedding, with subheadings for gift baskets, special meals, services, and many more, some that Jenny hadn't ever heard of before.

Her mother leaned across and touched the page with her fingertips. "I talked to your grandmother about what's been offered in the past and roughly what's been charged, and picked her brain about some of the new directions Krista has been talking about. Obviously it's just a rough outline, and there are a ton of details that we'll need to fill in, but I thought . . ." She clasped her hands together. "I answered a couple of calls, looked for this information, and realized it was scattered all over the place. So I thought I could help."

Jenny paged through, seeing blank spots. "You left room for graphics."

"Not my forte."

Maybe not, but the rest of it was pretty perfect. "You could've showed this to me on the computer."

"It felt more tangible this way."

Indeed it did, and as Jenny flipped through, she got that little excited shimmy in her stomach. "This is really good."

"You don't have to sound so surprised. This used to be my office, after all." Before Jenny could react to that, her mother barreled on. "So, do you think Krista will like it?"

"I think she'll love it. Better watch it, though, or she'll give you a to-do list."

"I wouldn't mind." It was said with more peace than Jenny had seen from her mother in . . . well, since she could remember. But then her expression shifted and she popped out of the chair, lit with sudden excitement. "I painted your room, too. Come and see!" She practically danced out of the office, leaving the folder behind.

Jenny sat there for a beat, staring at the chair on the other side of the desk as it swung in a pivot, then slowed and stopped. Then, wishing she knew what to say to her mom, how to get through to something deeper than this bright, brittle cheer, she followed her silently out the door.

Later that afternoon—after Jenny had *ooh*ed and *aah*ed at the cream-colored paint on her bedroom walls and put in a few hours touching up the white on the trim and clearing the decks in the office—she whistled to Rex, bundled up, and headed for the barn.

It was time to call in the big gun. Or at least ask him for a ruling.

Rolling one of the big double doors open just wide enough, she slipped through into the barn, where the warm, humid air was redolent with the scents of hay, wood shavings, and horses. As she muscled the door shut, a grizzled head popped out of an open stall about halfway down, near where a toolbox sat open next to several pieces of wood. Looking surprised, her father said, "Hiya, pumpkin."

Starting down the aisle toward him, past empty stalls that would be filled come summer, she said, "Hey, Pops. How's it going?"

"Well enough," he said, returning his attention to the stall door he was working on. "You going for a ride?"

"Not today." She leaned against the wall nearby. "Aren't you going to ask me how it went, being stranded in a snowstorm with Nick?" Gran had grilled her like a cheese sandwich.

He didn't quite wince. "That depends. Is there anything I really need to know? Anything you need to talk about?"

Charmed by the image of her dad toting a shotgun up to the vet clinic, she chuckled. "He's a good man, Pops, and I'm a big girl."

"Then I don't need to know anything else about it." He didn't put his hands over his ears and do a "la-la-la, I can't heeearrr you," but that was the impression she got.

But that was his way. He wasn't just the Switzerland of neutrality; he was almost completely hands-off until one of them got in trouble, and then watch out. He was as fierce a disciplinarian as he was a protective father, and when it came to the big stuff, he was her go-to guy.

Going on impulse, she crossed to him, went up on her toes and kissed his cheek. "Love you, Dad."

He set his tools aside and caught her in a one-armed hug. "Back atcha, kiddo, times ten."

"Why not a hundred?"

"Because you haven't asked me to be in your movie yet."

"Really? I didn't think you'd want to be on camera."

"I've still got a few moves."

"How about some stories? I could use more on the historical stuff, like cattle rustling and the Keyhole Canyon gang."

"I'm your man."

She kissed his cheek again. "You're hired."

He moved away and turned back to the stall door, where two old, chewed-down boards had been replaced with new ones. He swung it back and forth a little, cocking his head to judge the rasp of wood-on-wood where the replacements didn't line up quite right. After a minute or so of silence broken only by the soft noises the horses made in their deeply bedded stalls, he said, "Are you going to tell me what's bothering you?"

"It's not a what, it's a who."

"Your mother." It wasn't a question. "Take it from me, it's best to pick your battles." He shot her a wink. "I decided I could live with fabric on the walls and fake fur pillows that look like a sabertooth horked up some giant hairballs, but I drew the line at the water feature, because I knew I'd be the one in charge of maintaining the darn thing."

"Color me not reassured. But that's not what I wanted to talk about."

"Oh?"

"Not exactly. What I really wanted to ask . . . is she okay? The obsessive thing seems to be getting worse, not better. And please don't brush it off again, or tell me that she's got the right to try on a few hobbies, now that the two of you are retired."

He opened the door all the way, eyeballed the offending edge, and reached for a handheld planer. As he ran it along the door in smooth strokes, producing springy curls of wood, he said, "Well she does."

"I know. It's just . . ." How to put it that wouldn't sound like she was judging? Part of Krista's whole plan had been to give their parents and grandparents a chance to enjoy retirement. It had been Gran's choice to stay on in the kitchen, their parents' choice to hit the road. Who was Jenny to say that her mother wasn't handling it the way she should? Staring down at her gloves, where a thread had worked itself loose from the Velcro closure, she said, "Do you think she's happy?"

"I honestly do." He paused. "Are you?"

"Of course. Why? Are you telling me to mind my own business?"

The planer paused, then continued. "No, I'm saying to give her room, that's all. If I had to pick one thing I learned on the road, it's that no matter whether we're ten years old, fifty, or a hundred, we're still learning how to live inside our own skins."

"So I need to work on myself and leave Mom to her own devices?"

"Or at least let her figure out who she wants to be for the next twenty years or so. Not everybody's retirement has to look the same. I was the one who wanted to leave, so we left, and we wandered, and I got a chance to be someone new. After a while, though, your mother got tired of living in a little box. She wanted to come back, spread out a little and try her hand at some of the things she had studied on the road. So we winterized the *Rambling Rose* and hunkered down here so she could do what she needs to do."

"You're saying she's a work in progress." It was weird, thinking of her mom that way.

"Aren't we all?"

"I guess."

He chuckled. "What, you thought it was all over once you hit twenty-five?"

"Maybe thirty."

"Funny kid." He turned his back on her and went to work with the planer. "You want to help her, then do exactly what you're doing. Spend some time with her, and tell her you love her just the way she is."

"I . . ." Wow, that one hit her in the gut, not because it was a low blow, but because her first instinctive response wasn't "Of course I love her." It was far more complicated than that. "Okay, I'll do that. And thanks."

"You're welcome. And, sweetie?"

"Yeah, Dad?"

"Give yourself some time, too, okay? You don't have to figure it all out in the next few weeks."

That wasn't what she expected to hear, but it resonated. "Good talk, big guy." She kissed his cheek. "Have fun with your doors. Come on, Rex."

He bounded out of an empty stall, scattering shavings with infectious enthusiasm. *Oh, boy, we're going inside!*

"I envy you," she told the dog as they made the short, chilly trek along the plowed and shoveled pathways. "You always have so much fun."

Not that she wasn't having fun. It was just . . .

Sigh. Complicated.

Back in the office, she thumbed through her mom's binder once more, then plonked in the chair and went for the voicemail, where there were three new messages and two archived requests she was letting sit until she got a ruling from Krista. As she keyed in the password, though, the main line rang.

She connected. "Mustang Ridge Ranch, main office. This is Jenny speaking. How can I help you?"

"So official," Nick teased.

Sparklers lit in her stomach. "Hey, there. Done for the day already?"

"Yep. You?"

"I can be. Did you have something in mind?"

"You up for bowling?"

"Always." It was a Three Ridges winter staple, with all the nostalgia that went with it. "No leagues tonight?"

"They don't start until nine. I figured we could work around that, maybe grab a bite to eat after. Or, you know, some groceries."

"Count me in." And count her excited, far more so than a bowling date probably warranted. But that was one of the very nice things about having been away from Three Ridges for so long—all the stuff that had gotten old and tired by the time she escaped felt new again.

"Great. Pick you up in an hour?"

"Perfect."

There was a pause before he said, "There's one more thing. My dad wants us to come out to the cabin for dinner one of these days."

"Us?" She wasn't surprised that the word brought a quiver. Except it didn't exactly feel like dread.

"You and me. Well, I suspect it's more that he wants to meet you, and figures I'm part of a package deal." He cleared his throat. "In this context, I mean. And for the record, this isn't a meet-the-parents thing."

"Except that he's your parent, and I'm meeting him."

"Okay, granted. But it's a no pressure, no expectations sort of deal." He paused. "I think he misses seeing new people, living up there."

Her heart tugged. "Oh, that's a low blow."

"So you'll come?"

Had there ever been any doubt? "Count me in. When?"

"This Sunday. We'll leave around lunchtime."

22

Due to a rash of emergency calls and mechanical trouble with the Vetmobile, it was actually two Sundays later before they set out for the foothills. Which was good news and bad news, as far as Jenny was concerned.

It was good because she and Nick had been together pretty much every night over the past two weeks, enjoying each other. It didn't seem to matter what they did, they had fun. It was bad, though, because for all the fun they were having, now there was a countdown in the back of her mind. She was there for fifteen more days. Fourteen. Thirteen. Where before the days had loomed long, now they flew. And the last thing she ever expected was for part of her to wish she could have more time in Mustang Ridge.

She and Nick hadn't talked about it, though. The easy good-bye was part of their unspoken agreement.

They debated bad sci-fi movies as they drove to the foothills, and the two-hour trip passed in a flash. Before she knew it, he was turning off the mountain road onto the long, plowed path leading to his father's cabin. The dark green pine trees were heavy with snow, and dragged along the top of the truck in places, but then the forest opened up and they emerged back into the thin winter sunlight, into full view of the cabin—a small, snug log structure with fresh chinking, solar panels, and a curl of smoke coming from the stone chimney.

"How cute." Jenny pressed her nose to the passenger window. "It looks just like a gingerbread house!"

He grinned. "Don't tell my dad that. He thinks it's rough-and-tumble, and extra manly to live in a hunting cabin full-time."

"I'll keep that in mind."

As they tromped up the porch steps, knocking snow off their boots, the green-painted door swung open and out stepped an older, leaner version of Nick leading a big gray dog on a short leash. Age-stooped and grizzled, Bill Masterson had his son's piercing hazel eyes and long lashes. Or maybe that was vice versa.

Nick slung an arm around her shoulders, hugging her tight. "Dad, this is Jenny. Don't scare her off, okay?"

A funny sort of flutter worked through Jenny at seeing what her lover would look like in twenty-five years, followed by a queer twist at the knowledge that she wouldn't be around to see it. Telling herself to get over it—*hello, hormones*—she stepped forward and held out a hand. "Mr. Masterson. It's a pleasure."

He took her hand, but only to pull her into a hug. "It's Bill, young lady, and the pleasure is mine."

A whine-growl had her drawing back, but he gave

the big dog a reproving "Shush." Then, to Jenny, he said, "Let Molly sniff your hand."

Jenny eyed the creature, seeing the wolf in the shape of Molly's face and body. "I need both hands to work."

His eyes glinted. "Chicken?"

"Why, is that her favorite?" But at Nick's go-ahead nod, she obliged, holding out her hand for Molly to get her scent.

"Friend," Bill said to the dog. "She's a friend, got it?" When the long, thick tail gave a slow sweep, he nodded and unclipped the leash. "Okay, go on."

Molly barked and bounded away into the snow, making a fast circuit of the cabin with flowing strides that showed her feral heritage. It was like watching wild mustangs streaming across a grassy field, perfectly in their element. The snow sprayed with each powerful lunge, haloing the wolf-dog against the dark pine background and making Jenny yearn.

"Want your camera?" Nick asked with a chuckle in his voice.

"Later," she said, determined to be a good guest. "But, yeah. I'd love to film her." To Nick's father, she said, "Molly is absolutely gorgeous, Bill, as is your cabin. You've got a piece of heaven out here—that's for sure."

The dimples, it turned out, were hereditary. They came into view as Nick's father grinned and gestured them toward the cabin. "Come in, come in. Let me show you around!"

Over the next couple of hours, she learned very

quickly that the father had as much indefatigable energy as his son. He showed them around the surprisingly spacious three-room cabin, explaining the renovations he'd made to winterize the structure while minimizing his carbon footprint as much as possible. There were solar panels on the roof and another array higher up, as well as composting systems, water purification, and two wind turbines.

Jenny barely had time to marvel at each of the systems before they were off to the next, until they circled back around to the driveway so she could retrieve Old Faithful from the truck and snap away, delighted, as the men played with Molly in the snow. Later, after the quick night had descended and they had holed up in the snug cabin, they dined on fish Bill had caught just that morning from the fishing shack he had built at a nearby lake.

"You might think I'd be a vegetarian," Bill said, gesturing with his fork, "after so many years as a vet. But I never was a very good herbivore, and it's deuced hard to grow veggies off-season without a greenhouse.

"Is that a hint?" Nick asked.

A glint of humor entered those familiar eyes. "Maybe."

"Should make a fun summer project. Sign me up."

Bill transferred his attention. "How about you, Jenny?"

She kept it light. "Unfortunately, I'm only here for another couple of weeks." It was on the tip of her tongue to offer that she'd be coming back to the area to film, and maybe she could coordinate the timing with the greenhouse project, but she kept that to herself. Nick hadn't said anything about keeping in touch, and she didn't want to be the one to bring it up.

"Only two more weeks?" Bill said. "Is that when your new season starts?"

Apparently more information had changed hands than she had realized. What else had Nick said about her? "Actually, I'll get there ten days before I need to report. A bunch of the crew members are doing a Mayan ruin tour, really off the beaten track. We've even got a small grant to do some filming."

"It sounds warm."

"It will be. Though lately I've been seeing the appeal of cold weather more than I used to."

"You get accustomed to it. Right, son?"

"Humans are pretty adaptable. Is there more salad?"

The conversation bounced from vet stories to filming stories to local rumors and back again, and before she knew it, dinner was over and Bill was kicking them out to take a moonlit stroll while he dealt with the dishes. After a brief losing argument over the dishes thing, they followed orders. Jenny snagged Old Faithful on her way through the door.

This place made her want to take pictures. Lots of them.

"It's dark out," Nick warned as they took a wide loop around the cabin, following one of the trails Molly had cut in the deep snow.

"You don't say." She grinned up at him. "There's moon enough, and I'm a professional."

"So I've heard."

Her chin came up. "You want proof?" She stopped and lifted the camera. "Look a little to your left, focusing past me."

"I don't—"

She took two pictures in quick succession, *clicka-click*, and then checked the digital images. She gave a low chuckle. "You look very stern." And, with the fur-lined ruff of his hood framing the sides of his neck and the cold, harsh winter behind him, he could've been an explorer, a pioneer. The silver-blue light darkened his hair and his eyes, yet caressed the high, sharp planes of his cheekbones and the angle of his jaw. He looked shadowy and dangerous, yet at the same time solid, reliable, and like he belonged. Her heart took a long, slow roll in her chest. "Smile this time."

"I'm not—"

"Who's the professional here?"

"You are." His eyes took on an interested gleam. "But how about . . ."

She snapped a couple more shots, catching an expression that she thought could sell anything from chocolate to deodorant. "How about what?"

"You let me do you next."

"With your father watching from the cabin?"

"Ha-ha. I meant take your picture and you know it."

Her fingers tightened involuntarily. "You want to use my camera?"

"Oh. Touched a nerve, have I?"

"No, it's just . . . No." Changing angles, she snapped a frame and caught him just right, wearing a look of devilish challenge that no woman could possibly resist. At least she sure couldn't. "Okay, it's a deal. But you've got to do everything I say for the next half hour."

"Fifteen minutes, and I have veto power if things get too weird."

"Define weird."

"You know, nudity, marshmallow fluff, that sort of thing. Which, for the record, isn't the slightest bit weird for me in the bedroom, but crosses the line when we're talking about being out in my old man's yard in a couple of feet of snow."

"So noted. And it's a deal. Now, make a snowball and throw it past me. And so help me, if you hit the camera . . ." She let her warning glare finish the threat.

"Awww. Spoilsport." But he did as she asked, aiming way wide of her so she captured the spray of snow gone silver in the moonlight without catching the snowball in the face. "Good, good. Keep going. And remember, you're having fun!"

She took frame after frame, and damn, the camera loved him. He moved like a wild mustang, smooth and sinuous, yet so powerful that she wanted to stop and stare. But she had long ago learned that it was better to have the image in her camera than inside her head, so she changed angles and kept shooting.

Then, suddenly, he stiffened and stared into the trees. "Hear that?"

She froze, pulse kicking as she measured the distance between them and the cabin. She didn't hear anything, but that didn't mean there wasn't something out there with claws and teeth.

"I don't—" she began, but broke off as a distant howl rose up through the octaves. The sound shivered on the air, wild and boundless, sending tingly chills through her body. "Oh," she breathed. "It's beautiful."

The cry trailed to silence, but before she could do anything more than sigh, another, answering howl came from farther north. Then another. And another.

Within moments, the forest rang with wolf song that was far enough away that there was little danger, yet close enough that her throat tightened with emotion and her skin prickled with atavistic fear. She wished Old Faithful could capture the sound. That wasn't in the camera's repertoire, though, so she captured the look on Nick's face instead.

Alert and focused, he made her think of an alpha stallion testing the air and standing ready to protect his mares, only in this case the mare was her. She wasn't used to having someone put himself between her and danger, and sure wouldn't have expected to like it. But an electric thrill ran through her body as a chilly breeze moved his rumpled hair and the fur ruff of his parka, making the moment come alive.

Clicka-click.

And that was it. She had gotten the *a-ha*, the perfect moment, The Shot. Wow. She didn't need to look back at the picture to know it was right. Like that night in the storm when she was fifteen, she just *knew*. She lowered Old Faithful as the howls trailed off and the night went silent around them. Then she held out the camera. "Your turn," she said softly. "That was incredible."

He took the camera, fingers lingering on hers. "Yes, it was." And his full-on eye contact made her think again of the stallion, and realize that he wasn't just talking about the photos or the wolves.

The thud of her pulse stayed high, not from fear now, but from desire. He tugged on their joined hands, brought her in close, and brushed his lips across hers in the faintest, featheriest kiss.

She leaned in, seeking more. More flutters of desire, more of the heat, more of him. They kissed long and slow, until the night seemed warm and he wasn't so much holding her as anchoring her in a world gone surreal. Passion pounded through her—she wanted him naked, here and now, wanted him inside her.

Snow, she reminded herself. *Father in cabin. Big wolf-dog who doesn't like sudden movements in her territory.*

Still, she nearly whimpered when he eased away. It was gratifying to see the heat in his eyes, though, and hear the rasp of his breath. "Let's head in," he suggested. "It's getting cold."

"You don't want to take any pictures?"

"Not right now." He looped an arm around her and steered them back toward the cabin. "I could do with some coffee. How about you?"

There was no real reason for her to feel off balance as they reentered the cabin, no reason for her to want to give him a huge hug and then cling, feeling like the twelve days she had left weren't nearly enough. *This is good*, she told herself as she stripped off her scarf and gave it a little twirl. *We're good.*

Clicka-click.

She looked up at the noise and came face-to-lens with Old Faithful. "Ack! Don't—" She swiped at him as he took another couple of frames.

He dodged. "Why?"

Because I don't like having my picture taken. "Because it's adjusted for moonlight."

"Oh." He held it out. "Could you fix it for me?"

She took the camera and made the necessary tweaks, then hesitated before giving it back. Photos invariably made her look like she had the grace and IQ of a potato. Still, a deal was a deal, and she wasn't backing out now.

Handing the camera over, she said, "Just remember, you drool when you sleep, and I have Ruth's email address."

"More blackmail!" said a voice from the mudroom doorway. "That's perfect!"

Startled not just by Bill's appearance—and the flush that came from knowing he had heard the part about Nick drooling in his sleep—but also by his enthusiasm for the subject, Jenny turned. "Wait. What?"

"You want blackmail ammo, I've got some for you. It's waiting on the breakfast bar, along with coffee and dessert."

Nick's heartfelt groan came from behind her. "Not the photo album!"

Jenny went on whole-body alert. "Are we talking about family pictures here?"

"You betcha." Bill thumped an album lying on the wooden counter. Arrayed around it were a trio of steaming mugs and a plate piled high with brownies. "Come and get it."

Grinning, Jenny headed for the kitchen, not even minding the *clicka-clicks* anymore. "Tell me there are baby pictures." Not because she was particularly into babies, but because she had a feeling it would make Nick squirm.

"And the year he was a Ninja Turtle for Halloween."

"Awww."

"Kill me now."

She spared Nick a glance as she took her seat at the breakfast bar. "If it makes you feel any better, I'm willing to share a really bad prom picture."

"No Halloween Barbie?"

"Nope. Krista and I had Halloween down to a science from an early age—she was always a cowgirl and I was a paparazzo. Not sure if that was life imitating art or the other way around." She grinned over at him only to be met by the business end of Old Faithful and the familiar *clicka-click*. "Stop that."

"Nope. My turn, remember?"

She sniffed and turned to Bill. "I can't tell you how much I'm going to enjoy this."

His dimples deepened. "This is just my collection of favorite Nick pics. If you're a glutton for punishment, I've got a couple more boxes under the bed."

Nick's groan nearly drowned out her exclamation of "My hero!"

They spent the next half hour going through the album, which went chronologically from baby pictures to school photos and graduation snapshots, mixed in among candids that gave her glimpses of Nick as a jock, Boy Scout, and animal lover.

When she lingered on one of Nick as a young teen bottle-nursing a wobbly calf, Bill said, "He was never one to skip from one dream job to another. With him, even if he played with the idea of being an astronaut or a rock star, being a vet was always on the list."

Jenny eyed Nick. "I can see the astronaut. But a rock star?"

"I had an earring. Briefly."

Bill paused on a photo of Nick with a dark-haired beauty with a kind smile and eyes that reminded Jenny of her gran, where happiness mingled with humor. "This is Nick's mother, Mandy. She loved wildflowers, watercolors, and rooting for the Boston Red Sox, even when they stank." He cut a look in her direction. "She would have liked you."

That brought a pang, but Jenny kept her smile firmly in place and said, "She's a lovely woman. I wish I had gotten a chance to meet her." She didn't look in Nick's direction.

Through it all, he kept Old Faithful close at hand, clicking away, until Jenny more or less forgot about the camera and concentrated on the fun of poking at him for a couple of boy-band haircuts and the infamous earring. The photos got sparser once they passed the college years, with just a few from his years in vet school.

By then, she could hardly sit still. "Tell me you've got Africa pictures."

His father's face lit. "You want pics of Nick in Africa? You got 'em." He flipped the page to reveal two huge-seeming eight-by-tens of the same arrow-straight dirt roadway on a flat, dusty plain, with a baobab tree on one side and a small collection of thatch and plywood huts on the other. One was taken at dawn, with the pale blue sky dotted with pink-tinged clouds and a trio of skinny goats dozing near the houses. The other was taken during a gorgeous red-and-orange sunset that seemed to set the plains ablaze. "He sent me these the first week he was there. Took 'em himself." He skimmed his fingertips over the snapshots. "I thought they were damn fine."

"They're beautiful," she said truthfully. "Magical."

"It's hard to screw up an African sunset," Nick said dryly, but set aside the camera to lean over the pictures.

There were more photos of him in Africa than there had been from his school years, as if he'd been trying to make up for being abroad by sending lots of emails. She sure knew how that one worked. She marveled over pictures of him with friends, patients, and coworkers, and treating everything from a young goatherd's dog to a baby gazelle with a broken leg.

"This is my favorite." Bill turned to a two-page spread clipped from a magazine. Entitled "The Long Road to Twenty-Thirty," the article led with a half-page picture of a dozen or so men and women wearing Twenty-Thirty Project T-shirts and mugging for the camera, standing in front of a huge baobab tree—possibly the same one from the other pictures. In the middle, flanked by a blonde on one side and a dark-haired guy with a flyaway beard on the other, was Nick.

Jenny read the article, fingertips trailing over before and after pictures of a village, showing new livestock enclosures, tighter houses, and a working well. According to the article, those improvements were just the tip of an iceberg that included more productivity from the crops and animals, better schools and unprecedented access to health care. Swallowing past a lump in her throat, she said, "You changed people's lives."

He shrugged, doing an aw shucks. "It was—"

"He sure did," Bill said proudly, tapping his son's image, and then that of the pretty blonde beside him. "And Lily, of course." He said it like Jenny should know the woman.

Had Nick stiffened, or was she imagining it?

Cool fingers walked down the back of her neck and her stomach tightened. *Leave it*, she told herself. It wasn't her business. They were just having . . . *Damn it.* "Who's Lily?"

Nick hesitated before he said, "She was—still is—a hydroengineer in the Twenty-Thirty Project."

The quivers didn't go away.

Jenny studied the clipping, seeing the way Nick and the woman leaned into each other. "She was your girlfriend, I'm guessing." *I'm not jealous, I'm not*. She didn't have any right to be jealous, didn't have any claim to him beyond a winter-break fling.

Nick glanced away. "We were engaged."

Scratch that. She was totally jealous.

23

Nick got them out of there soon after, pleading a long drive and an early morning, and waving off his old man's apologies for having stepped in it.

Jenny had done her best to cover her surprise at the whole ex-fiancée thing, but she had obviously been rattled. And, just as obviously, Nick had screwed up by not telling her. His father had buttonholed him and made that one clear, in no uncertain terms.

"Sorry about that," he said as they trudged to the Vetmobile, with their shoulders bumping but their hands in their pockets. "I should've mentioned Lily before now. I just—"

"You don't have to explain. I'm the one who's sorry. Your exes are none of my business."

"Then why are you mad at me?"

She stopped and turned to face him, expression earnest. "I'm not mad at you, truly. I'm mad at myself for acting like this. And to be honest, I'm trying to figure out where it's coming from. It's not like I thought I was your first or something." She hunched her shoulders. "It's just . . . I don't know. I need some time to think."

"Whatever you want to know, just ask."

"Not yet." She turned and set out for the truck once more. When he caught up and got her door for her, she said, "Thanks. Now I've got a favor to ask."

"Anything. Well, within reason, anyway. I'm not too keen on walking home."

She rewarded him with a wan smile. "Could you give me the drive to figure it out? Normally when my brain gets all jammed up like this, I take a walk, have some alone time, and get my head straight. I don't want to leave things weird between us overnight, though, so I'm just asking for the drive time."

Something shifted in his chest. He moved in, hunkering close to her. "Jenny, sweetheart. You can have . . ." *Whatever you want*, he started to say, but that would've been too much, too soon, so he substituted "All the time you need." And even that wasn't entirely true, because their remaining days were numbered.

Her breath puffed out white in the chill air. "Thank you." She eased up and brushed her lips across his.

He didn't let himself think it was a good-bye kiss. But at the same time, he wasn't sure what to think. Did she feel betrayed, or was she truly mad at herself? *She's not a game player*, he reminded himself as he fired up the engine.

To his relief, the silent drive wasn't uncomfortable. In fact, it gave him a chance to settle down, too, and get his own thoughts in order. And, he realized, consider

what Jenny might be thinking and feeling, not just
about Lily but about him. About them. By the time he
pulled into the parking lot at Mustang Ridge, he
thought he had it figured out, thought he knew what to
say.

Killing the engine, he popped off his seat belt and
turned to face her. "I'd like to say something."

Her eyes widened. "I'm the one who owes you an
explanation."

"Maybe not." He took one of her hands, pressing it
between both of his, partly to warm the faint chill of
her skin and partly for emphasis. "I think I know where
you're coming from, Jenny, and I need you not to
worry. So I'd like to tell you about Lily and me, so
you'll understand."

"I'm not sure—"

He squeezed her hands. "Please."

She subsided. Nodded. "Okay. Go ahead."

He hesitated, searching for the right words. "Lily
and I went through the Twenty-Thirty Project's version
of boot camp together and hit it off. We were posted to
different rotations, but kept in touch now and then. A
few years later, and who walks into camp, but Lily. I
found out later she had requested the transfer. Anyway,
we got involved, got serious, got engaged. It was . . ."
heady, amazing, simpatico, "easy when we were traveling
together. We worked together, played together, ex-
plored together."

"In Africa." Jenny sighed. "It sounds like heaven."

"It was, in a way." In lots of ways. "We weren't in

any hurry to get married, but after a couple of years it felt right. We planned to have a simple ceremony before the end of our rotation, with our teammates and village friends as guests." He paused. "Then I got the call."

Now he saw a hint of sympathy. "That your mother was sick, you mean."

"That she was dying." The ache had mellowed some, but the scars still tugged, as did the memory of his frantic race home and that first sight of his mom, wan and shrunken, eyes dark and hollow with pain. "Lily and I decided to postpone the wedding. She visited a few times, and things were good when she was in town, but . . ." He shifted, trying to get comfortable on a truck seat that usually didn't bother him one bit. "I wasn't the same person anymore."

Instead of giving him the "yeah, I know how that is" that he halfway expected from her, Jenny frowned. "Well of course not. You had to prioritize your family for a few months. Surely she understood that."

It was hard now to remember back to those days, not because they were painful, but because they could've happened to someone else, another guy who had wanted to escape but got cut off at the pass. "Yes, she got that part. She stood by me, even flew back for the funeral with her project in a really tricky spot. But a few days later, when she started talking about us getting back out in the field, I couldn't see it."

"Your father needed you."

"At first. Then, I don't know. I got used to being

home. Before, I wanted to get away from the small-town thing. Now, I dig it."

She looked bemused. "More than Africa?"

"Yes and no. I miss it. The country, the animals, the people . . . they're amazing. But so is Wyoming, and I can't have both."

"Or Lily." Her expression had gone shuttered.

"Right. What we had worked while we were out in the field together, living the same lives. I asked her to move here, but . . ." He shook his head. "We tried the long-distance thing, but finally broke up a few months later. And, well, that's the end of the Lily-and-me story." He lifted her hand and kissed Jenny's knuckles, adding, "But this isn't even close to the end of the you-and-me story, I hope."

She straightened. "That's what I wanted to talk to you about."

But he kept going. "You need to know that I'm not hung up on Lily—it's over, truly. We still email every now and then, but like old friends. Nothing more."

"I wasn't worried about that." Her voice sounded funny, though, like that might not be the whole story.

"Okay, then, how about this? You also don't have to worry that I'm looking to get married, settle down, start a family, any of that stuff. Yeah, I was engaged, but that experience taught me just how tough it is for two people—especially two people who are driven by their careers—to make a life together. It also taught me not to ever expect someone else to change who they are for me—and that it's not fair for me to even ask."

Her shoulders dropped, but she didn't say anything.

Relieved that she was relieved, he continued. "So you don't have to worry. Yes, things have gotten pretty intense between us, but I'm not asking for anything here. When it's time for you to go, we'll say good-bye. No hard feelings. Just good memories."

She swallowed, then nodded. "Okay. I . . . Okay. That helps put things in perspective."

"Like I said, I figured you needed to hear that before you made any decisions to, you know, cut things off early." He wanted to keep touching her, but let go of her hand instead, giving her room. "I hope you won't. We've got twelve days left, nearly down to eleven now, and I don't want to miss out on any of them."

"Eleven days." She repeated the number with faint surprise, like she hadn't been doing the countdown.

"Almost. So . . . what do you say? Can I see you tomorrow? Or—and I'm probably pushing it—do you want to follow me back to the clinic?"

"Yeah, that's pushing it." But there was a flash of humor in her eyes, like she didn't mind that he had tried.

"Tomorrow, then. I'll think of something fun. Pick you up at seven?"

She hesitated, then nodded. "Okay. I'll see you then. And, Nick?"

"Yeah?"

"Thanks for telling me about Lily. I'd say I'm sorry it didn't work out, but that would be a lie." She leaned in and cupped his jaw in her cool, soft hand. "I wouldn't trade the past few weeks for anything."

He touched his lips to hers. "Me, either." And—thank God—it didn't feel like a good-bye kiss, after all. It felt like a see you tomorrow.

Okay. You're okay. Safely inside, Jenny leaned against the door and concentrated on breathing as the sound of Nick's footsteps faded on the path. *You can handle this.*

She hadn't thrown herself at him and clung, and she hadn't busted out with a chorus of "Why don't we stay in touch after I leave?" the moment they hit the driveway, which had more or less been her plan. In fact, she should be grateful that he insisted on going first in the explanation department, because his side of things had negated most of what she had come up with. All of it, really.

"Did you have a nice time?" The question came from the living room.

She looked over to find her mom sitting next to the fire with Rex at her feet, a book in her hands, and an empty wineglass at her elbow. Rose was still dressed for the day, in gray pants and a dusty pink sweater, with her hair up in a French twist that was only a little wispy around the edges. "Hey," Jenny said. "Is everything okay?" Was it bad that she was hoping for a problem? Ranch stuff would be a welcome diversion right now.

"Everything is fine. Can't I wait up for my girl?"

Roused from his fire-warmed nap, Rex padded over to Jenny, gave her a perfunctory sniff, and then did a doggy double take when he caught Molly's scent. Jenny patted him while he wriggled around her, his ridiculousness easing the tight knot in her chest.

Setting the book aside, her mom rose and headed for the stairs, beckoning with a sudden air of suppressed excitement. "Come on. I've got something to show you."

"Now?" A glance at the grandfather clock in the dining room clued her in that it wasn't nearly as late as it felt, closer to ten o'clock than midnight. "Okay, sure." *Please, no more painting.* She needed some time to herself, not another project.

The treads gave their familiar creaks beneath them both, seeming unusually loud, and Rex's toenails clicked a little on the wood, making Jenny think they were about due for a trim. Because it was easier to think about stuff like that than things like "I'm not asking for anything" and "When it's time for you to go, we'll say good-bye."

"Well?" her mom said. "Are you ready to see it?"

Jenny blinked, surprised to find them standing outside her bedroom door. "Ready to see . . . You mean it's finished?"

"An hour ago. Isn't it exciting?"

Guilt stung, because she didn't have an ounce of excitement inside her just then. "Don't you want to wait for Dad and the others, and we can film things and make a big deal about it?"

"We can do that tomorrow. I want this first time to be just the two of us. So go on . . . close your eyes."

"But—"

"Close 'em, or I'll do it for you. And keep your voice down. Your father is asleep."

Trying to get into the mood—her mom had put in a ton of work, after all, and deserved the *ta-daa* moment—Jenny put her hands over her eyes and nodded. "Okay. They're closed. Bring it on." *Be happy. Be grateful.* It wasn't her mom's fault that she and Nick had hit a fork and gone in completely different directions.

She heard the door swing open, and then her mom grabbed her arm and tugged, saying, "Come in, come in!" much as Nick's father had done when they arrived at the cabin.

They stepped inside the bedroom, which smelled like paint, fabric, and *eau de* day-old glue gun fumes, more like a craft store than the place where Jenny had spent countless hours hunched over her laptop, doing equal amounts of homework and instant messaging, or sitting cross-legged on the bed with Krista, deep in discussions of boys, music, and horses. Even the floor felt different, with thick padding beneath their feet, so the creaks stopped once they were past the threshold.

The door thunked closed, and then her mother said in a hushed voice, "Ready? On three. One . . . two . . . three!"

Jenny dropped her hands, opened her eyes, and blinked around in relief. *Hey, what do you know? This isn't half bad.* Despite her fears of tie-dye and shag, she had gotten a thick beige area rug and a padded brown-and-blue ottoman that worked really nicely with the pale cream walls and white trim. The pictures were gone from the mirror, but her photos of the storm had been mounted in shadowboxes and hung on the wall, and a small album on the desk was open to the crazy blueness of her prom dress.

The bed wore the pretty yellow spread and the yellow-and-blue pillows she had picked out, and the curtains were printed with yellow-centered daisies with curling green leaves. And standing there on the dresser was the crazy-ass ceramic horse from her mom's first design, only in mustard yellow rather than fire-engine red.

Darned if it didn't look kind of cool, the way she had it.

"Well? What do you think? Do you love it?"

"I . . ." Tears threatened out of nowhere, closing her throat and robbing her lungs of air.

The light trickled out of her mom's eyes. "Jenny?"

"It's . . ." She couldn't put the words together. The pretty room threatened to spin, making things worse because she knew she was blowing it. She could see the hurt she was causing, the confusion.

"You hate it."

"No! No, I don't. I love it. It's just . . . Give me a second here, okay?" She couldn't even wrap her head around enough of her thoughts to understand why she was stuck between wanting to dive onto that big bed and burrow into the pillows, and backing out, closing the door, and jumping on the first plane headed anywhere but here.

"It's the horse, isn't it?" Rose's voice sharpened.

"You said you hated the horse and I didn't listen. I thought if you saw it like this . . . Well, never mind. We can fix it." Whisking to the dresser, she swept up the ceramic beast and jammed it under her arm, so its bared teeth looked poised to take a chomp out of her breast. "There! Is that better?"

Jenny's blood heated. "Would you just listen to me for a second? I love the room. I even dig the horse. You were right about it, and I was totally wrong."

That got her a narrow-eyed glare. "You're just saying that."

"I'm not. Put it back."

Rex followed the back-and-forth with worried eyes.

Rose turned away, shielding the statue with her body, so it looked like the creature was peering around her to leer at Jenny with a ceramic *nyah-nyah.* "He'll look lovely on the mantel downstairs."

"Gran will have a cow." Jenny reached past her, grabbed the outstretched foreleg, and tugged. "Give him here."

"Stop it!" Her mom swatted at her, eyes firing. "You only want him because I'm taking him away from you."

Jenny pulled. "I want him because he's yellow and he looks awesome in here. And because you picked him out for me." There. That had almost come out the way she wanted it to.

Her mom wasn't listening, though. Eyes wild enough to make Jenny want to take a step back, she leaned in and hissed, "Let. Go."

"Jeez, take a breath, will you?" Jenny yanked on the horse. "You're acting crazy."

Rex scratched at the door.

"You're scaring the dog." Rose pulled back, nearly breaking Jenny's grip. "Knock it off."

"You knock it off. I'm trying to apologize, but you're not listening to me!"

"Let go!"

"I'm sorry that I jammed up. I should've told you right away that this room rocks. Which it does. Now give me the horse." With that, Jenny gave the kind of jerk she would've used to get a full-size horse moving when it wanted to stick all fours in place.

"No!" Her mom yanked back, teeth bared.

Crack! The horse's foreleg snapped off in Jenny's hand, sending her reeling. She backpedaled, bounced off the corner of the mattress, and plopped down on the edge of the bed, staring.

Rose's eyes filled with tears as she cradled the statue like a baby. After a second, the wetness spilled over and tracked down her cheeks.

"Mom, stop." It wasn't an order this time, more of a plea. Jenny dropped the broken piece in her pocket, rose, and crossed the room. It felt strange to reach out to her mother, even stranger to take her hand and find it soft, with none of the calluses she remembered.

"I can't . . . I don't . . ." Wet eyes met hers, confused and hopeless. "I can't do this anymore, Jenny. I just can't."

"Let's go downstairs." She took the broken horse

from her mother's unresisting grip, realizing that this wasn't about her, or at least not entirely. "We'll have some coffee or something, and talk." When was the last time she had said something like that to her mother? That was usually Krista's line, her sphere of comfort. Only Krista wasn't here, and Jenny was the one left with a sense of *what the heck?* and the feeling that this went way deeper than she had guessed.

Looking so much older than Jenny had ever seen her—older, even, than Gran—Rose simply nodded, turned for the door, and walked away from her latest project without a backward glance.

Jenny wedged the yellow horse under her arm and followed, wishing she could turn back the clock by twenty minutes or so and give herself a big kick in the ass just as she walked through the front door.

Downstairs, she hit the lights in the kitchen and set the broken horse on the butcher-block counter. Then she pulled out a stool and pointed to it. "Sit."

Rex, who had followed them down, plopped down instantly, then cocked his head. *Cookie?*

Rose, on the other hand, took her place at the counter, stared at the horse for a moment, and then put her elbows on the table and her face in her hands, finishing it off with a groan. "This is so embarrassing. I can't believe I just did that. What is *wrong* with me?"

"Well, if it helps, you didn't do it alone. I seem to have reverted to being fifteen for a few minutes there."

"When you were fifteen, I could've coped."

Jenny didn't know how to ask what happened without it sounding like an accusation. "Would you like some wine?" She could sure use some. First the thing with Nick, and now she was teetering on a familypoc-alypse. *But, hey, wine,* she thought, pulling a decent pi-not grigio out of the cabinet and trying not to notice that its color came very close to matching the horse.

"I've already had two glasses" came from behind her mom's hands.

Which would explain some of what was going on. Not all of it, though. "Have another." Jenny poured generous glasses for each of them, and plonked them down at the table. "You want to cook something?" Which could start a kitchen doomsday of its own, but right now she'd do pretty much anything to get that bleak, crushed look out of her mom's eyes.

Rose uncovered her face, looking like she was con-sidering it, but then she shook her head and reached for her wine. "Nah. Let's eat tomorrow's coffee cake in-stead."

Gran would be steamed over having her breakfast plans usurped, but Jenny headed for the fridge and pulled out the perfectly frosted ring cake, along with a bowl of whipped cream and a pint of sliced strawber-ries. "I'm not sure this goes together."

"Throw some Grand Marnier on top and it'll work." Her mom reached across to select a huge knife that said "butcher"—or maybe "slasher film"—far more than it did coffee cake. "How big of a piece do you want?"

"Let me." Jenny snagged the knife, whacked off a few slices, and set the knife out of reach when she went to get the liqueur. She poured a couple of hefty slugs over the cake, slapped on some berries and cream, and pushed one of the plates over as she took the stool beside her mother. "Dig in."

Her mom picked up her fork, but then just sat there, staring at a dessert that should've delighted her, not because it was a foodie's dream, but because the theft would annoy the bejeebers out of Gran in the morning. And if that wasn't enough to spark her interest, then this was serious.

"What's wrong?" Jenny asked softly after a long moment of silence. "What's going on with you these days? It's not just me, is it?"

More silence, lasting longer than a moment. More like a mini-eternity in which Jenny tried to think of something better to say, and her mom just sat and stared.

But then Rose moved, forking up a bite of the cake and eating it with a grudging expression of *not bad*. After chewing and swallowing, she said, "I've got a great life."

When nothing more seemed to be forthcoming, Jenny said, "Okay."

Way to rock the interview.

It seemed to do the trick, though, because her mom continued. "Most women my age would kill to have the opportunities I've had. I've traveled across the continent and back in both directions, taken classes, been to amazing workshops, seen things I never would've thought I'd see in person."

After a pause, Jenny said, "You sound like you're

trying to convince yourself." When her mom glanced over, she risked a small smile. "Been there, done that, recognize it. You . . . ah, getting bored with retirement?"

"Retirement." Rose made a face. "What kind of a word is *retire* anyway? Go to bed, leave the field of battle, withdraw from an argument . . . none of those definitions work for me. But your father loves it, doesn't he? He loves traveling, loves the *Rambling Rose*, loves meeting new people, seeing new things, going where the road takes us . . . And that's the problem."

Jenny's stool felt tippy, like one leg was shorter than the others. Centering herself and trying to find the right balance, she said, "Because you don't want to travel anymore and he does?"

"Because I don't know what I want anymore! I thought I did." She gestured around the room with her wineglass, sloshing the pale yellow liquid. "I thought I wanted to be in here with your grandmother. But it turned out I don't really want to cook."

"You don't?" Krista would undoubtedly be relieved, but Jenny was just confused.

"No. I want what your Gran gets out of cooking." Rose shot Jenny a sidelong look. "And if you ever tell her that, I'll deny it, and then get you back somehow. That's a promise."

"You . . . right." Jenny shook her head, not sure whether she was trying to clear it or rattle some of these revelations into place. Her mom might be a little buzzed, but this had the ring of truth. More, it made sense. Sort of, at least. "What about the decorating?"

"It's okay. I thought . . ." Rose shook her head, drained her wine and went for a refill. "I don't know what I thought I would get out of it. Doing the master bedroom was fun. So was your room, until . . . I don't know. I got caught up and went overboard, just like I did in the kitchen over the summer."

Jenny didn't dare agree with her on that one, but she wasn't going to argue, either. "Maybe something else, then?"

"What, like quilting? Stained glass? Write a book?"

"Maybe."

"I wish . . ." Rose glanced out the window, though there wasn't anything to see but blackness. "I wish this winter was over. Everything always seems easier in the springtime."

Impulsively, drawn by the sadness in her mother's voice, the slump of her shoulders, Jenny reached across and took her hand. "You'll figure something out. You always did."

"That was before. I'm not the same person I used to be."

"Sure you are." Jenny squeezed their joined hands. "If you want a reminder, I can go back outside and pretend to be just coming home way past curfew, so you can ground me."

"Hmm." Rose considered it for a moment, then shook her head with a faraway smile. "I'll pass. Thanks for the offer, though." Her eyes went to the yellow horse. "Poor guy, missing his leg."

"I've got it right here." Jenny produced the broken-off piece from her pocket and set it on the table between them. "And for the record, I really do love my room. It's amazing. I was in shock seeing it, I think, and caught up in my own problems. I'm sorry I didn't say the right things."

"Problems?" Her mom raised an eyebrow. "Did something go wrong with Nick? It seemed like you two were doing so well."

"He . . ." Maybe it was seeing glimpses of the mom she remembered, maybe it was the wine, but Jenny found herself swallowing past the sudden pressure in her throat to say, "We drove out to visit his dad today, and were having a great time until the subject of his ex-fiancée came up and things got weird." She stared glumly at her glass. "I think it wasn't so much jealousy, really, or the way it reminded me of how much I don't know about him. It was more . . . I don't know. Like it brought home what it looks like after things are over." And how they would soon be headed in that direction.

"Oh, sweetie." Her mom reached out and gripped her fingers. "Do you want me to be mad at him? I will, if you want."

Jenny's lips curved despite the sad echoes inside her. "That sounds like something Krista would say."

"Where do you think you two came from, a vegetable garden? Seriously, though, I'm sorry things got weird. Did you guys work it out?"

"I think things are going to be okay." As long as she played by their original rules. And she so didn't want to dwell on that right now. So she squeezed her mom's hand. "And none of that is an excuse for my flatlining when you showed me my new room."

Her mom hesitated. Then, apparently deciding to let her change the subject, she said, "It's okay. No biggie."

"Yes, it is a biggie. Thank you. Truly. It's wonderful."

"Well then." Lips curving, her mom focused on the horse. "I guess this guy's sacrifice wasn't in vain." She paused. "My .38 is upstairs. We could take him out back and shoot him. Might be a fitting way to end the evening."

Jenny snorted so hard she sucked wine up her nose, where it fizzed and burned. Coughing, laughing, she waved off the napkin her mother held out, and grabbed her own. "I was thinking more along the lines of Crazy Glue."

"Do you think it would work?"

"Worth a try. Better yet, we can give him to Dad and let him experiment. He's probably got some NASA-level epoxy he's been dying to use on something."

"Probably." But her mom gave the maimed statue a dubious look. "I could get you another one."

Jenny shook her head. "I like this one. Just think of the story we'll be able to tell about him, years down the road when your grandkids ask what happened to his leg." Her voice tried to wobble on the part about grandkids, but she didn't let it. She needed to get this right.

A smile bloomed on her mother's face, gentle and genuine. "Thank you for that, sweetheart." She stroked the gleaming yellow glaze, trailing a fingertip along the broken spot. "Yes. That's exactly what we'll do. We'll tell them that you had a tantrum and broke the horse."

Jenny laughed. "Oh, fine. Be that way." But inwardly, she thought, *Finally*. Finally, she had said the right thing at the right time, and she and her mother had managed to have a real conversation. Given how the rest of the day had gone, she would totally take it.

24

The following week passed in a blur. Jenny spent her days holed up in Krista's office and her nights at Nick's place. They went out some evenings, stayed in others, and put some serious mileage on his mattress. It was fun, easy, and everything she had thought she wanted six weeks earlier.

Now, though . . . she didn't know what she wanted.

"Five more days," she told Rex, feeling a sting that should've worn down by now, for all the times she had probed at the sore spot.

His tail thumped. *You're talking to me but it doesn't look like you're moving, so I'll just stay here if that's cool with you.*

"I'm going to miss you, buddy." She was having a hard time imagining a day without his cheerful floppiness and imagined backtalk.

He cocked his head.

"I'm not sad. I just . . . I don't know. Maybe I need to eat something." It was almost lunchtime, and her latest video edits were compiling. "Want to go find Gran?"

Rex leaped to his feet, tail whipping side to side. *Oh, boy, cookies!*

There was a tap on the door. "Jenny, dear?" It was her mom's voice, which was a bit of a surprise. Her parents had left midweek for a buying trip that she suspected was more of a clear-the-head getaway for her mom, who had been almost eerily reserved in the days following their heart-to-heart.

Jenny swung open the door, releasing Rex to dance around her mom's legs. "Hey! When did you guys get home?"

"Just now. Do you have a few minutes?"

"I was just going in search of food."

"Lunch is going on the table now, all hands on deck." Rose leaned down to ruffle Rex's fur. "Paws, too."

"As in, family meeting?" Jenny gave her mom an up-and-down, but didn't see anything out of the ordinary. "Is everything okay?"

"Absolutely. Come on, I'm starving."

Bemused, Jenny followed her mom into the dining room. Her father was at the sideboard, building a leaning tower of a sandwich from the sourdough and fixings that were laid out. Gran was in the living room, where she settled Rex next to the fireplace with a treat, and Big Skye was already at the table with a sandwich and mug of coffee.

Rose marched to the sideboard and started assembling an open-face sandwich. When Jenny hesitated, her mom looked back over her shoulder. "Come on. You said you were hungry."

She had been. Now she was just confused. "What's up?"

Gran came up behind her and gave her a nudge, saying in a low voice, "Whatever it is, I expect it'll go down easier with a sandwich."

"Words to live by," Jenny decided, and headed for the sideboard.

Ten minutes later, with everyone seated and lunch under way, Jenny's mom pushed her plate aside, dabbed her lips with a napkin, folded her hands atop the table, and said, "So."

The word hung there for a moment, seeming to require a response. Since nobody else stepped up, Jenny said, "Should we fire up the Skype and get Krista involved in this?"

"She knows," her father said. "Your mother and I took a ride over to Cali and ran this by her first." He was halfway through the first of two skyscraper sandwiches, suggesting that whatever game was afoot, he wasn't bothered by it. Unless he was stress eating.

"Well, then," Gran said, "what's the big news?"

Jenny said, "Mom?"

Rose pushed back her chair and stood, looking even taller than she usually did. She had her steel-dust hair pulled back, but was wearing jeans and a cable-knit sweater instead of her dressier outfits. Her shoulders were square, her eyes bright but not manic, and she looked like a very different person from the one who had wept over a broken ceramic horse.

With a quiver, Jenny realized that she looked like *Mom*.

After taking a long look around the table, lingering on Big Skye, Rose said, "First, I want to apologize for my recent behavior, especially to you, Barbara." That was aimed at Gran. "You're a truly amazing cook, and we're lucky to have you here. We always have been."

Gran blinked. "Why . . . thank you, Rose."

"No, thank *you*." She turned, focusing on Jenny, who froze midchew. "And Jenny, darling, I want to thank you for doing what you do best—providing an outside perspective on things."

She swallowed. "Um. What?"

"It wasn't until the other night, when I saw myself through your eyes that I realized how out of whack I had gotten. After that . . . well, I called Shelby, who knows the local therapists and recommended a woman I could go talk to. I had several sessions and then Eddie and I talked about things, and we went out to run them by Krista. And we've all agreed to make some changes."

Changes? A therapist? Jenny could only stare. But her father was working on his second sandwich, looking relaxed, even happy.

How had she missed this? Had she been so caught up in Nick and the videos that she had been oblivious to such a massive undercurrent? But maybe that was okay. This wasn't her deal, really. It was her mom's.

Rose pressed her fingertips into the smooth tabletop in a move that betrayed a hint of nerves. But there was no hesitation when she said, "So here it is. I ran the business end of this ranch for more than twenty-five years, and during that time I raised two wonderful daughters. I worked my butt off doing it, though, and when Ed first brought up the idea of the *Rambling Rose*, it sounded like paradise. I never really stopped to think about what it was going to mean for me. And I never really asked myself if I was ready to retire. Well, I'm not. In fact, I've decided that I'm going to un-retire."

Jenny wasn't sure whether to eat or gape. "You're going back to work?"

Humor glinted in her mom's eyes. "It's either that or pick a new hobby."

Yegad. "Do you know what you want to do?"

"That depends on you and your grandparents. Krista and your father have already given the okay, but this is a family ranch, which means a family vote." She looked around the table. "I want to create a new position: Head of Special Services. I would handle the weddings and other special events, centralize the extras, and add new services as they make sense." She folded her hands, as if to keep her fingers still. "Assuming the vote is unanimous, of course."

Jenny had given up on eating. Her mouth worked a couple of times before she managed to say, "That would be . . ." She blinked. "Perfect. You'd be amazing at it, and give Krista room to focus on other things." Wow. How hadn't any of them seen this? It was the right solution in so many ways. Except . . . "What about the *Rambling Rose*?" What she was really asking was: *What about Dad?*

Her father shot her a fond look that said *Don't worry about me. It's all good*. But she didn't just want good for him. She wanted the best.

"Your father and I will live here during the guest season, when the workload is heaviest. Probably March through October, or thereabouts. Then, come winter, we'll hit the road and head south until we don't see snow anymore. I can work remotely, with Krista backing me up."

"You're going to be snowbirds." Jenny's smile widened. "Mom, that's . . ." She had already said *perfect*, hadn't she? "I'm so happy for you."

"Is that a yes vote?"

"Absolutely yes."

Her mother turned to the other end of the table. "Barbara? Arthur? I'd really appreciate your support."

"You got it," Big Skye said. "You never let me down back in the day, Rosie. How could I let you down now?"

Jenny flashed back on memories of the two of them hunched over the accounts, or wrangling over the purchase of a new bull. *This*, she thought. This was what had been missing.

"Barbara?" Rose held out a hand. "Again, I'm sorry for being such a beast to you. I hope we can work together going forward."

Gran stood, rounded the table, and pulled her into a hug. "Of course, Rosie. How could you ever worry about it? Family is family, even when we drive each other nuts. As long as you stay out of my kitchen, we'll get along fine." Her bright, happy eyes went to Ed. "And you a part-timer! How perfect."

"I'm not a big fan of winter—that's for sure." Ed

touched his wife's hand. "But I'll always be my Rosie's biggest fan. I think it's a marvelous idea."

The vote was unanimous, with even Rex chiming in with an outdoor-voice bark when they all started cheering the new plan. Lunch turned into a celebration after that, with Gran producing a plate of berry tarts that had been earmarked for the senior center, and Big Skye popping the cork on a bottle of champagne he and Gran had gotten for New Year's and never gotten around to opening.

Lifting a half-full flute, he said, "To Rosie!"

Jenny's mom lifted her glass in return. "To Mustang Ridge and the Skyes, may they ever adapt when the situation requires it!"

The celebration wound down midafternoon, leaving Jenny with a slight buzz and zero motivation to keep working. On the pretext of taking pictures, she looped Old Faithful's strap around her neck, pulled on snow pants and boots, whistled up Rex, and headed out into a clear, bright day.

He barked and bounded ahead of her. *Oh, boy, we're going for a walk!*

Instead of following one of the plowed pathways or the trail that the wranglers' horses had packed leading up to the ridgeline, she set off across virgin snow. Her wide boots sank deep before finding any purchase, leaving her slogging along nearly to her thighs.

Rex wisely followed in her wake, letting her break a trail down past the guest cabins to the lake, where the wind had blown the snow off the ice and the frozen beach, and the action of a small spring kept a section of water open.

"Don't you dare fall in," she warned Rex, but he didn't seem interested in exploring. Instead, he stuck to her heels, tail waving gently.

She made for the small log boathouse, where the floating dock had been pulled up for the winter and lashed in place, and the windows had been covered with plywood. Plonking down on the steps, she leaned back against the door with a sigh. "Today was a good day, Sexy Rexy."

He leaned against her leg and stared out across the lake, and she looped her gloved fingers in his thick fur, reminded of the many times she and Rusty had sat together like this, back when she was a teenager and trying to figure out why she didn't fit in at Mustang Ridge, why she couldn't be content to stay put like all the others had. Now, as she stared out across the snowy fields to the distant mountains, she wasn't sure what she was trying to figure out. She had a great life, and she would be leaving her family in better shape than it had been when she arrived. Not that she was taking any credit there, but still.

"So what's the problem?" she asked herself.

Rex looked back over his shoulder at her. "Whuff?"

"That was rhetorical, more or less." Especially since she knew darn well that her problem was with a certain veterinarian, and the fact that she didn't want to lose what they had. Unfortunately, she wasn't sure how she could have that particular cake and eat it, too. She couldn't stay, he couldn't go, and he'd made it clear that he wasn't in the market for a long-distance anything. And maybe that was where she had gotten herself in trouble—she had seen how he was mostly camping out in his place and assumed his roots didn't go that deep, or that having lived the life, he'd be open to staying in touch. Maybe he had it right, though. If it hurt this much to think about being away from him, why prolong the pain? Then again, wouldn't it hurt less, knowing that she had calls to look forward to, emails to read, visits to make?

Rex surged to his feet, barked twice, and launched himself into a nearby snowbank.

"What the—" She looked around, but didn't see any reason for the sudden burst of energy.

Barking, the dog spun three-sixty and dove into the deeper snow that had collected up against the boathouse.

"You're a nut!" she called, but felt a grin stretch her face. Which might have been his intention.

For the next few minutes, the big goldie porpoised and played, leaping up in a glistening spray of snow and snapping at the crystals, and then disappearing again beneath the white surface.

She laughed as he submarined for a few feet and then popped up with an almost perfect cone of snow on his head. "Hold that thought," she said, then followed it with, "Stay, Rex."

She brought Old Faithful to life, tweaked the settings, and lifted the camera, just managing to get the shot before Rex shook his head, sending the snow flying, and galumphed toward her, tail wagging furiously. *Did you get it? Did you, did you?*

"I don't know. Let's see." She pulled up the preview panel on the camera's small screen, checked the image, and nodded. "Gotcha! And aren't you a handsome boy?"

Wiggling, he sat on her foot, panting happily.

Seeing a series of unfamiliar images in the preview tiles, she keyed over to those photos. "What the— Oh, right." She stared down at the pictures, stomach quivering with more of an *uh-oh* than an *aha*. Or maybe it was a combination of the two.

They were the photos Nick had taken that night at his father's cabin, while she had been looking at the old photos . . . and before they had gotten on to the topic of his ex. In some of them, she was bent over the album, exclaiming over this photo or that. In others, she was laughing up at Nick's father, or staring into the lens with a bemused look of *what's that camera doing there?* In each of them, though, there was a softness in her eyes and a curve to her lips that most definitely sparked an *uh-oh*.

It was a look she had seen on more faces than she wanted to count while filming *Jungle Love*. It was the one she and Jill called "cow eyes" when they were feeling snippy, or "stupid in love" when they weren't. But she wasn't stupid in love with Nick. She wasn't.

Except that when she paged back through the shots,

she saw the look over and over again. And when the screen went night-dark and she saw Nick standing in the moonlight, haloed in fur as he listened to the wolves howl, her belly knotted and her breath thinned out, and she was suddenly dying to text him, call him, drop in on him, be with him as much as she possibly could for the next few days. Plus a little voice inside her whispered that this didn't have to be the end of it—she could skip the Mayan trip and spend ten more days in Three Ridges.

She dropped her head in her hands. "Oh, damn." Now what?

25

Nick wasn't sure what to make of Jenny's request that he meet her out at the point, but he brought hot chocolate and brownies with him and made the drive, hoping for an adventure but fearing a Serious Discussion. Like the one that began with "I'm leaving soon" and ended with "better to just break it off now." He knew it was coming, but had been hoping they could stick to the fun script as long as possible. Like his old man always said, denial was more than a river in Egypt.

Her Jeep was already parked in the turnaround when he reached the point, so he killed his engine and hopped down from the Vetmobile, calling, "Jenny?"

"Down here" came the answer from below.

Tucking the brownies in one pocket and the thermos in another, he followed the narrow path down and around, finding it icier than before, treacherous in places. The little hollowed-out spot was clear, though, and warmed by the fire she had built in the stone-lined pit, suggesting that she had been there for a while.

She was wearing her heavy parka, but her gloves were off and the hood was thrown back, and when she looked up and smiled at him in greeting, her cheeks were flushed and warm. "Hey, there."

"Hey, yourself." He leaned in for a kiss that she eagerly returned, but still, he thought she seemed subdued.

"Sit." She patted the spot beside her. "I've got hot chocolate and brownies."

"Me, too." Chuckling, he pulled out his offerings. "Want to trade?" They made a solemn exchange and dug into their treats. As he sipped the still-scalding brew, he said, "Chocolate on chocolate. Are we celebrating something?"

"Yes. Maybe. I'm not sure."

"Which is it?"

"Maybe all of them." She nibbled at the corner of a brownie, staring into the fire. "For starters, my mom seems to have done a major turnaround." She described Rose's big announcement, finishing with, "I know it's too early to be sure, but I don't think this is just another 'ooh, shiny' moment that's not going to stick. I honestly think that this is going to be the perfect combination of her old job, her new interests, and the responsibility she's been missing."

"That's huge." He squeezed her hand. "I'd definitely say that's worth celebrating."

"True, but . . ." She hesitated and took a deep breath before continuing. "What she said about making adjustments got me thinking that maybe she's not the only one who needs to step back and take a look at things. Like you and me."

Oh, hell. Here it comes. Logic said the temperature couldn't possibly have just dropped five degrees. It also said there wasn't anything he could do to postpone the inevitable. Still, he didn't want it to end tonight. "Jenny, sweetheart, listen to me—"

"Not this time," she interrupted firmly, reaching over and stuffing half her brownie in his mouth.

He bit down reflexively, muffling his "What?"

"Shut up. It's my turn to go first." She waited, and when he nodded, said, "Thank you. Okay." She squinched her eyes and rubbed the center of her forehead. "I can do this. I can totally do this."

Her pep talk added to the knot in his gut. "You don't have to—"

"I'm falling in love with you."

That shut him up. Not just because it sucked all the oxygen out of his lungs, but because there wasn't anything he *could* say. Love wasn't part of the discussion. It wasn't supposed to be on the table. Yet there it was, thrown down like a gauntlet. A challenge.

He sat frozen. Numb. Angry, even, because this wasn't part of their deal. And, also, because a part of him leaped at the words. The man he had been would have known what to say. Hell, he might've said it first, as he had done with Lily, over a romantic picnic in their favorite spot at the river's edge. Back then, he had believed in love as a tangible force, something that could keep two people together no matter what.

It wasn't, though. It couldn't. And while his feelings for Jenny went far deeper than he'd ever meant to go, and the thought of her leaving tore at him, it couldn't be love.

"Jenny . . ." What could he possibly say to that? He didn't want to hurt her, but couldn't give the words back.

Her eyes searched his, seeming hopeful. "I know we said this was just short-term, just two people enjoying each other, but you've got to admit that it's gone way beyond that. We're good together, Nick. Fantastic. When I'm with you, I feel like a better version of myself." Something must have shown in his face, because she faltered. "Tell me you feel it, too."

He couldn't. He wouldn't. "After Lily, I swore I wouldn't fall for a woman who wasn't in the same place as me, didn't want the same things, the same kind of life."

"And I'm not that woman."

He wanted her—of course he wanted her. If she had handed him his brownie and announced that the show had been cancelled and she was in town for another month or so while she lined up another gig, he would've toasted the fates and told her to move some stuff to his place. But love was another story.

Love was messy. It hurt. It made people smaller than they ought to be.

Aware that the silence had gone on too long, he said, "You don't belong here, Jenny, and you don't belong with me, any more than Lily did."

Her expression hardened. "I'm not Lily."

"No, you're not, but you're like her in that you have important things to do away from Three Ridges." He took her hand, willing her to understand. "You want to change things up, like your mother talked about? Then get out of reality TV and find yourself a killer documentary to crew on. Better yet, build one from the ground up." He lowered his voice a notch. "You've got a gift, Jenny. Don't waste it."

Eyes firing, she yanked away and stood, pacing as far as she could in the small space. "I'm not wasting anything, thank you very much. And for the record, I wasn't offering to stay, or angling for you to ask me."

He stood and faced her. "Then what? A relationship can't survive different time zones."

"Why, because your last one didn't? You're the scientist here—since when does it make sense to draw a conclusion from a single data point? This is different, Nick." She thumped her chest. "I'm Jenny Skye, darn it, and I'm right here, asking you to give us a chance." She crouched down opposite him and cradled his face in her hands. "If it doesn't last, will it really hurt any worse to break up a few months from now than it will right now?"

Pushing to his feet, he walked to the edge of the drop-off. He stared down, feeling the cold in front of him, the warmth he was leaving behind. "I can't. I'm sorry."

"You mean you won't." There was a rustle of clothing as she rose.

He turned back. "Jenny . . ." But what was there left to say?

"I'm going to go." She bent to grab her thermos and set his next to the fire pit.

"Don't. Not like this." He reached for her.

She stepped back, shaking her head. Unshed tears made her eyes glitter in the firelight. "Sorry. I don't . . . I can't. . . . I'm going to go." She turned and fled, her footsteps kicking up rocks on the path.

Leaving him behind.

Jenny held it together until she got home, making it all the way to the safety of her room before she lost it. She barely noticed the grown-up decor or Rex charging in at her heels; she just slammed the door and flung herself on the bed, like she would have back when she was a teenager.

This was so much more painful, though.

Silent tears scalded her face and racked her body, and she curled in a tight ball of shock, shame, and misery, wrapping her arms around the center of her pain. It hurt more than she expected, more than she had believed could come from an injury that hadn't drawn blood, wouldn't show on an X ray.

"Stupid, stupid, stupid," she whispered between the sobs. Stupid to think that she had finally found a man who wanted her enough to stay in touch. Stupid to think that it would be okay because he understood her lifestyle. Stupid to think a man like him would be willing to put up with someone like her for the long-term. Turned out, his roots went deeper than she had thought.

"Whuff?" The mattress sagged and rocked as a heavy weight jumped onto the bed, and suddenly Rex was there, sniffing her and then gently pawing at her arms. *What happened?*

Shaky and raw, she uncurled her body and patted the bedspread beside her. "Come on, buddy. I could use a hug from someone who's going to be here the next time I come home."

The dog didn't do his two and a half circles, just dropped down beside her with a sigh of sympathy and a low whine at the back of his throat.

Wrapping her arms around the goldie's neck, Jenny buried her face in his fur, and wept.

26

Jenny slept like crap and woke up the next morning curled in a miserable huddle. Her body hurt. Her heart hurt. Everything hurt.

On some level, she had known that Nick would have made the move if he'd really wanted to. Now she knew for certain he didn't want to, didn't want *her*. Not enough, anyway.

Damn you, Nick Masterson. When her eyes filled with tears once more, she swiped the moisture away, irritated with herself. And with him. With all of it. Her just-for-fun relationships had never made her feel this way. There had been regret, yes, and the occasional wistful thought of *what if*. Never this ripping, tearing pain in her chest and roil in her stomach, this horrible vulnerability that made her feel naked and exposed even when she was buried under layers of blankets in her own bed . . . which wasn't nearly as comfortable as his.

She missed his mattress, missed being awakened by Cheesepuff in breakfast mode, missed feeling Nick's heavy, slumbering weight beside her or hearing his voice rumble "There she is" in her ear as he gathered her close against his warm, solid body. Missed the scent of him, the taste of him, the feel of him.

And, damn it, she was crying again.

"Never again," she told the ceramic horse, with its glued-on leg. "This sucks."

The horse just sneered. Rex, on the other hand, popped up with his front paws on the edge of the mattress and a hopeful look on his doggy face. *You okay? Need another hug?*

"Oh, Rex." She sighed. "What am I going to do?"

It was a rhetorical question, of course. She wasn't someone who could stay in bed all day, or even feel sorry for herself for all that long. Pretty soon she was up and getting dressed, with Rex dogging her heels and alternately bumping up against her in reassurance and bringing her dog toys in an effort to replace whatever it was she had clearly lost.

"Thanks, but I don't think a Kong is going to do the trick, big guy." She patted his head, then opened the bedroom door. "Come on. Let's get this day started."

Oh, boy! We're going downstairs! Worry forgotten, he charged down the stairs ahead of her.

She let the dog out to do his morning business, filled his bowl in the kitchen, and filched a muffin, all without encountering a single member of her family. Breathing a sigh of relief, she headed for the office, fully intending to bury herself in filmmaking.

Find yourself a killer documentary to crew on, a ghostly

voice whispered in her mind's ear. *Better yet, build one from the ground up.*

"Oh, shut up," she muttered, stiff-arming the door and striding through.

"What was that, dear?" The desk chair spun around from the window, and her mother looked up at her. As if realizing—finally—that she was in the chair Jenny usually used, she said, "Am I going to be in your way? I can work at the dining table, if you'd prefer."

"I . . . No, you stay. I'll work at the table." And maybe disappear for a really long walk, or a drive, or something. "As long as you don't mind manning the phones?"

"Happy to, dear." Her expression shifted. "Is everything okay? You look . . ."

"Pissy? Tired? Like a dead thing the dog dragged in?"

"I was going to say sad. Did something happen with Nick?"

Darn it, Jenny thought as tears prickled, burning her eyelids and fighting to break free. She didn't want to talk about it, though. Not even with her mommy. "I'm just tired. Didn't get much sleep last night." She collected her laptop and headed for the other room.

Her mom's voice floated after her. "Nick called a little while ago. He'd like you to call him back. He said it was very important."

Jenny didn't trust her voice. Not to answer her mom, and not to call him back. A check of her cell phone showed that he'd left two messages there, too, starting an hour ago. Which meant . . . What? Had he woken up lonely and reconsidered?

Ha. She was done being a stupid optimist and putting herself out there. She had said what needed to be said, and that was that for now.

She would deal with him later, maybe. But not now.

So, with Rex curled at her feet, she got to work on the footage she had shot in Kitty's Kountry Kitsch, determined to lose herself in the images. She had done two interviews, one with Kitty talking about Mustang Ridge through the eyes of a teenage girl, and another that focused on the store. Thanks to Kitty's mom, Jenny also had several photos of Kitty in pigtails and Wranglers, riding along with the herd.

Jenny was frowning over one of them, trying to decide if it fit better *there* or *there*, when her cell phone rang. The noise dragged her out of her self-induced filmmaking fugue, and her heart flip-flopped. It wasn't either of Nick's numbers, and she didn't recognize the area code.

She hesitated, then thought, what the hell, and answered. "This is Jenny Skye."

"Oh," said a startled voice. "It's you! I'm so glad you answered! This is Miranda Solace." The woman paused as if that explained everything.

"Um . . . I'm sorry. Do I know you?"

"Didn't Dr. Masterson call you?"

A chill shuddered down Jenny's spine. What was going on here? "We haven't connected. Can I help you?"

"We . . ." She paused, and Jenny heard children's voices and a chirpy song in the background. Then the woman said, "I'm sorry. This is going to be a shock if you haven't already spoken to your vet. You see . . . it seems that you have our dog."

Maybe she said something else after that. If so, it got lost in the sudden roaring noise as Jenny clutched the phone, mouth working in a silent wail of *Noooo!*

Rex was her dog. Hers.

He had been sacked out under the table by her feet, but now scrambled out, all paws and floppy ears, looking around for the danger. *What? What? Now what's wrong?*

Jenny dropped to her knees and wrapped an arm around the big goldie's neck while he thumped his tail and tried to lick her. "Rex," she whispered, her throat so tight, she almost couldn't get out the word. "Oh, Rex."

"You call him Rex? Wow, his real name is Red. What a coincidence." The woman's voice warmed; the kids had gone quiet. "I can't begin to tell you how happy we were when our vet called. We were on vacation this past August, going from campground to campground in our RV, and somebody broke in while we were out to dinner. They took the kids' games, our computer, some little things . . . and Red. At first, we thought he had gotten out, but then we found his GPS collar down the road. It had been cut off."

She paused like she was waiting for Jenny to say something, but what was there to say? The story hung together, and Nick must have believed it, if he had passed along her name and cell number.

And then he had called her to try to break the news himself, despite everything.

"Anyway," Miranda continued, "we kept the telephone chain going, along with Web postings . . . we even consulted an animal communicator. You can't imagine—or maybe you can—how excited we were when our vet saw Dr. Masterson's post about a goldie being found."

"Are you sure it's him?" Jenny's voice wobbled.

There was a long pause. "I'm sorry. You're very attached to him, aren't you?"

"Are you sure?"

"We saw the pictures. It's him. Your vet said he was sure you would be happy to keep him . . . but we miss him like crazy. You understand, don't you?"

"Of course." It was barely a breath, leaking out of Jenny like it was her last. She looked down at the adoring brown eyes that stared up at her, trusting that she was there and there was a warm spot by the fireplace, just like she had promised him. "Do you . . . I guess you're going to come and get him."

"We're in the car right now. Our GPS says we'll be there in an hour!"

It was the shortest hour of Jenny's life. She went through the motions—telling her parents and grandparents, collecting Rex's favorite things into a small mountain on the porch, and stuffing him full of cookies with only a small twinge of guilt that he might barf it all up on the long car ride.

He stuck to her side through the preparations, bumping against her legs and arms like a young colt in a scary situation, looking up at her with big, worried eyes. *Why are you upset? Is something bad happening? What can I do to help?*

The reassurances stuck in her throat, lumping into a hard ball of emotion as her mom hugged him good-bye, sniffling back tears, and Gran added a bag of homemade biscuits to the pile on the porch. Even Big Skye patted the goldie's upturned head, muttering, "Good dog. Sorry to see you go." Her father hung back with his hands stuffed in his pockets, looking longingly at his shop.

Jenny could relate. She wanted to go back to bed, burrow in, and pretend the past two days hadn't happened. Or load Rex in the Jeep and go someplace where Miranda Solace and her loud children couldn't find them, and where she wouldn't keep bumping into things that reminded her of Nick.

With five minutes to spare on the hour she'd been given—and GPS always lied, anyway—she patted her thigh. "Hey, Rex. Want to go for a walk?"

He leaped up and danced in a circle. *Oh, boy! Walkies!*

They set out across the parking lot, heading for the path beside the barn, but hadn't gone more than a hundred yards when the sound of an engine broke the winter silence, and a minivan came over the hill.

Jenny's instincts said to run. Her conscience had her turning back. "Sorry, Rexy. False alarm. Want to go see—"

As the minivan pulled into the lot, the goldie lit up like a firecracker had gone off beneath him. He lunged away from Jenny and raced toward the vehicle, barking his fool head off. And even before the car had come to a complete stop, doors flew open and kids hurtled out—two boys and a girl, the three of them seeming more like a dozen as they pigpiled on Rex.

Jenny started toward them. "Don't . . . his ribs . . . oh, damn."

Rex nearly turned himself inside out trying to greet all of the kids at once. *Ohboyohboyohboy! You're here! Where have you been? Oh, let me lick you!*

The driver's door swung open and out stepped a middle-aged, middle-size woman with middling brown hair and a smile that lit her entire face when she looked at the melee. "Red! It's really you!"

Rex—or Red—gave a happy bark, ripped away from the kids, galloped a wide circle around the woman, and plonked his furry butt in a sit-stay belied by his excited whole-body quiver. Miranda laughed, dropped to her knees, and wrapped her arms around his neck. "There's my big boy!"

The kids shrieked and piled back on with lots of hugging and laughter, and piping shouts of "Red!" and "No, it's my turn!"

Jenny felt a touch on her arm. Turning, she found her mother and father on one side of her, Gran and Big

Skye on the other. They were looking at her with so much sympathy that she was tempted to curl up in a tiny ball and wail. She didn't, though. Been there, done that, hadn't helped things any. "I'm happy for them," she said through numb-feeling lips. "It's not like I could take him with me when I left."

The woman rose and turned toward them, eyes glistening with unshed tears. "It really is him, isn't it?"

Jenny jammed her hands in her pockets. "We, um. He's got some beds and toys and stuff. We'd like you to have them."

The other woman's eyes went to the avalanche on the porch, and widened. "Why, thank you." Then she looked back at Jenny. "I mean it. Thank you from the bottom of my heart. Dr. Masterson told me how you rescued Red, and everything that you've done for him. I want to reimburse you, of course."

"We don't want the money." *We want Rex.* Jenny swallowed, fighting to keep her composure. "We would've done the same for any animal in need."

"But . . ."

"Give it to a local shelter, if you like." The kids were wrestling with their dog in the snow, shrieking with laughter as the powdery white flew everywhere.

Under any other circumstance, Jenny would've been dying for a camera. As it was, she was dying for this to be over.

Miranda's expression was heading toward stricken. "I'm so sorry. I wish . . ." She shook her head. "If it was just me, I would leave him with you. Where better for a dog than a farm? But the kids love him. They need him, now more than ever. My husband's cancer—"

"It's okay," Jenny interrupted, knowing it was rude but unable to listen anymore. "You don't have to explain. He's yours. Take h-him." Her voice broke on the last word.

Things moved fast after that, blurring into a rush of bodies and dog toys, and Miranda's raised voice as she herded the kids back into the car. Then she opened the back deck to reveal a dog gate and a worn bed flecked with red-gold hair. She patted the deck. "Come on, Red. In you go."

Oh, boy. Car ride! Rex bounded toward the vehicle, but stopped halfway, and looked back at Jenny. *Aren't you coming?*

Last night she had told herself her heart wasn't broken, that she had kept enough of herself intact that she was going to be just fine. Now she couldn't even find that lie. She was empty. "Go on, buddy. It's okay."

Instead, he turned and came back toward her, tail wagging.

Damn, damn, damn. Eyes stinging, she crossed to him, crouched down, and wrapped her arms around his ruff. "You're a good boy." Her words were muffled by his fur. "I love you."

He wriggled and whined, simultaneously trying to lick her face and offer her all his itchy spots. And when she walked over and patted the back deck of the minivan, and said, "Come on, buddy. Back where you belong," he hopped up, did his two and a half turns, and sank down with a happy sigh, as if all was right with his world.

Well, that made one of them.

Feeling like it was tearing holes in her lungs to breathe, Jenny kissed the top of his head and backed away. "Bye, buddy. Be a good dog."

His tail thumped. *I'm a Good Dog!*

Miranda closed the hatchback, turned to Jenny, and gave her a big hug. "Thank you," she whispered fiercely. "You don't know how much this means to them."

Jenny didn't argue that one. She just drew away and nodded. "Have a safe trip." She wanted to tell the woman—this stranger who was taking her Rex away—that he liked his kibble slightly moist and his cookies fresh out of the oven, but she didn't. He was going back to his old life, his old routine.

So instead, she raised a hand in farewell, and watched as Miranda drove the stuffed-full minivan up the hill leading away from Mustang Ridge.

When the vehicle crested the ridge and disappeared, the silence was deafening.

Swallowing hard, Jenny dug her nails into her palms.

Finally, Gran said, "Have you talked to Nick?"

Ouch. "No."

"You should call him."

"We broke up." She heard a chorus of indrawn breaths, felt the change in the air. "And, no, I don't want to talk about it."

"Baby . . ." That was her mother, voice full of the sympathy she couldn't bear right now.

She held up a hand. "I'm okay. Really." Or she would be, anyway. Eventually.

The sound of an engine came from the main road, growing stronger.

Jenny wheeled around. Had Miranda changed her mind? Had Rex barfed so grandly in the minivan that she wanted to delay things?

But it wasn't the minivan. It was the Vetmobile.

Any remaining warmth in Jenny's veins went cool, and from there to a faint churn of nausea as Nick parked and killed the engine. When the driver's door swung open and he emerged, the others melted away, with her father saying, "We'll be inside. Give you two some privacy."

She wanted to tell them not to bother, that she didn't have anything more to say to Nick. But the words froze in her throat as he approached.

The sunlight picked out the burnished highlights in his hair and the shadows showed in his eyes, which were filled with grief, regret, and the sympathy she had managed to resist coming from the others. She couldn't resist him, though. Not even now.

When his arms opened, she walked straight into them. When his grip closed on her, she burrowed into the familiar space and scent, the safe place. And when he whispered, "I'm sorry, Jenny. I'm so damn sorry he's gone," she burst into tears.

He had been there at the beginning with Rex, so it seemed only right that he was there at the end.

She dug her fingers into his parka and buried her face against his throat, sobbing because everything *hurt*, deep down inside. She didn't know how much of the pain was from him, how much from Rex, and how much from the growing realization that she couldn't have everything she wanted, not this time. And that when she left, she would be leaving part of herself behind.

The sobs racked her body, tore at her throat, and twisted her stomach. But Nick just held on to her, stroking her hair and murmuring things like "Easy, there" and "Just breathe" like she was a terrified puppy getting its first shots.

It worked, though. Little by little the great, gulping tears eased and her breathing settled. Her body relaxed some, so the aches overtook the tight spots and she became conscious of a crushing exhaustion. Not so much one that made her want to go to sleep, but rather made her want to pretend that she didn't exist for an hour or two. Maybe longer. She let go of his coat and patted down the crumpled places. "Thanks. I, uh . . . I guess I needed that."

"No problem."

Then, as though she hadn't spent the last ten minutes clinging to him and soaking his jacket, she stepped back and looked up at him. "What are you doing here?"

A corner of his mouth kicked up, but his dimples

stayed hidden, his eyes dark with regret. "I wanted to make sure you were okay."

"Define okay." There was nothing okay about any of this.

"Yeah. That was about what I figured."

With the first rush of desperate emotion past, the other stuff filtered back in, making her take another big step away from him and draw her coat tighter around her body. "Well, thanks for coming." Sort of. She wasn't sure if seeing him again had made things better or worse.

He cleared his throat. "Do you want to get out of here? Go for a drive or something? Might be better than being around all the memories right now."

A disbelieving laugh tore at her throat. "No offense, but driving around with you doesn't count as avoiding memories." Was it really so easy for him to drop back into the friend zone, or wherever he was? Well, good for him, but she wasn't playing along. "In fact, thanks for coming by—truly—but I think you should go now."

He studied her for a moment, expression shuttered. Then he nodded. "If that's what you want."

No, you idiot! I want you to hold me while I cry. I want you to tell me over and over again that it's going to be okay, that those kids love Rex and they're going to take the very best care of him. And I want you to admit that what happened between us was more than you expected, too. I want you to want me enough to take a stab at staying together, even if it means months of phone sex and Skype. I want you, damn it!

Balling her hands at her sides, she repeated, "You should go." As an afterthought, she added, "Give Cheese-puff a pepperoni from me, will you?" And oh, how it hurt to know she probably wouldn't see him again.

Nick hesitated, turning toward her as if he were going to hug her again, or go in for a good-bye kiss. But he didn't. "Okay. But call me if you need anything, Jenny. I mean it. Anything."

"I will," she said, but they both knew he didn't mean the offer any more than she meant the acceptance—because what she needed from him wasn't something he was willing to give.

She told herself not to watch him walk away, but she did it anyway, even knowing that the others were no doubt spying from the house, both grieving for Rex and debating what they should do to help her. Sure enough, as the Vetmobile disappeared over the hill, her phone rang, Krista's name flashing on the display.

Jenny answered. "Hey, there. I take it you've been briefed?" She was proud that her voice was only a little ragged, the tears barricaded deep inside.

"There's a ten thirty flight tomorrow out of Laramie. A quick hop to Denver, and you're on your way south."

Oh, damn. There went the tears. "I can't bail on you."

"You're not. You're being good to yourself. And, besides, Mom can cover the last few days. You can be in Belize City in time for a late dinner, back at base camp the day after that."

Base camp. The words made Jenny yearn for humid

warmth, the color green, and a camera to hide behind. "I wanted to see you, and hear all about the fruity drinks and pool boys." She tried to keep it light, but the tears made hot tracks down her cheeks. "I can stay, really."

"Another time. Maybe I'll even come down and visit you. How does that sound?" Krista's voice went wry. "With Mom in the office, time off won't just be an option, it'll be a necessity." She paused. "Want me to book your ticket?"

Jenny looked around the cold, white world and felt her heart break. She didn't want to leave, not like this. Not really at all. She wanted to turn time back a week or two, to one of the many mornings she had awakened in Nick's arms, roused by Cheesepuff's insistent "Mmrph?" and treated to Rex's infectious joy. *You're awake. Yippee!*

"Book the ticket," she said, and felt her heart rip cleanly in two. "I need to get out of here."

27

The next morning, Nick headed for his father's cabin before dawn, on the theory that if the drive didn't help him work out the mental kinks, a few hours of ice fishing—a mind- and body-numbing hobby if ever there was one—should do the trick.

The cabin was empty when he arrived, but he followed the well-worn path down to the lake, where a thin tendril of smoke threaded from the pipe of his old man's fishing shack, and Molly lay on a big woven mat in front of the door. Her head came up as he approached, her lips rippling in a silent growl.

"I'm a friend, remember?" He debated pulling off a glove and letting her sniff his hand, but didn't like the look in her eyes and preferred his hand attached to his wrist. Stopping a safe distance away, he called, "Dad? You want to tell your wolf that I'm a-ok?"

The door swung open. "Nick? That you?"

"You got anyone else likely to call you Dad?"

"Come in, come in. Molly, let him through. He's a friend."

The big wolf-dog immediately plopped her head back down and gave a couple of tail thumps.

"Oh, fine. He's the only one who gets to do the friend password, huh?"

Her unimpressed look said *Yeah. Pretty much.*

"Good dog." Nick stepped over her, careful not to slip on the ice, because he wasn't sure her benevolence would extend to being sat on. He was having a bad enough day and didn't need a bite in the ass to cap things off.

The fishing cabin was roughly the size and shape of a two-hole outhouse, with a pair of folding chairs, a potbelly stove up on a platform in one corner and a couple of shelves on the opposite wall that held snacks, bait, and beer. An auger and a chainsaw sat below the shelves, their handiwork evident in the vaguely oval-shaped hole that had been punched through the foot-thick ice. The air smelled of coffee and fish, and his father had returned to his chair to take up position next to the line he had dangling in the dark, cold water. He had his eyes on Nick, though. When their gazes connected, he said, "You want to talk about it?"

"Can't a guy just drive up to see his father on his day off?"

"Sure, but why would he want to, when he's got a lovely woman in his bed?"

"Yeah. That." Nick scowled at the far shore.

"You and Jenny having problems?"

"Not anymore."

"Oh?"

"We broke up."

Instead of sympathy, he got a scowl. "Why the hell did you go and do a fool thing like that?"

"It was going to be over in a few days anyway."

"How so?"

"She's got a career, Dad. This was only a vacation for her." Sort of. "She'll be back down south by next week."

"So? You've got a computer. And I was reading the other day about this thing called sexting."

Okay, this was so not helping. "Can we not talk about it right now? I came to fish."

His old man snorted. "You did not."

"Give me a flipping pole."

"I'm using a hand line."

"That'll do." Grimly, Nick fixed on a sinker, baited the hook with a chunk of frozen whatever, and dropped it in, careful not to foul his father's line. Then he stared at where the line met the water, watching for telltale vibrations.

After a good stretch of chilly silence, his father said, "Coffee?"

"Are you offering me some or putting in your order?"

"Offering. Jeez, you're touchy."

"Coffee would be good." He knocked back his first cup in three deep swallows, got a refill, and sucked back half before he let out a deep, gusty sigh. "Sorry I'm being a prick. She's hurting, I'm hurting, and the whole situation sucks."

"So why didn't you want to keep things going once she left?"

"Do you really need to ask? You were the one who said there was no way I could make it work with Lily."

"Jenny isn't Lily."

"Of course not, but there are more similarities than differences."

"Are we talking about the women or the situation?"

"It doesn't matter."

That earned him a faintly pitying look. "You're smarter than that, son."

"Shut up and fish," Nick said, figuring that would be the end of it. His father had never been big on giving advice in the romance department.

After a few minutes, though, his old man refilled his own coffee, took a sip, and said, "Your mother left me once."

"She . . . *What?*"

"She left me. We had been married a few years, but she didn't like Laramie much, or even Wyoming. She missed New England, missed her family, and got it in her head that I should buy into a practice back east. Even found me a couple to choose from."

Nick stared, not quite comprehending the words that were coming out of his old man's mouth. "I . . . I don't know what to say."

"Neither did I. Wyoming is in my blood, my bones. I didn't see how I could be happy anywhere else, and I didn't understand how she could ask me to try. We fought about it, we discussed it, we even tried flipping a coin. But in the end we couldn't agree—she wanted to go and I wanted to stay. So she went, and I stayed."

"When was this?"

That got a grin out of his old man. "'Bout ten months before you were born. I lasted two very long weeks before I realized this was more about my pride than anything. So I sucked it up and hopped on a plane." His teeth flashed. "Got there just as she finished packing to come home, having decided that home wasn't home unless we were together."

"In Wyoming."

"That was how it wound up, sure, but I would've stayed there if she had wanted to. The other stuff just didn't matter if she wasn't there." He glanced over. "That's what I've been working on lately, figuring out how to make the other stuff matter without your mother in the picture."

Nick did some of his own staring into the water, but then shook his head. "You guys were already married. Jenny and I are just getting to know each other."

"So what's the harm in continuing the process?" His father wiggled the line experimentally. "Or, to put it another way, what's the worst that could happen? If the two of you stay in touch and things go sour in a couple of weeks or months, is breaking up then really going to be any worse than what you're going through now?"

Jenny had asked him something similar and he hadn't answered her, mostly because his gut said that it would be far worse in a few weeks or months, but his head wasn't entirely sure why. Now, though, having slept on it, he was able to say, "What we've had together here worked perfectly because we both knew that it was just a short-term thing. It was easy."

"Look, you lost your mom, Lily, and your old life all within a few months of each other. It's only natural that you're going to want to be a little careful putting yourself out there again. But if you don't ever try, you're going to wind up growing old alone." His father made a pained face. "With a cat."

"What's wrong with falling for someone who wants to marry the local vet and live happily ever after above the clinic?"

"Absolutely nothing. Didn't you say Ruth wanted to set you up with some locals?"

"Not interested," Nick said flatly.

"Exactly. You might like small towns, son, but you're not a small-town boy. That's not saying you couldn't find someone else to love, but in my experience, the kind of connection you and Jenny share isn't something that comes along every day. I think you need to give it some credit, because the way I see it, Lily liked the adventure better with you in it. What if it turns out that Jenny likes you better than the adventure?"

Yeah, but what if she doesn't? The thought was instinctive, and came from deep inside, along with a sharp stab of the hurt he'd taken to bed with him, the one he'd awakened with. The one that said he just plain wasn't *enough* for her.

But that was Lily talking, not Jenny.

Jenny loved his country-vet lifestyle, his zip-tied end table, and his bratty cat. She loved snow days, French Toast, and his mattress-on-a-box-spring bed. Most of all, she loved the guy he was now, not the one he used to be.

At least, she had.

Quivery shock ran through him, then punched him in the gut with the sudden certainty that he was an idiot. An ass. And he was on the verge of throwing away something very special. Yes, the distance thing was an issue. Potentially an insurmountable one. But they wouldn't ever know if it was solvable unless they tried.

Dropping his handline, he lurched to his feet. "Thanks, Dad. I've . . . I gotta get out of here."

"Go." His father waved him off. "And don't step on the wolf!"

By the time Nick rolled through the WELCOME TO MUS-TANG RIDGE archway a couple of hours later, he still didn't know what he was going to say to Jenny, but he knew damn well that he wasn't leaving without seeing her. He got out of the truck and felt a pang at the memory of what had happened here just the day before, and how when he knocked, there wasn't going to be any skittering claws or a welcoming bark. But while he couldn't bring Rex back for her, he thought he could make some of the other stuff better. He hoped.

When he knocked, though, and Gran opened the

door, her eyebrows rose. "Is something wrong with one of the horses?"

Had he been relegated to just the vet so quickly? He sure hoped this was her way of saying she was on Jenny's side. "I need to talk to Jenny."

"Oh, but she already left for the airport!" She glanced over her shoulder at the wall clock. "Her plane takes off in an hour."

Damn, damn, damn. There was no way he would make it. But he had to try. "What flight?"

Sixty seconds later, armed with the information, he peeled back out onto the main road while his phone rang through to the cabin. When his father picked up, he skipped the preliminaries and said, "Dad, it's me. I need a huge favor."

Jenny's plane was delayed almost three hours by weather. Normally, that wouldn't have been a big deal—winter in Wyoming, and all that—but she really wasn't happy having the extra time to sit and think about everything she was leaving behind.

Not that she regretted the decision—she was dying to get back down south and put her cameras to some serious work, the kind where she didn't have to think about anything other than the light, the shot, and the action. Her upcoming ten-day trip was seriously going to rock, and being away from Wyoming would be good for her. She would be able to put things into perspective. She hoped.

But the more she sat there, popping Tums and sipping bottled water as the delay edged back yet another half hour and she got close to having to rebook her connection for the second time, she knew—deep down inside, where honesty lived—that this wasn't like any of the other times she had left home. This time, she wasn't just heading toward something; she was running away. And this time she was going to desperately miss the people and things she had left behind.

She wasn't just going to miss Rex and Nick, though those were the two big holes that ate at her gut and had her buying antacids rather than M&Ms at the gift shop opposite her gate. She was also going to miss her parents and grandparents, and she wasn't going to get to hear all of Krista's stories from her weeks away. Sure, they would Skype, but it wouldn't be the same. And she supposed she could keep in touch with Shelby, and maybe even Kitty Cosgrove, but that wouldn't be the same, either. And, well, yeah, maybe that had been Nick's point about the futility of trying to keep their relationship going long-distance.

"That doesn't mean breaking up was the right thing to do." She said it out loud, even though there wasn't even a flea poster to talk to. "We could've found some kind of a compromise if he had wanted to."

"Oh, he wants to, all right," a deep, resonant voice said from directly behind her.

She stiffened, body going hot-cold-hot as footsteps rang on the polished floor and Nick came into view, wearing jeans and a crisp button-down shirt beneath his parka, and his sturdy boots on his feet. It was the luggage that caught her, though, locking her in place.

Over his shoulder was slung the battered knapsack she had seen him wearing in almost all of the Africa photos, and he carried a matching duffel of many-times-washed canvas, wearing faded patches and MASTERSON written in big letters in permanent marker. Like he was going somewhere.

She whispered, "What are you doing here?" She didn't care that her voice shook, considering that she was shaking all over.

"I'm coming with you," he said simply, then spread his hands away from his body. "That is, if you'll have me." It wasn't quite a question.

"If I . . ." She stopped and closed her eyes. *Don't freak. Don't babble.* "What about the clinic?" Krista would kill her if she kidnapped the vet.

"My dad is covering." He grinned, dimples putting in a brief appearance. "Guess your mom wasn't the only one ready to come out of retirement." He set down his duffel and knapsack, sat in the chair she had just vacated, and tugged her down beside him. Turning to face her, he took her hands in his. "I was wrong, Jenny, about so many things."

She couldn't breathe, couldn't think. But somewhere inside her, hope kindled. He was there. He wasn't shutting her out. And he had his Africa bags with him. "You can't stay away forever."

"No, I can't. But I can take a couple of weeks. So, what do you say? Can I tag along on your side trip? I make a mean Sherpa."

Yes, she wanted to say, *a million times yes!* She wanted this to be their answer, wanted the hurt to stop. But could she trust the one-eighty? What was to say he wouldn't do another U-turn a few weeks or months down the road? "I'm going to be gone longer than a couple of weeks."

"So we'll Skype. Email. Do whatever it takes. It won't be perfect, granted, but it'll be a whole lot better than not having you in my life." His expression flattened enough to let her know that he wasn't just ignoring the issues. They were still there, but he had decided he wanted her enough—wanted *them* enough—to take the risk. To give it a try.

"What changed?"

"I opened my eyes this morning, and you weren't there. I went up into the mountains and you weren't there. And when I went to the ranch to talk to you, you weren't there, either." He squeezed her hands. "I don't want to live without knowing you're somewhere in my life, even if it's far away."

"Oh . . ." She breathed the word as the pain drained away.

"Is that oh, good, or oh, bad?"

"It's good." The smile seemed to begin deep inside her, then grew to take over her face. "It's very good." She bounced a little in her chair. "You're coming with me! I can't believe it!"

Relief loosened his body and put a gleam in his eyes. But he lowered his voice to say, "Wait. There's one more thing I need to say."

"What's that?"

"I love you."

Her heart shuddered in her chest. "You don't have to say that."

"Yes, I do. Not because you said it to me, or because I think it's what you want to hear, but because when a man realizes that he's been an asshat to the woman he loves, he wants to make up for it as soon as possible." He stood, spread his arms, and proclaimed, "I love this woman! I'm going to follow her to another country because I love her!"

"Shh!" Laughing, she pulled him back down beside her while a couple of whoops and a smattering of applause came from the harried-looking travelers around them. She bumped him with her shoulder. "You're nuts, Doc."

"Nuts about you." Expression going serious, he drew her in for a kiss that started soft and lingering, then turned deep and dark. When they parted—to more applause that they both ignored—he rested his brow on hers and murmured, "I love you, Jenny Skye."

She wanted to close her eyes and bask in the marvelous words and the dawning wonder that this was really happening. But she wanted to see it all, too, and store it in her heart, so she looked into his eyes, and said, "I love you, Nick Masterson, at home or abroad. And I can't wait to see what's in store for us."

Straightening, he raised their joined hands, and proclaimed, "Next stop, Belize City!"

"Actually, it's Denver."

He kissed her hard and fast, then grinned and said, "I don't care where we're going, as long as we're together."

23

One year later

The Steak Lodge had been redecorated since the summer, Jenny saw as the hostess led her and Nick—followed by twenty of their nearest and dearest—to a back room, where tables had been pushed together for the party. The new decor was sleeker and more modern in places, with brushed stainless at the bar and fewer boots on the walls, yet maintained the cheerful kitch of the original. They had even added a stuffed grizzly and a couple of pine trees with knotty eyes that followed Jenny as she walked by. She glanced back over her shoulder. "Is this your work, Mom?"

Rose's lips curved in satisfaction. "I might have made a few suggestions."

"That's an understatement," Krista whispered from the other side of Jenny. "She and Kitty turned this place upside down for nearly a month."

"Why does this not surprise me?" Jenny said it with

a smile, though. Their mother had taken on her new responsibilities at Mustang Ridge with a vengeance that might've been daunting if she hadn't been so darn effective. As promised, the *Rambling Rose* had rolled south before the snow hit, but Rose and Ed had flown back for the party. And, no doubt, so she could check on a few of her pet projects.

Like the Steak Lodge, Jenny thought. *And us*. She squeezed Nick's hand and got a quick glance and a couple of dimples in return, putting a happy flutter in her belly.

The bison head that had goaded them into a kiss during their first date—and again when they had visited the restaurant during her summer break—had been moved into the private room, centered on the back wall, where it emerged from a painted bison's body. Around it was painted a panoramic view of fields and mountains, and above it hung a banner that read: WELCOME HOME, JENNY . . . FOR GOOD!

And it really was good. Better than good. It was the best.

Nick had been wrong about distance being death to a relationship, but Jenny had definitely found that their relationship had made distance a whole lot less fun. Even with him flying to Belize for a week here and there, and her spending part of the summer back home, she had missed him like crazy when they were apart. More, she had missed Three Ridges. And that had been a wonderful surprise.

"Nice to see our bison is still around," Nick said, and

steered her to a chair directly beneath it, pulling it out and seating her like a gentleman.

That was one of the things she loved about him—that he was a gentleman. But she also loved that he had a naughty streak that made him drag her out of their tent in the middle of the night for skinny dipping, an adventurous side that had wound up with the two of them taking skydiving lessons on their last side trip, a softer side that meant he talked to cats as seriously as he did research vets with an alphabet soup of letters after their names. . . . Face it, she flat-out loved him for all his facets, and for the knowledge that there were still more parts of him left to discover.

For example, she had a feeling he had something more planned than just a dinner party tonight. In the couple of days since she flew in and he met her at the airport with both their families in tow, she had walked in on enough instantly interrupted phone calls to know there was something afoot. She was trying not to build up her hopes too far that it was a ring.

That was a kicker, wasn't it? A year ago, she would've howled if someone had suggested she'd be moving home for good, freelancing for Shelby's ad agency, putting in applications for documentary grants, and hoping for an engagement. But here she was.

Across the table from her, Krista wiggled her eyebrows in a silent *Well? Has he said anything?*

She gave an almost imperceptible headshake. *Not yet.*

Nick took the chair next to her while the others

sorted themselves out around the table, with the gang from Mustang Ridge—including Shelby and Foster—bumping elbows with Nick's father and Ruth, who had been an item since about five seconds after Dr. Bill had walked into the clinic. Michelle, Kitty, and their husbands rounded out the party, giving things a lively air.

Dinner was a loud, cheerful family affair, with lots of teasing up and down the table, along with several toasts to Jenny's return, her and Nick officially moving in together, and life in general. By the time they ordered dessert, she was starting to unwind from her expectations and just go with the flow. She *ooh*ed over the arrival of her brownie sundae with extra nuts, and was about to dig in when there was a mechanical whir from overhead, and the bison came to animatronic life.

The fringed eyelashes blinked, the big head shook, and the creature looked down at them. Mouth moving a hint faster than the soundtrack, it said, "Is it time, Nick?"

Jenny's mouth dropped open. "What did he say?"

Nick nodded to the bison, all serious, like they were carrying on a conversation. "It's time. Tell them to bring him on in."

Heat rushed to Jenny's face. Anticipation. Was this what she thought it was? "What's going on? Bring who in?"

Nick stood and held out a hand. "Come and see."

Pulse thudding, she followed him around the table

while the others watched. Ruth and Nick's dad were beaming, making her think *This is it*.

A moment later, the hostess reappeared in the doorway, leading a new guest.

A four-legged guest, with a gorgeous honey-colored coat and a long brush of a tail that swept side to side like an overcharged metronome, while liquid brown eyes looked around, then locked on Nick in recognition.

Jenny's. Heart. Stopped. "Is that—" She broke off because it wasn't Rex—this dog's coat was lighter, his nose narrower. But he looked so much like Rex, right down to the eager wiggle and the expressive eyes, that it reawakened the little voice in her head when he looked from Nick's face to hers with an expression of *Do you like me? Do you? Can we be friends?*

"Oh." She leaned down and wrapped her arms around the wriggling dog, heart going pitter-pat at the feel of soft fur over the strong, sturdy body. "Oh, look at you. Who are you?"

Nick crouched down at her feet, caging the eager goldie against his body. "This is Roger. He's Rex's full brother, a few litters younger."

"Oh." She straightened and covered her mouth, throat tightening. "How did you . . ."

"I called Miranda, partly to check on Rex—he's doing great, by the way, as is her husband—and partly to see if I could get info on his breeder. Turns out, Rex had been partway trained as a service dog, but flunked out because he had focus issues."

A laugh bubbled up. "You don't say."

Roger was doing his best to hold the sit-stay, but his body vibrated with the effort. *Can I play now? Can I? Huh? Huh? Am I a Good Boy?*

Nick grinned. "I do say. And, lo and behold, his breeders just happened to have a younger brother of his in the same predicament." He paused. "So, what do you say, Jenny? You ready to put down another set of roots?"

"Cheesepuff will be annoyed."

"He'll adjust." His eyes bore into hers. "Will you?"

She leaned into him and brushed her lips across his. "I already have. You gave me the time and the room to figure out what's really important, and I've got it down now: You're important. Our life together is important." Grinning, she looked down. "And Roger!"

Yippee! The dog leaped up to lick her face, almost knocking her down in the process.

Laughing, she fended him off. "Okay, enough. Roger, sit!"

His butt plonked down, but it was more of a contained wriggle than an actual sit, and his eyes had gone to the table, prospecting the desserts.

Deciding that was close enough, she patted him, then laid a big, smacking kiss on Nick's lips. "Nice work, Doc."

"You like your present?"

"I love him." She kissed him again. "And I love you."

"Love you, too, sweetheart." He stood and moved

away to rummage in his coat. "Check his collar for me, will you? It felt a little loose just now."

"What? Oh, sure." She worked her fingers through the dog's silky fur and found the soft nylon collar. "It feels okay to . . ." She stopped. Stared.

Stitched into the nylon, where Roger's name or a phone number should've been, were the words: MARRY ME.

She gaped as the air rushed out of her lungs, and she whipped up her eyes just in time to see Nick go down on one knee in front of her and the dog.

He had a ring box balanced on his palm and a wicked gleam in his eyes. "What do you say, Jenny Skye? You willing to take a chance on a landlocked vet who promises to play hooky with you as often as humanly possible, and when he can't, swears he'll cheer for you from back home?"

"I . . . Yes! Of course, yes!" She flung herself at him, trusting his strong arms to catch her, his tough body to absorb the impact, and his heart to hold her close no matter what. "I love you. Yes, I'll marry you."

They embraced and kissed while the others whooped and clapped, and Roger whirled around in dizzy, excited circles.

I've got a family of my own. Oh, boy!

Read on for a preview
of the next book in the series,

HARVEST AT MUSTANG RIDGE

Coming from Signet Eclipse in
August 2014.

A quiver ran through Krista at the sight of that brown felt Stetson—its wearer was turned away from her, with his boots planted even with his shoulders as he gestured toward the horse pens. She caught a glimpse of dark hair that had a touch of red to it, like a black horse that had bleached in the sun.

It's not him, she thought. The cowboy was taller and broader than Wyatt had been, and big enough that she couldn't picture him as a champion bull rider. The center of balance was all wrong.

Exhaling a relieved breath—she would rather deal with a stranger than the Ghost of Boyfriends Past—she approached the huddle just as it broke up and the two younger men headed into the barn, presumably to shoo her mare into the chute.

"Hi, there," she said to the big guy's back. "I'm here for hip number forty-one."

"Figured you might be." The familiar low baritone of his voice wasn't nearly enough warning before he turned.

Krista froze at the sight of dark brown eyes and the seam of a faded scar running alongside his square jaw. The electric-fence zap from before hit her again, only a thousand times stronger, while something in her head went *bzzzzt*, like her brain had just short-circuited. So much for the whole *it's not him* thing. Because it totally was, from the ends of his trail-worn boots to the top of his Stetson, with a plain leather belt in the middle, clasped with a geometric brass buckle, which was understated for the crowd, but still drew her eye to dangerous territory.

"Wyatt." She hadn't meant to say it out loud, but that was definitely her voice, headed for a squeak.

He nodded slowly, keeping his eyes on her like she was a spooky horse and he was waiting to see which way she was going to bolt. "Hey, Krista. Long time no see."

Her pulse pounded in her ears and her tongue glued itself to the roof of her mouth. Which was okay, really, because talking was probably a bad idea. After all, what was a girl supposed to say to the guy she had almost married, eight years after they broke up instead?

"Um, hey," she said, the words sounding like they were coming from far away. "Nice belt buckle."

Wyatt had known she would be there, had figured they would cross paths. He had tried to picture how it would go, and had decided not to overthink it after all those years. And even when he had seen her across the crowd and felt the gut punch of too many memories threatening to bust through, he had told himself it wouldn't be a big deal. Just a tip of the hat, a "good luck with your horse," and moving on.

Except that now, when he was face-to-face with her, his arms were suddenly too heavy to do the hat thing, and that "good luck" had turned into "long time no see." And he was having trouble looking away from her, like he'd gotten caught staring at the sun.

She gleamed like the sun, too, with her white straw hat, yellow-blond hair and pale honey tan. And she looked exactly the same as he remembered, fresh and vibrant, like it had been eight days rather than eight years.

How was that possible? Sure, there were small differences—her hair was a shade or two darker beneath the sun streaks, and the co-ed bounce had turned to a woman's poise—but he could've picked her crazy long legs and cowgirl swagger out of a crowd. Heck, he *had* picked her out of the crowd. But now that he had her right in front of him, he didn't have a clue what came next.

Tearing his eyes off a pair of baby blues the color of the wide-open Wyoming sky, he looked at the woman beside her, who was a carbon copy done in brunette and a T-shirt that had *I'M STARRING IN MY OWN REALITY SHOW* splashed across the front.

Jenny, he thought, though he'd never met Krista's identical twin. There was a harder, sharper edge there, one that made him think she wasn't one to pull her punches. Or maybe that was because of her narrowed eyes and the way her lips shaped his name, making it look like it was something that would've gotten his mouth washed out with Ivory back in the day.

"So," she said dangerously. "You're Wyatt Webb."

Well, that answered one question. She clearly knew the whole wretched story. Or at least one side of it.

He tipped his hat. "At your service."

She bared her teeth. "How about you take your service and—"

"Time out!" Krista made a T with her hands and stepped between them. To her sister, she said, "I've got this. How about you get the truck ready to roll? Sounds like they're getting our new horse out of the pen."

Deep in the barn, clanging gates and agitated whinnies said she was on the mark. There was no telling whether it would take Sam and the others thirty seconds or thirty minutes to get the mustang onto the trailer, but things would move fast after that.

"You sure?" Jenny demanded.

Krista nodded. "Positive."

Moving off, the sister shot Wyatt a warning look that he could've told her wasn't necessary. He wasn't trying to start anything—far from it. He had just figured it'd be best for him and Krista to get the "hey, how are you" over with in relative privacy rather than bumping into each other in town, when they'd both be shocked down to their boots.

Not that she had looked particularly shocked, except for those first few seconds, when her eyes had widened and her cheeks had flushed like she was happy to see him. That had faded fast, though, and he didn't blame her for it.

When Jenny was out of earshot, Krista turned back to him, hooked her thumbs in her pockets, and stood with her elbows akimbo, making her outline larger than her petite frame. "I didn't realize you were in town."

"I'm spending a couple of weeks with Sam."

"Thinking about going into the oil business?"

"More looking for inspiration." When her brows furrowed, he added, "The Independence Pioneer Museum commissioned a big piece for their rededication ceremony, and it's been a while since I've had trail dust in my teeth." Too long. "I wanted to get back up into the high country and see the sights before I got to work."

Expression blanking, she said, "You're an artist?"

"Metalworker." Art wasn't his thing. Forges and hammers were. He was just lucky that the pieces he liked to build had struck a chord with the money crowd.

She shook her head slowly, like her brain was going "does not compute." Not that he could blame her. It'd taken him a while to wrap his head around the idea, too. After a moment, she said, "I didn't know."

"No reason why you should." Also no reason to mention that he'd looked her up, and had seen the success she had made of Mustang Ridge. What was the point? They weren't catching up so much as passing by. "Anyway, they asked me to build—"

He broke off as a rapid-fire thud of unshod hooves came from the barn area, intensifying as pebbles kicked up against the pipe panels. There was a flash of movement in the shadows of the barn overhang, and then the trailer rocked as the mustang hit the closed-in end and doubled back.

"Oh!" Krista said, surging forward. "Don't let her—"

Wyatt was already on the move, ducking through the pipe panels to shut and latch the back gate of the trailer. The moves were automatic, ingrained, though he'd been off the rodeo circuit since before he and Krista had been a thing.

The horse gave a high, frightened whinny, which was echoed immediately from the pens as the rig shuddered, then started rolling. Moments later, Jenny leaned out the window and waved. "Krista, come on! Hurry!"

"I—" Krista threw him a baffled look, then took off after the truck, calling back over her shoulder, "Bye, Wyatt. Have a good visit."

Her boots kicked up dirt as she jumped on the running board. Her laughter trailed back as she popped the door and ducked in the cab, and then the truck accelerated away, turned past a falling-down corn dog stand, and disappeared behind the caution-taped grandstands.

And she was gone.

Telling himself that it wasn't a letdown, that he'd done what he had intended on the get-it-over-with front, nothing more or less, Wyatt turned back to the barn. He bit back a groan to find Sam standing there, wearing battered jeans and a work shirt in place of his new-money clothes, along with the sort of look he usually reserved for coiled-up rattlers and explosives, like his friend might blow any second.

Which he might've been entitled to eight years earlier, when he'd gotten in Wyatt's way during the post-breakup fallout, and the two of them had pounded each other to a pulp. But that was a long time ago, damn it.

"Shut up," Wyatt growled. "We've got horses to move."